JOANNA'S HUSBAND AND DAVID'S WIFE

Books by Elizabeth Forsythe Hailey

A WOMAN OF INDEPENDENT MEANS
LIFE SENTENCES
JOANNA'S HUSBAND AND DAVID'S WIFE

Joanna's Husband
AND
David's Wife

Elizabeth Forsythe Hailey

DELACORTE PRESS/NEW YORK

Published by Delacorte Press
1 Dag Hammarskjold Plaza
New York, N.Y. 10017

Manufactured in the United States of America
First printing

Library of Congress Cataloging-in-Publication Data

Hailey, Elizabeth Forsythe.
  Joanna's husband and David's wife.

  I. Title.
PS3558.A327J6   1986   813'.54
ISBN 0-385-29436-0
Library of Congress Catalog Card Number: 85-16117

For my father and my mother,
who were there at the beginning,
and for my husband,
who had better be there at the end

JOANNA'S HUSBAND AND DAVID'S WIFE

Julia darling,

I've been awake all night trying to write you a letter, but after half a dozen futile attempts, I've decided to leave you these journals instead. I never planned to show them to anyone—certainly not my daughter. However, if there are any answers, I have to believe they're here.

I've kept a journal beside my bed all through our marriage, writing in it openly, never considering locking it as I did my teenage diary. Your father doesn't have the slightest interest in reading the year-by-year history of our marriage—he thinks he knows what happened. In fact, I can't imagine that he would ever take the time to look at these pages unless I were to die and they were all he had left of me. Even then, he would probably only be interested in seeing if they were worthy of posthumous publication.

As you read—and even now I shudder to think of things you'll discover—I want you to keep at the center of your thoughts how much I love you.

Mother

Dearest Julia,

I found your mother's journals while you were still asleep and started reading them immediately. I had hoped to finish before you woke up. However, I had to stop. It's not fair for you to read such a one-sided version of our marriage. So I'm going to calm down, start over, and add my own point of view. After all, there was a day when I was the writer in this family.

Promise me you'll read this version before making any decisions you may regret. By then you'll have come to your own conclusions about what marriage is like—for both the man and the woman. Or at least for your mother and me.

I'll do my best to make my additions reflect how I felt at the time, so it will be a fair fight. After all, Joanna was reading the meter as it ran—something she was much better at than I. I was always too impatient to get to my destination and know the fare. Now I'm beginning to wonder if she wasn't right. What matters is the trip—and the sights along the way.

Whatever happens, nothing will change how much I love you.

Dad

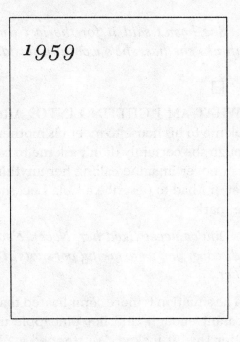

1959

I DID SOMETHING TODAY I've never done before—asked a boy for a date. I can't fall asleep for wondering why. Maybe if I write down what's happening between us, I won't be so frightened. I promise this won't turn into another of my mushy high school diaries. That phase of my life is behind me! Besides, I don't feel mushy about him at all.

Well, thanks. I had never felt so mushy about a girl in my life. And what's wrong with a little mush? Hate the word, love the feeling. In fact, I still feel mushy about her even now. Are there tears in these old eyes?

My motives for asking him for a date were innocent enough. When I drove down to the newspaper to reclaim my summer job, I discovered he'd taken my place in the city room and I'd been assigned to amusements, where he wanted to be. So I offered to share the free tickets to *The Pajama Game* which came with the job, hoping somehow that would make it up to him. But is that all I really want to happen?

I think of all the plans I have for my life after college—and yet I still find myself wanting to end this entry by saying "Good night, David." Why?

She hasn't said it for the last time either—and if she thinks she has, she's woefully mistaken.

☐

WHAT AM I GETTING INTO? After the show tonight, he took me to his house to meet his mother. Her name is Eula Lee, though she certainly didn't ask me to call her that, and, frankly, I can never imagine calling her anything but Mrs. Scott. However, if I had to describe a Eula Lee, she'd come pretty close to the mark.

You've never liked her. Never! Never! Never! And now I discover you were taking pot shots at her the night you met her.

The situation is more complicated than I realized. But she was pleasant enough, and her pineapple upside-down cake tasted better than it looked. We stopped at White Rock Lake on the way home—first time I've ever been kissed by a boy who wasn't drunk. I asked him to go with me to *Wish You Were Here.*

First time I'd ever kissed a girl who hadn't already picked out her china and silver patterns. I was stunned to discover how much better they kiss.

☐

I TOLD HIM it was happening too fast—that I wanted to go to graduate school after college, then travel. But he told me he'd just been accepted at the Yale Drama School and was leaving the newspaper at the end of the summer.

Yale impressed her. Thank God.

☐

I THINK HE MUST WORRY a lot about money. We've been seeing each other every night, and even though we eat casually —usually Mexican food or pizza—I suppose it adds up.

A girl who expected courses *at a Mexican restaurant? You bet it added up.*

4

□

TONIGHT David told me he's saving his money for Yale, so we have to find cheaper ways to be together. I wish he'd let me pay my share when we go out to dinner—then I could order what I want without having to look at the price first—but I'm afraid I'll hurt his feelings if I suggest it. I offered to cook dinner for him tomorrow night. My family is on vacation in New Mexico, so we'll have the house to ourselves.

Money couldn't buy an evening like that. I wanted to stay the night in that beautiful blue bedroom, but her parents had taken care of that the way they would take care of so many things. Made her promise she'd sleep every night at the neighbors.

□

ON THE WAY HOME from *Kiss Me, Kate* tonight, David asked me to marry him. He must be crazy. I said I loved him—and I think I do—but we shouldn't make promises we're not sure we can keep.

I was crazy—crazy with the fear of losing her. Even then I knew she was the smartest thing I'd ever do.

□

HE'S asked me again! This time I said yes. Why not? I have another year of college in case I change my mind. I like the thought of being engaged—but I'm not telling my parents. Not yet.

I knew she was stalling, but I didn't care. Besides, I knew her better than she knew herself. She may have made the promise lightly but she wouldn't break it lightly.

□

MY FAMILY is back home, so we have nowhere to be alone. Just a car—and no matter where we park, I feel so exposed.

Tonight David borrowed the key to a friend's apartment. We only had two hours, so we waited till afterwards to eat.

Hard to imagine me making love for two hours on an empty stomach. Not that what we were doing then was making love. But it was close. I was ready to marry her, but I wasn't ready to start another family—not until she'd learned to live with the one I already had.

☐

MY PARENTS insisted I invite David to dinner tonight so they could get to know him. What a mistake! I'm glad I haven't said anything to them about being engaged. The very thing I love about him—his passion in defense of anything that matters to him—puts my parents on edge. They prefer people with double vision, who can manage to see both sides of a question at the same time. If only he hadn't gotten started on what a great president Truman had been.

"That ordinary-looking little man!" protested my mother. "This is the first time a kind word has ever been uttered at this table about Harry Truman." Dinner went downhill from there.

After David had left, I asked Mother to take a good look at me. How would she describe her daughter to a stranger? "Well, you have a wonderful smile," she began hesitantly.

"That's because I have too many teeth," I replied. "That's all anyone sees when they look at me. I'm ordinary-looking too— just like Mr. Truman. And so is David. But he makes me feel beautiful."

Wait a minute! I liked Truman, yes, but I never thought I looked like him.

☐

TIME'S RUNNING OUT. I go back to college next week, and David leaves for New Haven. I invited him to a big Labor Day picnic some family friends give every year. I thought he'd like the free food, if nothing else. But we didn't even stay till dinner was served. Everything about the party upset him. He acted as if he'd never been waited on before.

6

*She called it a picnic—what I saw was a family of slaves,
including little black children, passing hot hors d'oeuvres
on silver platters. I didn't want any part of that world and
if she did, I wasn't sure I still wanted her.*

□

DAVID TOLD ME tonight he can't marry me—he doesn't
approve of the way my family lives. What is he talking about?
My family doesn't live that differently from his. Neither of our
mothers can cook. The only difference is, my mother has a maid,
so she doesn't have to keep trying.

*She really couldn't see much difference, but a friend had
told me her father was one of the five richest men in Dallas.
How could I marry someone who was used to getting everything she wanted?*

He must think we're rich. Where would he get an idea like
that? I told him my father had to borrow money from his father
to go to college and on to law school, but all he said was, "Just
because your father married for money doesn't mean I can do
it." We sat in the car talking for a long time, then he came
around and opened my door. He didn't touch me once all night.
At the front door I offered my hand for him to shake. When I got
to my room, I cried myself to sleep. I didn't even want to marry
him until he said he wanted out of it. Now I feel so empty and
afraid.

*I hated what I was doing to her—but I couldn't help
myself. If only she'd been born poor—a poor orphan. Then
I could've come into her life like a hero. My friend turned
out to be woefully wrong about her father's money. Still, he
had a lot more than anyone I'd ever met.*

□

YESTERDAY I thought David was ready to end it. Today he
asked me to marry him secretly right away. He said I was the
best thing that had ever happened to him, and even though he
didn't deserve me, he was terrified of losing me. Does that mean

7

he thinks I'll change my mind before next summer—or he'll change his? How can I marry a man who's so unpredictable?

Poor, naive Joanna. Nothing in her safe, comfortable childhood had prepared her for the roller coaster ride ahead of her. She didn't even know about my temper until it was too late for her to change her mind. I made sure of that.

☐

TONIGHT David took me to the Cattleman's Restaurant for a farewell dinner and told me to order a porterhouse—so I knew he was serious about wanting to marry me. He said if we couldn't be married secretly, at least we could be engaged secretly—and he gave me a silver ring.

I didn't have to wear it, he assured me, and we didn't have to say anything to our families—but he wanted me to have the ring to remind me that in his eyes I was the only girl in the world. I was too touched to think about eating, so as soon as we finished our salad, David told the waitress I wasn't feeling well, and we drove to White Rock Lake and necked till dawn.

In those days nothing turned me on like not *having to pay for dinner.*

☐

DAVID ASKED ME to drive him to the train station so he could tell his mother good-bye at home—in private. I waited in the car, but she came out with him and broke into sobs as we drove away. I've never cried leaving home—nor has anyone in my family shed a tear telling me good-bye. But when his train pulled out of the station, I cried harder than I've ever cried in my life. What's happening to me?

She was brought up to hide her feelings like dirty pictures, the way everyone in her family did. That's going on the assumption they had any feelings to hide.

☐

8

COLLEGE is like a prison sentence after last summer. I keep touching my ring, which I wear all the time, to remind myself how happy we were. I write David every night just before I fall asleep. Today I finally heard from him—for the first time in a week—a frantic note scribbled between classes. He thinks I should cancel the trip I'm planning to New Haven at the end of the month. His first writing assignment is due—a one-act play— so he says he won't have any time for me. Oh, God, am I losing him again?

I'd been on a high from the day I got to New Haven. After registering for classes, I took a train back into New York to see Geraldine Page in Sweet Bird of Youth. *Christ, what a performance. Tennessee Williams was—and is—the reason I got into the theater. I caught a late train back to New Haven, my head exploding with what I'd just seen and everything I was about to see. For the first time in my life I was where I wanted to be—and there wasn't time for anyone else. Or need.*

☐

TONIGHT I called David and told him I was coming to New Haven whether he had time for me or not. I just want to be in the same room with him, even if it means sitting quietly and watching him work.

I'd done everything I could to discourage her, but when she said she was coming anyway, I started counting the days. I hate making love to a pillow.

☐

WHEN I SAW DAVID waiting on the platform, I knew I was right to come. He looked so much younger than I remembered. I've been telling my friends at college that I'm engaged to an older man, but he looked as eager and excited as a kid just out of high school. When he hugged me, I could feel how much he needed me. I can't wait to start sharing his life. It's already so much more exciting than mine.

She wasn't in love with me, she was in love with some fantasy—an older man, a playwright, someone with an exciting career ahead—no one I knew. Yet. But with her believing in me, I could believe it might happen. Alone, I had my doubts.

Walking from the train station to the campus, we were like polite foreigners trying to find a common third language in which we could communicate. We hadn't seen each other in a month, and here we were struggling to make conversation. What do married people find to talk about night after night?

David took me to his room. Then we didn't have to talk and everything was a lot better. Later we had hamburgers in front of a roaring fire at a wonderful place called George and Harry's. I love New Haven.

Did she ever in her life sit in front of a fire that wasn't roaring? She always saw what she wanted to see. Maybe I wouldn't be in so much pain right now if I'd learned that trick.

☐

DAVID WORKED through the night finishing his play and this morning after breakfast announced he was going to read it to me. "Can't I just read it to myself?" I asked. I didn't want him judging my reaction to every line. But I didn't say that—I said if I read it to myself, he would have time to do something else.

He saw right through me said plays were not meant to be read in silence. A playwright needed an audience, and I was going to be his. I was terrified.

It wasn't hard to see through her. She wanted time to come up with the words she thought I wanted to hear. She wasn't used to telling the truth because she wasn't used to facing it.

What do I know about the theater? I grew up going to the starlight operettas with my grandmother. When I got older, my parents took me to Margo Jones's theater-in-the-round to see Shakespeare, but never the new plays which made that theater's reputation (Mother, who thinks of herself as a character out of Noel Coward, considers Tennessee Williams "sordid"). I thought it was exciting to watch costumed actors singing and dancing at night under the stars and later to sit close enough to touch them and see them spitting soliloquies.

But this wasn't a theater. There were no costumes or scenery —and no audience so I could disappear into anonymity. It wasn't even dark. I felt as exposed as David. And just as much on the line.

Hard as I tried to concentrate when he started reading, I couldn't keep the characters straight. Nor could I understand why they kept getting so upset with each other. They were supposed to be a family. How could they say such terrible things and continue living under the same roof?

When David finally finished, I was so depressed I didn't know what to say. I told him I had to be alone for a while; I just couldn't talk about it. He said he understood completely; he felt the same way when he saw *Long Day's Journey Into Night.* This afternoon while David took a nap, I went to the library and read *Mourning Becomes Electra.* I wouldn't have known what to say to Eugene O'Neill either. I wondered if he cared what *his* wife thought.

> *At the time I assumed she was overwhelmed by the power of my first play. Apparently not.*

☐

I CAN'T SLEEP. I feel like such an outsider in New Haven. David took me to a party tonight but spent more time talking to our hostess than he did to me. She's a published poet named Elaine West who got a huge scholarship to study playwriting and seems to have spent most of it on an apartment in a new high-rise building at the edge of campus.

When David and Elaine weren't talking to each other, they seemed to be competing for the attention of a rather dull-looking man named Brad Savage. I learned later that he's a directing student. An original play's best chance of being produced at Yale is to be chosen as a thesis production by a graduate director, so they're very popular at parties—until they make their choices.

Pouring myself a glass of wine from a gallon jug, I was wondering how soon we could leave when I heard David telling Elaine about his play. To my amazement she asked if she could read it. Why would she want to do that? Suddenly I felt very jealous and possessive. I wanted to shout that I was David's audience—the only one who got to hear his plays before they were finished. But the next thing I knew, he was making a date to read it aloud to her tomorrow as soon as he puts me on the train. David was right—I should never have come to New Haven. I don't belong here.

I knew what she was feeling, but I wanted her to see there was no place for a wife in my life—before I had to tell her —and leave quietly without making a scene.

When we left the party, I kept hoping he would take me back to his room. All I could think about was how long it would be before we saw each other again, probably not till Christmas. I'm not sure I know how to talk to David anymore, but alone with him in his room, I don't feel so inadequate.

However, he began talking immediately about his play, saying he had some great ideas for revising it before reading it to Elaine tomorrow. Sensing he was about to test them on me, I said I was sleepy and asked to go back to the room he'd arranged for me in the graduate women's dormitory. I still can't believe how gratefully he kissed me good-night. What's going to happen once we're married? What am I going to do with my life while David writes plays?

Who would ever have guessed? Not I.

☐

I HATE BEING BACK in a girls' school after a weekend at Yale. No one here thinks it's possible for men and women just to be friends. They wouldn't understand how David could be alone with someone like Elaine West in her apartment and do nothing more intimate than talk about his play. I have no trouble believing that all they do is talk, but what worries me is that their talk may be more intimate than anything I do with him.

I thought David would call tonight to make sure I got back safely. I stayed in my room to study instead of going to the library so I wouldn't miss his call. But he didn't, and I couldn't study, so I wrote him what Mother calls a "bread and butter" note thanking him for the weekend. I didn't mention his play. I still don't know what to say.

I went down to the pay phone to call her a dozen times that night. But how could I tell her I was leaving school and going home to Texas?

☐

DAVID FINALLY CALLED. Now I understand why I haven't heard from him all week. Sunday, while she served him tea and scones, Elaine West told him his play was hopeless. She said his characters were cardboard and his plot melodramatic. How could she be so cruel? No matter what I thought, I could never tell someone to his face that his work was not good, especially when I knew he was doing the best he could. But suddenly I heard David saying he would be grateful to her for the rest of his life. She'd saved him from making a fool of himself in front of the class.

Grateful to her! I couldn't believe what I was hearing. If he was grateful to *her*, then what did he feel for *me?* He did admit, however, that he'd left her apartment in something of a stupor. In fact, he even wrote a letter to the Dallas city editor asking for his old job back. Fortunately he didn't mail it. By the end of the week he had an idea for a new play and spent the weekend drafting it. Tomorrow he's reading it to the class. I asked if he was going to show it to Elaine first. "Oh, no," he said. "I don't need to. This one works."

I was sure I had something that time. When I finished reading, my playwriting professor, John Gassner—the reason I had saved for five years to get to Yale—called for a show of hands. "How many liked this play?" No hands. "How many think this play has potential but needs work?" No hands. "How many like the premise but think the approach is wrong?" No hands. "Then let us discuss what is causing you to withhold your latent enthusiasm for this play."

I crawled away from class. To think how I'd struggled to get to Yale. Gassner was never unkind—but when he got through dissecting my play, it was clear he had even less "latent enthusiasm" for it than my classmates.

I was walking back to the dorm alone when Tom Morris, Gassner's student assistant, caught up with me. He said he wasn't allowed to comment in class but he liked what I'd written. "You gotta remember Gassner grew up in New York. He doesn't understand the way people talk in Texas. It's just one man's opinion. Don't let it get you down. The play has promise. And so do you."

I hung on to his words like a lifeline—and never stopped to reflect that he too was only one man. But sometimes one good man is all you need.

I'm the wrong girl for David. I know that now. He needs someone who can stand up to him, who knows the difference between good and bad and won't be afraid to tell him. So I've decided to apply to Stanford for graduate school—and not to write David again until he writes to me. I also just took off his ring and put it in my desk drawer.

At first it was a relief not getting letters I didn't have time to answer. But by the weekend I was worried. I finally called, only to be told Joanna was out of town. That was the first time I got caught taking her for granted. Unfortunately, it wasn't to be the last.

☐

MY FRESHMAN ROOMMATE got married today, and I was her maid of honor. As I walked down the aisle, I kept imagining the wedding I will probably never have. It was a storybook setting. The only thing missing for me was David. And yet I knew he would've hated it.

I watched my former roommate dancing with her new husband. Barbara and Bruce Honeywell. Even their names are compatible. Her family is from Long Island, New York, his from Lake Forest, Illinois. The two families met for the first time this weekend but were laughing and talking as if they were old friends. Bruce is in his first year at Harvard Business School. Barbara plans to keep busy decorating their apartment and learning to cook. They make marriage look so easy and so inevitable—and so impossible for David and me.

I should've known from her silence that I wasn't the only one having doubts. Whenever something went wrong between us, I got loud and she got quiet. So quiet sometimes it seemed as if she were trying to disappear from my life before I had time to notice. Perhaps she was.

☐

I CALLED DAVID TONIGHT and asked if he could meet me in New York for the Thanksgiving weekend. I even offered to pay for our hotel room. I thought it might put us back on the track if we could spend a whole night together. We just seem to grow further apart writing letters and talking over the phone, measuring the minutes by a dwindling stack of coins. But when we're naked under the covers, I don't have to be told how much he wants me with him. Sometimes I wonder if going to bed together if we do finally get married would be as exciting as it is now when we have to stop short for fear of getting into trouble.

Your mother always enjoyed talking about sex as much as doing it. I'm just the opposite, so don't expect me to have a lot to say on the subject. When I think of the passages I've had to edit in what she wrote for public consumption, I shudder to imagine what lies ahead in these private pages.

I got so aroused just thinking about being alone in a hotel room with David, I was sure he would say yes. Four days together to see shows, act like tourists. I thought even if we didn't have a future, we could still have a present.

I had a hard time holding back the tears when he said no, explaining that he could afford neither the time nor the money. When I asked what he would do for Thanksgiving, he said Elaine West had invited him to dinner. Does he really expect me to believe she'll be cooking a turkey?

Elaine and I ended up having pastrami specials at the Yorkside. Then she asked me back to her apartment to hear her play. I hated it but didn't know how to tell her. By the time she finished explaining all the levels, I thought maybe I was wrong. So I just said it didn't work for me. She burst into tears and accused me of trying to get even. That night I went to a double feature—alone—and faced the possibility that no woman could be part of my life if I was determined to have a career in the theater.

My roommate, Kate Greenfield, found me huddled on the floor of the pay phone booth, crying my eyes out, after I hung up from David. She invited me to come home to Washington with her for Thanksgiving. Well, why not?

☐

I HAD A DATE TONIGHT with Kate's older brother Adam, who lives in Georgetown and works for the State Department. Kate thinks I've broken my engagement to David—and I suppose I have. I just haven't told David. However, when I packed for the weekend, I left his ring in my desk drawer.

Adam is very attractive and cosmopolitan, speaks five languages. Kate adores him, and he's always fixing her up with his friends. And vice versa, I suppose.

All through Thanksgiving dinner yesterday I kept thinking how I would love to be part of the Greenfield family; if I were married to Adam, I could have Kate as a sister. Adam stayed late to help Kate and me wash the dishes. We put a stack of Ella Fitzgerald records on the stereo and sang along. Then Adam began to dance with me, and suddenly I realized Kate had left us alone. When he kissed me, I started crying, then lied and said I was exhausted from schoolwork.

Today at noon Adam took me to his office in the State Department. I couldn't help wondering what it would be like to be married to a man who went to an office every day and knew from promotion to promotion exactly where he stood in his career. When he asked me what my plans were after graduation, I said I was going to Stanford to study comparative literature so I would feel at home anywhere in the world. He's in the State Department for the same reason, he said. Tonight when he kissed me, I kissed him back.

Kissed him back? Jesus! If it was anything like the first time she kissed me back—and I'm sure it was—he probably thought they were engaged. And poor, innocent me, working my butt off in New Haven while she was playing "Hi, sailor" with the State Department. What really bugs me is that I never even suspected. I thought having her in a girls' school in the South was the safest way in the world of keeping her on hold for a year. And look who ended up holding her!

☐

WHAT A ROTTEN WAY to begin Christmas vacation! First I find out the Roanoke airport is shut down because of bad weather, which means I have to take a train to Washington and stand by for a flight to Dallas. I can't give anybody an exact arrival time because I don't know in advance which flight I'll be on, but David promises to meet all of them. I tell him I'll take a taxi but he insists he'll be there. So when he's not—even though it's 4 A.M.—I can't help being disappointed. Why do we make foolish promises to each other?

I took his ring out of the desk drawer when I was packing and put it back on my finger, but it doesn't help. I just don't feel engaged anymore.

I knew she was mad about not being met, but she would never admit it to my face. Why couldn't she have been as honest in person as she is in these pages?

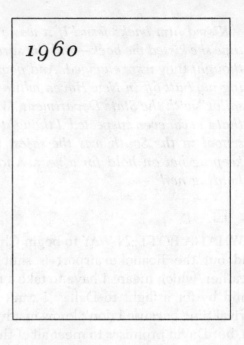

1960

A NEW DECADE—and I'm entering it alone. David invited me to spend New Year's Eve at his house so he wouldn't have to drive me home in the wee hours. His mother made a bed for me on the living room couch, but as soon as we had welcomed in the New Year with ginger ale and frozen egg rolls—

Have pity, Joanna. Do you have to include every depressing detail?

she retired for the night and David took me into his bedroom and closed the door.

Putting a record on the stereo to disguise any noise, he began to undress me. I tried to respond, but my mind kept wandering. I wondered what Adam was doing tonight in Washington. Then I wondered what David and I would be doing if we were in New York. I love him, at least I think I do, but I want love to expand my world, not contract it. I looked at that single bed in that grim little bedroom in that claustrophobic tract house, and suddenly I was fighting for breath.

I was so frightened by what I was feeling, I grabbed my clothes and ran through the house to the carport, climbed in his car and sat there shivering, choking back sobs. David slid in beside me and put his arms around me. I couldn't admit what a vain, shallow creature I am—one New Year's Eve with his mother, watching Guy Lombardo on television and eating frozen egg rolls, and I'm out the door. So I said I thought we should start the New Year with a clean slate, unencumbered by earlier promises—that the last thing he needed as he launched his career in the theater was a wife tagging along behind him.

And like a fool, I believed her. Now I learn she wanted out worse than I did. What a little snob she was! Tract house? I was still gazing in awe at the all-electric kitchen, the wall-to-wall carpeting, the tile bathrooms. It was the first house I'd ever lived in that didn't have permanent scars from previous occupants. I was so proud that Mother finally had the house she deserved. I never guessed it had sent Joanna running for her life in the opposite direction.

Then I gave him back his ring and told him I'd been nominated for a Woodrow Wilson fellowship for graduate study.

I don't remember anything about the fellowship. However, I must admit at that time her ambitions were of no interest to me. All I remember is my relief at getting off the hook.

☐

I LEARNED TODAY that I'm a Woodrow Wilson finalist. The scholarships are designed to encourage promising students to become college teachers. I can't imagine teaching as a career—at least not in the immediate future—but all the scholarship obligates you to do is consider the possibility. I have to go to Washington for an interview this weekend. Kate has invited me to stay at her home. Except for a Christmas card, I haven't heard from Adam since Thanksgiving.

Apparently Adam didn't know a good thing even when it kissed back.

☐

I THINK I'VE GOT THE FELLOWSHIP! When my interview was over today, I wanted to celebrate with somebody. David. Even though we're no longer engaged, I thought he'd be happy for me, maybe even proud. The interviewing committee had asked if I had any immediate plans to get married. I said no —but couldn't help wondering if they asked their male candidates the same question.

When I finally reached David, he said he was just about to write me—with good news. A friend had put him in touch with Audrey Wood. He'd sent her his play and she'd written back a nice note, asking him to call her the next time he was in New York. He paused, obviously waiting for me to congratulate him. Finally I had to ask, "Who is Audrey Wood?"

The connection went dead. I waited for him to call me back. When he didn't, I called him.

"She represents Tennessee Williams and a lot of other important playwrights," he said in a strained voice. "It could be the beginning of everything."

"When are you going into New York?"

"Monday," he confessed, adding with a laugh, "before she forgets who I am."

I wished him luck and hung up. He hadn't bothered to ask why I'd called, and I forgot to tell him. Besides, his news makes mine seem trivial. He's made his first professional contact. He's on his way.

On my way to where? If I'd known at the time, I wonder if I would've had the stomach to keep traveling.

☐

I BEGAN CALLING DAVID at five o'clock, as soon as the rates changed, to find out what happened with Audrey Wood. Yesterday I didn't even know her name. Today her opinion could change our lives. But David was not at the dorm. I decided he probably stayed in New York to see a play. I called him every hour until the switchboard closed at eleven, finally leaving a message for him to call me collect tomorrow.

☐

AT LAST I REACHED DAVID. He refused to discuss his meeting with Audrey Wood. And told me never to ask him about it again.

It took years to teach Joanna the cardinal rule of civilized behavior in the theater—never ask anyone how anything went. If it went well, they'll tell you soon enough. If it went badly—which it probably did—skip it.

☐

I GOT A LETTER TODAY from the Woodrow Wilson Committee regretting to inform me that I would not be receiving financial aid for graduate school but congratulating me on my academic record and hoping I would still consider a career in teaching. Fat chance!

To tell the truth, I'm relieved. I can't imagine ever feeling I know enough about anything to teach anybody else. Thank goodness I didn't tell David I was a finalist. Now I don't have to tell him I lost.

If she'd been more open about her failures, maybe it would've been easier for me to share mine.

Suddenly my plans for graduate school seem colored by defeat. If I go to Stanford, will I just be turning my back on life instead of seizing the chance to live it?

☐

CHILDHOOD IS OVER! As long as I love David, I will never feel comfortable with my parents again.

I was amazed to find him waiting for my plane when I arrived home today for spring vacation. I thought he was staying in the East. He took me in his arms right there in the airport and said he wasn't going back to New Haven next fall unless I went with him. He gave me back the ring so I could wear it home to my parents. Suddenly I knew the only thing I wanted to do with my life was be his wife. His dreams are bigger and bolder than any of mine.

My parents invited him to stay for dinner and I kept waiting for him to say something about wanting to marry me. But no one got anywhere near the subject—in fact, I was beginning to wonder if everyone was deliberately avoiding it.

So after dinner—before David could change his mind again—

Or Joanna could change hers. I now realize that the decision was never mine alone—though at the time, of course, I assumed it was.

I showed him the vacant servants' quarters above the garage and said if we got married in June, we could fix it up and live in it till we left for New Haven in the fall. He seemed to like the idea, and we began figuring out what it would cost to paint the apartment and get it in shape. I said we'd better talk to my parents before they went to bed.

We were discussing the cost of wallpaper and paint when Daddy suddenly interrupted. "Does this mean the two of you plan to get married?" I could see David was not about to go down on bended knee to ask for my hand, so I said quickly that we didn't want a large wedding, just the immediate family. Everyone appeared relieved—especially David.

But the interrogation had just begun. "I want you to know I've had you investigated," Daddy said to David. What did he mean "investigated"? Why didn't David explode? When he continued to sit there, smiling politely, I saw for the first time what marriage to me was going to cost him. I wanted to challenge my father, to ask what right he had "investigating" the man I loved. But I've never talked back to my parents and if I start now, they'll blame David.

Then Daddy smiled and assured David the word on him was good. I breathed a sigh of relief. Apparently the "investigation" was nothing more than a few casual inquiries among friends on the newspaper. But David was still rigid with shock. I realized with a sinking feeling that, no matter what the future brought, David would never trust my parents. They had put him on the defensive in the first round, and he would never forgive them.

I almost called Joanna later that night and ended our engagement yet again. It wasn't as much the thought of her father having me investigated as it was the putting. They had this thick, green carpet on their living room floor, money-green, and the entire time he talked he kept putting golf balls into a little metal object. He was wearing a cashmere cardigan and plaid wool pants. And he kept putting instead of looking at me. Joanna and her mother accepted it as perfectly normal behavior. He putted and we watched. And he never missed. I was way out of my league. I knew it and he knew it. And he enjoyed it.

□

I WROTE STANFORD and said I was getting married instead of going to graduate school. I decided not to tell David about it. I don't want him to think I'm making any sacrifices for him.

Were you making a sacrifice for me—or were you letting marriage get you off the hook? Forget about me. What about you? What did you really want to do with your life— or didn't you know? I always knew what I wanted and I suspect it was that, more than anything, that kept you with me, whatever the cost.

□

I STOOD IN OUR COLLEGE cafeteria line tonight and realized that this was the last time in my life I would be able to take dinner for granted. All that food set out, with no thought or preparation on my part, ready whenever I felt like eating. It was a luxury I'd never stopped to appreciate. Tomorrow my parents arrive for graduation. Then home to Texas, marriage, and groceries.

□

MY PARENTS ARE NAPPING in the next room—and David and I have just had our first long-distance fight. I called to tell him we were in Texarkana and would be home by lunch tomorrow. He was furious, said he couldn't believe we'd stopped for the night at five in the afternoon when we were only a couple of hours from Dallas. In fact, he took it personally. We haven't been together since spring vacation. Wasn't I as crazy to see him as he was to see me? I said of course I was—but I couldn't ask my father to keep driving after dark.

Our road trips always follow the same pattern. We awake at sunrise, drive for a couple of hours in the coolness of early morning, stop for a big breakfast, drive a few more hours, stop for lunch, and arrive at our night's destination in time for my parents to have a drink and a nap before finding the town's best restaurant for dinner. It's an agreeable way to travel—one I'd never thought to question until David demanded to speak to my father. I said my parents were resting, and promised I'd call him as soon as we got home tomorrow. "But how am I going to get through tonight?" he asked. I said if it was any consolation I wouldn't be able to sleep either, he'd gotten me so upset.

☐

DAWN. David just left, and I'm alone in our first apartment. I can't wait till we can start sharing every minute of our lives!

Last night when my parents and I returned to the motel after dinner, David was parked in front of my room, eating a hamburger to go. I burst into tears when I saw him and ran into his arms. "No one has ever loved me as much as you do," I said loudly. I saw my parents exchange a glance and knew they'd heard. Good.

And I saw the look her mother gave her father. They knew what I knew—that no one would ever be able to love her as much as she wanted to be loved.

I could see that my parents did not know how to deal with someone as impulsive as David. Finally Daddy offered to pay for another room at the motel. David thanked him but said he would be driving back home tonight. "And I'm going with him," I announced. "We want to be together."

Suddenly Mother whispered something to Daddy. He took a key off his key ring and handed it to David. "This is to the garage apartment. We fixed it up for you. Hope you like it."

While Joanna was packing, her father took me aside and gave me strict orders not to stay in the apartment all night until after the wedding. The neighbors, you know.

24

It was after midnight when we pulled into the driveway of our house. I woke the baby-sitter who was staying with my younger sister and brother and told her not to worry if she saw a light in the garage apartment. Then David and I climbed the stairs to our first home. All spring vacation we'd discussed how we would decorate it. But my parents had made it look like just another room in their house. I felt cheated.

Cheated? We had a roof over our heads rent-free. Painting the walls might have given Joanna the illusion of independence but I couldn't forget who owned the property. Besides, I liked the way her parents' house was furnished. What if it wasn't my taste? I still wasn't sure what my taste was. Her mother had even rented an original oil painting from the art museum. I'd never lived with an original work of art before. I liked it.

However, this morning I'm feeling a lot better about everything. I just hope David and I will be as happy here all summer as we were last night.

□

I WISH DAVID AND I could run away to New Haven—and get married on the way. Our wedding is going to be as small and simple as a wedding can be—a morning ceremony in a chapel, with only the immediate family present (in David's case that means his mother—he has no idea where his father is), then a reception at our house. And since both of us are working at the newspaper again this summer, we will only have a three-day weekend for our honeymoon.

But everything is already getting so complicated. When Mother asked David how many announcements his family wanted to send, he said none—a wedding announcement was nothing but a way of asking for a present.

Mother said he was being ridiculous. Her friends planned to give us presents whether they received announcements or not. Then she told us to be sure to register our china and silver patterns at all the stores.

This upset David even more. He said if people wanted to give us something we could use, why didn't they give us money. He had no intention of choosing patterns for something we had no interest in owning. He couldn't even foresee the day when we'd have a dining room.

I kept my integrity—and so Joanna chose our china pattern without me. We still eat off it and I still hate it. I vowed that as soon as we could afford to, we'd buy a new set of china—together—but within a few months, china and silver were the least of our differences.

☐

OUR HONEYMOON—EARLY EVENING. We were supposed to spend our wedding night in Corpus Christi on the Gulf of Mexico, but it was raining so hard when we left Dallas after our morning ceremony, we decided to stop at a motel in Waco—even though it was only four in the afternoon.

I went in the bathroom and put on my new nightgown and matching robe. I felt like an actress dressing for a part. The wardrobe was right, but where was the script? Opening the bathroom door, I felt more awkward and vulnerable in the once-in-a-lifetime role of virgin bride than I ever had lying naked beside David, aching to finish what we started. Now there was nothing stopping us, and I wasn't sure where to begin.

Then I took one look at David and began to laugh. Clad in his new paisley bathrobe, burgundy pajamas, and leather slippers, he stood posed by the bed like a male model. And just so I wouldn't miss the point, he was holding the latest issue of *Esquire*.

If Joanna was hoping for a husband who would take sex seriously, she had the wrong fellow.

I guess he was as nervous as I was about what was expected of him.

Me? Nervous?

But at least he could count on making me laugh. I didn't know what I could count on doing for him. However, when we went to bed, he seemed to enjoy every minute of it, and I felt warm

26

and happy when it was over, knowing I'd pleased him. Until he asked if I'd had an orgasm. I said I felt wonderful.

"But does that mean you've had an orgasm?"

I said if I felt wonderful and he felt wonderful, what else could it be, so please stop asking questions before he ruined everything.

I knew she hadn't had an orgasm. I just didn't know what to do about it—except keep asking.

I finally said I wanted to take a bath before dinner, but what I really needed was time alone to think. What if there's something wrong with me and David is forced to go to other women for the satisfaction a man expects?

How many years into the marriage were we before she started demanding satisfaction for herself—and not just in bed?

☐

I HAVE NO IDEA what time it is. David is sleeping soundly and I'm back in the bathroom, alone with my thoughts—and my journal. No one would believe how we spent our wedding night —not that I plan to tell anyone!

On our way into the motel restaurant for dinner, David bought a newspaper and began glancing through the amusements section while I concentrated on the menu. I hadn't eaten all day and I was starving. I'd just decided to order a T-bone steak when David looked at his watch. "We can make it if we hurry," he said, returning the menus to the waitress.

"Make what?" I asked in dismay.

Then he told me that *Babes in Arms* was playing at Paul Baker's theater at Baylor University. The theater is famous for its original design—with comfortable armchairs that swivel 360 degrees. David was so pleased about the chance to see the theater I almost suspected him of engineering our impromptu stop in Waco.

"I never would've planned to go to the theater on our wedding night," he said as if reading my mind, "but as long as we're here . . . and if you're not too hungry . . ." He hadn't eaten anything all day either. If art could sustain him, then I'd be damned if I'd admit to a hunger so mundane it could be satisfied by food.

I was hungry too, but I wasn't about to let my stomach— or any other part of my anatomy—rule my life. And it was a good production, as innocent and optimistic as we were that night.

☐

NEVER SPEND A HONEYMOON at the beach. By this afternoon we were too sunburned to touch each other. I took it better than David. Frankly, I'm not sure the main event lives up to the promise of the preliminaries. David said if we couldn't go to bed, it was silly to spend money on a motel room. We might as well drive home and get settled in our new apartment.

It was after midnight when we reached Dallas. The house was dark, but David wanted to see if any mail had come for us while we were away, so I opened the front door with my key. When I turned on the hall light, I heard a shriek. My younger sister Diana, wearing shortie pajamas, her hair in curlers, was creeping up the stairs with a late-night snack. "I can't live like this," she screamed, "with strangers coming in and out of the house at all hours." Then she slammed the door and disappeared into her room.

"Strangers?" David looked as if he'd been slapped. "You're her sister and I'm your husband. What kind of family is this?"

He stormed out of the house just as my parents came down the stairs to see what the trouble was. "What are you doing home?" they asked in dismay. I guess they thought I'd been abandoned on their doorstep after three days of marriage.

"Isn't anybody glad to see us?" was all I could think of to say before I ran after David.

Is this what marriage is like? Will he forever hold me accountable not just for what I say and do, but for the actions of anybody related to me by blood?

I feel like a homeless refugee. I no longer have a place in my parents' house, but I'm not sure I belong with David either. How could I have married a man without finding out first if I could live with him? I knew he felt deeply about things, but what a temper! I had no idea. He should be labeled "Highly explosive. Use extreme care in handling." I have got to have a larger goal for my life than how to get through it without upsetting him.

I deliberately deceived her. I admit it. She knew I was— what was her word?—"unpredictable," but I'd managed to convince her that artistic temperament was an asset in my chosen profession. However, I was careful to keep my temper hidden till after we were married—then, once she'd promised to love me for better or worse, I felt free to show her worse.

□

I WOKE UP THIS MORNING with my stomach in knots, wondering what to do about all the unopened wedding presents that arrived while we were away. As much as David hates the idea of wedding presents in principle, he gets as excited as a child at Christmas each time another package arrives—unless it's from his side. He dreads opening anything from anyone he knows.

I was humiliated when her mother cleared the furniture from their sun porch and set up card tables covered with white tablecloths so our wedding presents could be put on display. The single silver teaspoon from my mother's best friend, which I knew cost more than she could afford, was engulfed by complete place settings from her parents' crowd.

I prayed there would be nothing this morning to embarrass or upset him. I'm just beginning to realize how hard it is to make another person happy. I tiptoed into the bedroom to see if he was awake enough for breakfast and he pulled me back into bed.

When we got around to the wedding presents, he spotted a package from his former neighbors in the little West Texas town where he grew up. "I'm going to close my eyes," he said, "and you're going to describe it to me. If you can."

I unwrapped the package and stared at it. "Well, it's round," I began, "and wooden—and there's a picture of a cow painted on top." I looked in the box again, hoping for instructions or at least an explanation, but all I found were matching salt and pepper shakers.

David opened his eyes and began to laugh. "Don't you know a hamburger press when you see one?"

Thank goodness the wedding was behind us—and those damn display tables gone. Though I would've enjoyed watching her mother try to hide that hamburger press among all those silver serving dishes.

□

HOW CAN TWO PEOPLE who agree on almost nothing be so much in love? Marriage is truly an unnatural arrangement. It's a miracle any marriage lasts.

Here is a list of things I love that David hates: breakfast, baths, airplanes, lists, mushrooms, morning, Leslie Howard, ballroom dancing, horses, bicycles, novels, solitude, and trying things I've never tasted.

I don't hate baths, I just don't feel they have a place in a daily *schedule. As for Leslie Howard, every time I see* Gone With the Wind *he gets worse. I keep thinking the next time it's shown, surely he will have been replaced.*

Here is a list of things David loves that I hate: scary movies, staying up late, vanilla ice cream, Joan Crawford, chocolate milk, biographies, ballet, tapioca pudding, going to movies in the middle, licorice, marshmallows, and falling asleep fully clothed on the couch.

You must realize this entry was written long before Mommie Dearest *told all. And* Psycho *is* not *a scary movie, it's* art.

Here is a list of things David and I both love: words, the ocean, travel, books, chili, snow, children, mountains, pecan pie, Bette Davis, plays and movies that make us laugh, plays and movies that make us cry, plays and movies that make us laugh and cry.

It's easy to say you love children before you have them. What's important is how much more we love you today— seventeen and thirteen years after the fact.

Here is a list of things we both hate: alarm clocks, anything that involves striking, throwing, catching, or chasing a ball, cocktail parties, country clubs, not knowing where the other one is.

Does this marriage have a chance?

It never entered my mind we wouldn't stay married for- ever. It still doesn't—or I wouldn't be slogging my way through this damn journal now.

□

I LIKE GOING TO WORK every day with David. How must it feel to be married to a man who tells you good-bye after breakfast and doesn't come home till time for dinner? Thank goodness the newspaper relaxed its rule against hiring married couples so we could both have jobs this summer. We need the money. David pleaded our case, pointing out that we were working at the paper separately before we were married. This time he got the job he always wanted—in amusements—along with season tickets to the summer musicals, and I'm back in the city room.

This leaves me only weekends to practice domesticity. I keep cookbooks stacked on my bedside table and mark recipes that require more than a half hour of preparation to try on the weekend. Saturday is "simmer night."

Today we slept late. I was kneading bread when David an- nounced he was driving over to spend the afternoon at his mother's house (which I suspect he still considers his house— will he always? I wonder). Feeling abandoned, I asked plain- tively how I was supposed to get to the Laundromat with our week's laundry.

David muttered something about what an inconvenience it was being married to a rich girl whose mother always sent her laundry out, then asked why I was spending time and money at a Laundromat when his mother had a washing machine. Why didn't I come with him and do the laundry while he mowed the lawn? I said I couldn't be gone that long; I had bread rising and a pot roast simmering. David shrugged and said to give him the laundry; he'd take care of it.

The bread was in the oven, and I was in the tub shampooing my hair, looking forward to a cozy dinner for two, when David suddenly burst into the bathroom. "You've got to do something to make up to my mother for expecting her to do your laundry—I've brought her home for dinner."

I turned on the water full force so we couldn't be heard in the next room and whispered angrily, "It's not *my* laundry, it's *our* laundry, and I never expected your mother to do it. You said you'd take care of it."

"I did," he said. "There's a basket of clean clothes in the bedroom. But now she expects dinner."

So much for a Saturday à deux.

The next Saturday I took Joanna with me to do the laundry. She was hanging underwear on the clothesline when Mother pulled me aside and whispered, "The clothespins are upside down and she doesn't even know it. I'd tell her but I'm afraid of embarrassing her." There was no way to explain to Mother that her daughter-in-law took no pride in knowing how to use a clothespin. In fact, when I pointed out her mistake, Joanna just laughed and suggested we give Mother an automatic dryer for Christmas.

☐

WE INVITED MY PARENTS for dinner tonight. Mother begged me not to go to any trouble and suggested that, since it was a hot summer night, I just serve cold cuts from the delicatessen. But David wouldn't hear of it. He insisted we serve my parents the kind of dinner he enjoys—pork chops, french fries, biscuits, gravy, salad, and dessert. Mother, who never serves potatoes or bread or dessert, ate almost nothing and asked me privately afterwards, with a look of enormous sympathy, if David expected me to cook like that every night.

And her father told me it was the best meal he'd had since he left the farm. He asked me who taught Joanna to cook like that. Not her mother, that's for sure.

After dinner Daddy leaned back expansively and said that since we'd had such a small wedding, he and Mother would like to give a formal dinner dance at the country club to introduce us to their friends. David grimaced but said nothing. I could see it was going to be up to me to get us out of it. I began by saying we were opposed in principle to country clubs. But that didn't stop Daddy.

His next suggestion was a catered cocktail buffet at home for their hundred closest friends, all of whom, it seems, were dying to meet my new husband. I explained that David didn't want to be put on display, but they kept insisting until David finally stood up and announced, "I don't want to meet your friends. I already have all the friends I want."

And that is how I came to be known among their hundred closest friends as David the Difficult.

□

DAVID TOOK ME WITH HIM last week to a screening of a horror movie he has to review. Thank God I'm not in amusements anymore. I kept my hands in front of my eyes for most of it, but what I saw through my fingers appalled me. David was equally appalled—but for artistic reasons. He wrote a scathing review and turned it in to the amusements editor yesterday.

Today the stars of the movie came to town on a promotion junket. The amusements staff, including David, was invited to join them for a fancy lunch at a downtown hotel. When they got back to the paper, the editor returned David's review and asked if he couldn't do better by the movie now that he'd met all the nice people who made it. In reply David said we would be leaving for New Haven sooner than we thought. I have a feeling neither of us will ever work for the newspaper again.

I also, of course, rewrote the review, was polite about the movie, and over the years have grown to wish that all critics had editors who made them behave.

☐

OFF TO NEW HAVEN AT LAST! I've never been so happy to board a train. This summer has felt more like a rehearsal for marriage than the real thing.

Elaine West has offered us the use of her high-rise apartment in New Haven until we find a place of our own. She is spending the summer in London, not returning till school starts in another two weeks.

Today, on the train, David confessed we could've had the apartment all summer. Why didn't he tell me? How different our first months of married life might have been away from our families. I made a silent vow that if I had anything to do with it, we would never go back to Dallas again for longer than a visit.

She knew why we had to keep returning—I'd always feel responsible for what was left of my mother's life. But since it wasn't a pretty story, Joanna chose not to think about it.

☐

WHEN I'M HAPPY, I never seem to have much to say here. And yet it shouldn't go without saying. These last two weeks in Elaine's beautifully furnished, air-conditioned apartment have felt like the honeymoon we never really had. We sleep late, eat out a lot, go to movies—and look for an apartment.

Why don't I feel compelled to describe what it's like to wake up slowly in David's arms, knowing he can make whatever I was dreaming come true? Don't I trust my happiness enough to talk about it? Or is it enough simply to live it?

☐

LATE THIS AFTERNOON we finally found an apartment—and just in time. Elaine comes back tomorrow. All the best places were taken in the spring by graduate students willing to pay three months' additional rent to hold them. David felt we should save the money and take our chances on finding a place in the fall.

Besides, he didn't want to go apartment hunting without me.

34

I'm glad he waited, though it's a shock to discover how different our attitudes are toward what constitute the necessities of life. Fortunately for the future of our marriage, there are so few available apartments we were in complete accord today—and greatly relieved—when an elderly widow whose husband just died agreed to rent us the third floor of her house.

It is located in a residential neighborhood not zoned for renting, so we have promised to pay the rent in cash every month and to have our mail addressed to her care to keep the postman from getting suspicious.

Two male design students from the drama school are sharing the second floor—which means their lives are open to our inspection every time we climb the stairs. But they don't seem to mind, so I guess I shouldn't either.

Our bedroom is directly under the eaves. In fact, the ceiling slopes at such an angle we will have to crawl in and out of bed to avoid hitting our heads. The only standing room is between the foot of the bed and the door to the hallway.

What amazes me, looking back, is how little that bothered us. Apparently it was a very horizontal time in our lives.

☐

TODAY I BEGAN TO THINK about getting a job. David says I should only look for work that would interest me if I were single. The problem is, I had no plans to work until I'd gone to graduate school, so there's not much I'm qualified to do. The supply of English majors on the job market greatly exceeds the demand. Taking Elaine West's advice, I applied to the Yale University Press—and said I'd settle for the most menial position just to get into publishing. Unfortunately, there are no job openings at present but my application is on file.

After dinner tonight while I was looking through the want ads, David got out his budget for the year to prove that his savings, reinforced by his afternoon job at the alumni office, could meet our expenses. He said I shouldn't worry about working this year—I'd worked hard enough through high school and college, and deserved a year off.

*I only told her what I wish someone had told me when I
finished college. I was rarely as kind to her as she was to
me. It's good of her to record one of my better moments.*

☐

I ENVY ALL THE ACTIVITY on the floor below us—and
wish I could be part of it. This afternoon as I climbed the stairs
with a bag of groceries, I was struck by how many people
seemed at home in the big living room.

In my only previous experience of family life, a clear line was
always drawn between company and family. Company arrived
at appointed hours, usually in response to an invitation, and
required food, drink, and undivided attention. But here people
gather without invitation and receive no particular show of
attention; they just seem to enjoy the simple comfort of being in
the same room.

As I set two places at the small dropleaf table in our living
room, I began to wish there were more of us each night around
the table. I grew up in a family that never had much to say until
dinner was served. Then everybody talked at once. But David
always brings a book to the table. If I protest, he says he has too
much work not to accomplish two things at once whenever
possible. He says we have plenty of time to talk in bed.

Doesn't he understand that he is my whole life? I wake up
every morning wondering whether he still loves me. Why do I
have to be constantly reassured? David takes it for granted that
I love him, so spends his time thinking about more important
things. When am I going to have a larger goal in life?

*I knew she was lonely, but she had no idea what married
life was costing me in hours as well as dollars. I had begun
to doubt that there would ever be enough time in the day or
money in the bank for all the things I wanted to do—and
all the things I wanted to do for her. How much time would
she give me to make good on all my promises?*

☐

I'VE FINALLY MADE CONTACT with the second floor!
Tonight for dinner I decided to try a new recipe that called

for two cloves of garlic. I always take my cookbook to the grocery store so I can be sure to buy all the ingredients. I had no idea what garlic looked like, but a clerk pointed it out to me, and I bought two. Since garlic resembles a strangely-shaped onion, I decided to treat it like one, peeling and chopping each bulb.

Soon the most overpowering aroma filled our tiny kitchen, which is actually just an open space at the top of the stairs. Opening all the windows in the living room and bedroom didn't seem to help. I was assembling the rest of the ingredients when a friendly male voice shouted up from the second floor to ask what was cooking. From our stove I could look straight down the stairs into the smiling face of Wyatt Blair, the designer who occupies the bedroom just below ours. Our first-floor landlady had introduced us but we'd never exchanged more than a greeting on the stairs. And I'd never stopped to consider how really attractive he is—the kind of man who is clearly comfortable in his own skin and has grown up taking his good looks for granted, secure in the knowledge they will get him anything he wants.

I always told myself looks didn't matter to Joanna. Now I find she's apparently her mother's daughter in more ways than one.

Wyatt bounded up the stairs, took one look at the mess I was busy sauteeing in olive oil, and burst out laughing. Then, turning off the flame under the skillet, he told me not to make a move until he got back. He ran down the stairs and quickly reappeared with a big garlic, which he began to tear apart with his bare hands. "This is a clove of garlic," he said, holding up a smooth, curved shape. "You cut off the ends, peel away the skin, and do with it as you will."

He asked to see the recipe to make sure there were no more pitfalls ahead, and before I quite realized what was happening, he was chopping onions alongside me. We were both laughing, struggling to balance slices of white bread on our heads—Wyatt's trick to prevent tears—when David came home. He seemed a little disconcerted to find Wyatt sharing our kitchen but said he had to read *The Wild Duck* and to call him when dinner was ready. Impulsively, I asked Wyatt to join us. If David could bring *The Wild Duck* to the table, I could bring Wyatt.

It's hard to believe that someone who became such a wonderful friend later irritated me so much in the beginning. It's not that I was threatened by him, pretty boy that he was. But I didn't marry Joanna so that some fellow could suggest adding endive to our salad.

However, something very interesting happens to a married couple in the presence of a sympathetic third party. You start vying for the stranger's attention, then begin seeing each other anew through the stranger's eyes and finally find yourselves falling in love all over again. Alone with Joanna, I read at the table and often fell asleep on the couch. I don't know what it was about Wyatt—whether it was the wine he contributed to the meal or the way he responded to Joanna's laughter—but I couldn't wait for him to leave so I could take her to bed. I didn't even give her time to do the dishes.

□

TONIGHT ON TELEVISION Kennedy debated Nixon—and David and I had our first public fight. Kennedy won the debate hands down—the outcome of our fight is still undecided.

Wyatt came upstairs to watch with us and brought Susan Armstrong, a second-year costume design student. They're working on a project together, but I think there's more than that between them.

Susan is a striking redhead with offbeat good looks and a dramatic style. She was wearing a boldly striped shift with a matching scarf around her neck. When I asked her where she got it, she said she designed it herself. She's been making all her own clothes since she was sixteen. Then she lifted her scarf and showed me why—her outfit was cleverly designed to hide an ugly scar that starts just beneath her left ear and continues along her neck. She told me she was in a car accident as a teenager and went through the windshield. She considers the scar a small price to pay for still being alive, but finds it hard to be friends with anyone until they know.

After the debate Susan and I made a cake. While it was baking, I asked if she would consider designing a dress for me.

"What are you trying to hide?" she asked. Smiling uncomfortably, I replied, "Nothing—except maybe myself." I hate shopping—trying on clothes, looking at myself in the mirror—and David hates what I buy without him. When he saw my trousseau, he said now that we were married, we couldn't afford mistakes, and the next time he was going shopping with me.

Saying that I had a beautiful figure and should wear clothes that showed it off more, Susan sketched me quickly in a tight-waisted red dress. "With your long dark hair and fair skin, you should wear bright colors," she advised. "Then people will notice you when you walk into a room."

While she took my measurements, I kept staring at the sketch, wondering if I could ever look the way Susan saw me. I finally got up the courage to ask how much a dress like that would cost. She said she could get the material wholesale for very little money and would design and make the dress as a gift. I was protesting, saying the dress would be a present, but not from Susan—I'd use my parents' birthday check—when suddenly I smelled something burning. Hurrying into the kitchen, I opened the oven door and gave a shriek.

David raced in from the living room. Pointing to the smoking cake, I began to cry. He put his hands on my shoulders and I thought he was going to hug me. Instead he began shaking me as hard as he could. "Don't ever scare me like that again," he said in a furious whisper. "I thought *you* were hurt—I nearly had a heart attack."

Seeing Susan trapped uncomfortably in the hallway, not knowing how to get past us into the living room, I tried to laugh off the incident, saying I screamed because I was so mad at myself for forgetting the cake. "It's not funny," shouted David. "How can you laugh after what you've just put me through?"

I was wishing I could sink out of sight when Susan crossed to David and put her arms around him. "I thought I was the only one in the world who got so frightened," she said. "I'm always expecting the worst. In fact, I never send out a bag of laundry without telling it good-bye forever."

David calmed down when he saw that Susan understood his behavior. Then Wyatt went downstairs for a six-pack of beer while Susan and I made a big platter of french fries to replace the cake.

Perhaps it's just as well I don't have a job. Being married to David is turning out to be a full-time career. I wake up every morning wondering if this is the day I'll get fired.

Why didn't I worry that one day she might just quit? Because in the beginning I was calling all the shots. How did I get away with it? Looking back at how I behaved when we were first married, I realize I was constantly testing her love. I had to be sure she saw me clearly—for exactly what I was—and loved me anyway.

☐

WYATT WANTS TO MARRY SUSAN but he's afraid to propose. He came upstairs this morning while I was going through David's clothes, checking for missing buttons. He said how much he envied David and me for being able to share our lives. He never knew his mother—she left him with his father when he was a baby and never made contact again. He grew up having to take care of himself. How wonderful it must be to have a wife, he said, as I took down David's good suit, checked the pockets for torn linings, brushed off the lint, and returned it to the closet.

I decided not to confess that David woke me this morning to report a missing button on the shirt he planned to wear—and would not leave for class until I'd gotten up and sewed on a new one. After he left I was too depressed to go back to sleep. No matter how hard I try, I seem to fall short of his expectations. I was an honor student in school but I'm failing the most important subject of my life—marriage. I'm lost without assignments and test scores to tell me where I stand. When I read *The Ladies' Home Journal*, I feel hopelessly inadequate. None of their readers would allow a shirt with a missing button to make its way into her husband's closet.

I resolved to spend the day trying to be a better wife, and now Wyatt says he wants one just like me. That may be as good a grade as I'll ever get. I advised him to go right over to Susan's apartment and ask her to marry him.

How nice it would be for me to have a best friend living on the floor below us.

□

WHAT A FOOL I WAS urging Wyatt to propose to Susan—or anyone! How could I have been so stupid and naive?

He saw me climbing the stairs with groceries yesterday afternoon and said he'd taken my advice and asked Susan to marry him—but she just laughed. She was pressing a skirt and didn't even take him seriously enough to unplug her iron.

Furious that she could be so unfeeling, I hugged him and said some day she'd realize her mistake. Then I invited him to share our meat loaf but he said he didn't feel like being around married people. He didn't want to think about what he was missing. He started down the stairs, then stopped midway, sat, and put his head in his hands.

I brought him a mug of coffee and sat beside him on the step. He took a couple of sips, then suddenly turned and said he would find it very easy to love me. I was stunned—but before I could respond he said he would also find it very easy to love David.

Wyatt was attracted to me? Well, a person can't help but be flattered.

Then I *think* I heard him say he'd actually slept with both men and women and wasn't sure which he preferred. I could hardly concentrate on anything after that. Is it really possible to love *both* men and women—physically, I mean? I think he could tell I was wondering who, because he quickly added that he couldn't name names. I nodded, embarrassed to be caught with my thoughts so naked. As frightened as I was by Wyatt's confession, I was also fascinated by how much more complicated people are than I'd been led to believe growing up in Texas.

Putting his free hand casually on my knee as he continued to sip his coffee, he said he'd always dreamed of getting married and living in a big house filled with children. But after what happened with Susan, he'd never have the courage to ask another woman to marry him—he might as well face the fact that he's homosexual.

His hand continued to rest on my knee, while I became more nervous by the minute. I'd seen *Tea and Sympathy* and loved it —but I wasn't prepared to live it. I was about to stand up and pour myself another cup of coffee when we heard the front door open and footsteps coming up the stairs. I prayed it was David. But it was John, Wyatt's roommate, or should I say his lover? I no longer know what to think about anyone.

"Be right there, John," Wyatt called. "God, you'll never believe the day I've had." He handed me his mug, thanked me for the coffee, and headed down the stairs. I could hear the two of them laughing as I washed the mugs.

Now it's twenty-four hours later—and I still haven't left the apartment. What do I say if I pass them on the stairs? And how do I tell any of this to David?

She didn't have to tell me. In three years at the drama school I met more people struggling with their sexual identity than I had in all my years in Texas. Or were they just more open about it?

☐

OUR FIRST DINNER PARTY. My mother would have been shocked at how I behaved but I'm rather proud of myself.

David informed me at noon that he'd invited Elaine for dinner. He said he needed her help plotting an Alfred Hitchcock show. He's taking a television class from a CBS story editor who thinks he has talent and has encouraged him to write a script on spec. So as soon as he left for class, I set off for the grocery store, determined to cook a meal that would prove to Elaine I had *some* talent.

Wyatt saw me climbing the stairs balancing three bags of groceries and hurried to my rescue. When I confessed how tense I was about cooking for company, he insisted on lending a hand. I invited him to stay for dinner. Not that I thought Elaine was his type—or vice versa—but I felt he should be around girls whenever possible.

However, David and Elaine made it clear from the moment

we sat down to dinner that this was not a social occasion. They talked character and plot and motivation as if it was a language neither Wyatt nor I could understand. I came up with what I thought was a great plot twist and David seemed to be considering it until Elaine explained why it wouldn't work. Of course he agreed with her. Then she reminded David of something someone said in class, and they began laughing at what was clearly a private joke—I couldn't see anything funny about it. David and Elaine have their own language, and when I'm around them, I feel like a foreigner just off the boat in a country where they've lived all their lives.

How do I compete with someone who looks right through me? Her indifferent attitude toward her appearance mocks the time I spend curling my hair and deciding what to wear. The irony is, her casual style—straight hair parted in the middle, the same wool skirt and silk blouse every time I see her—results in a kind of unstudied elegance that makes a strong statement about the kind of woman she is. If I didn't envy her, I wouldn't hate her so much.

Why was Joanna so determined to make it into a contest? I couldn't imagine being married to Elaine, but I desperately needed someone in my life who wouldn't pull punches about my work. Joanna was too kind—or was it too frightened?—to risk it.

The truth was, I needed both of them. Elaine understood. I was so naive about marriage at that point, I expected Joanna to understand also. I'm still naive about marriage, I suppose, or what's just happened wouldn't have happened. But at least I no longer need two women in my life (daughters excepted, of course).

Elaine ate the food I'd worked all afternoon to prepare without comment, and when I stood up to clear the plates, Wyatt was the only one who accompanied me into the kitchen. But I was too angry to stand dutifully at the sink washing dishes. I put on my coat, announced I was going to the movies, and invited Wyatt to go with me.

David came down the stairs after us and asked me what I thought I was doing, leaving in the middle of dinner.

"Dinner's over. You've had your dessert," I stormed. "I've waited on the two of you all night, but I can't go on playing Alice B. Toklas, sitting in a corner while the writers talk about their craft."

When I got back just now, the dishes had been washed and put away, and David was already asleep. I couldn't help smiling as I brushed my teeth, thinking of Elaine up to her elbows in soapsuds.

Elaine never got near soapsuds. She didn't even help me clear the table. I did the damn dishes—out of guilt—while Elaine talked. How could Joanna have possibly thought I'd even consider marrying someone like that?

☐

I HAD A JOB INTERVIEW with the New Haven *Register* today, but the only opening was on the night desk, so I turned it down. I know what I'm doing with my life when the sun goes down—it's only during the day that I have doubts.

On the way home I stopped by Susan's apartment for a fitting of my new dress. She lives alone on the top floor of an old frame house, and has converted the living room into a studio, filled with easel and canvases.

She hugged me warmly, saying after what had happened with Wyatt, she wasn't sure I still wanted to be friends.

I said what goes on between a man and a woman is too private for anyone on the outside to pass judgment. I wasn't just thinking of Wyatt. If David and I split up, we would have a hundred and one reasons apiece.

As she pinned the hem on my dress, Susan said Wyatt asked her to marry him for the wrong reason—he wasn't in love with her, he was afraid to live as a homosexual. She also suspected he felt sorry for her because of her scar and thought she would agree to marry him for fear no one else would ask her. "And I almost did," she confessed. "I'm as eager to get married as Wyatt—and also for the wrong reason. I don't want to have to get a job when I graduate. I want someone to take care of me so I can stay home and paint." I said she sounded like the perfect wife for David.

44

I already had the perfect wife—and I already knew it.
And in those days I even said it out loud rather frequently.
Why did I stop saying it aloud? Because I thought she
finally believed me, dammit!

☐

I VOTED FOR THE FIRST TIME in my life today—for John
F. Kennedy. Until now I've always thought of politicians as
members of my parents' generation—or older. But Kennedy is
one of us. I wonder if we'll do a better job of running the
country. I spent the afternoon getting my hair styled in a bouf-
fant, and I'm planning to buy a pillbox hat.

The East Coast story editor for the Hitchcock show loves
David's script and has sent it to the West Coast. No one in his
class has come this close to a sale; we're keeping our fingers
crossed.

☐

THE DIRECTOR OF THE YALE PRESS called this afternoon to offer me a job as an editorial assistant, starting next
week. I told him I'd be there. For the past month I've been
stopping by once a week to see if anything was available. I even
wrote several of my college professors for letters of recommendation. I'm so excited at the prospect of having a job—somewhere to go every day while David is in class and enough money
to buy the things at the grocery store he never feels we can
afford, like mushrooms and artichoke hearts.

I put down the phone, gave a squeal of joy, then grabbed my
coat and set out to find David. He said he would be in the library
all afternoon, and I found him stretched out on a couch reading
The Dance of Death. I raised my hands above my head to signal
victory. He quickly collected his books and, as soon as we were
outside, threw his arms around me in a bear hug.

"Where was the call from?" he asked. "New York or California?"

And then I knew. He thought his script had sold. Why else
would I have come looking for him? He had no idea how much I
wanted to work. I hadn't told him about my weekly visits to the

45

Yale Press. He'd probably even forgotten I'd applied for a job in September.

Taking a deep breath, I tried to downplay what had happened, erasing any sign of enthusiasm. But it was too late. Once David realized the good news had nothing to do with him, he heard very little of what I was saying. When I finally stopped for breath, he said slowly, "If you start work next week, how can we go home for Christmas?"

I didn't have an answer. I guess I thought we *were* home. Tonight, as David and I sat facing each other in silence across the dinner table, I began to regret he no longer read as he ate.

I know I behaved badly, but when I look back on all that, what I still feel is the pain at not making a sale to Alfred Hitchcock. Even now, late at night, I watch the damn reruns and keep thinking mine was better. Mine was better.

☐

CHRISTMAS NIGHT. Our first Christmas as a couple—but I feel less married every day we spend in Dallas. We took the train to Texas as soon as classes ended. I told the Yale Press I couldn't start work till the first of the year. Family complications. What an understatement!

David refused to stay in the garage apartment, saying since we made the trip to be with our families, we should be with our families. So we're staying in his old bedroom, with his mother in the next room.

Early Christmas morning we drove to my house to be with my family as they opened all the presents under their tree. My mother had continued to shop for me as if I were still in school. Unwrapping package after package of clothes that reflected her taste, not mine, I wondered if I could exchange them for cash without telling her.

My sister had brought home her Jewish roommate from college and my family was determined to make the girl's first Christmas an unforgettable experience. For every present Diana unwrapped, there was a matching gift for her roommate. Two of everything—sweaters, skirts, even jewelry. She was overwhelmed. But not as overwhelmed as David, who sat staring at his single gift: a cheap beige pullover, so ordinary and nondescript it was embarrassing. I told my parents I wasn't feeling well and asked David to take me home. They didn't have any idea what they had done, and there wasn't any way to explain it to them so they would understand.

Sure there was. The same way I explained it to my mother. In advance of need, as they say in the mortuary business—before she had a chance to make any mistakes. I told her that for Christmas and birthdays, Joanna and I were to be treated equally. What she spent was her business —as long as it was the same for both of us. All I wanted was for Joanna's parents to treat me like a member of their family—or a Jewish roommate.

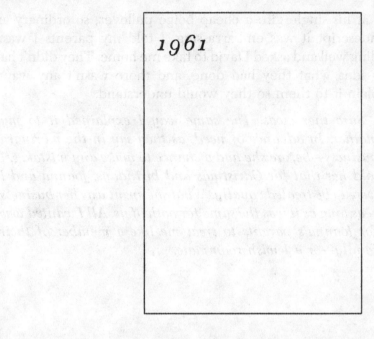

1961

IT WAS SNOWING so hard this morning—Inauguration Day
—that offices were closed and classes canceled. Now that I go to
work every day, it's an incredible luxury to sleep late—especially when David can sleep late with me. The best feeling in
the world is to look at the clock, then remember you don't have
to wake up, and to fall back asleep in the arms of someone who
has promised to love you all your life.

We didn't leave the apartment all day. I made French toast,
which we ate in front of the television watching the inauguration. When Kennedy spoke, I felt he was challenging all of us
who'd come of age in the comfortable 1950s. It's time to stop
taking and give something back. But how? Where? To whom?
I'm working long hours now, plus keeping house and looking
after my husband, but I still feel part of me is being held in
reserve for some unknown purpose.

I tried telling David how I felt, but he couldn't relate to what I
was saying. Finally he asked in alarm if I was pregnant. I assured
him that I never took chances. He seemed relieved, then said
Kennedy's speech had started him thinking. He's decided it
would be selfish to have children of our own, even in the far-

away future when we can afford them. He thinks, when the time comes to start a family, we should adopt. Not babies—older children that nobody wants. I agree, but frankly I can't imagine us with children of any age. We're still children ourselves, learning to live together. Marriage is an almost impossible balancing act; how could I ever manage to juggle children too?

It took her years to understand that marriage is like riding a bicycle. A family adds extra wheels—so you don't fall rounding the curves.

☐

TODAY MARKED THE END of my third week on the job. Though it's hard getting up in the morning, leaving David asleep, and even harder going to bed at night, leaving him awake, once I get to the office I feel so organized and efficient.

David and I are so different. He abhors routine—and goes out of his way to avoid doing *anything* exactly the way he did it the day before. Often I'll have dinner in the oven and he'll come home from class in the mood for a movie. The first time it happened, I made the mistake of saying we had to eat dinner first, but David told me to stop acting like his mother.

Now I've learned to take whatever I have in the oven and put it in the refrigerator overnight. Dinner, like almost everything, can be put on hold for twenty-four hours to no ill effect.

Why do I think that's some kind of sexual crack?

Never knowing what to expect from David makes me welcome the predictable pattern of my work week. I was so proud today when I finished copyediting my first manuscript and sent it off to the printer. At home I never finish anything without thinking it will have to be done all over again the next day or the next week.

☐

I COULDN'T STOP CRYING last night when the curtain came down on the drama school spring production, *Look Back in Anger*. David was furious at my reaction, demanding to know how I could go all to pieces over John Osborne when I've never cried at the end of one of his plays? How did I think that made him feel?

I tried to explain that it wasn't John Osborne's writing that made me cry, it was the bleak picture he painted of marriage. The man and the woman came from two different classes—two different worlds—and as passionately as they love each other, their differences finally destroy the marriage. As hard as I tried to resist, I couldn't help identifying with the wife. But then I began crying again, and David sent me to bed. When I woke up this morning to go to work, he was asleep on the couch in the clothes he was wearing last night.

At the time I refused to see any parallel between the play and our marriage. I took it at face value as an attack on the English class system. Joanna only saw what was on the stage—a bitter, violent man unleashing all his anger and frustration on the innocent, loving wife trapped into passivity by a background she cannot escape. So she cried herself to sleep. And I stayed up half the night rewriting my new play, both challenged and intimidated by Osborne's skill.

What's ahead for David and me? I love him for his passion—but it's so foreign to me, I'm frightened by it. I've never met anyone who allowed his emotions to consume him as David does. In love, our bedroom becomes a world of its own, and we exist in the moment, oblivious to any differences that divide us by daylight. Angry, he's a madman, deaf to argument. I've learned to wait for the fire to burn itself out before attempting to speak for the defense. At work, his energy is awe-inspiring—he approaches a blank page with unabashed confidence in his ability to fill it.

Did she really believe that? What bravado I must have displayed. Where, oh, where has it gone?

Part of me feels unworthy of him, but another part of me thinks I'm the best thing that could have happened to him just because we're so different. Opposites attract—we're living proof of that—but then what? Sometimes I think we're as mismatched as the hare and the tortoise.

Whoever said anything about the hare and the tortoise getting married? As I recall, they had a race—and we all know who won.

When David is angry at me, he accuses me of having no passion. In the beginning I believed him. Restraint was bred into me. I never heard my mother and father raise their voices, and I soon learned that any sign of emotion with David would cost me the argument. Then I discovered that keeping my emotions in check gave me a tremendous sense of power.

When he swept into my life, he overpowered all my defenses. I realize now I started this journal the day we met because I was terrified of what was happening. I knew from the way he looked at me that I was about to be violated in some irrevocable way. I couldn't change what was happening, but at least I could record it. But what tight-assed entries! Have I always been afraid of revealing my feelings—even to myself?

Yes, my darling. Yes, yes, yes.

What I loved from the first about David was how different he was from me. He revels in his emotions, while I hide from mine. And yet I know they're there, just waiting till everything is quiet and safe before they come out of hiding. It is ironic that the more he rages at me for my lack of passion, the more controlled I become. Is it because I feel I have surrendered control of everything else in my life to him? The only thing left for me to control is my feelings.

I was convinced she was holding back passions that would astonish us both if she could ever unlock them. I was determined to teach her to start talking back, to stand up for her rights, to value what made her unique—and to scream bloody murder when anyone took advantage of her endless hunger to be loved. What I failed to foresee was that when she began to do as I encouraged, the person directly in the line of fire was me.

☐

TONIGHT ELAINE GAVE a big end-of-school party. This time I knew everyone by name—even if they only knew me as

51

David's wife. When Brad Savage found out I worked for the Yale Press, he took me aside and asked a lot of questions about publishing. He plans to go into teaching but is already dreading the "publish or perish" pressure that accompanies an academic career. I always thought he was rather arrogant and opinionated, but tonight I began to see how vulnerable he is beneath that facade. Just as he was telling me he'd decided to direct *The Rivals* for his thesis production, hoping his research will lead to a book on Restoration comedy, David appeared out of nowhere, grabbed my hand, and said we were going home. Then he told Brad what a fine thing he was doing giving Richard Brinsley Sheridan a break in the theater.

What a kick in the ass for David! He's spent all spring rewriting his play, *Beside Myself,* in an attempt to please Brad, hoping he'd choose it for his thesis production.

> *So had Elaine and half a dozen other playwrights. What we all failed to realize is that an untried director is a lot more secure with a dead playwright than with a live one looking over his shoulder. Unfortunately, that has also proven true of experienced directors. They all prefer dead playwrights. When he was alive, even Shakespeare had to produce his own stuff.*

☐

EVERYONE WE KNOW is leaving for the summer. Wyatt is designing sets for a summer stock theater in Rhode Island. If it weren't for my job, we'd be going back to Dallas. But what would we do once we got there? David swore last summer he would never go back to the newspaper. I can't imagine another summer in my parents' garage apartment. We would probably have ended up in David's old bedroom. I can't bear the thought of being back in that room, in that house, in that city. David has just got to make it in the theater.

This summer he will be working afternoons in the alumni office, trying to save enough money for next year's tuition in case the scholarship he's hoping to get falls through. He plans to spend his free time drafting a new play.

☐

DAVID LEARNED TODAY that he's lost out—for the third year—on one of the big scholarships. This afternoon he paid to mimeograph twenty copies of *Beside Myself* and got a list from a magazine of every playwriting contest in the country. Apparently he's entering all of them. If Yale won't take him seriously, he's determined to find someone, somewhere, who will.

☐

HOW DOES DAVID really feel about our marriage? I confide my doubts and fears to this journal. Where does he confess his?

Today I got my answer. I ran into Elaine at the grocery store. To my surprise, she asked if she could come home with me. I couldn't help being flattered.

As I was putting away the groceries, she began talking about David's new play and how harshly the class had treated him when he read it aloud last month. All I heard was "new play." Had David finished a new play without telling me? I always assumed *I* was his first audience. I couldn't admit to Elaine that I knew nothing about the play. She said the class all felt he was too close to the subject to be writing about marriage. All except her, of course.

I asked why she'd waited so long to say anything to me. She said she couldn't get the play out of her mind but hesitated to encourage him to do any more work on it without finding out first how I felt. She wouldn't want anything to hurt our marriage. I told her David was free to write anything he chose.

The minute she left, I began to rifle through his desk drawers. Finally, hidden in a stack of blank typing paper, I found it—a new play, still untitled. Terrified of what its pages might reveal, I began to read.

At first I didn't understand what had troubled Elaine. The play was about an orphan whose childhood sweetheart reappears twenty years into his marriage and asks to move in with him and his wife. What did all this have to do with David and me? But when the husband began telling his wife how lonely he was, insisting that taking in another woman was the only way to save their marriage, I realized David had put into words something I've been afraid to face: living with another person can be lonelier than living alone.

I waited till after dinner to confront him. If that was really how he felt about marriage, maybe we should just divorce now. He told me to stop acting like a child, called Elaine a bitch for telling me about it, and said it was old news anyway—Gassner had told him to put the damn thing away for at least ten years. Then he might know enough to write a good play about marriage and divorce. About marriage and divorce? In ten years? Is Gassner only giving us ten years? God, what an awful day. David made it a better night.

I've obliterated the bottom half of this page because I see no need for your mother to go into detail about what it took from me to make it a better night for her.

☐

DAVID BROUGHT ELAINE HOME for dinner last night, and she announced to our surprise that she's spending the summer here too. I was making spaghetti for dinner, and she insisted on contributing a bottle of chianti and a cake for dessert. She was very nice about the spaghetti and even helped me wash the dishes. But when I began yawning at eleven o'clock, David insisted I go to bed, since I had to be at work at nine. I waited for Elaine to leave but she just thanked me for dinner and continued to sit there. They were still talking at 2 A.M. when I got up to go to the bathroom.

Elaine spent most of that evening telling me how much she admired Joanna—for not losing herself in marriage. She said she didn't think she was capable of being a wife, and then she began to cry. I didn't know how to console her. Finally she asked if she could sleep on our couch. She said she felt safe knowing Joanna and I were in the next room.

☐

I'M TERRIFIED THAT DAVID AND ELAINE are having an affair. If they are, it's my fault. If I hadn't been so determined to get a job, we'd be in Dallas now, spending a quiet, air-conditioned summer with our families. Our apartment under the eaves, which seemed so cozy and charming in September, is an oven. David says it's too hot to concentrate, so when he finishes work, he goes to Elaine's apartment to write. At least that's what he says he does. All I know for sure is that he doesn't come home till eight or nine at night. Tomorrow is our first anniversary. I wonder if he even remembers.

Of course I remembered—but you wouldn't know from reading this. I surprised her at work wearing a coat and tie and took her to Kaysey's—the restaurant across from the Shubert Theater where all the show people used to eat. I couldn't afford it, but I thought she deserved it. We each ordered lobster—the first we'd ever eaten—and when the waiter asked what the occasion was as he tied the bibs around our necks, I said it was a religious holiday, for men who worship their wives. I figured with that speech I'd won her for at least another year.

When she started to cry, I thought it was sentiment. Now I realize she was crying because she thought I was having an affair. Well, let me tell you something about unfaithful husbands—you don't have to wonder. Sooner or later, someone rings your doorbell and tells you more than you want to know. My mother could have told Joanna exactly how it feels to be a betrayed wife—that is, if they'd ever talked about anything that mattered. How could Joanna have imagined that I was capable of infidelity after what I'd lived through with my father?

One afternoon soon after I turned thirteen a man Mother had never met knocked at our front door and asked if she knew where her husband was. She said he was at work. He said no—in his house with his wife. And in case she didn't believe him, he gave her the address. She screamed at the man to go away, then told me to put on my coat, we might have to stay in the car a long time.

I was just learning to drive but I didn't have a license so I was surprised when she handed me the key and said she was too upset to take the wheel. We parked across the street from a little shack of a house and waited for a couple of hours. Just as it was getting dark, Dad came out the front door. I thought there was going to be a scene but instead Mother told me to drive home. Dad never even saw us. I prayed she was going to leave him, go home to my grandmother in East Texas, but instead she cooked dinner as usual and had it waiting when he came home. Not until I went to bed that night did I hear their shouts and screams coming from the bedroom.

I vowed that night that if I ever had the courage to get married (believe me, there was nothing about my parents' marriage to recommend the institution), I would be faithful to my wife even if I failed as a husband in every other way. Looking back, I realize I may have set my standards a little low. I excused a lot of impossible behavior by saying to myself that at least I was a better husband than my father had been—I'd never been unfaithful. And I never have. But apparently it doesn't count for much.

☐

ELAINE CALLED ME at work this morning and said she had to see me. Could we have lunch? I couldn't see myself choking down a meal while she told me she was having an affair with my husband. Trying to stay calm, I said David expected me home for lunch but I could meet her somewhere after work, while David was writing in her apartment.

Elaine was waiting in a booth at Hasselbach's when I arrived. She asked if David knew we were meeting and seemed relieved when I shook my head. Suddenly beginning to cry, she said she needed help and I was the only one she could ask. Would I go with her overnight into New York while she got an abortion—and promise not to tell David anything about it?

Before I dared ask who the father was, she began talking about the divinity student who'd pursued her all spring, begging her to marry him. She'd sent him home for the summer with the promise of an answer in September. Two weeks later she discovered she was pregnant. That was the night she slept on our couch, but she'd been too confused and frightened to tell either of us. Since then, she'd thought about all her options and come to the conclusion that marriage would put an end to her writing career.

I've never known anyone who had an abortion—or even considered the possibility. I didn't know what to say. She didn't need me to tell her that it was not only dangerous but illegal. Once I got past my relief that David was not the father, I felt like offering condolences—except I wasn't sure to whom. Thinking of that divinity student who wanted to take a wife with him to his first ministry, I was filled with sadness.

A year ago I would've urged Elaine to get married and have the baby. But now I know firsthand how hard it is to make a marriage work—even when you plunge into it as wholeheartedly as David and I. How could I plead with her to put aside a career and marry a man she wasn't sure she loved, just because she happened to be pregnant?

But how could I go with her to get an abortion? It would mean spending the night away from David for the first time in our marriage—and lying about the reason. Elaine could see me hesitating but said she couldn't trust anyone else. She added that I owed her a favor; she'd put in a good word for me with the editorial director of the Yale Press when she met him at a cocktail party last fall. She knew how much I wanted to work and thought I was too bright to make a career out of just being a wife.

I was surprised and touched to learn that Elaine had gone out on even a small limb for me. She wanted me to have the chance to be everything I could be. How could I do less for her?

Tonight after dinner I told David I had to go into New York tomorrow to meet with an author. He asked if I couldn't wait till the weekend so he could go with me, but I explained that the author was leaving for Europe, and I had to go over his copyedited manuscript with him before he left. David was dubious about the trip—especially when he realized I'd be gone overnight. I thought quickly and said my boss at the Yale Press had an unmarried sister in New York with whom I'd be staying—to save paying my hotel expenses, I suspected. David bought it. I promised to call him as soon as I arrived.

□

WELL, IT'S DONE, and Elaine is fine—but I'm not sure I am. The doctor's office was located just across the street from the Actors Studio. Shelley Winters passed us on the sidewalk, hurrying to class. Sometimes the theater seems pretty silly compared to life.

While we waited for the nurse to take her inside, Elaine handed me her new play to read. She said maybe it would take my mind off where I was. I just hoped it would justify her decision. And my coming with her. And lying to David for the first time in our marriage. But the more I read, the more convinced I became that what she ought to be aborting was her play.

I never knew any of this. Joanna not only lied to me but made it stick—and kept Elaine's secret all these years. I can't imagine her holding someone's hand through an abortion. Even now, with all her pro-choice talk, she still thinks having a baby is the ultimate creative act. Or am I the one who thinks that?

I do remember her turning away from me in bed the night she came home from New York. I'd never known her not to want to make love before. Or since. Till now, of course.

□

TODAY David got a long-distance call from Kansas, informing him that *Beside Myself* had won first prize in the contest he entered at the university there.

Hallelujah! This is the first mark of approval he's gotten as a playwright since his acceptance at Yale. I know it's just the first of many prizes his plays will receive. Today Kansas, tomorrow the Pulitzer! How exciting to be the wife of a prizewinning playwright—that's career enough for any woman!

58

I can hardly bear to read this. How young and naive we were! But even at that time, my hopes were seldom as high as hers. I never started a race without knowing the odds. My mistake perhaps. You shouldn't leave the starting gate thinking about anything but winning. Joanna always believed in the promise of each new day. If she was disappointed, so what? There was always a new promise on the horizon. I've never been able to live like that. My loss.

I was hugging and kissing him when I suddenly heard him promising to be in the audience opening night. Now, how are we going to manage that?

The prize is a hundred dollars, but it will cost us five times that much to get there and back. Plus I risk losing my job. I've only been working seven months, so I'm hardly due for a vacation. David expects me to ask my boss for an unpaid leave of absence so I can come with him, then home to Texas for a visit before school starts. I suppose I'd feel worse if he didn't want me in the audience for his first opening night—but not a lot.

To her credit she kept all these second thoughts to herself. In fact, she had me convinced the trip to Kansas was going to be the highpoint of her life.

☐

MY HEART BROKE for David tonight. I remember reading once about Scott Fitzgerald taking Sheilah Graham to a production of his play *The Vegetable* in Pasadena while he was making his living as a screenwriter in Hollywood. He wore a tux and made her put on a long dress. They arrived for the gala opening night only to discover the production was an amateur effort taking place in a basement with makeshift scenery and a handful of people in the audience. The only difference for us in Kansas tonight was that we didn't overdress. Thank goodness David doesn't own a tux.

Were we really in a basement? I have no memory of anything except the ecstasy of hearing my words spoken aloud by actors. For the first time in my life I felt like a playwright.

☐

CLASSES BEGAN TODAY, and when David learned that a timid director named Lewis Brill still hadn't decided which classic to direct for his thesis production, he cornered him, trying to convince him he would get more attention directing a prizewinning original play.

Lewis asked if there were any reviews from the Kansas production. David lied and said no. Finally Lewis agreed to read the revised version of *Beside Myself*. But David had a better idea. He'd assemble a cast to read the play aloud for Lewis in our living room. And after the reading, I'd fix dinner for everyone.

The plan worked. By the time we'd finished dessert Lewis had agreed to direct the play. I don't think anyone has had him to dinner since he came to Yale. It's amazing to watch David in action. I can't believe the way he's made that pitiful production in Kansas work for him. Maybe the trip was worth it after all— even if we are still paying for our train tickets. Thank goodness I didn't lose my job.

After the reading David asked Wyatt to join us to talk about the set. Wyatt said our living room furniture had just the drab look the play needed. We'll have to sneak it down the stairs at night after our landlady is asleep. Lewis loved being part of the conspiracy and left the house thinking we were all going to become the best of friends.

Poor Lewis. I wonder whatever became of him? On second thought, I don't.

☐

THE WHOLE CAST came over for dinner last night—minus Lewis, who David says only gets in the way. I made a Texas-style taco casserole. Everybody said it was different from anything they'd ever tasted—I don't think anyone liked it. We had to use our double bed as a dining table since our living room furniture is making its stage debut.

After dinner David asked the actors to help him improvise a scene he feels is needed to end the first act. I couldn't believe he could just abandon his play to a bunch of actors who were still learning the lines. But he followed them around like a besotted grandparent, telling them how completely they understood their characters and writing down every word they uttered.

At the end of the scene one of the actors was actually sobbing. I felt as if I were in a giant playpen with a lot of self-absorbed infants. I don't belong in the theater. At least I'm only related by marriage.

I told David I wasn't feeling well, brushed the corn chips off the bedspread, crawled under the covers, put a pillow over my head so I wouldn't hear the screams and sobs coming from the living room, and went to sleep. What am I doing with my life? Most of what goes on in my living room since David's play went into production has nothing to do with the life I want to live. Thank goodness for my job. At least it makes sense!

> *We could've rehearsed in the theater. I invited the cast for dinner so Joanna would feel included. My mistake. One I continued making over the years, obviously.*

□

BESIDE MYSELF opened last night and we had a terrific two-floor party to celebrate. Wyatt iced tubs of beer and wine in his kitchen, and I fixed a baked ham and potato salad in ours. Our living room was still packed with people at 2 A.M. when I slipped into the bedroom, crawled under all the coats piled on the bed, and went to sleep. The coats were gone when I woke up this morning, but David was still awake, talking to Elaine.

I made coffee while they thrashed over a new opening for Act Two. I hated having to go to work, but once I'd washed all the dishes from the party, I really wasn't needed. I had no idea what to do about Act Two.

> *For twenty-four hours I tasted success, until a sophomore reviewed the play for the Yale paper and called my writing sophomoric. I didn't show the review to Joanna; I was afraid she might agree.*
> *Remind me to tell you some time about the fool your mother made of herself the night an actress in my play became ill and she tried to take her place. Or has our*

marriage reached such a point that I can no longer risk telling foolish tales about her?

☐

MY MARRIAGE has cost me my job, but I'm not telling David. When I went in to ask my boss for another unpaid leave so we could go home for Christmas, he said, "Another leave? Who do you think you are? Do you know how many applicants are on file for your job?"

I said I loved the work, but I loved my husband more and if I had to choose, I wouldn't hesitate. So now I have the afternoon free for Christmas shopping, but my heart sinks at the thought of spending money when there won't be any more where that came from. I'm not going to say anything to David till after Christmas, but I think I'll suggest that this year, instead of surprising each other with presents, each of us should choose something we really want and say it's our gift from the other one. That way we won't end up spending money on things we don't like and won't use—like the antique bracelet he gave me last year, which has already come apart at the hinges, or the Irish fisherman's sweater I gave him, which he says is so heavy he can't breathe when he wears it.

At the time I had no idea she'd lost her job. I just thought she was trying to get out of shopping.

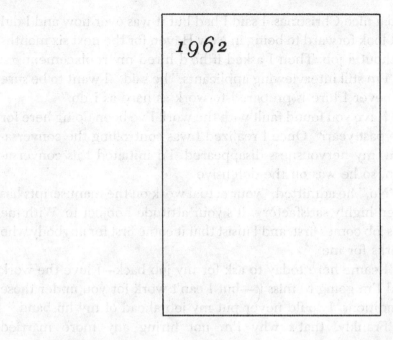

1962

I CAN'T WRITE ABOUT CHRISTMAS. Living through it was hard enough. I was waiting till we were back in New Haven to tell David I'd been fired, but when we got here I lost my nerve. I told him I wasn't going to work today because I was sick. And I am—but it's nothing physical. I'm filled with anger at having lost my job. If only I could tell someone—but I don't want David to feel responsible.

☐

MY THIRD DAY IN BED. Wyatt came upstairs to bring me some soup after David left for class, and I began pouring out my heart to him. He asked if I'd do anything differently if I had it all to do over, and I said no—my only regret was all the things I didn't say.

"Then say them," Wyatt suggested. "Write your boss a letter. Or better yet, get out of bed and go over there and say them to his face. It can't hurt—you've already lost your job—and it might make you feel better."

As nervous as I was about confronting my former boss, he looked equally tense about seeing me. He began by asking if I'd had a nice Christmas. I said I had but it was over now and I did not look forward to being in New Haven for the next six months without a job. Then I asked if he'd hired my replacement.

"I'm still interviewing applicants," he said. "I want to be sure whoever I hire is prepared to work as hard as I do."

"Have you found fault with the work I've been doing here for the past year?" Once I realized I was controlling the conversation, my nervousness disappeared. I'd initiated this conversation, so he was on the defensive.

"No," he admitted, "your actual work on the manuscripts has been highly satisfactory. It's your attitude I object to. With me this job comes first, and I insist that it come first for anybody who works for me."

"I came here today to ask for my job back—I love the work and I'm going to miss it—but I can't work for you under those conditions. I could never put my job ahead of my husband."

"Frankly, that's why I'm not hiring any more married women."

"Your loss," I answered—and then left the office quickly before I began to cry.

Walking home, I realized I meant it. I've lost a weekly salary, but he's lost a valuable source of labor. Men have ruled the working force for so long, they think they can make all the rules. Has it ever occurred to them that women who put family ahead of job might bring some important human values into the marketplace? How many men have looked back on their lives and wished they'd devoted more time to their families? I've never heard of anyone saying on his deathbed that he wished he'd spent more time on his business.

David was happy to see me out of bed when he came home from class. He had a letter in his hand from Audrey Wood. She's agreed to represent *Beside Myself* and wants ten more copies immediately so she can begin submitting them to producers.

I said I'd start typing tomorrow—then confessed I'd lost my job. Staff cutbacks, I said. Since I was leaving in June anyway, I was the first to go.

"Well, we'll miss the salary," David said with a shrug, still jubilant over his good news. "But you've had your turn at bat.

Now it's up to me to start earning a living." And we went out to dinner to celebrate. Marriage is wonderful!

That night after Joanna was asleep Wyatt told me what had really happened at work. The next day I stopped by the office and told her boss personally what I thought of him. I don't think I changed his mind about hiring married women—probably just the opposite. I was furious that he'd hurt her feelings, but other than that, I didn't feel too badly about Joanna losing her job. I was sure that, with Audrey Wood showing my play, I'd soon be needing a full-time editorial assistant myself.

☐

AFTER MONTHS OF WAITING for her to call him—I could see it in his eyes every time the phone rang—David finally called Audrey Wood today. She was polite but terse, which is apparently her style. She explained that clients do not call agents, agents only call clients—which she will do as soon as there is any news to report. I wonder if that rule applies to her successful clients—or just those who are about to give up and go back to Dallas? David graduates at the end of the month—and no production in sight. We can't go back home. We just can't. But David says we're not moving to New York unless he gets some professional encouragement before he graduates.

☐

A RAINBOW in sight at last! With any luck at all, we'll be able to follow it right into New York. I don't care about a pot of gold —I just want to make the trip.

I'd been confiding all my fears and frustrations to Wyatt. I thank God every day that he's homosexual—or at least thinks he is. Otherwise, David would have been much too jealous to allow us to become best friends, especially considering how handsome Wyatt is. I love knowing that all I have to do is shout down the stairs and he'll come running—to share a cup of tea or a laugh. I'm going to miss him so much when we have to leave New Haven and live in separate houses. But at least, whatever the

65

future holds, it looks as if we'll be together this summer—and David will have a production.

At my suggestion—though David of course has no idea I had anything to do with it—Wyatt showed *Beside Myself* to Martin Mills, who runs the summer stock theater in Rhode Island where Wyatt has designed sets for the last two summers. Mills has ambitions to break into the New York theater and Wyatt convinced him that an original play is his best chance.

> *After Joanna convinced Wyatt—apparently. Christ! She really didn't trust my career to take off on its own steam. But probably better I didn't know. I might've blown it— and then what would've become of us?*

□

MARTIN MILLS took us to dinner, along with Wyatt, to discuss his plans for the play. He wants to try it out in Rhode Island this summer, then, if all goes well, take it off-Broadway next season.

David was wonderfully cool. He said Audrey Wood was showing the play in New York, and several producers had already expressed interest. This was news to me, and I was about to ask who when David accidentally overturned a glass of wine in my lap and I had to go to the ladies' room to repair the damage. By the time I returned to the table, it was agreed David would be playwright in residence for the summer, and I would work in the box office in exchange for our room and board.

□

BESIDE MYSELF went into rehearsal today. Willa Crane, the actress playing the lead, has only done musical comedy bits, but David thinks she's going to be a big star. Frankly, I'll put my money on her leading man, Paul Gaines. He may be short, but he has a brooding intensity and animal energy that really do things to women. I think Willa is as attracted to him as I am.

> *I was too excited by Willa and her talent to notice how Joanna was responding to Paul. But it turns out we were both right.*

66

Willa is only ten years older than I am, yet treats me as if I were David's daughter instead of his wife. Her husband left her for another woman five years ago when she was pregnant with their first (and only) child—and now she seems determined to prove that marriage is an unworkable arrangement for anyone.

She asked David to have dinner with her alone tonight to discuss the part—and suggested I baby-sit with her four-year-old daughter Molly. Actually, I didn't mind. I like the daughter better than the mother.

Molly wanted to play her favorite game, wedding. I made her a bridal bouquet out of wild flowers and pinned a bed sheet to her hair for a veil. She asked me to be the bridegroom, then demanded that I take off my wedding ring and put it on her finger. When I refused, she burst into tears and said she was going to tell her mother. But she was saved the trouble.

When Willa came through the door and saw Molly in tears, she assumed I was responsible. I quickly explained that Molly wanted my wedding ring but I wouldn't give it to her.

"Children are like artists," said Willa. "They're very sensitive."

"So are wives," I muttered.

☐

I'M APPALLED by the scene I witnessed today at rehearsal—a scene much too blatant for David to have written. There's more honor among thieves than there is among actors. What kind of a world have I married into?

The drama began when an attractive young man came to the box office where I was working and asked to see Paul Gaines. I said that he couldn't be interrupted, he was inside the theater rehearsing. The next thing I knew, the young man had burst into the theater, jumped onstage, and grabbed Paul by the throat. Paul was on the floor gasping for breath by the time the stage manager got them separated, so we only heard one side of the story—but I think one side is all there is.

It turns out the fellow—also an actor—roomed with Paul in New York. They both auditioned for Martin Mills when he was casting his summer season, and the part went to Paul's room-

67

mate. However, when the call came, the roommate was out of town, so Paul took the message—and the part. A casual remark by a casting agent tipped off the roommate and he caught the next train for Rhode Island—apparently intending to kill Paul and reclaim the role.

Unfortunately, time—and Willa—are on Paul's side. The play opens tomorrow night, and she refuses to go onstage without him—a position no doubt reinforced by the fact that she no longer goes home without him. And far from being shocked at his unscrupulous behavior toward his roommate, she seemed stimulated by it. At least I've never seen her more eager to end a rehearsal.

David and I felt so badly for the fellow, we offered to take him out to dinner, but he said that since he wasn't getting the part, he'd have to return to New York tonight—he has another audition tomorrow. Ah, the life of an actor. They make writers look stable by comparison.

Thanks.

□

THE PLAY OPENED TONIGHT, and Audrey Wood was in the audience along with one of her famous clients, Hunt Townsend. He's currently writer in residence at some Ivy League college, but it's been ten years since he's had anything produced in New York.

When the curtain came down, David grabbed my hand and we made a run back to our cabin. He said not to turn on any lights. He didn't want anyone to know where we were.

As he peeked from behind the window shade at the opening-night audience pouring out of the theater, I asked if he thought it went that badly. Instead of replying, he suddenly released a curse and yanked me into the bathroom, locking the door behind us. "It's Audrey Wood. She's on her way over here."

There was a peremptory knock at the door and a stern, schoolmistress voice said, "David, a party in your honor is in progress onstage. If you don't make an appearance within half an hour, I'll be back—and bring the party with me. Now vomit or cry or do whatever you have to do—then pull yourself together." Then in a softer tone she added, "And don't be embarrassed, darling. I know how you feel. Don't forget, I've been through all this with Tennessee."

David turned on the shower full force, stripped, and got in. There was nothing for me to do but take off my best dress and get in with him.

And there's nothing for me to do but obliterate another page of this journal.

When we appeared at the party, our hair still wet from the shower, we were greeted with a round of applause. David pretended we'd gone for a night swim in the ocean, and we were toasted by the crowd as if we were some glamorous, young reincarnation of Scott and Zelda climbing dripping wet in our evening clothes from the fountain in front of the Plaza Hotel.

Hunt Townsend shook David's hand in congratulation, then put his arm around his shoulder, took him off to one side, and engaged him in an intense conversation. How thrilling it must be for David to be treated like an equal by such a distinguished man of letters.

The son of a bitch told me to put the play away in my trunk. When I was older, he said, I would take it out and reread it and see that it was the work of a very young man. Twenty years later I was asked to speak at his funeral. I declined. Joanna never knew why.

☐

BRAD SAVAGE SHOWED UP last night for the closing performance—married to Susan Armstrong. I had no idea they were even dating. Neither did Wyatt, apparently. He said if they mentioned going out with him after the play, I should say he'd be too busy striking the set. However, they didn't ask.

To our surprise Brad was full of praise for the production and told David how much he regretted not directing the play at Yale. If he had, maybe he'd be headed into New York in the fall instead of to Greencastle, Indiana, to teach drama.

However, he said he wouldn't have had the courage to ask Susan to marry him without the prospect of steady employ-

69

ment, so perhaps it was all for the best. He and Susan fell in love when she was designing the costumes for *The Rivals.* When I told Susan how happy I was for her, she squeezed my hand and said Brad was giving her everything she ever wanted—time alone to paint.

When Brad said they were driving back to New Haven, David impulsively suggested they stay overnight in our cabin. I wondered what he had in mind. We only have one room—and one double bed. But Brad and Susan accepted gratefully, confessing how much they'd been dreading the long drive back to New Haven, yet knowing a hotel room was out of the question on their budget. Before I could ask David his plan, he'd put our mattress on the floor for Brad and Susan and said we'd sleep on the box springs. Susan and I were still talking long after Brad and David were both asleep.

The next morning when Martin Mills saw two couples emerging from our cabin, he gave me a wink and said the next time I threw an orgy, be sure to invite him and his wife. The nights got pretty long in Rhode Island.

☐

DAVID AND I are staying with Willa in her apartment on Central Park West while we look for a place of our own. She thinks we would get more space for the dollar on the Upper West Side, but today I bought *The Village Voice* and circled half a dozen possibilities. It's enough I live in her shadow; I have no intention of living in her neighborhood.

Am I going to have to take second place to another woman for the rest of my marriage? In New Haven it was Elaine. In New York it's Willa. I can't even admit how jealous I am, because each of them has something to offer David that I have no way of giving him. How can I want the best for him yet resent his reliance on Elaine's mind and Willa's acting? Each of them challenges him to do his best work—so my future depends on them as much as his does. Why then does my stomach tangle in knots when David sits at the table with Willa for hours after dinner talking about Stanislavski and Artaud and how to transform illusion into truth while Molly and I sing songs and wash dishes?

David will only agree to sublet an apartment—he refuses to sign a lease until he sees what happens with *Beside Myself*. Martin Mills has found a prospective angel, a wealthy, stage-struck businessman who he hopes will put up the money for an off-Broadway production. Meanwhile we're living off the option.

It was only a $500 option. We were surviving because her parents were sending us money again. And she, of course, was trying not to notice.

□

FINALLY A PLACE OF OUR OWN—a sublet on Perry Street in the Village, three rooms for just sixty-five dollars a month. David thought I'd be depressed when I saw the bathtub in the kitchen and kept reassuring me that we could leave on a month's notice, but I'm determined to stay here until *Beside Myself* opens off-Broadway. Then we can talk about moving uptown. Life in New York is so exciting—who needs a house with an entrance hall?

Everything is falling into place so fast. By the new year David is sure to be the toast of the town. Sometimes my heart stops to think how close I came to missing all the bright lights! What would I be doing now if I'd gone off to graduate school alone? I find it hard to imagine a life that revolves around the library.

Did I realize when I asked Joanna to marry me, I was also asking her to buy my dream? By the next year, she had grounds to sue for breach of promise.

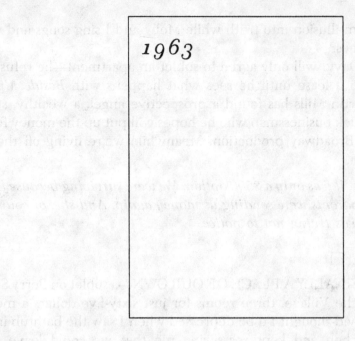

1963

OUR ANGEL DISAPPEARED soon after Christmas. Martin Mills suspects his accountant talked him out of investing in a play. I was crushed, but David took it better. He says no responsible accountant would allow a client to put his money in the theater—the odds are better at the racetrack. But Mills did renew his option—he hopes to raise the money for a production from other sources. So, with the Christmas checks from our families, we have enough money to scrape by for a few more months. Sometimes I feel our marriage is as much a month-to-month commitment as this apartment. Are David and I just playing house?

It may have seemed like a game to her, but it was life or death to me. I'd given myself a deadline—two years to make it as a writer. If I failed, I'd do what half the people in my graduating class had already begun to do—teach.

☐

ELAINE WEST came for dinner tonight. At the last minute we asked Wyatt too. It was the first time we've had Elaine to our new apartment, which she pronounced unique and charming.

We've been at work all winter fixing it up. Wyatt helped us paint it. How I miss having him on the floor below! He's sharing a place on Riverside Drive near Columbia with three other designers—one male, two female. I hope he's found happiness with at least one of them. Each cooks dinner for the others one night a week, and the other three days they're on their own. He likes the arrangement; there's always someone around when he feels like talking, but nobody takes offense if he wants to be alone. Why doesn't marriage allow people to be so easy with each other?

Most of the furniture in our small living room we found abandoned on the sidewalk and dragged home. Once we scrubbed and sprayed and recovered and repainted, it all looked quite presentable. When Elaine asked where we found everything, I said we'd been combing the Village ever since we moved in.

She's not had any luck finding an agent to represent the plays she wrote at Yale. I seem to remember that as she was writing them, she prided herself on the fact that they were so uncommercial. But she resents it when an agent tells her the same thing. So she's abandoning playwriting to become a critic—as soon as she convinces a new underground weekly newspaper to hire her to review theater. Happy thought: if she gets the job, we can count on at least one good review for *Beside Myself*.

☐

EVEN THOUGH WE COULD USE the money, how can I get a real job when the man I love likes to work at night while the world is asleep? He usually finishes just as the sun is rising. Then we get dressed and go for a long walk down to Wall Street. Sometimes we stop at Chock Full O'Nuts for doughnuts and coffee. David takes a perverse pleasure in being surrounded by people on their way to work, knowing that we're heading home to bed.

If we have to go to the bank or a grocery store, we do that on the way home, then tumble into the double bed which completely fills our tiny bedroom. We sleep until dark, when I wake up and fix dinner. If it's not too late by then, we try to make a ten o'clock movie. At midnight David starts work. And I reach for another novel. Sometimes I think I'm just reading about life instead of living it.

I understand why David is in hiding. We had such big plans when we moved into New York. Now it's nine months later and his play is still unproduced. No wonder he doesn't want to face anybody. I feel as if I'm married to a man who's had to go underground for political reasons.

People wonder why they can never reach us by phone. They don't know that we only answer it at dinnertime and not even then unless we're in the mood to talk. Sometimes when it rings, we play a game. For every ring, we take turns naming a likely caller—someone with whom we have no interest in talking. I always name Willa first and Elaine second. If we run out of names before the phone stops ringing, we answer. But that seldom happens. And so I have what I thought I always wanted —David all to myself. Why am I so restless?

Restless? Restless is going to three double features in one day—something I used to do regularly until I married Joanna. I assumed she was content curling up for hours with John Updike. I admired his writing in the beginning too, but grew to hate him when I imagined he was satisfying my wife more than I ever had. Or was she just using him the way I once used double features—as an escape from what was not happening in her own life?

☐

HOME TO TEXAS for the summer. How am I going to get through the next three months? David seems undaunted by the fact that *Beside Myself* is still unproduced—and is already drafting a new play, which he's calling *Jack Fell Down*. He says he can work better away from New York.

I was always lying to Joanna. The truth was, I wasn't working well anywhere. But I kept returning to Dallas because of Mother—my compulsion to fill up her emptiness.

God knows there are no distractions in Dallas. We never go anywhere or see anyone outside our families. Why do I feel like a soldier coming home from a war we lost?

So what did she want me to do? Stay in the front lines and keep taking it? I was shell-shocked from rejection. The prospect of a summer in hiding was the only thing that kept me going.

I've begun to suspect that David likes his characters better than he does me. He spends more time in their company, but why not? They surprise and delight him with their reactions in a way I no longer can.

☐

TONIGHT MY PARENTS gave a big dinner dance at the country club for their anniversary. They wanted to make it a joint occasion—we will have been married three years next week—but David said we preferred to celebrate in private. The truth is, we don't have much to celebrate beyond the fact that we've made it through another year. Martin Mills has dropped the option on *Beside Myself,* so David says he can't see any reason to go back to New York. He wasn't in a swell mood before we left for the country club, then at dinner my father's law partner made the mistake of asking if he was still writing plays. "Are you still practicing law?" David retaliated. "Or did you quit when you lost your last case?" Fortunately, at that moment the orchestra began to play, so I quickly asked him to dance.

All I could think about that night was how much it had cost me to rent a tux—just to be insulted.

☐

MY MOTHER IS GOING to Europe for three weeks—an art museum tour of Greece—and tonight at dinner (David got out of it by pleading illness) she asked me to go with her. The friend who was planning to share her room had to cancel at the last minute. All the arrangements have been made, and Mother would pay for everything. There's just one catch—David. Much as I would love the trip, I don't know how to tell him. I have to decide by tomorrow.

Greece? I don't remember anything about Greece. When was this? What was her mother trying to do to us? She knew

I wouldn't let Joanna go to the grocery store without me if I could help it.

□

LAST NIGHT I LAY AWAKE for hours beside David trying to imagine what it would be like to go anywhere without him. Except for my trip into New York with Elaine, we haven't spent a night apart since we were married. How could I even contemplate sleeping alone for three weeks?

I finally fell asleep and dreamed I was walking alone down a cobblestone street in a country where I couldn't speak the language—yet I felt completely at home. It must have been some Mediterranean country, because I was the only woman on the streets. A few shy faces framed in black shawls stared in censure from doorways or shuttered windows, but I paid no attention and continued walking toward the center of town, where tables of men sat drinking and laughing. Without understanding any of the words, I moved among them as if I'd known them all my life.

One pulled me into his lap and began to kiss me. I kissed him back, then moved to the next one. Finally I came to a table where a man was sitting alone, his back to the crowd, indifferent to all the laughter. Drawn to his despair, I began to caress him, using tricks I didn't even know I possessed to arouse him. The crowd seemed to disappear into the shadows, but I could sense they were all still watching from somewhere. I grew desperate, as if my life depended on making this man respond. Without shame, I undressed and offered myself to him. Slowly he removed the black cape he was wearing and wrapped me in it. Then he picked me up in his arms and strode to the edge of the water, where a small sailboat was waiting. Not until we were sailing on the ocean, away from all the curious faces watching us from the shore, did he begin to make love to me—and then I saw that it was David. I didn't care where he was taking me, I just knew I didn't want to go anywhere without him.

When I woke up, I did something I've never done before—I began to make love to him while he was still sleeping. He didn't seem to mind. Later, while he was taking a shower, I called my

76

mother and told her I couldn't go to Greece—or anywhere—with her and made her promise never to let David know I had considered the possibility. He is foreign country enough for me.

I never guessed Joanna would even sleep on the idea of going anywhere without me. However, it did lead to one of the best mornings of our marriage.

☐

FALL IN NEW YORK—my favorite season. David has been showing everyone his new play, *Jack Fell Down*, but so far no takers. He says if it hasn't been optioned by the end of the month, we'll go home to Texas for Thanksgiving. Without a production pending, there is nothing to keep us in New York.

Usually my spirits sink whenever he starts planning an exodus, but through a friend at the Yale Press I just got a free-lance indexing job. The pay is minimal but I can work at home and my hours are my own. Maybe now David will relax enough about our finances to start another play. We can't just wait around for a production of *Beside Myself* or *Jack Fell Down* to change our lives. He has to keep writing!

Where did she find the courage to keep believing in me? Do I hear you asking if I would have given her that kind of support had the situation been reversed? Or is it just my conscience?

☐

WE DID SOME early Christmas shopping at Brentano's today—mostly trying to select a game to keep us amused on the long train trip to Texas. Tentatively decided on The Web.

Our big effort of the afternoon: taking the laundry. David never lets me go alone, which I used to think was silly, but since we heard about the Greenwich Village Laundromat where a man takes off all his clothes and sits naked while they wash and dry, I prefer being escorted.

Spent all evening playing The Web. We didn't buy it. David memorized the directions while standing at Brentano's, then came home and drew his own board. Tomorrow we have to go back to the store to check a few rules. So far neither of us has been able to win.

□

ON BOARD THE DOME CAR somewhere in Pennsylvania. Tomorrow morning we're getting off at Greencastle, Indiana, and spending the night with Brad and Susan. Though we exchange frequent letters, we haven't seen them since Rhode Island—over a year ago. I'm so looking forward to being with them. They're still the only married friends we have.

□

THIS IS EASILY the most horrible day I've lived through—we've lived through—the country's lived through. I've stared at the television for hours and slept for hours, but there is no escape from the terrible reality.

We were having lunch on campus with Brad and Susan when someone began shouting that President Kennedy had been shot. Then someone turned on a radio and I heard an announcer say "Dallas." I barely made it to the bathroom before I began to vomit. When I returned to the table, David told me the gun had been fired from the schoolbook depository just blocks from the newspaper where we met.

No one felt like eating, so Susan and Brad took us back to their apartment and we spent the rest of the day huddled around the television set like cave dwellers around a fire, keeping our backs to the threatening darkness.

Assassination! The word sounds so archaic to me—a word out of history books describing something that happens in other centuries or other countries. Not in 1963 in the United States! And especially not in Dallas, a city where I've never once felt frightened.

□

"HOW CAN YOU GO to Dallas after what's happened?" Brad asked bitterly this morning as we stood on the platform waiting for the train. "Aren't you ashamed to call that city home?"

I began to cry. Susan suddenly threw her arms around me and

78

said she couldn't bear to see us go, knowing it might be years before we were together again. Then she told Brad she was going to take the train as far as St. Louis and stay with us during the five-hour layover. She would be back in Greencastle by bedtime.

On the train to St. Louis, Susan told us she's pregnant. Brad doesn't know. They were planning their first trip to Europe next summer, but the baby is due in July. She doesn't know how to tell him. I said she was acting as if the baby didn't belong to him. And Europe will not go away.

I can't help envying the way Brad and Susan seem to be building a life together and setting goals, even though things don't always work out as planned. David and I have never saved for a trip to Europe—there's never been anything *to* save—and I can't imagine when our life together will be ordered enough to accommodate a child, planned or unplanned.

We took Susan to dinner in the Harvey Girl restaurant in the St. Louis station before putting her on the train back to Greencastle. She said how lucky we were to have both our families in the same town. Brad's parents live in Philadelphia, so Brad and Susan visit them whenever they go east. But Susan's family lives in California; she hasn't been home for a visit since she married. Brad doesn't like being with her family, and when she's with him, Susan doesn't like being with them either. Last summer she planned a trip alone by Greyhound bus to see them, but on the morning of her departure, Brad began to vomit. It turned out just to be a 24-hour virus, but she lost her reservation and never made another.

Maybe thinking about Susan will make it easier for me to get through a few meals with my parents while we're home. If only they won't ask David about his plans for the future.

Poor Joanna. I could literally see her getting more tense with every mile of track that brought us closer to Dallas and her parents' dinner table. If I remember correctly, that was the year I bought a pair of hedge clippers, named the two huge bushes outside my mother's front door after Joanna's parents, and found myself trimming them at least twice a day.

☐

I THOUGHT once we got to Dallas, the horror of the assassination would be assuaged by all the familiar sights and faces. But we continue to live our lives clustered around the television screen—as if the images it projects are more real than anything we can see through our doors or windows.

Today Lee Harvey Oswald was killed leaving the jail surrounded by a police escort. Our friends in the East are convinced we live in some untamed frontier town. Wyatt called tonight from New York urging us to come back for Christmas. He's never been to Texas but said it was clear to him from everything he'd read and seen on TV that our lives are not safe if we stay. How absurd! This is our home. The people we know and love here had nothing to do with the madness of the past few days. It could have happened anywhere.

☐

BOTH DAVID AND I planned to get Christmas jobs, but when he applied at the post office, he found all the seasonal help had been hired. However, I was luckier. Tomorrow I start work selling toys in a neighborhood department store. Poor David feels so guilty that I got a job and he didn't, he insists he's going to drive me to work every day—though I could easily take the bus.

Guilty, yes—but also relieved. The last thing I wanted was to sort mail when my head was full of a new play. So for three weeks I led a typical nine-to-five life—driving my wife to work at nine, picking her up at five, and depositing her paycheck of $28.50 a week after taxes in our joint account. To her parents' credit, they didn't have me arrested.

☐

DAVID HAS NOT MADE LOVE to me since Kennedy was assassinated. Until now we've never gone longer than a week and that was only once, after his option was dropped. I think

Kennedy was a symbol for him—as he was for me—of the way our generation was going to change the world. Now he's gone and my parents' crowd is in charge again. No wonder David is in despair.

What noble motives she always assigned me. The truth was, like characters out of Chekhov, I was in mourning for my life . . . with no dream of Moscow to sustain me. I'd been to New York—and back. The bright girl who put aside her plans to travel and study in order to stay at my side was now on her feet eight hours a day selling toys, while I was stuck halfway through Act Two of my latest opus. Whatever had made me think my career would be big enough for both of us? It couldn't even keep me going. I kept waiting for Joanna to leave me. The more determined she seemed to stay, the worse I treated her, giving her every possible pretext for abandoning me as a lost cause.

☐

FOR CHRISTMAS David gave me a chain made of two strands—one gold, one silver—that come together in a Gordian knot at the neck. He said it represents the two of us and our marriage. I gave him the new Oxford dictionary inscribed "Somewhere in here you will find your next play."

Brad and Susan called from her parents' house in California to wish us merry Christmas and to tell us they were expecting their first child. We pretended surprise. After a big turkey dinner David feigned sleep and signaled me to meet him in the bedroom. He wasn't sleepy at all. Merry Christmas.

Reading this entry, I have to wonder which she enjoyed more—doing it or writing about it. I can tell you what I enjoy least—reading it. So my black felt pen has once again spared you her excesses.

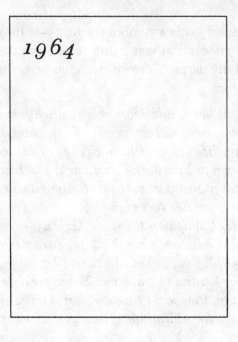

1964

NEW YEAR'S DAY. David and I celebrated New Year's Eve in an observation car speeding through the Ozarks. We're traveling by day coach from Texas back to New York. So few people take the train on New Year's Eve we each have two seats to ourselves, which allows us the illusion of being able to lie down —at least from the head to the waist. We've made this trip over a dozen times since we married, and I still haven't figured out what to do with my lower half while my top half tries to sleep. The worst part is knowing we could've flown for the same price. But David considers it irresponsible to run the risk of flying when there are other lives dependent on us, namely his mother.

I was having nightmares that I died and Joanna's parents locked my mother in a cattle car and shipped her off to the poor farm. Actually she was supporting herself as a substitute teacher and trying to slip me a little cash whenever she could.

☐

SPRING. I bought a pink wool coat at Bonwit Teller's. I've never had a spring coat before—I always go from my heavy winter coat to my khaki raincoat. Maybe a new coat is the key to enjoying each season as it comes. I've tried everything else.

There must be ten pages torn out of this journal here. What memories was she trying to erase? What was happening to us in 1964? Nothing! At least not to me.

I remember the pink coat. I just wish I could forget my reaction to it. I wouldn't be seen with her in it—is that what I shouted at her? What was she doing, I demanded, throwing away money on something so impractical?

She had been at the breaking point all that spring. Sometimes late at night I would find her crying in the bathtub for no reason. She was behaving like a woman going through a change of life—at twenty-six, for God's sake! I mean how else do you explain the pink coat?

But when I tried to make her see what a ridiculous choice it was and suggested she return it to the store the next day, she grabbed it and started out the front door, saying she'd bought it on sale and couldn't take it back.

At first I was too angry to go after her. I figured she'd cool off and come home and ask me to forgive her. I still hadn't even asked how much the damn thing cost. But when she didn't come back, I got worried and went looking for her. I found her in the Laundromat, holding an empty box of black dye while behind the glass door of the washing machine her coat tumbled in an inky ocean.

She wore that black coat—which had shrunk into a very short black dress—for years. Every time she put it on, I felt both of us were in mourning for our lives. She never wore pink again.

Is that all that's missing here? The saga of her one and only spring coat? The next entry is dated 1965. What happened that summer, that fall? Why can't I fill in the blanks between the events Joanna has chosen to record? What irony that during all those years when she thought of herself only as an observer, she was in fact shaping the story of our marriage. I never realized she was exercising the power of life and death every time she opened her journal—and I doubt she realized it any more than I did, at least not at the

83

time. We thought what happened, happened, and we would remember it. But I realize now that's not true—from this distance, it seems that what happened is what Joanna chose to record—nothing more.

I can't keep reading feeling like a victim of Joanna's view of our marriage. Those missing pages were torn from my life too. I can't go on until I remember what happened that year—to both of us.

She did leave me for three weeks when her mother had a hysterectomy. She said she was going home to take care of her. Could there have been another reason? Until I started reading these journals, I would have said impossible. But now I'm no longer sure of anything. I'm beginning to feel I was married to a stranger all these years.

Did she have reasons of her own for making that trip to Texas? I remember that she had a doctor's appointment the week before she left. She said it was just a checkup, that everything was fine.

A thought keeps coming into my mind and I can't get rid of it. Did the doctor tell her she was pregnant? She knew we couldn't afford a child. I'm making myself crazy staring at the binding, trying to see how many pages are missing, trying to imagine what she tore out of her life—our life— without a trace.

I have to be wrong. Her parents would never have allowed her to have an abortion. But what if they didn't know? What if she had it somewhere else? Could she have called on Elaine to return the favor? If I hadn't introduced them, Joanna would never have even known anyone who had an abortion—at least not in 1964! How do I know she was even in Texas during those three weeks? She said that's where she was when she called at night, but what proof do I have? She always did the calling—so her parents could pay, she said. Could she have gone somewhere else first, then home to recover? And told her parents she was thinking of leaving me? God knows, they wouldn't have had any problem believing that.

Will I ever know what was written on those missing pages? Do I want to know?

84

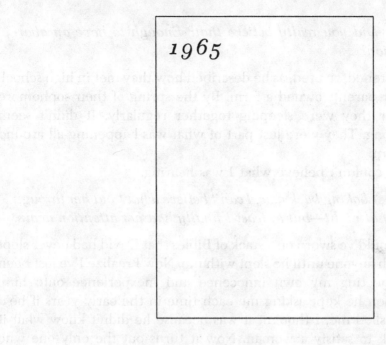

1965

I'M NOT David's first wife! Is it possible?

Thank God I finally shocked her into writing again. I can't believe how much of our lives got lost between entries.

We'd just finished dinner last night and I was working on an index when he confessed he'd been married before—right out of high school. I began to laugh. Was this a joke? But he just shook his head and said he couldn't go on keeping it a secret. I asked what happened to her, still not convinced but beginning to wonder just how much of his life a husband can withhold from his wife.

Or a wife from her husband.

Fighting tears, he said she had died in childbirth. Could it be true? I knew it could when I thought of how much I've kept from David this past year.

How much, Joanna? How much?

Suddenly I understood why David has always said if we wanted children, we'd have to adopt.

85

Did you really believe that? Enough to have an abortion?

I listened, riveted, as he described how they met in high school. Her parents owned a farm. By the spring of their sophomore year they were sleeping together regularly. It didn't seem wrong. They were just part of what was happening all around them.

I couldn't believe what I was hearing.

Looking back now, I can't believe what I put her through that night—but at least I finally had her attention again.

I would've sworn on a stack of Bibles that David had never slept with anyone until he slept with me. Now I realize I've just been projecting my own innocence and inexperience onto him. When he kept asking me each time in the early years if he'd satisfied me, I thought it was because he didn't know what it took to satisfy a woman. Now it turns out the only one who doesn't know is me.

After his confession he took me to bed. I felt as though a stranger were making love to me. I kept thinking of a younger David discovering love with someone else, possessing her so completely and insatiably she finally died from it. And here I am, as far as I can determine from five years of reading, frigid. At least I've never had an orgasm—and I don't even know enough to know what I'm missing.

☐

I FINALLY WENT to a doctor today—on the pretext of having a yearly checkup. After he told me everything was fine, I asked what I had to do to have an orgasm. He said the worst thing I could do was worry about it—just relax and enjoy myself and let the orgasms take care of themselves. Then he said there was no scientific evidence to prove that the female of the species was even *supposed* to reach a climax during the sex act, since it was hardly essential for procreation. "Women nowadays are getting themselves all worked up over nothing," he assured me with a patronizing smile. "After all, cows don't have orgasms."

I looked so depressed when I came out of his office, David assumed I was dying of some dread disease. I kissed him and said I was nowhere near death. There are too many things I want to do first. And having an orgasm heads the list! I may not have a past like David, but I'm determined to have a present—and to prove how much I love him with every response.

As with everything else, she may have been a slow starter —but when she got there, she really got there.

□

ELAINE WEST WAS FIRED last week—for writing a good review of a play no one else liked, including her publisher. We felt badly about her public dismissal, especially since we agreed with her about the play, so David called and invited her to dinner tonight.

Elaine probably has the best mind of anyone we know, but she can't seem to connect with anyone, either personally or professionally, who appreciates it or knows what to do with it. What a pity.

After dinner, while we washed the dishes and David was out of earshot, Elaine confessed that she'd gotten a Christmas card this year from the divinity student, now a minister with his own church somewhere in West Virginia—a family photograph of him, his wife, and their three children. It was the first time she'd heard from him since New Haven.

If he already had three children, I tried to joke, then it was a good thing Elaine hadn't married him; she wouldn't have had time to do anything on her own. "And just what *have* I done on my own?" she asked abruptly, not bothering to wipe the tears from her cheeks.

I didn't know how to comfort her. Glancing in the living room to make sure David was still watching the late news on television, I whispered to Elaine that I had a problem and needed advice. No words of consolation could have cheered her faster. Then I confessed that I'm still not sure what an orgasm is—so how can I know if I've ever had one or even come close?

Elaine hugged me warmly and said I'd been reading too many novels. What happens is not nearly so mysterious and awesome as you're led to believe before you actually experience

87

it yourself, she said, then described a simple exercise I can start doing right now—to strengthen something called the "magic muscle." It was first used by women trying to get back into shape after pregnancy. When they were able to have sex again, they discovered to their surprise they were enjoying it more.

Suddenly I feel as if Elaine just crawled in bed with us.

☐

TONIGHT DAVID READ me his new play, *Detours*—about a girl and a boy who meet in high school. She lives on a farm, and they start sleeping together in the spring of their sophomore year.

By the end of the play, when the wife dies in childbirth, I was sobbing and David was elated. I couldn't understand his excitement until he confessed that he'd lied to me about his early marriage. He said that during the past year he had lost faith in his powers of invention.

Little wonder now that I realize that during the same time Joanna had lost faith in me.

The characters didn't become real for him until he'd convinced me everything in the play had actually happened. Would I forgive him?

I hit him across the chest as hard as I could and swore I'd never believe anything he told me again. His deception unlocked all the anger and frustration I've suppressed these five long years of our marriage. I told him I could not go on living a secondhand life. I wanted things to happen to *me*.

But something did *happen to you. Something you didn't have the courage to confront. How else do you explain the missing pages?*

☐

IT'S FINALLY HAPPENED—that elusive interior explosion I was beginning to think I'd never experience, except in fiction. At last! I wish I could share my excitement with David, but I can't tell him it happened tonight without admitting it never happened before.

As if I didn't know. Though I, of course, gave full credit to my increasingly sophisticated technique. Joanna wasn't the only one picking up pointers from books and movies during those years. I still feel I deserved the credit to make up for all those years when I blamed myself for what wasn't happening for her—*even though she kept assuring me it was. I came to my wedding night filled with those myths of the fifties about women having to be "played like violins." I knew I was out of my depth—I'd never even taken piano lessons. But I did my best—though there were nights when I thought the responsibility for making a woman happy could sure take the fun out of sex for a man. I just wish to God someone older and wiser had told us about the "magic muscle" before* the wedding. *But better late . . .*

□

CHRISTMAS CAME EARLY this year. *Detours* has been optioned for Broadway. The producers plan to open it in the spring. They want rewrites, so we'll be staying here over the holidays.

□

I WENT TO THE DOCTOR today and confirmed my Christmas present for David—I'm pregnant. How will he take the news? If his play hadn't been optioned, I'd be afraid to tell him. In fact, if he weren't finally getting his first New York production, I'd be afraid to have this one, too.

Oh, God—my worst suspicions confirmed.

The play just has to be a hit. It's the only way we'll be able to afford a baby—and all the things that go with it.

I'm going to wait till Christmas morning to tell David—never again will he be able to say I'm no good at surprises!

No—never again.

□

WE WENT CHRISTMAS SHOPPING tonight, not buying anything, just browsing in all the stores, feeling like characters out of Dorothy Parker, imagining what we'll buy next year if the play is a hit.

We were looking at the model rooms in Bloomingdale's, furnishing our dream house in our imagination, when I suddenly saw the perfect room for a child. Before I realized what I was doing, I clutched David's elbow and said that was the room I wanted for our baby. He hugged me and I was so happy thinking he understood, but then he asked with a grin, "You want a house *and* a baby? You really expect a lot out of life, don't you?"

So I had to confess that the house could wait—but the baby couldn't. It would be arriving next summer—whatever happens with the play.

David's eyes filled with tears, and suddenly I was terrified of what he would say next. What would I do if he said we couldn't afford a baby?

She had to know me better than that.

I ran to the escalator and kept on running down the moving stairs, pushing people out of my way. When I got to the street, I tried to hail a cab—though I had no idea where I was going. David finally caught up with me, put his arm around me, and steered me across the street. Then he pulled me into the doorway of a small stationery store and kissed me so passionately I could hardly get my breath. "You idiot," he whispered. "How could you think I would be anything but happy?"

Happy, yes, my darling Julia. But as terrified as I'd ever been in my life, too.

I felt as if a hundred pounds of fear had fallen off my back. Whatever happens with the rest of our lives, David and I are going to have a baby—something we had an equal part in creating. My life has finally begun! Joy to the world!

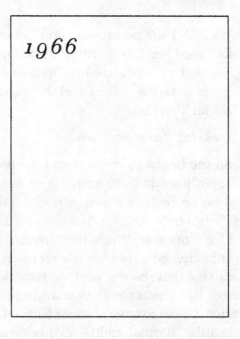

1966

FINALLY HEARD from Brad and Susan Savage for the first time since the announcement of their daughter's birth almost two years ago—and understood why she has stopped answering my letters. And why she sounded so funny on the telephone when we called at Christmas to tell them about the baby. Their daughter is retarded. What a tragic discovery!

They've suspected for months that something was wrong; at the age of twenty months the baby still can't walk or talk. The doctor finally confirmed their suspicions. Susan was trying to find the courage to tell us when she found out I was pregnant, and she didn't want to frighten us. But now she's pregnant again and Brad wants her to have an abortion. She says she'll leave him first. She asks what I would do. I don't know what to tell her.

Why couldn't that letter have gotten lost in the mail? I was already a wreck worrying about whether our baby would be perfectly formed. Everyone I passed on the streets, I checked to make sure they had two eyes, one nose, a pair of arms, a pair of legs. So many did, why not ours?

☐

I'VE SPENT the past twenty-four hours thinking about Susan. I finally called her this morning while David was still asleep and told her that no matter what Brad said or did, she had to be strong and have the baby. I said she would regret it all her life if she had an abortion.

Speaking from experience.

Then she began to cry and said she couldn't help feeling she was being punished for praying so hard that their first child would be perfect. "I was so afraid she'd be born with a birthmark," she confessed, "and have to go through life hiding it the way I have my scar. When they handed her to me in the hospital, I kept checking for blemishes. I made the doctors and nurses swear to me that she was perfect. It made up for everything I've suffered. But it was too important to me—and now I'm paying the price. I have to have another baby—to prove I can give birth to a healthy, normal child—for my own sanity, if for no other reason."

The more I tried to reassure her, the more frightened I became for David and me. Even a perfect child is going to change our lives completely. Could our marriage survive a less than perfect one? Please, God, don't put us to the test.

We both prayed more that winter than we had in all the years of our marriage—though we didn't join a church or make any outward show. I was a churchgoing Methodist when I married and your mother assured me she was an equally devout Episcopalian, but we both felt closer to God sharing a bed on Sunday morning than we did sharing a pew.

☐

DETOURS went into rehearsal today. I was thrilled when David asked me to come to the first reading. He has always included me so completely in his life—much more than my father ever did my mother. She has no idea what he does all day at the office—and as far as I can tell, no interest in learning. I seem to serve as a witness for David—making whatever is happening to him seem more real.

He also invited Audrey Wood. Her manner is so imperious she makes me very tense. And frankly, I think she scares David too.

Not since my ninth-grade history teacher had I been so terrified of a woman.

When Miss Wood entered the theater, she crossed the stage to David and instructed him in a whisper, "Kiss me, darling, for luck."

Though we've become accustomed to how effusively (and insincerely, I think) people in the theater greet each other, both David and I are uncomfortable kissing people we hardly know —and he would sooner have kissed the queen mother than Miss Wood. But having spent a lifetime in the theater, she understood instinctively the significance of a theatrical gesture. When I looked around, I saw that the kiss—and the intimacy it implied —was not lost on anyone, from actors to director to producers.

Willa is playing the lead. David continues to insist he wrote the part for her. Am I the only one who thinks she's at least ten years too old?

You and the critics!

□

WE'RE KEEPING MOLLY for the weekend while Willa—we pray—learns her lines. Molly is an open, loving child—which reassures me that parents have very little to do with how their offspring turn out. Thank God! I'm terrified at the thought of being totally responsible for a new and unformed life. How do you communicate with a creature who can't talk or reason? If only the baby could be born eight years old like Molly. It's such fun having her here, and I think she feels the same way—at least she always cries when Willa comes to take her home.

□

DAVID'S MOTHER arrived yesterday. Opening night is a week away but this is her first trip to New York and we want to show her the sights—most of which we've never seen ourselves.

We took her to our apartment from the train station. I'd spent the previous day cleaning, scrubbing, putting little bunches of fresh flowers everywhere to welcome her, but she could not hide her dismay at the way we live. She thinks Greenwich Village is a tenement section of New York City—and cannot imagine why we would choose to live here.

We had invited her to stay with us, but she insisted we reserve a hotel room for her—at her expense. She said she was afraid she'd get in our way in the apartment, but I suspect it was the idea of bathing in our kitchen that made her spring for a hotel room. She said she couldn't afford anything fancy so we found her a room at an unpretentious midtown hotel for twenty-five dollars a night.

However, this morning she complained that she was kept awake all night by a rat running across the room. When she called the desk to complain, the manager assured her coldly that "at best what you heard, madam, was a mouse."

She finds New York uninhabitable—and was appalled when David told her that if the play is a hit, we're going to buy a brownstone. He assured her that it would have plenty of room for her whenever she wanted to visit. To which she replied that she was counting the days till she got back to Texas and, once she was home, never planned to cross the Mississippi again. She said one trip to New York was enough for a lifetime.

I thought she was being small-minded and small-town at the time. But I now realize she was preparing me, albeit unconsciously, for the end of my love affair with New York City.

☐

TODAY, while we were showing Eula Lee New York from the top of the Empire State Building, David got an idea for rewriting the end of his play to make it more affirmative. He hurried back to the apartment to type the scene while I took her on to Radio City to see the Rockettes. The new ending was in for the first preview tonight. The audience was responsive, but the actors, especially Willa, felt a happy ending compromised the intent of the play. She considered the play a tragedy when she first read it and that is how she intends to play it—despite the fact that the audience has discovered a lot of laughter in the lines. David is much funnier than he realized, but Willa insists she is not onstage to give the audience a good time. Tomorrow the old ending goes back with the wife once again dying in childbirth, just the way Willa likes it.

□

WE MADE A BRIEF APPEARANCE at Sardi's last night for the opening night party, then took refuge in Eula Lee's hotel room before the reviews started coming in. We thought if no one knew where we were, no one would be able to reach us with bad news. Unfortunately, however, Eula Lee made the mistake of turning on the television set for the late news and got the first review right in the face. Why do all those damning adjectives sound even worse out loud?

David unplugged the set, then told the switchboard to hold all calls till morning. We didn't dare leave the room the rest of the night for fear of encountering more bad reviews. The only way we could get any sleep was to keep ourselves ignorant of our fate till morning.

There were only two twin beds in the room. Eula Lee had one. David took the mattress from the second and, pushing aside the dozen rattraps his mother had insisted be set all over the room, made a bed for himself on the floor, leaving me the box springs.

None of us slept very well. But in my nightmares all my anxieties about the play were transformed into grotesque visions of childbirth. I gave birth at least ten times—to dead or malformed infants—before I woke up sobbing in David's arms. I didn't dare tell him what I'd dreamed, but wondered where I would find the strength to get through the day ahead of us, let alone the months and the years.

David ordered a big breakfast from room service to put us all in a cheerful frame of mind. But when the waiter rolled in the table, there was a *New York Times* lying beside the orange juice. The play had taken such complete possession of our lives I half expected to find the review on the front page.

David grabbed the paper and disappeared into the bathroom. Then I heard sounds that made my morning sickness seem like child's play. My own stomach began to contort in sympathy. I pounded on the bathroom door, which David had locked behind him. When he finally let me in, the paper was spread open on the floor and I vomited on the review without reading a word of it.

Over the years we've found that much the best way of dealing with them.

As soon as we dressed, David and I left Eula Lee to enjoy the room service breakfast—if she could—and returned to our apartment. A telegram from the producer—who had tried unsuccessfully all night to reach us by phone—was waiting in the door. It said negative reviews were forcing him to close the play. Opening night turned out to be closing night as well.

It took me years to put it into perspective. But now when I speak of my first Broadway play, I boast that "it ran all evening." The line invariably gets a laugh—from everyone but me.

□

WE'RE RETREATING TO DALLAS. David says when the entire New York Drama Critics Circle demands you leave their city, you'd best leave it.

I finally got one wish. I'm riding home to Texas in a reclining position. David is traveling by day coach, but he bought a single bedroom for me next to the one his mother had reserved in advance.

At first I thought it was my condition that entitled me to such luxury, but then I realized I'd be sharing my small compartment with two chairs and a footlocker, plus five shopping bags filled with furnishings from the Greenwich Village apartment we'll never see again.

This morning David turned in our keys to the actor from whom we've sublet since we arrived in the city almost four years ago. When he asked where we were going, David said to try our luck further west. The actor assumed he meant Hollywood and said to save him a place. The truth is, we have no plans beyond getting home to Texas and hiding out until the baby is born.

□

I HAVE A FATHER-IN-LAW after all. Going through the mail that had accumulated in her absence, Eula Lee discovered a picture postcard of a trailer camp in West Texas addressed to David and containing a one-line greeting, "How you been, boy?"

The card was dated the night the play opened—and closed— on Broadway. David couldn't get over the coincidence until Eula Lee remembered it was also his father's birthday. "I wonder what poor fool he's talked into marrying him," was her only comment when she read the card. "You can be sure he's not living in any trailer park alone."

Tonight David wrote his father, telling him he was about to become a grandfather.

I couldn't think of anything else I'd done in the decade since I'd seen him that would've been of any possible interest to him.

□

I'LL FOLLOW DAVID anywhere—but if I have to stay here with him much longer, I'll go mad.

My parents took us to Sunday lunch today—and offered to help him find a teaching job for fall. He seemed very appreciative, but when we got back to the house we're sharing with his mother—he calls it home but I'll be damned if I will—he said he never wanted to see them again. I asked what they said to him when I was out of the room to make him so angry. He replied that I was right there—and I should be as angry as he was. If my parents believed in his talent, how could they insult him by offering to help him find a teaching job?

I pointed out that David had begun the conversation by saying he'd had all the pain he could take from the theater and had to find something else to do with his life. So Daddy suggested teaching, offering to call a friend at SMU.

"Oh, he'd love that, wouldn't he?" David exploded. "Having

me stuck in some damn teaching job—playing it safe in Dallas for the rest of my life, like him and all his friends. I suppose you'd like that too. A husband you could call to heel like your mother does."

I wanted to hit him but couldn't, seeing in his anger all the pain he'd been suppressing since the play closed. I hid in the clothes closet so his mother wouldn't hear me sobbing. In a few minutes David opened the closet door and knelt on the floor beside me. He took me in his arms.

"I thought if I married you I could make you happy," I said, choking back sobs.

He just shook his head and said everybody expected too much of marriage. "You can make me unhappy by leaving, but you can't make me happy by staying. I don't think one person can ever make another person happy. It's something you have to do for yourself. Stop worrying about me," he said, unbuttoning my blouse. "Save yourself."

Later, lying on a pile of coats in the closet, I finally found the nerve to ask him, since he didn't want to write for the theater anymore and he didn't want to teach, what exactly he did want to do. He said if I weren't pregnant, we could join the Peace Corps. I breathed a sigh of relief. However ill-defined his plans are, at least they involve me—and they don't include spending the rest of our lives in Dallas.

☐

DAVID HAS DECIDED we should devote our lives to the migrant workers, living among them, educating our child with theirs. However, I've persuaded him to wait until the baby is born to break the news to our families.

The obstetrician who delivered me is going to deliver our baby. I like him much better than the doctor I was seeing in New York, who didn't know anything about me. Maybe it was fate that brought us home to Dallas for the birth of our first child. All I know is, as the time grows near, I'm happy to be surrounded by people who love me.

☐

I'VE ENDED IT with my parents! They'll be lucky if they ever get the chance to *meet* their first grandchild.

Where was I when this happened? I don't remember Joanna ever reaching a breaking point with her parents— though God knows I did everything in my power to provoke one.

I should've suspected something funny was going on when Daddy said he had a friend who was trying to write a play and wanted some professional advice from David. Could he drop by for a chat?

That was suspicious—any friend of theirs wanting professional advice from me.

David refused to talk to him when he telephoned this afternoon—

As I remember, I said something tactful about not having time to give advice to amateurs, which Joanna no doubt translated into a more palatable excuse.

but the man would not take no for an answer. He said he was going to be in the neighborhood and would just stay for a few minutes. David was furious. He said he would be working in the bedroom and did not want to be disturbed. I would have to get rid of the man by myself.

I was determined to turn the would-be playwright away at the door, but he seemed so pleasant and sympathetic I invited him into the living room. I said David was working, but I'd be happy to talk to him. If he didn't mind secondhand information, I could tell him a lot about what it took to be a playwright.

To my surprise, he didn't want to talk about himself—which should've been my tip-off that he had no connection with the theater. However, he asked such sympathetic questions I found myself pouring my heart out to him. It's been a long time since anyone asked me how *I* felt about anything—it seems as if David and I have concentrated all our attention from the day we married on his career in the theater. Even in my most private moments, alone with my journal, I think of little else—at least little else seems worth recording.

But suddenly I began confessing to this stranger how frightened I was of the future, not knowing where we would be living or how David could afford to support a wife and a baby. I also worry about what I'm doing to the baby by worrying so much. I even told him how much I miss my parents. I know marriage has cost us our friendship. I'm constantly on guard for fear of being disloyal to David.

Finally, after listening to me for almost an hour, the man said he thought he could help us—but he really had to see David too. Would I please ask him to come into the living room?

"What do you mean help us?" I demanded. "I thought you wanted David to help *you* write a play."

That was just an excuse to get through the door, he explained. He had no interest in the theater—frankly, he thought plays were boring compared to life. He was here because of my parents. They thought David needed help—in fact, they were afraid he was on the verge of a mental breakdown—but they knew he would never agree to see a psychiatrist, even if they paid.

"Is that what you are—a psychiatrist?" He nodded affirmatively. I would've screamed in outrage but I was afraid David would hear me in the next room.

My in-laws were trying to set a shrink loose on me? Thank God I never knew. It turns out Joanna is a better actress than I thought.

"Then I take it my parents are paying you for this house call?" He nodded again.

I opened the front door. "Get out," I whispered indignantly, "before I have to call my husband. How dare you come into our home and take advantage of me like this? My husband doesn't need anything but a little encouragement. Of course he's close to losing his mind—who wouldn't be after what he's been through?"

"Your parents are just trying to help," he said as I slammed the door after him.

When I looked into the bedroom, I saw that David had fallen asleep with his steno pad open beside him. If he can have the courage to start a new play, then I have to find a way for him to finish it.

The first step is getting out of Texas—but how?

Is she saying she engineered our exit? How many other surprises does she have in store for me? Talk about your life not being your own.

☐

WHILE DAVID was at the bank today, I went through all the opening-night telegrams he'd stuck in his desk, which he's been too depressed to answer. I finally found the one I was looking for —from Ben Weisman in Hollywood. He and David were rival playwrights at Yale—Ben was always a scholarship and a production ahead of him—but he went directly from New Haven to Hollywood. Writing to the address on the telegram, I thanked Ben for his good wishes, told him I was pregnant, and we were broke. Did he think David could make a living in Hollywood? I told him David didn't know I was writing, so please not to mention my letter when he wrote back.

Even Ben? No wonder he seemed so embarrassed when I told people how he'd come out of nowhere to save my life. I always thought he guessed from reading my reviews that I was on my knees. What would I have done differently if I'd known Joanna had written him for help? Nothing, I hope.

☐

FINALLY! A PHONE CALL from Ben telling David he'd invested a thousand dollars in his Broadway play, so he was probably taking its failure worse than David. I haven't heard David laugh that hard since the play closed. Then he asked Ben why he would risk that kind of money in the theater. He should know better.

Call it conscience money, Ben laughed. He then said he's making $550 a week as a screenwriter under contract to a studio, his first novel has just been published, he has a house with a swimming pool and a Jaguar in the garage, and the maître d' at Chasen's greets him by name. "But," he added, quoting La

Rochefoucauld, " 'it is not enough to succeed. It is also necessary that your best friend fail.' " He thanked David for providing him with a perfect life—and asked if he'd be interested in writing for the movies. He thought he could get him a job. Hallelujah!

☐

BEN WAS STUNNED to see me getting off the plane with David. "Couldn't you have left her at home?" I heard him say as I stepped onto the moving sidewalk headed for the baggage claim. Home? My only home since I married is with David wherever he goes. Did he think when I asked him for help I was planning to stay behind in Dallas? Ben was married when we knew him in New Haven but likes being single in Los Angeles. I'm not sure he's actually divorced; his wife has a job in the East, which apparently he has encouraged her to keep.

Whatever I did, Ben was convinced he could do better. Except marriage. That's why he didn't like having Joanna around. He didn't like being reminded that when it came to wives, he had not outclassed me.

Not only did I not fit into Ben's plans to show David the swinging side of Los Angeles, I barely fit into his two-seater Jaguar convertible. David had to hold me on his lap all the way into town.

We're staying in an old hotel in Hollywood called the Montecito, run by a man whose face I recognized from a hundred movies but whose name was unfamiliar. A lot of actors stay here; there's a board beside the front desk on which current celebrity residents are billed. Julie Harris is due next week. Apparently she's never learned to drive and likes to stay within walking distance of the Huntington Hartford Theater, where she'll be performing.

By the time he left us at the hotel, Ben had recovered sufficiently from his disappointment that David was still very much married to invite us to dinner. David clearly did not relish the prospect of riding anywhere with 150 pounds of me on his lap and suggested we meet somewhere within walking distance of our hotel.

Ben said we might as well take in a little Hollywood history with our meal—and told us to meet him at Musso and Frank's on Hollywood Boulevard.

This venerable institution actually has a brass plaque on the outside wall announcing that it was established in 1919. How they would laugh at that in New England. But living in a town this new does make you feel anything is possible.

Easy for her to say. My whole future was riding on a good meeting with a man I had yet to meet. Somehow I had to convince him over lunch that I alone could save a script on which he had already spent so much money the picture would probably never get made. And first I had to convince myself that six newspaper critics who had assured New York I was without talent had holes in their heads.

☐

DAVID GOT THE JOB. Thank God! Maybe now he'll begin to believe in himself again.

So she did know what I was going through. Why didn't we ever talk about it? Why couldn't I tell her that there were days when I found her optimism a real pain in the ass? Because her faith in me was still the only thing in my pocket.

☐

BEN PICKS DAVID UP in his Jaguar every morning, and they drive to the studio together. I'm usually still dozing when David kisses me good-bye. At the beginning of our marriage I tried to interest him in breakfast but he said food at that hour made him nauseous, so I soon gave it up too—though it was my favorite meal before I married. But now my life belongs to someone else besides David. So as soon as he leaves for work, I fix me and my baby a big breakfast.

Though technically we are only renting one room, it is large and airy with a full kitchen and dining area. At night we pull two

Murphy beds down from the wall to convert our living quarters into a bedroom. Ordinarily I hate not sleeping in David's arms, but my present bulk makes separate beds a blessing. However, we still manage to share one on occasion—though lovemaking at this stage of pregnancy requires a certain amount of ingenuity, not to mention agility.

I was very turned on by her changing shape. So far it was the only place I had made my mark.

After breakfast I put on one of my two tent-shaped sundresses (one advantage of being pregnant is that it doesn't take any time at all deciding what to wear) and go for a walk. Sometimes I walk along Hollywood Boulevard with its endlessly fascinating stores—books, records, magic tricks, still photos from movies, and just plain junk. Other days I explore the hills behind the Hollywood Bowl.

Hollywood is not at all what I expected. When I look out the window of our hotel room and see all the stucco houses perched precariously on the hillside, brightly blooming flowers spilling out of the clay pots that make only a pretense of containing them, I think I must be in Italy. But strolling Hollywood Boulevard, I feel I am passing the side shows on my way to a main tent just out of sight where I will be a spectator at the greatest show on earth.

I come back to the hotel room in time for lunch. I now drink milk with every meal, managing to get it down, even though I hate it, because I know I'm drinking it for someone else. Then I stretch out on the couch with a book (I'm reading Fitzgerald's Pat Hobby stories, trying to recover from the week-long depression I was in after finishing Nathanael West's *Day of the Locust).* I usually fall asleep after a few pages—the warm breezes wafting through the room work like a sedative, making me feel I have nothing to fear. Do the final stages of pregnancy induce this kind of euphoria in everyone? I do absolutely nothing all day long—yet I've never felt more important or productive in my life.

And Freud thought women envied men a puny penis. I've never in my life felt what Joanna is describing.

□

THE MONTECITO IS DIFFERENT from anywhere I've ever lived. Not since college have I been on such friendly terms with the people living around me. Most of them are actors on the road with plays. They perform at night and spend their days around the swimming pool, hoping for phone calls from their agents with news of jobs that will get them off the stage and into movies or television.

I go down to the pool every afternoon and swim for an hour. What luxury to have access to a pool in my present inflated condition. The water is the only place where I feel weightless. After I swim, I lie in the sun ripening like the bananas on the trees overhanging the pool.

I couldn't afford a maternity bathing suit, so before we left Texas I borrowed a wide-girthed suit from my grandmother. The best I can say for it is that it is comfortable and covers me in all the right places. A fashion plate I am not, but my unthreatening appearance has made me more friends than if I looked my best. Actors do not hesitate to approach, script in hand, to ask if I will run lines with them. Several are traveling with their families, treating Hollywood as a summer vacation. I've made friends with some of the children, and they're very excited at the prospect of a new baby on the premises. Every afternoon when I arrive at the pool, they come splashing over to ask at the top of their lungs if I've had my baby yet.

The baby swims night and day—the butterfly stroke, I think. David can no longer watch television with his head on my lap. We are both getting anxious for its arrival. Sometimes I worry about how much a baby will keep us at home, but David just wants to begin enjoying it. Last night he dreamed that it stood up inside my stomach and reached out its arms to hug him, then curled back down and went to sleep. If I think about that when the pains come, maybe I won't feel them.

I was so frightened of what she was going to have to go through, but she never seemed to doubt that when the time came she'd be able to handle it. Where do women get such confidence—not to mention courage?

□

THIS HAS BEEN A WEEK that changed our world. It began at the Hollywood Bowl. David and I were watching the Bolshoi Ballet perform *Swan Lake*. As the dying swan folded her wings, I felt something take flight inside me. I clutched David's hand and told him I thought I was in labor—two weeks early.

David called Ben in a panic to drive us to the hospital—only to discover Ben was about to lend us his car for two weeks while he went east. David and I had to laugh, thinking of all the trips we'd planned to take if we ever got a car. A trip to the hospital was not one of them.

Ben brought the Jaguar to the hotel, then handed David the keys, saying he didn't think this was any night for me to sit on my husband's lap. When he kissed me good-bye, he said I was right to come to California with David. If his wife had insisted on coming with him instead of staying docilely behind, he wouldn't be going back now to ask her for a divorce.

The labor room nurse was very skeptical when I told her I'd taken a natural childbirth class at the YWCA and wanted to stay conscious through the whole experience. She said I could play all the games I wanted till the going got rough. Then the professionals would take over.

David's nervousness increased when the nurse left us alone. I suspect he paid no attention the night I made him go to class with me. I'd been reading a lot about how excluded husbands feel during childbirth, and I wanted to make sure he shared the experience. I realize now I wasn't doing him any favor. I should've just kissed him at the door—the way my mother always did my father—and left him in the waiting room to get through it on his own.

The night seemed to go on forever. Finally at dawn, when the doctor said I was still several hours from delivery, I asked for a saddle block for myself and something stronger for David. The nurse brought him a pill called Valium, which put him right to sleep on a couch in the waiting room.

I remember thinking just before I passed out that I had to get a prescription for Valium before I went back to Broadway.

David was awakened by Ben, who'd stopped by the hospital on his way to the airport. When David realized it was 10 A.M., he raced to find our doctor, who explained that the baby was not in the right position to be born. If the head didn't drop within the next hour, he would have to do a Caesarean.

I couldn't believe what Joanna had to go through. We might as well have been living in the Middle Ages. Men had learned to split the atom and destroy the world in a matter of seconds, but women were still forced to endure, as they had for centuries, hours of agony to produce a single human life.

Ben canceled his flight to New York and took David to breakfast, offering to lend him money if I needed a Caesarean. When they got back upstairs—ready to face the doctor and his decision—they saw me being wheeled on a bed down the hall. Assuming I was on my way to surgery, David rushed to kiss me good-bye. I asked where he'd been—didn't he know he had a beautiful baby daughter waiting to meet him?

No woman ever kept me waiting longer than you did, darling.

I had to wait till the next morning to be alone with my baby. We've named her Julia—not for anyone we know but because we like the name. She was brought to me right after breakfast—swaddled in a pink blanket, only one arm allowed to be free, her wristband matching her to me. The nurse just handed her to me and left the room, but Julia didn't have to be taught why she was there. She nursed eagerly. It hurt a little, but I was so happy she wasn't disappointed in me I didn't mind.

David arrived for visiting hours laden with perfume and flowers and a copy of John Steinbeck's novel *The Winter of Our Discontent*, which he'd inscribed, "For bringing us into the summer of our content." I hated it when eight o'clock came and he had to leave. But then the nurse brought the baby again, and I wasn't lonely anymore.

Except for being away from David, I've loved these days in the hospital, but the doctor says I can go home tomorrow. Then no more visiting hours—hallelujah! The three of us will be together all the time.

☐

IT'S THE MIDDLE OF THE NIGHT, and Julia is wide awake. What am I doing wrong? I can't believe they actually let us leave the hospital this morning—and take this baby with us. I can't help feeling that someone in charge got very careless. We're not allowed to drive a car without taking a test, we can't get married without a license. Being a parent is a much more awesome responsibility, yet no one checks to make sure we're up to it. Frankly, I'm beginning to have my doubts.

I'm so unprepared for motherhood compared to my mother. She was a professional. Next to her I feel like an amateur. When she was expecting a baby, she devoted her pregnancy to preparing for its arrival. The baby would come home from the hospital to a freshly painted and wallpapered room containing a crib equipped with bumper pad and mobile, a bureau filled with baby clothes, and a playpen, high chair, pram, and stroller all waiting to be put to use. A nurse would be in attendance for the first two weeks, presenting the baby to my mother for feedings at regular intervals but otherwise not intruding on her life while she lay wearing new nightgowns and bedjackets and receiving visitors.

We bought nothing in advance. In the first place, David was not sure his week-to-week assignment would last through the birth of the baby. But more than that, he was terrified something would go wrong and did not want me returning to face a roomful of baby supplies. He finally got around to buying the essentials this morning.

Julia didn't seem to realize she was being turned over to amateurs—and slept all the way home from the hospital. When we entered the lobby of the Montecito, a bouquet of flowers from the manager and his family was waiting at the front desk and the name of Julia Scott had been listed on the board as the newest celebrity resident.

While I showed Julia around her first home, David drove to Wilcox's Pit Barbecue in Hollywood to buy chopped-beef sandwiches for lunch. He had to spend the afternoon at the studio but said not to worry about fixing dinner, he would pick something up on the way home. I was nursing the baby when he arrived with a deluxe pizza loaded with peppers and anchovies.

He's taking such good care of us, but Julia doesn't seem to appreciate it. Now she's crying again. I just fed her an hour ago —but I guess I'll try it again. I don't know how else to keep her quiet so David can sleep. This room has never seemed so small.

You were getting a steady secondhand diet of barbecue and pizza—yet we couldn't understand why you cried all the time. It's a miracle we weren't charged with attempted infanticide.

☐

DAVID FINISHED his rewrite yesterday, and tonight his producer invited us to his house for dinner to celebrate. He and his wife have been married fifteen years and have five children— hardly a typical Hollywood marriage. The youngest is a two-month-old boy, so they included Julia in the invitation. Her first Hollywood party turned out to be the stuff of which fan magazine copy is made—she and the son of the producer ended up sharing a bed.

Tomorrow Ben returns. David is meeting him at the airport. Then we will be without a car—and also without a job. The rewrite is finished to everyone's satisfaction but there are no further assignments in sight. What do we do now?

What we always did. Hang on to each other and the few dollars we'd managed to save—and wait.

☐

BEN THINKS David and I should stay in Hollywood, job or no job, and gamble that something will come along. He introduced David to his agent, Eliot Rich, who seemed impressed with his ability but could not promise to get him work. We've paid the rent on our hotel room till the end of the month. If nothing has turned up by then, David thinks we should take the baby home to Texas. He's going crazy trying to live in one room with a wife

109

and baby. He wants to start a new play but can only write in the bathroom with the water running.

We both need to get out of this room on occasion but don't feel safe leaving Julia with a baby-sitter—even if we could afford one. Today David decided we would start taking turns seeing movies. If he's going to have a career as a screenwriter, he should see the latest releases, so he'll go to everything first. If he likes something, he'll stay with the baby while I go.

☐

SO FAR David has seen six movies but doesn't consider any of them worth my time. Tomorrow I'm leaving Julia with him and going *somewhere* for two hours—even if I just end up riding the escalator at a department store.

Going to the movies separately put a new strain on our marriage. When we went together, Joanna always agreed with me. But once she was on her own, she seemed to enjoy everything she saw—while I liked almost nothing.

☐

BEN BORROWED a station wagon from a neighbor and drove us to the train station last night. We'd reserved two single bedrooms so the baby wouldn't keep both of us awake on the two-day trip to Texas. Ben assured us his agent would find David an assignment and we would be back within a month, but I still felt as though we were Adam and Eve being driven out of the Garden of Eden by some avenging angel.

Ben could see how depressed I was. After we checked our luggage at the station, he took us across to Olvera Street to wander through the Mexican market that takes place every night outside the adobe houses where Los Angeles began. He insisted on carrying Julia, who was wide-eyed with wonder at all the activity. Suddenly I felt David's arm around my waist. It was the first time the two of us had walked anywhere as a couple since the baby was born. We sat at an outdoor table, drinking margaritas and eating spicy taquitos dripping with guacamole sauce. By the time we boarded the train, we were feeling almost festive.

It was dark when we pulled out of the station. Julia was asleep in her portable bed, lulled by the chugging rhythm of the train. We put her in one of our two single bedrooms, then David pulled down the bed in the facing bedroom and we shared it. I've been so busy being a mother this past month, I've almost forgotten how to be a wife. Fortunately, like riding a bicycle, it all comes back very quickly.

☐

JULIA HAD TWO GRANDMOTHERS and one great-grandmother waiting at the train station to greet her when we arrived in Dallas today. I was anticipating a custody battle for the first grandchild on either side of the family, but once everybody had hugged and kissed, my mother seemed quite relieved that we were going home with Eula Lee.

David urged her to visit often—and bring Grandmother—but she just smiled evasively and said, with a pointed look at Grandmother, that if she'd done nothing else for her children, she'd always allowed them to live their own lives, without any interference from the older generation. Now that my little brother has left for college, I think she and Daddy are looking forward to having the house to themselves and forgetting they have children—or even a new grandchild.

☐

WE'VE BEEN HOME A WEEK and Mother and Daddy have only come by once to see Julia. How can they stay away? I can't understand it and neither can David. Eula Lee paces the house waiting for Julia to wake up from her naps. She wanted to keep the crib in her bedroom, but we decided to convert the laundry room into a makeshift nursery.

It was my plan, once we were settled, to get the baby on some semblance of a schedule, putting her to bed at the same time each night, letting her cry until she fell asleep so she would know who was in charge.

The first night under the new regime, I put her down, then headed for the bathroom to take a shower so I wouldn't hear the howling. David was typing the first act of his new play in our bedroom with the cast recording of *Gypsy* playing at full-volume on the stereo, so I knew he'd be oblivious to the chorus of complaints coming from Julia. When I finished bathing and stepped into the hallway to listen at the door of the laundry room, I was greeted by absolute quiet. Smiling in triumph, I tiptoed into the room to check on her. The crib was empty.

I headed down the hall to Eula Lee's room. She was rocking Julia in her arms, singing a lullaby of unknown origin off-key. The infant eyelids were heavy with sleep but before they closed completely, I could swear my daughter winked at me. Eula Lee turned to me, smiling proudly at her accomplishment. "Don't make a sound," she warned. "I've just gotten her to sleep."

I bit my tongue and felt like the villain of the piece. How can I live in a house ruled by a two-month-old infant? However, an hour later, when David emerged from the bedroom and suggested a late movie for the two of us, I felt very grateful to have a mother-in-law who considers it a privilege living under the same roof with her first grandchild. Sharing a house with David's mother has allowed me to become his wife again.

I now realize that if Mother and Daddy were as obsessed with the baby as Eula Lee—which David expects them to be—we'd have a war on our hands. And I'd be caught in the middle. I have to believe my parents are sensitive enough to understand my dilemma and are trying to make it as easy for me as possible.

And as easy on themselves. I know I was being unreasonable. I was no more eager to live with them than they were to have us. And yet I wanted them to know what they were missing not waking up every morning to the miracle of my baby in their house. I think I honestly expected them to be camped on our doorstep each day waiting to pay homage— to risk appearing as foolish and doting and possessive as my mother because nothing mattered more than being with their grandchild. But that was asking much more of them than they were interested in giving—the mistake I'd made from the beginning. Still, I suppose I should be grateful. Remembering how they kept their distance during those desperate, lonely months allowed us to keep ours

*once we were living in California. And to turn down with-
out guilt their annual invitations to visit them in Texas.*

□

WE'VE BEEN BACK in Texas over six weeks now—without a
single phone call from the West Coast (or the East Coast, for that
matter). How long are we to be stranded here in the middle of
the country? I would gladly travel in any direction that offered
the prospect of employment and peers.

I no longer have any friends of my own in Dallas. The people I
grew up with seem more like my parents' friends than they do
mine. David and I used to have a lot of friends on the newspaper, but he feels they all expected him to hit it big when he left
Texas, and until he does, he prefers to remain incommunicado,
working on his new play.

□

A WOMAN PHONED DAVID long-distance last night to say
his father was in a hospital in Amarillo with a severe case of
pneumonia. Her name was Mabel, she said, and she was married
to him—but didn't act as if that made her any relation to David.
She reported that Bartlett had gotten a big kick out of the baby
picture we sent him from Hollywood and talked of little else but
his first grandchild. It would mean everything to him to see her
before he died. David promised we'd start driving immediately
—and be there by noon.

Eula Lee cried when David told her his father was dying—but
refused to discuss the possibility of going with us. Insisting we
needed her help with Julia, David promised to keep her presence a secret from his father. Finally she agreed to make the
trip. I pray I'll always want to see David at the end, no matter
what intervenes.

What year was this written?

David drove like a madman through the night. I kept wondering what was going through his mind and what would be going
through mine when this moment arrived for me with one of my
parents.

At the hospital we discovered Mr. Scott asleep under an oxygen tent. A motherly-looking woman with glasses and gray hair, who sat holding his hand, whispered in his ear as we entered the room.

He opened his eyes and smiled but appeared too weak to talk. However, he turned his head, as if looking for someone else. David explained that hospital rules kept us from bringing the baby into the room but said he would hold her up outside the window.

While he went to get Julia, I stayed with Mabel. Eula Lee has never had a kind word for her ex-husband, but Mabel seems to adore him. She said she didn't know how she would get through the rest of her life if anything happened to him. How could two women be married to the same man and feel so differently about him? Is a good marriage really just a question of the right casting?

No—you've got that confused with a good play.

Standing beside the bed, I gazed down at my father-in-law fighting to breathe. I'd heard so many stories of his cruelty to David as a boy, I was prepared to hate him, but he looked so frail and helpless, I felt only pity. He opened his eyes, and despite the oxygen tent, I could feel him giving me the once-over.

Then David appeared at the window holding Julia. Bartlett broke into an enormous grin and raised both fists in a gesture of victory.

Getting married and fathering a child was the first thing I'd ever done to make him proud of me. Probably because it was the only time in my life I ever followed in his footsteps.

When David returned to the room, Bartlett suddenly announced in a loud voice that he wanted to see Eula Lee. David asked what made him think she'd come with us, but Bartlett just shook his head insistently. Finally Mabel took David aside and said she knew Eula Lee had to be in the car taking care of the baby. She also realized David was afraid of hurting her feelings by bringing his mother into the room, but she wanted Bartlett to have anything that might help him recover.

Reluctantly entering the hospital on David's arm, Eula Lee

muttered, "If I say good-bye to that man and he doesn't die, I'll never forgive him. Or you!"

I stepped to the window with Julia, determined to witness the scene that was about to take place. Crossing to the foot of the bed, standing slim and erect, my mother-in-law suddenly became the only person in the room. Mabel seemed to fade into the background and David stood tentatively in the doorway, like an intruder. He told me later that he could actually feel the physical attraction that still existed between his father and mother—he was almost embarrassed to be in the same room.

Then Bartlett said something I couldn't hear and Eula Lee turned away sharply, the connection broken. She was fuming as she returned to the car, mumbling that he couldn't even die without insulting her one last time. I asked what he'd said. "He told me I had the map of Ireland on my face." And she broke into sobs. I said I didn't understand what it meant. "My wrinkles, all my wrinkles," she moaned, continuing to sob.

When I went back inside to say good-bye, I told Bartlett I'd been waiting a long time to meet him and we had a lot more to say to each other, so he'd better get well. He smiled, but his mind was still on Eula Lee. He said she looked so young and pretty standing there, he'd repeated to her what he'd said the first time they met—that she had the map of Ireland on her face. Why did it make her so angry now? She'd loved hearing it forty years ago. He was still shaking his head in despair as I leaned over to kiss him good-bye. "I never could do anything to make that woman happy."

Mabel walked to the door of the hospital with me while David told his father good-bye. He promised we'd come to see him again when he was feeling better—joking that he was too mean to die without causing us a lot more trouble. Later, when we were alone, David told me the last thing Bartlett said was, "Tell my wife good-bye for me." David corrected him. Eula Lee was no longer his wife. He was married now to a wonderful woman who was devoted to him. Bartlett gave David a hard stare. "I don't care how many times you get married, boy, you only have one wife. If you never learn anything else from me, learn that."

☐

BARTLETT IS MUCH BETTER and will be out of the hospital at the end of the week. David and I brought Julia back to Amarillo yesterday and are staying in the trailer Bartlett and Mabel call home. This time Eula Lee has remained in Dallas.

The trailer is small but cozy. Even though it's been parked in the same place for several years now, you have the feeling each day that whether you go or stay is up to you. Not a bad way to live—at least in my present mood. How do people get through life knowing they're going to wake up in the same place every day?

David says if his father weren't coming home from the hospital, he wouldn't mind staying here indefinitely—or at least until he finishes his new play, *Anybody Home?* Finally—after ten years of trying—he's been able to get his father down on paper.

And out of my nightmares.

□

WILLA CRANE CALLED tonight from New York—the first we've heard from her since *Detours* closed, though we did send her a baby announcement. She's just gotten her first movie role and will be filming on location in Texas this fall. She's bringing Molly with her and plans to enroll her in school in Dallas. I was stunned when David invited her to stay with us. Where? In the laundry room with Julia?

□

WILLA AND MOLLY arrived yesterday. We offered them our bedroom—David assured me they wouldn't take it but they did, without even a polite protest, so we're sleeping on a Hide-a-Bed couch in the living room. Willa had to be in the makeup trailer on location by 5 A.M., so David woke up at four this morning to drive her to work. She offered to rent a car, but David assured her he likes to wake up early and write. Since when?

With Willa in the house, I had at least a tenuous connection with show business. Driving her to location every morning, I talked about the play I was writing. She offered

116

to show it to the director of her film as soon as I was finished. He was looking for a new play to take him back to Broadway. And I was looking for a ticket out of Texas— heading in any direction.

□

WITH SO MANY PEOPLE living in this little house, David and I can't even have a fight, except in whispers. Just as well. If I said everything I was feeling now out loud, it would end the marriage. The only thing that keeps me from walking out the door is knowing that David is in more pain than I am—and unlike me, has no one to blame for it.

Thank goodness for Julia, who provides our only sense of forward motion. Every week she seems able to do something she couldn't do the week before. The first year of life is one miracle after another. The first day she turned over, David was so thrilled he couldn't wait to wake her from her nap to see if she still remembered how to do it. What a pity that babies have no sense of their accomplishments—and no memory of these early triumphs to sustain them in their adult years when there is no longer any guarantee that each morning may bring a new skill.

□

LOCATION FILMING ended today. Tomorrow Willa and Molly are flying back to New York. Willa is taking David's new play with her to read and, if she likes it, has promised to pass it on to the director.

Even though I'll be glad to have our bedroom back, I'm going to miss them—and all the complications they brought with them. I've grown especially fond of Molly—and she's been like a big sister to Julia, playing with her for hours at a time. She is desolate about leaving Dallas and this morning, as she was getting ready for school, begged David and me to adopt her. She loves living in a house with a husband, a wife, and a baby, as well as a grandmother. This house, which seems uncomfortably crowded to me, feels cozy and safe to her. I felt the same way about my family when I was growing up. Now I wonder if there were as many unspoken tensions between my parents as there are among the adults sharing these rooms.

I doubt it. Tension requires a certain amount of passion.

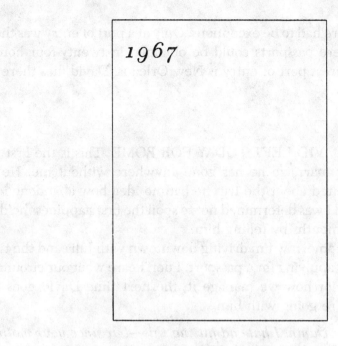

1967

JUST AS WE WERE beginning to give up hope, David got a phone call from Irwin Fletcher, the producer he worked for last summer. Last summer? It seems like a decade ago. Fletcher wants David to fly to Rome at the end of the week for a fast rewrite on a film that goes before the cameras next month. David agreed immediately. "You do have a current passport?" Fletcher asked.

"No problem," David replied, trying to be both honest and affirmative. When he put down the phone, he whirled me around the room then called Hollywood to tell his new agent about the forthcoming deal.

And had to remind the son of a bitch who I was.

Next he called the post office to see how fast he could get a passport. It wasn't a matter of renewing an old one, he explained, he was applying for a passport for the first time in his life. But he had to have it by the end of the week, when he was scheduled to leave for Rome. "Impossible" was the official response; a new passport takes at least a month.

Seeing the assignment slipping through his fingers, David said there had to be exceptions. Only at a port of entry was the reply. There passports could be obtained in twenty-four hours. The nearest port of entry is New Orleans. David flies there tomorrow.

□

DAVID LEFT TODAY FOR ROME. This is the first time in our marriage he has gone anywhere without me. He was so excited about the trip he had no idea how abandoned I felt—and I was determined not to spoil the first happiness he'd known in months by telling him.

Tomorrow I'm driving downtown with Julia and the two of us are applying for a passport. I don't care what our circumstances are or how we manage it, the next time David goes abroad, we're going with him.

Damn, I hate admitting this—but since your mother so faithfully recorded her truths, I don't see how I can in good conscience omit my great lie. I didn't go to Rome.

Fletcher called the night before I was to leave and said the studio had suddenly insisted on a big-name writer for the job. But I couldn't bring myself to tell your mother—or her parents. So I pretended I was leaving for Rome, took a bus instead all the way to West Texas. Stayed with my old girlfriend's mother. Poured out all my failures to her. She said I'd made two wrong choices: marrying above myself and aiming too high. Her daughter had married a sanitation inspector—and lived happily in Indiana.

It was the worst week of my life—until now, that is. Finally I slinked back to Dallas, stopped at Neiman's for a couple of "made in Italy" gifts for you and your mother, came home, and spent days describing sights I still dreamed of seeing. Which, years later, we finally did see together, didn't we, darling? A much better way, of course.

□

JULIA AND I are staying with my parents while David is in Rome. How strange it seems to be sleeping in my old bedroom

120

with a baby in a crib beside me. When I'm here in the house where I grew up, I don't feel old enough to be a mother.

Will I ever think of myself as an adult around my own mother? In her house I seem to fall short of the mark in everything I do. She never criticizes me aloud, but I'm sure she must know that my underwear is unraveling at the seams and my shoes are run over at the heels. She seems so completely in control of her life; why do I feel at the mercy of mine?

Tonight I think I may have discovered the secret of her serenity. When she kissed me good-night, she disappeared not into the master bedroom she always shared with my father but into the bedroom which had belonged to my sister. She must have seen me watching her with surprise, because she turned around at the door and said with a smile, "Once all the children left home, I started sleeping around." Then she explained that she needs less sleep than my father, but it disturbs him if she comes to bed later or gets up earlier. Once she started sleeping in a separate room, she could set her own hours—for the first time in thirty years of marriage. "There are so many more hours in the day for me now," she said. "Sleeping alone has added years to my life—literally."

I couldn't help asking if Daddy didn't miss having her in bed with him. "He misses having a warm body beside him," she confessed with surprising candor. "I doubt if it has anything to do with me."

Suddenly I wanted to crawl in bed beside her, turn out the lights, and talk all night, the way I used to do with my friends when I was still in school. Sometimes I miss falling asleep beside another female, discussing the mysteries of the male. I remember reading that in an earlier century when travel was more difficult and families more isolated, a man would move out of his wife's bed to make room for a visiting female friend or relative.

I was about to follow her into the bedroom to ask how children had changed her marriage when I heard Julia crying. So I kissed my mother good-night and hurried to quiet my daughter before she woke my father.

Mother gave me a look of such sympathy before she closed the door into the room where she now sleeps happily alone, I decided it was just as well I'd missed the opportunity to question her. Perhaps it was better to acquire the knowledge I sought through experience, just as she had. The marriage vow seems to contain within it an unspoken pledge of silence.

Why did Joanna always have to make marriage so complicated? I rarely thought about being married, I just was. Forever.

□

TODAY DAVID got a seasonal job here in Dallas—in a printing plant that specializes in high school yearbooks. When he returned from Rome last month, I assumed we'd be living in Hollywood by now, with producers clamoring for his services. But there is no continuity in the life of a writer. One assignment seldom leads to another—or so we're learning. And we're also running out of money.

I was waiting for Anybody Home? *to change our lives. I had thirty copies mimeographed and sent one to everybody I knew who had any connection with show business.*

□

IRWIN FLETCHER CALLED DAVID to say he's ready to invest in *Anybody Home?*—just tell him where to send the check. David thanked him but explained that the play has not been shown to producers yet; he was just giving Fletcher an early look at it, as a friend. Fletcher was eloquent in his enthusiasm and said he had a few ideas about producers. We could use them.

Audrey Wood refuses to show *Anybody Home?*—saying it suffers from the same excesses as his Broadway failure, *Detours*. David was so stung by her criticism, he wrote asking her to release him from his contract. She replied with a terse telegram officially ending their relationship and wishing him good luck.

At the very least I hoped for a phone call from her asking me to reconsider. My career was zooming. Straight down.

David also got a positive reaction from Paul Gaines, who thinks he's perfect to play the lead. He just made his off-Broadway debut in a Pinter play and got great reviews (which he enclosed—I'm no longer alone in thinking he's going to be a big star).

At my insistence David wrote him back and said we thought he'd be perfect for the lead too—opposite Willa. That should whet his appetite. As far as we know, she hasn't had anything to do with him since Rhode Island, but he's never stopped pursuing her—along with every other actress who crosses his path. Apparently Willa is the only one who doesn't come running when he snaps his fingers.

I think we've got our two leads. Now all we need is a production.

□

TODAY THE OFFICE MANAGER of the yearbook plant offered David a permanent job in the executive training program. His temporary employment comes to an end next week when the yearbooks are shipped.

David told me about the offer very matter-of-factly—then asked what I thought he should do. I couldn't believe he was seriously considering it. How could we stay in Dallas when he had a new play?

But he growled that a new play is worthless without an agent or a producer, and he had neither; what he did have was a wife and child to support, in case I hadn't noticed. If he were alone, he could afford to gamble, but he was weighted down with responsibilities—and I was not helping by pretending they didn't exist and doing nothing to share the load.

Tears streaming from my eyes, I ran into the laundry room and began to pack a diaper bag for Julia. Then I called my mother and asked her to come get me. I said I wanted to bring Julia home for a while. There was a long pause on the other end of the line. Then she said my sister just cabled that she's coming home from London. My brother is due home from college for summer vacation at the end of the month. In her silence I could hear what she was thinking: if I came home with a baby, the last empty bedroom would be occupied and she would once again have to share my father's hours along with his bed. I told her I'd changed my mind and hung up the phone.

Then I called my grandmother and said I was bringing the baby for a visit. She sounded delighted and asked no questions. Julia was asleep in her portable bed. I loaded it into the back seat of the car, along with the diaper bag. Funny, I never once thought about packing a suitcase for myself. Julia's needs are so overwhelming my own seem insignificant. But as I climbed behind the steering wheel, I realized I didn't even have a purse.

I marched into the bedroom, determined not to be dissuaded from my purpose, but David was typing and didn't even glance at me. Announcing with all the control I could manage that Julia and I were going to my grandmother's, I promised I would get the car back in time for him to go to work—or wherever he wanted to go. From this day forward, he was free of all responsibility. I wouldn't even ask him for child support. I was perfectly capable of getting a job and taking care of myself and our baby. I'd always planned to work after I married—until I fell in love with a man who wanted me with him wherever his work took him. But by doing what he said he wanted, I'd become a burden to him. I still loved him and was willing to prove it by doing the one thing I'd never imagined I would do—leave him.

I started for the door but David blocked my exit, dropping to his knees and wrapping his arms around my legs so that I couldn't move. He said if I left him, his life was over.

I never dropped to my knees so fast in all my life. Everything that mattered to me was walking out the door. It's an important lesson to learn, Julia—when to drop to your knees and how long to stay there. Preferably, until you get what you must have. As for me, if your mother had gone out that door, I fear I'd still be on my knees today. In fact, I may be on them again by the time I finish reading this damn journal.

He had his arms around me, kissing me like a soldier just back from the war, when I suddenly remembered Julia asleep in the car. I raced through the kitchen to the garage, David right behind me. Julia was still sleeping peacefully, but sitting in the back seat beside her was Eula Lee. "If you leave, I'm going with

you," she announced firmly. "You're not taking my only grandchild away from me. And there won't be any living with David if
you leave him."

David assured her I was staying, then carried Julia back into
the house. Eula Lee told him not to put her bed back in the
laundry room—from now on Julia is staying in her bedroom.

It is now 2 A.M. David fell asleep soon after we made love, but
I'm more awake than I was this morning. Thoughts keep crowd-
ing my head. What can I do to lessen his burden? How can I get
a job when I don't even know where we'll be living in another
month? Somehow I have to find a way to work.

*So that was when she took the vow. Amazing to realize
how many years passed before she had anything to show
for it.*

□

WE FINALLY HEARD from Brad and Susan Savage, congratulating David on *Anybody Home?* and both of us on Julia. They
moved to Chicago last fall, and Brad is now teaching at Northwestern. Their second child, a boy, was born soon after Julia
and, to their great relief, is developing normally.

They're keeping their daughter at home, against the advice of
their doctor, who thinks she could learn to function more inde-
pendently in an institution. Brad agrees with him, but Susan
feels it is more important for a child to be loved than to be
independent.

Brad wants to recommend David for the post of playwright in
residence at Northwestern next year—which would culminate
in a student production of his play. Brad made it clear he would
be going out on a limb for David but said the new play would
give him a stronger case. He asked David to have John Gassner
write him a letter of recommendation. I'm praying it will happen—it would be wonderful to live in the same town as Susan—
especially with a new baby.

*Any other time I would've told Brad to shove it, but I was
on my knees, spending my days in that damn yearbook
factory, checking the spelling of names on football teams*

*and in honor societies and choral groups till I thought I'd
go blind. If I didn't go mad first. So I swallowed my pride
and wrote Gassner, asking for his help.*

☐

A FRIEND from the newspaper called David to say news of
John Gassner's death had just come over the Associated Press
wire. We didn't even know he was ill. He was only sixty-four.

*I'm ashamed to say my first thought was "There goes my
recommendation."*

Then a letter from Mrs. Gassner, written last week, arrived in
the afternoon mail. She said a recommendation, which her husband had dictated to her from his hospital bed, was on its way to
the university. She sent us her best wishes on the birth of our
daughter and said a baby present was in the mail. David said if I
ever got to wondering what he wanted in a wife, I didn't have to
look any further.

*Talk about a working marriage! I remember one winter
afternoon at Yale, fighting my way home through a snow-
storm. Mr. and Mrs. Gassner were coming from the opposite direction—she was walking ahead of him, taking the
brunt of the blizzard; he was directly behind her, holding
on to her coat, following hesitantly in her footsteps. He was
the one with the reputation, but she made it possible. He
knew it and she knew it.*

☐

BRAD SAVAGE WROTE that with Gassner's recommenda-
tion, David is virtually assured the playwright-in-residence post.
We should hear officially in a couple of weeks.

Now that I know we'll be departing Dallas at the end of
summer, I've begun to realize how much of value I'll be leaving
behind. Like any child, I grew up taking my family for granted.
But now that I've moved outside the charmed circle of childhood and realize what an ambitious and difficult enterprise
starting a family is, I look with increased respect at what my
parents and their parents before them accomplished.

Especially my grandmother. Her family is her proudest achievement in life, and yet she has always been her own woman—and much more independent than I've ever dared to be, especially since I married. For the first time I'm beginning to see my grandmother as a wife and mother like me. Unlike me, however, she insisted from the beginning on her right to travel and see the world even when her husband found it inconvenient to accompany her.

My grandmother takes more pleasure than anyone on my side of the family in the presence of the first baby from the next generation and plans her social life, which is still quite active even at the age of eighty-three, to allow at least two afternoons a week in Julia's company.

David and I have no social life in Dallas—he turns and flees in the opposite direction if he sees a familiar face headed our way in the grocery store. It used to annoy me when he acted like a fugitive from justice, but last week, coming out of a movie, we ran into one of my best friends from high school, accompanied by a husband I'd never met. When we'd gotten through the introductions, she asked David what he was doing in Dallas. Didn't he write for the movies anymore?

I explained that we'd brought the baby home for a visit, but she looked at us suspiciously and asked when we were going back to Hollywood. "Any day now," I lied, adding that David was waiting to hear about an assignment.

Driving home, David said nothing—but my heart ached for him. Even the most innocuous social exchange is agony for a man without a job. Women are used to making conversation on all manner of irrelevant topics—from clothes to children to cooking—but a man's whole identity is tied to what he does for a living. When he's unemployed, he might as well be walking around naked.

So my grandmother, who doesn't find it the least bit strange that a man would rather be at home with his wife and infant daughter than in an office, has become our best friend. She arrives in the afternoon around two, sending her maid off to do errands in the car while she plays with Julia. She refuses all offers of food and drink and never expects or even wants me to stay in the room with her—which makes her a most welcome guest indeed. She finds Julia, at the age of ten months, an enchanting companion.

Since her back is supported by a steel brace, Grandmother cannot attempt to lift Julia. However, she pulls a chair close to the playpen and talks to her, handing her toys, teaching her patty-cake, reciting nonsense verses, and singing little songs. Ordinarily Julia becomes bored after half an hour in the playpen and cries for someone to lift her out of it, but she seems to understand that her great-grandmother is doing all she can.

Today I looked in at four o'clock to see how the two of them were getting along. It was so quiet I was suspicious. Then I saw that Grandmother was asleep in her chair, and Julia had stretched out on the floor of the playpen and was singing herself to sleep, repeating the song I'd heard Grandmother singing to her earlier.

From the day we brought her to this house where a doting grandmother danced attendance, Julia has made it clear she expects to be rocked to sleep, and she almost always gets her way. None of us can stand to hear her cry. But today she seemed to understand that what she wanted was impossible. Watching that squirming little creature try to get comfortable on the playpen pad, without audible complaint, I suddenly saw twenty years into the future and dared imagine what a remarkable woman my daughter could become—a direct descendant of her remarkable great-grandmother.

When the maid returned, I explained that Grandmother was sleeping and said we would drive her home after dinner. Then I suggested the maid take the rest of the day off. She thanked me so profusely I realized Grandmother must hold her to rather strict hours. I grew up in a house with a live-in maid and my mother continues to have day help five days a week to do all the cleaning and cooking, but I have never had anyone work for me. What would it be like to have someone around all day to do my bidding?

To do her bidding? What an awful phrase. I hate the idea of hiring someone else for services we are capable of performing ourselves. I always assumed Joanna agreed with me. Apparently not.

128

Joining us at the dinner table, Grandmother kept marveling that I'd put a complete meal on the table without help from anyone. "It's so difficult to be a young woman today," she said. "So much more is expected of you than was expected of me when I was a bride."

I was amazed at this statement. We've all been led to believe that modern conveniences have made life much easier for women. How could my grandmother, who set up housekeeping without electric appliances or supermarkets, think my life was so much harder than hers?

"But you've had to learn to use all those things," she explained, surprised at how slow I was to see her point. "I always had a maid for the housework, a cook in the kitchen, a laundress to wash and iron, and a nurse for the children. You do everything. I marvel at your ability to handle so many different jobs at one time—but can you really call it progress?"

She really knew how to hit where it hurt. But she had a point—and at least she had the good grace to blame the times, and not me personally.

Julia was seated in her high chair beside Grandmother at the dinner table. She seldom submits to such confinement for an entire meal; I usually end up balancing her on my lap while I finish dinner. But tonight Grandmother captured her attention by feeding her bites of food from her own plate with her fingers. With Julia amused, I was looking forward to a civilized, relaxed meal for once when Grandmother suddenly gave a yelp, held up her hand, and said Julia had just bitten her. We all hurried to look, and sure enough, a tiny, sharp pearl of a tooth had broken through the soft pink lower gum.

Grandmother gave her first great-grandchild a hug, and Julia waved her fist in the air proudly, as if to put us all on notice she was armed now and could defend herself against violations of her person. It seemed appropriate somehow that my grandmother was the one to discover my daughter's first tooth. Three generations apart, they embody the same joyfully independent spirit. When I forget who I am, I have only to look backward into the past or forward into the future. My grandmother and my daughter provide the two spiritual poles between which I must locate an equator for my own life.

☐

IT'S OFFICIAL. David will be playwright in residence at Northwestern starting in September. My parents seem pleased that he finally has a job their friends can understand, and we are getting along with them better than we have in the past. Our friendly relations may have been reinforced by the fact that my sister has returned from a two-year stay in England speaking a different language, at least as far as my parents are concerned. Oh, they understand the words, but her meaning eludes them. She becomes hysterical at any mention of making her debut in the fall, saying she doesn't give a damn about being introduced to Dallas society, since she has no intention of spending the rest of her life here. However, unlike us, there is no place she would rather be at the moment. She is tired of trying to make friends, plus a living, in a foreign country. She just wants to fold her tent for a while—and be with people who will take care of her without making demands or asking questions.

Life is so much easier when you make conventional choices; once you fall into a previously established pattern, your path is clearly marked. But Diana is trying to lead an original life, even more original than mine, since apparently she is determined to do it alone, and the effort is taking its toll. Though I admire her, I don't find it easy being around her. Every time I defer to David in anything, she gives me a look that makes me feel like a spineless creature with no mind of my own.

The only blood relative with whom I really feel comfortable is Grandmother. Unlike my parents, she seems to appreciate our financial straits, and never arrives at our house empty-handed—though some of her offerings are rather bizarre, to say the least. If she has spent the morning straightening out her desk, her purse will be filled with letters or photographs, often of people I don't even know, containing some detail she thinks will interest me. Once, when she had been sorting through her jewelry, she brought me an amethyst ring that had belonged to her mother. If she and her maid have stopped at the grocery store on the way to our house, she buys a sackful of things she thinks we might enjoy but would never buy for ourselves. She has always had a maid to do her grocery shopping, so she now finds the supermarket a great adventure. While the maid buys staples, Grandmother goes merrily up and down the aisles, filling a cart with anything that strikes her fancy, which ends up in a sack for us. She gets as excited as a child showing me her purchases—curiosities like jalapeño jelly, frozen crepes, angel food cake mix. Today she pulled from her sack a huge prime rib roast, saying she hoped I would know what to do with it. Actually I don't. I have never bought such an expensive piece of meat. But I'll try to be worthy of it.

David and I are grateful for her good intentions, even when they disrupt the tenuous emotional balance of our household. Last week she arrived with a huge authentic Audubon bird print which used to hang in the two-story entrance hallway of her home. It had been a wedding present to her from a favorite aunt, so its sentimental as well as name value obscured the fact that it was grotesquely ugly.

Unable to find a place for it in her new apartment, she had decided we had just the wall for it in the living room of the house we share with Eula Lee. The fact that the wall is already occupied—by an original painting executed by David's grandmother, on his mother's side—did not deter my grandmother from her unspoken objective, which was to find a new home with one of her heirs for her beloved Audubon birds.

She probably suspected that, being in the most financially precarious position of any household in the family, we were the least likely to object to her unsolicited offering (I can just imagine what Mother would've said if Grandmother had given her those birds and told her where to hang them).

Her instincts were shrewd—as always—and her opening thrust glistened with guile. "If you hang the Audubon in your living room," she said to David, "your mother can keep her mother's painting in her bedroom. I can imagine how much it must mean to her, and if she's the way I am, she wants the things that mean the most to her in her bedroom, where she can see them last thing before she falls asleep and first thing when she wakes up."

*What a wily old silver fox she was—but a worthy oppo-
nent till the day she died. Frankly, since her death, I am no
longer afraid of my own, for she has never ceased making
her presence felt in our lives.*

Then she sat in the living room until David had hung the print
to her specifications.

*I remember carrying my grandmother's painting into
the bedroom where my mother sat red-eyed with outrage
and promising that once Joanna and I left Dallas, it could
be returned to the living room.*

*Three months later, on Joanna's birthday, her grand-
mother sent her a Hallmark card with a short message
scribbled on the back, words to the effect of "Since you and
David liked the Audubon print so much, I've decided to
give it to you in place of my usual check. It is actually
worth a great deal more than a hundred dollars, so this
year you came out ahead. Happy birthday! Nana."*

*What I will never cease wondering is what would've
happened if we'd said at the outset how we really felt about
the print. Did she deliberately set a trap to test our integrity? Only she knows the answer.*

☐

CHANGE OF PLANS. We're getting out of Dallas sooner
than I dared hope. *Anybody Home?* is being given a staged
reading at the Eugene O'Neill Theater Conference in Water-
ford, Connecticut, next month. Usually the plays are submitted
through the playwright or his agent, but David was not even
aware of the conference and no longer has an agent to represent
him in the theater. Fortunately, however, he still has friends.
Paul Gaines was asked to be part of the acting company and
agreed to come only on the condition that *Anybody Home?* be
given a reading—with Paul playing the lead. Willa will be playing the wife, which is just what Paul hoped would happen. So
what if he's using the play to serve his own purposes? We're
using him to serve ours. But as long as everyone comes out
ahead, why not?

We've decided to drive east. Eula Lee is buying a new car and will let us have her old one for the trade-in price. From Connecticut we'll drive to Chicago and get settled for fall. I feel as if our life has been on hold for the past year. I can't wait to get moving again!

For once I was as eager as Joanna to hit the road. No pioneer family in a covered wagon could have headed west more hopeful of what lay ahead than we were driving east that summer in our secondhand Chevrolet.

The actors will be rehearsing in New York, and Willa has invited us to stay with her, which seems only fair, since she lived in our bedroom for two months last fall.

□

WE ARRIVED in New York City last night at midnight. Molly and Willa were waiting up for us. We took Julia and all her equipment up to the apartment, then David parked the car on a side street. When he returned to unload our two suitcases and his typewriter, they were gone. Stolen. I guess we were lucky the car was still there. Welcome back to Manhattan.

When you've been betrayed by someone you once loved, you never trust them again. That was the way it was between New York City and me. A love affair gone wrong.

When David asked Willa how rehearsals for *Anybody Home?* were going, she mumbled something evasive and changed the subject. But this morning over an enormous breakfast of pancakes, fried eggs, and sausage, she finally confessed that she'd withdrawn from the play to accept a role in a movie which starts filming next week. She said Paul made her feel as if she'd betrayed all of us, and David had to admit he was disappointed too.

However, when he met Willa's replacement at rehearsal today, he felt a lot better. She's an unknown actress from Oklahoma who he thinks is more right for the role than Willa. That wouldn't be much of a trick.

Less than thrilled at how well David was taking her defection, Willa hardly said a word during dinner. She'd insisted on cooking a huge meal, which we found almost impossible to eat in her

133

hot, unair-conditioned apartment. At first we assumed she had thrown herself into the role of hostess with her customary enthusiasm, but then she confessed as she served herself a second helping of mashed potatoes that the director had ordered her to gain twenty pounds for her new movie role. She is apparently determined to have us get fat alongside her—or at least keep her company while she eats her way into her new character.

☐

I CAN'T BELIEVE how much has happened in the past twenty-four hours. Was it just yesterday Julia and I were sitting at the breakfast table with Willa and Molly? David was sleeping late, and when I woke him to get dressed for rehearsal, he whispered that I had to get him out of dinner every night for the rest of the week before Willa killed him with her cooking. I suggested that he confront her himself, but he said he already had enough pressure at rehearsal—besides, I was better at handling Willa. Better at handling her? If it weren't for David, I wouldn't even have to know people like Willa.

When I saw her making out a grocery list, I quickly assured her she didn't have to cook for us—in fact, we were planning to have dinner with friends every night for the rest of the week. Her reply was that we should feel free to invite anyone we wanted to her apartment. She loved cooking for a crowd.

I'm not an actress. I've never been able to lie convincingly. And Willa did nothing to make it easier for me. In fact, I could swear she enjoyed watching me squirm. The more I explained, the more hostile she became—finally exploding that she was not running a hotel, that guests had certain obligations, and if David and I were unwilling to accept them, perhaps we'd better find somewhere else to stay.

Fortunately Julia began to cry at that moment—which is the only thing that kept *me* from bursting into tears. I was in the bedroom changing her diapers when there was a knock at the door. Molly, looking wise beyond her nine years, assured me that her mother was just getting in character for the movie. At least that's how she'd apologized to Molly earlier in the week after calling her the "bane of her existence" and saying women didn't have a chance to become artists because they were cursed with children.

I quickly forgot how upset I was with Willa in my concern for Molly, but she explained that she didn't mind so much anymore when her mother lost her temper because she always made up for it by letting Molly do something she would never have been allowed to do otherwise. Then Molly began to laugh, remembering her third birthday. Willa had taken her to see *The Sound of Music*—her first Broadway show. At the end Molly was so overcome with delight, she stood in her seat to applaud. The rest of the audience was also standing. Outraged by the audience response, Willa suddenly stood in her seat too—and began to boo. Molly burst into tears, and then Willa felt so badly, she let Molly wait at the stage door to get Mary Martin's autograph.

Poor Willa. All the things that made her such an exciting actress made her an impossible parent. Those violent mood swings between anger and guilt. I recognized them in myself—but fortunately I had Joanna to serve as a buffer between me and my child. Willa had no one. And so by the age of nine, Molly had become the adult in that relationship. No wonder she and Joanna were best friends, Joanna being the adult in ours.

When David called from rehearsal, I told him Willa had asked us to leave. He sounded almost relieved and promised to make other arrangements by dark.

Willa was on the telephone with her agent when David arrived, so our exit fortunately escaped her attention. Molly helped us load Julia's things into the car and begged us tearfully to write to her. I hated leaving her there alone with her own mother. When I see how treacherous and complicated blood ties are, I wonder that a civilized society can entrust children to the sole and often arbitrary authority of a parent. Surely there should be someone older and more objective looking out for them.

Our small Chevrolet felt like an air-conditioned refuge after the heat and tension of Willa's apartment. I didn't care where we were going, it just felt good to be moving again. But when we stopped in front of what appeared to be a deserted warehouse on lower Broadway, I began to get curious.

At the front door above the name of the manufacturing company that occupied the lower floors was a single name next to a buzzer—W. Blair. "Wyatt?" I asked curiously. David just smiled and pressed the buzzer. There was an answering buzz, and David pushed open the front door.

When we stepped off the freight elevator at the top floor, Wyatt was waiting for us. Beyond him was a vast space undefined by walls, bounded only by floor-to-ceiling windows on all sides. It was a set designer's fantasy, transformed by dozens of hanging plants with winding graveled paths below into a secret garden where it was possible to work and eat and sleep. Theatrical posters suspended by fine wires were placed back to back to separate the work area—where Wyatt had his drawing board and art supplies—from the living quarters. A massive bed was built into the back wall of the loft, with a canopy suspended from the ceiling to create a tentlike effect.

I was enraptured. Wyatt explained that a lot of artists were moving into downtown lofts to get more space for their money. He was paying less for this than he had for his Bleeker Street apartment, one fifth the size.

While we sat talking on pillows in the living room, Julia amused herself by taking tentative steps between David and me. Wyatt paid no attention to her, which made him unique in her experience and therefore irresistible. Accustomed to adoring adults who applaud her every move, she would crawl into his lap, then when he continued to ignore her, crawl down again. Finally, as if accepting that nothing less would attract his attention, she walked from me across the room to Wyatt—without once falling—just as the phone began to ring.

Oblivious to the miracle that had just occurred, Wyatt walked to the far end of the loft to answer a phone beside his bed. When he came back, he swooped Julia into the air and said if we still needed a place to stay, we could have his bed and he'd take the couch. David and I knew better than to ask who was on the phone and what had been said, but I suspect Wyatt doesn't spend many nights alone. I started to protest that we didn't want to interfere with his life, but David silenced me with a look that made it clear we were lucky to have a bed for the night.

Putting Julia on his shoulders, Wyatt suddenly turned to David and me and asked how long it had been since we'd had any time alone. He suggested we take a walk around the Village, maybe even catch a late movie—and leave Julia to keep him company while he worked. Then he confessed how lonely he gets at night—so lonely he lets in people who mean nothing to him only to wake up in the morning wondering how to get rid of them. Having the three of us there made it a lot easier to tell anyone who called that he was busy.

David took my hand as we stepped into the elevator—and held it the rest of the night. I can't remember the last time we walked anywhere holding hands—it felt as if we were falling in love for the first time, with everything ahead of us.

I could sense his excitement about *Anybody Home?* How ironic that in finally coming to terms with the most important figure from his past—his father—David has provided us with a future. No telling where this play will take us!

We stopped in at the Cookery for the spicy barbecue sandwiches we used to love. I was glad to see they were still on the menu, even though the price has gone up. It made me feel we still belonged.

Gazing at me across the table, David said he didn't know what he'd do without me, thank God I was willing to travel with him, whenever and whatever the cost.

I thought of all the places we've lived since we married—my parents' garage apartment, our third floor in New Haven, a cabin in Rhode Island, our apartment in the Village, our one room at the Montecito, Eula Lee's house—six homes in seven years of marriage. What do the next seven years hold?

Whatever happens, David and I have a longer history of shared experiences between us than many couples accumulate in a lifetime. I find him more exciting now than I did the summer we met. We've seen each other at our best and at our worst. The experts are always stressing the importance of keeping the mystery in a marriage. But what attracts me to David is what I know about him—his courage, his passion, his tenacity. This is supposedly the vulnerable year in a marriage—when the seven-year itch strikes. But why would a couple split up just as they acquire a vocabulary of shared references? I can no longer imagine life without him.

And all I did was hold her hand. Seven years into this journal and I have yet to see sex inspire such a soliloquy.

When David and I returned to the loft, it was after midnight. Wyatt was snoring on the couch, Julia asleep in her crib beside him. His favorite aria from *La Traviata,* which I haven't heard since New Haven, was still playing on the stereo as we climbed into his huge double bed and closed the curtains.

☐

LIFE IS FILLED with possibilities again. Who could ask for anything more?

Anybody Home? played to a packed house tonight at the O'Neill. Paul was magnificent, but to give credit where credit is due, it's a star-making role.

Nice of you to notice.

Julia—bless her heart—stayed asleep in the car for all three acts. I went out at each intermission to check on her. David, who was much too nervous to remain seated during the performance, watched from the wings and kept slipping out the stage door and circling the parking lot to look through the car window and make sure she was all right. He said later it kept him calm having her there. Looking through the window and seeing her peacefully asleep made what was happening inside the theater seem less like life or death.

The audience was filled with important people—agents, critics, producers. I didn't spot Audrey Wood until the play was almost over, then I had a hard time taking my eyes off her— especially when the audience gave the play she had refused to represent a standing ovation and she was forced to choose between remaining conspicuously seated or joining the crowd. Afterward she sought David out and told him she had made a mistake. She asked if he'd found a new agent to represent him in the theater. He lied and said yes.

The most important person in the audience turned out to be a man we'd never met—the producer of a new theater opening in Los Angeles in the fall. Irwin Fletcher had sent him the play last spring. He read it but apparently didn't realize how much he liked it until he saw the standing ovation. He told David he wanted to do it in November. If only we weren't going to Northwestern!

☐

DAVID HAS DECIDED he'd rather be a playwright in production in Los Angeles than a playwright in residence in the middle of the country. So he called Brad Savage, told him about the L.A. production, and said he hoped Brad would understand. Of course Brad didn't.

Brad took my decision as a personal betrayal. However, before he hung up, he asked if I could suggest a replacement. I mentioned Elaine West, saying her credentials carried a lot more weight in the academic world than mine. She'd never had a play produced but she'd published plenty of bad reviews.

Next David called his Hollywood agent and told him we were on our way back to California—at our own expense—and he needed a job.

☐

THE MANAGER at the Montecito greeted us on our arrival yesterday as if we were family and gave us top billing on the celebrity residents board. We set up Julia's bed in the large closet adjoining the bathroom. In her first year of life she has gone from a laundry room to a closet. How old will she be before she has a room of her own? Fortunately, she's still too young to feel deprived. In fact, she seems to be thriving on the uncertain, unconventional life we're leading. Packing is her favorite game. She has an assortment of shopping bags in different sizes which she packs and unpacks endlessly with her toys.

David had a good meeting with a producer who wants him to write for television. He'd seen *Detours* on Broadway and read *Anybody Home?* (which Irwin Fletcher has apparently shown all over town). None of the Hollywood producers we've met are anything like the stereotype of the old-fashioned cigar-chomping movie mogul. The Louis B. Mayers and Samuel Goldwyns and Harry Cohns have been replaced by a new breed of literate, well-traveled men at least as bright as anybody I've met in the theater.

I wonder if she would've felt that way if I hadn't gotten the assignment. But I did—so I have to agree. My agent even got me "top of the show" when he negotiated my price, trading on the fact that I was a Broadway playwright. "But he's never written for television," the producer protested. "Exactly," Eliot replied. So to write an hour script I was paid six times what I made in twelve weeks at the yearbook factory. Hooray for Hollywood!

☐

WE JUST GOT A LETTER from Elaine West thanking David for recommending her for the playwright-in-residence post at Northwestern. Until September she'd never been west of Philadelphia, but to her amazement she's fallen in love with the Midwest. She says she would've lost her mind if she'd had to spend another winter in New York. She hopes we can be friends again the way we used to be—and begs me to write and send a picture of the baby.

Joanna sent her your picture and I sent her a copy of Anybody Home? *She sent back a copy of* Winnie-the-Pooh *for you and a five-page letter full of astute comments and compliments for me. Sometimes I think friendship is as complicated as marriage—you certainly have to work just as hard at the ones you care about.*

☐

I BROUGHT JULIA to rehearsal today. The theater is so large I can keep her quietly occupied at the back without anyone except David even realizing we're there. It's rather embarrassing to still be breast-feeding a child who now walks everywhere and announces in words what she wants—but it does keep her quiet. There are times I resent the constant appeasement policy David insists I practice with her, but I suppose it's a small enough price to pay for being able to share his life—especially when we have to live so much of it in one room. I go cold with fear trying to imagine what my life would be like if I weren't sharing his. So, for now, I keep my blouse unbuttoned and my mouth shut.

Paul has come to California to repeat his role in the play—and hopes it will lead to a film offer. He says he would be happy never to go back to New York again—except on location for a movie.

He has a room at the Montecito just down the hall from ours, and after rehearsal all of us usually have dinner together. He flirts with Julia as outrageously as he does with older members of her sex—and she is just as susceptible to his charms.

Tonight we went to Chinatown for dinner. On the way to the restaurant we stopped at a souvenir store. David bought me a silk kimono which makes me feel like a geisha, and Paul purchased a dozen different trinkets for Julia, which he gave her at ten-minute intervals during dinner to buy her silence so we could talk about the play.

☐

IT'S DAWN. David and Julia are sleeping soundly but the dream that just woke me has left me so frightened and confused I'm afraid to risk falling asleep again. I feel as if I've been unfaithful to David. Nothing has changed on the outside—but I can't answer for what's going on inside my head.

What's this?

It all started yesterday. The actors were off, but David had to meet with the director about rewrites, so Paul asked me to drive to the beach with him—and bring Julia. David was a little surprised when I accepted. It never occurs to him that I might occasionally like to go somewhere besides rehearsal.

The weather was glorious and we drove all the way to Santa Monica with the top down. I was pretty sure Paul had asked every available female in the cast before saddling himself with

Julia and me for the day, but I didn't care. I was just happy to be along for the ride.

David hates any form of recreation that takes place out of doors. He doesn't trust the elements—probably something to do with growing up amid all those dust storms in West Texas. I'm not very athletic but I love stretching out on the grass or the sand with the sun shining down on me and the wind stirring the landscape into motion.

I sat at the water's edge helping Julia build sand castles and watching Paul swim. Then we took Julia into the ocean together, swinging her into the air to jump the waves. I lost all track of time, but the sun was setting when we finally gathered up our towels and started for the car.

Julia was exhausted from all the activity. I cuddled her in my arms, hoping the motion of the car would put her to sleep, but she kept crying for the breast, so finally, trying to be as European about it as possible, I pulled up my sweater and pulled down one side of my bathing suit. I tried to make a joke of it with Paul, but he could see how embarrassed I was. Suddenly he put his hand on my cheek and told me to stop blushing—what I was doing was as natural as breathing. Then he said I should stop apologizing for still nursing Julia, adding that his mother had nursed him until she got pregnant again, and he didn't seem to be any the worse for it. He adored his mother and she adored him and frankly he thought that was the key to his success with women.

What an ego! So far, however, none of this surprises me. I never knew Paul to put any woman off-limits, including my wife. Which was why I didn't like the idea of her going to the beach—or anywhere—with him without me.

Except Willa, he confessed sadly. He fell in love with her the summer they met in Rhode Island and thought the feeling was mutual, but once the play closed, the affair ended. She explained it was only their characters that had fallen in love. If she'd stayed in the cast of *Anybody Home?* and come to Los Angeles with him, he felt it probably would've happened again —the only time she allows herself to become emotionally vulnerable, he said, is within the context of a character. But she decided to make a movie instead, so "here I am on my own," he said with a smile, "doing my best to enjoy being uncommitted. I know I have the reputation of just adding notches to my belt," he continued, his hand caressing my cheek while Julia suckled contentedly, "but the truth is, I like women and enjoy being with them. Frankly, I think women are a lot more interesting than men—maybe because they're not afraid of their feelings."

Why didn't I just take his hand and put it firmly back on the wheel, where it belonged?

That's what I'd like to know.

Dare I admit how much I liked what was happening? Marriage seems to put an end to touching for its own sake. I knew Paul didn't have serious designs on me, but for the first time since I married, I felt attractive to another man, and I liked the feeling.

When Julia fell asleep, her mouth finally relinquishing the nipple, I started fumbling with my free hand for my bathing suit strap. Paul reached over to help me, his hand brushing my exposed breast. But instead of apologizing, he just smiled and said he could never understand why women worried about ruining their figures by breast-feeding their children—I'd never been more beautiful.

By the time we pulled into the Montecito parking lot, my knees were trembling so that I could hardly stand. Paul took Julia, who was still sleeping soundly, from my lap and carried her up to the room. When I opened the door, I saw that David had fallen asleep on the couch, pages of his script scattered on the floor beside him. Paul put Julia in her crib, then gave me a quick kiss good-bye as I whispered a thank-you for the afternoon.

Still tingling from the attention, I stripped and stepped into the shower to wash off the sand. David came into the bathroom just as I was reaching for a towel. Maybe it was my imagination, but I felt he looked at me standing there naked, dripping wet, as if he were seeing me for the first time. Suddenly brazen, I held out the towel to him and ordered him to dry me off. As he toweled me gently, I unbuckled his belt and unzipped his pants. I felt his mouth on my breast and then my knees buckled and we were on the floor astride a pile of damp towels. Neither of us said a word—it was like sex in the middle of the night, intense and impersonal. But just as I was exploding inside—wave after wave of pleasure breaking on the beach of my body—I remembered the way Paul smiled at me as his hand brushed against my breast.

"I thought you'd never get home," David said finally, pulling me to my feet. "That's the last time I'm letting you go anywhere without me."

To think my only concern was for her physical safety—I had no idea the real danger was inside her head.

I lay awake for hours with Julia sleeping soundly in her closet and David lost to consciousness on the bed next to me. I kept thinking of Paul, and when I finally fell asleep, I had the most erotic dream of my life, with Paul doing things to me I never imagined one person doing to another.

I woke up filled with guilt, as if I'd actually betrayed David by dreaming about Paul.

Is it possible to feel betrayed seventeen years later? The blood's rising—I think it is.

David is right not to want me to go anywhere without him. I'm not to be trusted.

I never suspected. Fortunately, however, that was her only outing alone with Paul. At least I think it was. Of course I've got pages to go before I sleep.

☐

AT 1 A.M. WE LEFT the opening-night party and drove downtown to the *Los Angeles Times* to get an early copy of the morning paper and read the review. Finally a review we can send home—to everyone except David's mother. The reviewer misunderstood and thought *Anybody Home?* really happened. In fact, David never met any of the other women in his father's life, but to read the review, you would think he actually fell in love with one of them. Eula Lee is going to find the play hard enough to forgive—without the added embarrassment of people thinking it has *anything* to do with her.

144

☐

DAVID'S PICTURE is in *Time* magazine. We were so excited till we read the article, which repeated the mistake from the *Los Angeles Times*. David did *not* grow up watching his father in bars with other women, and just because some staff researcher found an article that says he did does not make it true. David was able to clip the offending paragraph from the Los Angeles review before mailing it home to Eula Lee, but she subscribes to *Time*. We're in for it now.

☐

UNIVERSAL STUDIOS wants to buy the film rights to *Anybody Home?* and there is talk about Lee Marvin playing the lead. David called to celebrate the sale with Eula Lee, who's been a movie fan all her life. But as soon as she heard his voice on the phone, she hung up. David called back. She hung up again. *Time* had gotten to her first.

I was in agony. It was the high point of my life—a successful play and a movie sale—all I'd ever wanted—and my mother wasn't speaking to me.

David called home again. This time he only said two words, "Lee Marvin." He waited for a click at the other end of the line, but instead there was an anticipatory silence, so he pressed his advantage. "He may star in a movie based on my play." More silence. But he could tell Eula Lee was still on the line. Finally she spoke. "Who'll play the wife?"

That was the closest she ever came to acknowledging that the play had any connection with her life—or mine.

☐

TONIGHT DAVID CALLED HIS FATHER to tell him his life was turning out to be worth more than either of them had ever imagined. How would he feel about coming to Los Angeles to see it on the stage? Bartlett said that might just get him on a plane for the first time in his life. David promised to send a pair of round-trip tickets for Thanksgiving week and to reserve a room at the Montecito.

☐

WE GATHERED TOGETHER for a family Thanksgiving today, with a cast of characters that would never make the cover of *The Saturday Evening Post*. Bartlett and Mabel arrived yesterday. We drove them around Los Angeles, showing them sights until Bartlett begged to be allowed to return to his hotel room and watch television. The size of Los Angeles overwhelmed and depressed him. He's never lived in a town he couldn't cross in twenty minutes. After we'd been driving for an hour, he muttered, "I'd leave this place if I could find the edge."

But he cheered considerably this morning when we took him and Mabel to a champagne brunch. Even in his heyday as a drinking man, he'd never had anything alcoholic for breakfast, and he kept the waiter busy refilling his glass. By midafternoon Julia was ready for a nap, and David felt his father could use one too, before the play. Mabel stayed in our room talking with me while Julia slept in her closet. David decided he should prepare his father for just how personal the play was—and showed him the *Time* article. David told me later that after Bartlett read it, he handed it back with a shrug and said, "Well, it's true—isn't it?"

My mother graduated from college, my father left school in the sixth grade, but like any born storyteller, he understood instinctively that just because something didn't happen exactly the way you told it doesn't keep it from being true.

When the play ended, Bartlett and Mabel led the applause for the actors and couldn't wait for David to take them backstage to meet the cast. Mabel shook hands politely with the actress playing the other woman but hugged the wife as if she were her stage counterpart. Bartlett slapped Paul on the back, told him how proud he felt seeing himself on the stage, then said, "I'd still be laughing if the damn thing weren't about me."

☐

146

EULA LEE HAS COME to Hollywood for Christmas. She says the reason for her trip is not the play but Julia. Their reunion was heartwarming. Julia flew into her arms at the train station and will not leave her sight.

The cast of the play was, of course, anxious to meet her; since meeting Bartlett, they've looked forward to getting a look at the other half of the "real story." However, Eula Lee made David promise not to tell them that she was in the audience today at the matinee. A wise decision—because by the curtain call she was crying so hard Julia got scared and began to cry along with her.

In a final attempt to get her to go backstage, David told her that his father had been happy to meet the cast after the play. Between sobs she moaned, "The fool! Has he no pride?"

With that David gave up, hurried us to the car, and didn't stop until we were in the parking lot at Ohrbach's. With Eula Lee and Julia still crying in the back seat, I couldn't imagine a worse time to go shopping. But David does know his mother. Choking back sobs, she chose a new winter coat and matching accessories —and by dinner time was absolutely dry-eyed. After dinner she even urged us to go to a movie while she baby-sat with Julia.

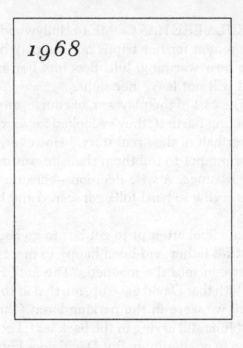

1968

WE JUST RECEIVED the final check from Universal for the film rights to *Anybody Home?* For the first time in our married life we have money in the bank. So, at my insistence, we're looking at houses.

David sees no reason why we should not continue living in our one room at the Montecito, but I think Julia deserves better than a closet. Of course, real estate is incredibly expensive here; even in the Valley, where houses are a bargain compared to Beverly Hills, we haven't seen anything we like for less than forty thousand dollars. When you think we were paying $65 a month in New York and are now paying only $125 a month for our room at the Montecito, a house does seem like a huge financial obligation, especially for someone who never knows where the next job is coming from—or if there'll even be one.

For the first and perhaps only time in our lives we do have enough for a down payment, and once Julia starts nursery school, I can get a job to help meet the monthly payments. However, David will continue to be opposed in principle to the idea of homeowning—just as he was to marriage—unless or until we fall in love with a house as irrevocably as we did with each other.

She forgets that I fell in love with her long before she allowed herself to fall in love with me. But when it came to our first and only house, she was the one who gave her heart. All I saw was the hideous pink color ("We'll paint it," she said), the aging bathroom fixtures ("We'll remodel," she suggested), and the enormous dead oak tree in the middle of the backyard ("We'll take it out, dig the hole a little deeper, and have a fishpond," she proposed). I could have no more gotten out of buying that house than I could have gotten out of marrying her. Thank God.

□

I'VE FALLEN IN LOVE with a house—but David says we can't afford to make an offer unless Eula Lee agrees to share it with us. We've waited eight years to have a home of our own—and finally be able to unpack our wedding presents—and now he's asking me to share it with his mother. It's not fair!

The only fair I know features prizes for livestock.

Unfortunately, however, it does make sense. If Eula Lee sold her house in Dallas, we could apply the proceeds as a down payment on the house we want here—and use our savings to remodel.

Of course, she may not agree. Ever since her mother died and left her a small inheritance, she's been scrupulous about keeping her money separate from ours. She insists on paying her own way wherever she goes—and we pay our share of the expenses whenever we stay with her in Dallas. Eula Lee would only give up her independence for one person—Julia. When she hugged Julia good-bye after Christmas, she said to David, "No one in my life has ever loved me like this child—not my mother, not my husband, not even you, David. I understand for the first time why I've lived this long."

If she's willing to come—to sell her house, which represents the only independence she's ever known, and invest in our future—how can I object?

And there is a bright side. If Eula Lee moves in with us, we'll never again have to visit her in Texas.

Our friends were always saying to Joanna, "I could never live with my mother-in-law. How do you do it?" I could have used a little more sympathy for my role as ringmaster. Oddly enough, the only one who really understood how hard it was on me was Joanna. She said whenever she lost patience with my mother, she would remind herself how much harder it would have been if her mother were living with us and she felt accountable to me for everything that woman said or did.

☐

ALBUQUERQUE, NEW MEXICO. We left Dallas at dawn, our Chevrolet loaded like the Joads' pickup. We never seem to be able to exit a city with any style; there are always too many things we want to take with us. The house in Dallas finally sold, and its contents are on their way to California by moving van— except for Eula Lee, who occupies the back seat with Julia.

My parents remain behind in Dallas, along with my grandmother, who, since her second stroke in April, calls Julia by my name and has no idea who I am. I cannot imagine ever thinking of Dallas as home again and can't wait to get back to Los Angeles —which has felt like home from the day we arrived, even though we've never lived anywhere but in a hotel.

☐

PALM SPRINGS. We stopped for the night after hearing on our car radio that Robert Kennedy had just been shot in Los Angeles. I cannot believe that such horror could happen again.

I slept for a while, but when I heard the television in the adjoining room, I got up and kept vigil with Eula Lee, watching the footage of another Kennedy getting shot over and over again. The more I watched, the less real it seemed. I'm afraid that if I fall asleep again, the newsreel footage will turn into a nightmare—a nightmare that will seem worse on waking when I have to acknowledge it's true.

Where is home now? Where do we go to feel safe? Not Dallas, where I was born. Not Los Angeles, the promised land. I guess I have to face the fact that home is nothing more or less than an idea we carry within ourselves. Home is not a place, it is people. Here in this motel, with David sleeping beside me and Julia safe in the next room in her grandmother's care, I know I am as at home as I will ever be anywhere again.

☐

WHY WAS I SO DETERMINED that we own our own home? Having a baby didn't change our life nearly as much as buying a house. When Julia was born, we continued to live like nomads, packing her up and taking her with us wherever we went. But this house seems to chide me as reproachfully as a neglected relative whenever I turn my back on it.

The word *housewife* is more appropriate than I ever imagined. There are days when I feel more married to this collection of shingles and brick than I do to David. But instead of being jealous, he encourages my single-minded devotion to an occupation rapidly becoming more time-consuming than a career. Housekeeping! No matter how much I do, there is always more to be done. And my two-year-old assistant wants to be included in everything.

The day we brought Julia home from the hospital, my obstetrician advised me to use the hours she was asleep for my own pursuits, to wait until she was awake to sweep and dust and wash dishes. He said I'd be a better mother when she was awake if I was my own person when she was asleep. It was good advice and easy enough to follow until I also had to run a house.

David and I spent the summer painting the exterior. He finds domestic chores a welcome change from writing and prefers building shelves or pruning trees to outdoor sports, which he considers a waste of time. He likes having some tangible change in the status quo to show for his efforts at the end of the day. So do I. But most of what I do has to be done all over again the next day, which leaves me with very little sense of accomplishment.

David has lots of ideas about how a house should be run, which he must have gotten from magazines. He certainly didn't get them from me. Or from my mother, who had a maid from the day she came home from her honeymoon. Or from his mother, who made it quite clear when she moved in that this house has nothing to do with her. Now she considers herself retired and gives me nothing more tangible in the way of support than a sympathetic look as she steps over the vacuum cleaner cord on her way to the sanctuary of her bedroom.

I don't say anything, but David sees me seething, and the next thing I know he's shouting at her that she has no right to live like a guest in the house. Why can't he just ask her politely to give me a hand with the housework? Or does he stage the whole scene for my benefit, wanting to make sure I hear how loudly he stands up for me? Does he think by playing the heavy, he eases the tension between his mother and me? Is that how he wants me to behave with my parents, taking his side so loudly the whole house shakes?

Damn right—but I'm still waiting.

After a showdown like this, Eula Lee retreats to her room in tears, and I expect to see her emerge with her suitcase packed. But when I call her to come to dinner, she's all smiles, and she and David start chatting as if nothing had happened. No one apologizes or promises to change, and everything goes on just as it was before. So it doesn't get anybody anywhere to ask for more than she's willing to give—she made her terms clear when she moved in, and that's that. If I didn't get so mad at her, I'd have to admire her stubbornness. I keep thinking how beholden I'd feel in her position—if I were living with my children, I'd do anything to ensure my welcome. But Eula Lee just seems to take everything for granted.

For granted? She made the down payment on our home, didn't she? She was entitled.

I worry sometimes that, except for Julia, she has no life of her own here, but she doesn't seem to want any friends and shuns the company of anyone her own age. In fact, she seems relieved to be free for all time from social obligations. When we have friends for dinner, she sits at the edge of the living room listening to the conversation without comment until it begins to bore her, then escapes unobtrusively to her room.

An escape I often envied her.

152

☐

RAIN AND MORE RAIN. I haven't left the house in a week. Valley streets are flooded and canyons impassable. A contractor friend says if our house can hold up through all this, we'll be okay for the next twenty years. We had no idea when we bought it what a well-built house we were getting. It had to be tested by storm.

Like marriage. The house at least is still standing.

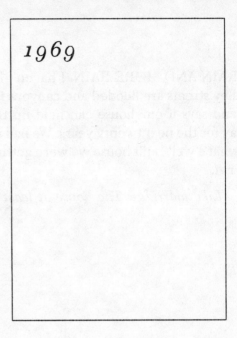

1969

I DIDN'T EXPECT CANDY, I didn't expect flowers, I didn't even expect a card, but it is Valentine's Day, damn it. Where did this love affair go wrong?

I'll never stop loving David, but sometimes I wonder what marriage has to do with love. The problem with family life is, it's so convenient for everyone—someone to bring home a salary and pay the bills, someone to clean and cook, a full house for every holiday. We lose sight of how it started—and why.

David and I got married for only one reason—because we loved each other so much we couldn't bear to be apart. I used to get physically ill when I had to tell him good-bye. I would count the hours till his telephone call, then begin to cry as soon as it was over because no matter how long we talked, there was still so much left to say. We knew a lifetime together wouldn't be enough. Now, unless he wants to make love, he doesn't even kiss me good-night.

Why did meaningless gestures mean so much to her? She knew I stopped breathing when she was out of my sight.

☐

154

WHAT'S GOING ON in Woodstock? They say it's a rock festival, but it looks to me more like an invasion of aliens. Tonight on the television news I saw a close-up of a girl I knew at college. What a shock! We're the same age—thirty-one—but looking at her in her beads and headband, a baby strapped to her back, I felt as old as my parents.

How can I be so out of touch with my own generation? I'm in sympathy with people marching for peace and moving into communes, but I dress like a member of the establishment. And I can't imagine depending on drugs to expand my consciousness in a world where music and art and children exist.

How did I take such a different path from a girl who seemed so much like me in college? Did she fall in love with someone and follow him as blindly as I've followed David?

Blindly? You never even close your eyes when we kiss.

Sometimes I try imagining how his life would be different if he'd married someone else; at best it would only be a matter of degree. My life, on the other hand, like the lives of most of the women I know, has been completely shaped by my choice of a marriage partner. Where would I be now if I hadn't married David? I have to confess that the answer would depend entirely on the man I'd chosen in his place. The only women I know making their own decisions about where and how to live are either unmarried, divorced, or widowed.

Bullshit! If it had been left up to me, I'd still be at the Montecito—paying rent once a month and no mortgage hanging over my head. Joanna was the one who decided how we would live. All I did was make the living.

Men take it for granted that they're entitled to the support of a loving companion as they make their way in life. Women have to be prepared to sacrifice this support—at least in the beginning—in order to have any control over their lives. Few men would be prepared to pay that high a price, and neither are most women, myself among them. But somehow, in the years ahead, while continuing to lead David's life, I must find a way to reclaim my own.

Do I accept his decisions too easily? Am I honestly trying to make him happy—or am I afraid of losing him if I get in his way?

I remember in college the headaches I used to get contemplating all the options that awaited me on coming of age. Once I married, the headaches disappeared. It's really very easy living with David. He has strong opinions about everything—which saves me a lot of time and thought. I never have to worry about whether I'm pleasing him. He doesn't hesitate to tell me when he's unhappy and why. But if I even hint that I'm unhappy, he takes it as a slap at him and gets very upset. So I've learned to express only happiness openly—and allow my silence to indicate discontent. That way we avoid an argument, but the signals are there if anyone is interested.

Nothing frightened Joanna faster—at least in the early years—than the prospect of a fight. I often exploited her fear in order to get my own way. But in my heart I ached for the day she'd finally want something more than she wanted to avoid an argument. Well, I've gotten that wish, haven't I?

Early in our marriage I learned that when David wants to go somewhere, he makes plans and we go. But if I initiate anything, he gets defensive and hostile. And he won't hear of my going alone.

The appointed hour inevitably finds him immersed in work, which he puts aside reluctantly to dress and take me wherever it is I now greatly regret having expressed any interest in going. And if the event, usually just a movie, turns out to be a disappointment, I feel personally responsible and spend the rest of the evening apologizing for wasting his time when he could have been working.

No comment—because she happens to be telling the truth.

The problem with being married to a man with no regularly defined office hours is that—unless *he* declares a time-out—he always manages to give the impression that he ought to be working. Or am I just jealous because his work gives him more pleasure than I do? I see very little evidence that I make David

156

happy anymore, so for now I'm concentrating on not making him unhappy. Is that enough? It seems to be for him, but I'm not sure it is for me.

Perhaps because I have to live so much of my life within the boundaries imposed by his tastes, I delight in the few activities that are entirely my own, like cooking. Thank goodness David has no interest in the subject, aside from likes and dislikes. He finds fish boring and has forbidden me to serve chicken at home, since we inevitably find it on our plate at every dinner party we attend.

This leaves only meat for the main course, so I amuse myself finding new ways to serve vegetables. In the process I've lost my taste for red meat and become a vegetarian without anyone even noticing. I still eat whatever is put in front of me when I go out, but when the choice is mine, I eat only salad and vegetables and feel, at least at the dinner table, that I have become my own woman again.

I saw what she was doing, but as long as she could find ways of asserting her independence without inconveniencing me, why interfere? Or deny her the pleasure of thinking she had taken some kind of stand behind my back? As long as that was all she was doing behind my back.

☐

I DON'T KNOW WHY I'm even keeping a journal—every day is just like the one before. Why bother?

So what happened to the rest of 1969? How could she let it get away without a trace? At least when there were missing pages, I knew something had happened that she was trying to forget. But this time the binding is intact. Somehow it's even worse to think nothing happened that she felt was worth remembering. The terrible thing is, I don't even remember her being unhappy. However, I also don't remember 1969.

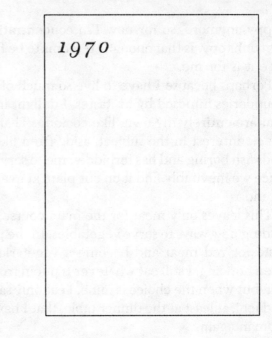

1970

MY PARENTS CALLED to wish us a happy new year and a prosperous new decade—and to announce they're getting a divorce. Apparently the decision is entirely mutual. They wanted to spend one more Christmas as a family before breaking the news to their children but, as it turned out, celebrated the day with only each other for company. My brother and his wife have just bought their first house and wanted to have their own tree and turkey. My sister is so happy in San Francisco she decided to stay there with her friends. Now that their children no longer need a home to which they can return for the holidays, Mother and Daddy apparently feel free to go their separate ways.

They've talked about selling their house—it goes on the market tomorrow—ever since my brother got married but could never agree on where they'd move. Daddy always said when his children were grown, he wanted to hang out his shingle in the little East Texas town where they go on weekends. Mother, on the other hand, would like an apartment in one of the elegant condominiums springing up in the Turtle Creek area. Not that she intends spending much time there, but she needs a home base from which to travel. She's already planning to rent a villa in Italy this spring. For the last few years each has tried to persuade the other to his point of view, but in the course of this long-running argument, they've just grown further apart. Now they've finally acknowledged the fact and agreed to separate.

They say they're still the best of friends—though I find that hard to believe. Mother is not even asking for a divorce. She's quite happy to let Daddy continue handling her affairs, as long as she's free to travel and live where she pleases. She says as far as she's concerned, the only reason to divorce is to remarry— and she has no intention of repeating that experience in the years left to her. However, Daddy has devoted his life to upholding the spirit as well as the letter of the law, and the idea of marriage in name only is abhorrent to him. He refuses to deal with the paperwork of marriage for an absent partner and feels they should divide their property legally before parting company.

They both sounded very cheerful and civilized over the phone, but after they said good-bye, I burst into tears. I wanted to fly to Dallas to be with them. Even though I've been home very little since I married, I always knew it was there if I needed it. I took comfort in the knowledge that there was a sanctuary— a place where I could go with my daughter to be safe and sheltered—if anything happened to my husband or my marriage. But from now on, the life I'm living will be the only one open to me, like it or not.

Your grandmother provide a "sanctuary" for you and your mother? Hah! She had even less interest in being a live-in grandmother than she did in being a live-in wife. Nothing would've sent her packing faster than the sight of her daughter and granddaughter coming home to stay.

David can't understand why I'm so upset about my parents. He says his mother has been much happier since he talked her into leaving his father, and he's sure my mother will be too. There are times when I wonder if David really believes in marriage.

159

Absolutely! Until something better comes along—which I pray it will, dear Julia, before you and Jessica make any lifetime promises.

Eula Lee seems to take comfort in the fact that my parents are getting a divorce—as if that somehow vindicates her. Sometimes I have the uneasy feeling that she is waiting for me to walk out on David to feel truly vindicated, but I'm determined never to give her that satisfaction.

Bravo! If only you'd stayed determined.

□

TODAY I GOT A LETTER from the Woodrow Wilson Committee asking what I've done with my life in the ten years since graduation. They're conducting a survey on all the finalists from 1960—trying to make sure, I suppose, that they gave their money to the right people. There were spaces in which to list graduate degrees, awards, professional societies, publications. There were no spaces in which to list years of marriage or number of children, so the fact that I am pregnant again went unnoted. It is clearly not considered an accomplishment.

I tore up the letter and went to bed right after dinner. When David asked if anything was wrong, I said I was just tired. And I am. But sleep no longer seems to help. I wake up more exhausted than when I fell asleep. I look back on how happy I was being pregnant the first time—when that was all I was doing with my life. Now I wonder how I will get through the next six months.

The only one who took Joanna's second pregnancy worse than she did was my mother—who acted as if we had deliberately set out to sabotage her plans for an early retirement. However, Jessica came into the world with a single purpose—to give her grandmother a second chance at the happiness life had so far denied her. Mother referred to her from the beginning as "my baby"—and it seemed more often true than not.

It has always been hard for me to believe I had anything to do with my daughters. Nothing I took credit for creating

*has turned out half so well. No wonder there are so few
female artists, and those few usually childless. Compared
to childbearing, most creative efforts are pretty pathetic.
Why would someone with the power to create life waste
time and energy on anything less? I watched Joanna swell
with promise—and started a new play.*

☐

JULIA AND I spent the day packing. Once more David's
career has provided a welcome diversion from my own prob-
lems.

Willa has found a Broadway producer who loves *Anybody
Home?* She always regretted giving up the play to do a movie
and wants a second chance at it. So we'll be spending the winter
in New York.

Willa also wants Paul to star opposite her—the original cast,
together for the first time—but he's just been offered the lead in
a big movie that starts shooting next week.

*Most men in my position would have welcomed a legiti-
mate excuse to leave a pregnant wife and four-year-old
child at home and indulge in a temporary escape from
domestic routine, but I couldn't imagine life without the
two (almost three) of you. I always wondered, if the situation had been reversed, would Joanna have felt the same
about me. Now, of course, I have my answer.*

☐

IT SEEMS STRANGE to be on a train headed back to New
York with another play. And to be pregnant again. Twice now
David and I have gone into production at the same time, but as
much as I complain about pregnancy, I wouldn't trade places
with him. However, he can't wait to get into rehearsal.

I love being alone with him when he's so excited—so filled
with confidence and anticipation. We have two single bedrooms
again, directly opposite each other. As soon as Julia went to
sleep tonight, I crossed the hall to David. We raised the shade
and made love very slowly while the night landscape rushed by

outside our window. Now that we can afford a sleeping compartment, I love the train.

☐

WE CALLED WYATT as soon as we got to New York to see if he knew of an apartment we could sublet—and he offered us his. He's moving to Los Angeles with the soap opera for which he designs sets, but keeping his loft. Since he won't accept rent, we suggested he stay in our house in Los Angeles while he looks for a place of his own. Now how do we tell Eula Lee that a strange man is going to be sleeping under the same roof with her?

Once I assured Mother she wouldn't be expected to cook for him—and that he was homosexual—she seemed to like the idea of having a man in the house. On those terms she might have stayed with my father.

☐

WHAT AM I DOING in New York? David spends all his time with Willa. For all I know they're having an affair. She insists on having dinner alone with him every night after rehearsal. To talk about the play, he swears. Why don't I believe him? Maybe because he's stopped sleeping with me. He says it's because I'm pregnant—he doesn't want to take chances—but that didn't stop him the first time.

I loved the way Joanna looked when she was pregnant—and it was just as much a turn-on the second time. The problem was Willa. There was nothing left for sex after a day with that bitch. She kept demanding that we fire the leading man, not because he wasn't a good actor, but because he seemed determined to remain faithful to his wife.

Every night at dinner I listened to Willa rant that she had yet to meet a man who was worthy of her, either personally or professionally—and prayed that she would get through opening night without sinking the play. Taking her to bed would have been easier.

No, that's not true.

162

☐

DAVID HAS NEVER SUGGESTED that I bring Julia to rehearsal, so we take the bus uptown every morning and spend the day at the Central Park zoo. Today Molly met us for lunch, then took Julia for a ride on the merry-go-round. Being a good mother takes a lot more time and effort in New York than it does in California.

David thinks I spend too much time trying to make Julia happy. I could say the same thing about him and Willa. But just when I get ready to have it out with him and tell him how neglected I feel, he crawls into bed beside me, exhausted from whatever he's been through with Willa, and falls asleep with his arm enclosing my waist. Do I really wish I were sleeping alone in Los Angeles? Never. I just wish I had more of David, but the only alternative is less. At least he wants me with him—and there is nowhere else I want to be. If the play's a hit, all this will be worth it.

And if not?

☐

OUR LIFE HAS BEEN LIKE A PLAY the past twenty-four hours, full of dramatic twists and turns.

Anybody Home? opened last night. I didn't know what to expect when I took my seat next to Molly in her best party dress. All I knew was that Willa had put everybody involved through hell during the four-week rehearsal period. I prayed for David's sake that the performance would go well.

Suddenly Paul Gaines slipped into the seat beside me, saying he'd flown in from Los Angeles for the opening and David had given him his ticket to the play. I explained that David was keeping Julia backstage—he was too nervous to sit through the performance. I almost was. When the curtain went up, Paul took my hand for good luck, and I could feel myself relaxing.

I bet.

Willa gave an inspired performance from her opening line. David, with Julia in his arms, rushed out at intermission to celebrate. The only one who didn't seem surprised at the miracle taking place onstage was Paul. He said that was exactly the performance he thought Willa would give. Wasn't it what David wanted when he wrote the part?

Molly put her arms around Paul and asked innocently if he was going to stay at their apartment again tonight. David and I exchanged glances. The miracle of Willa's opening night performance had just been explained. Paul answered hesitantly that he didn't know.

"Oh, please," begged Molly.

"Yes, please," added David as the bell sounded to signal the end of intermission. "The magazine critics come tomorrow night."

The first television review was a pan, aborting the opening-night party. A few out-of-town angels lingered at Sardi's, determined not to be denied the gala opening night their investment had promised. David shepherded Julia and me over to Eighth Avenue to escape the chic crowd gathered outside the restaurant waiting for taxis, and we started walking uptown. I had no idea where we were going—the loft was in the opposite direction. Then I realized that David just wanted to keep moving. Suddenly, waiting to cross Forty-ninth Street, he leaned over a trash can and began to vomit.

At that moment an occupied cab screeched to a stop. Paul opened the door to reveal Willa and Molly in the back seat. Molly pulled Julia onto her lap and I climbed in beside them as Paul steered David toward the front door. "You can't get in here. The law only allows four passengers," said the cab driver gruffly.

In a tone perfected by his years as a soap opera doctor, Paul shouted that this was an emergency. And David did indeed look like a man who was about to breathe his last.

"Sorry. The law's the law," said the driver, stepping on the gas and speeding uptown, leaving Paul and David to find another cab.

I told Willa again how wonderful she was in the play, repeating everything I'd said backstage—before the television review.

"I know I was," she answered matter-of-factly. "But it's a

wonderful part. David is a wonderful writer. Don't let anyone take that away from him. Ever."

"I won't," I promised, leaning over and kissing her on the cheek. I had kissed her a hundred times in the meaningless greeting I've perfected since marrying into the theater, but this time I meant it.

To my surprise she put her arms around me. "Poor Joanna," she murmured. "It's so much harder just having to watch—not being able to do anything."

To my embarrassment I began to cry. Willa continued to stroke my back. "Cry now. Let it all out. Once we get to the apartment, you have your role to play just as I had mine tonight. Don't let David know how much this matters to you. It already matters too much to him."

What irony, I thought. Willa was still in character, playing my mother-in-law, the woman who was supposed to love David more than anyone except me. And yet I couldn't imagine playing this scene with Eula Lee. I would never let her see me cry— and even if I did, I cannot imagine her comforting me as Willa did.

Paul went with David to get the morning papers. *The Times* was a pan, but there were extractable quotes for the actors. The other reviews were mostly good. I made breakfast for everybody while Paul and David laid out an ad. We were feeling quite cheerful when the producer called to tell Willa he was closing the show.

He had three more plays under option. I had no prospects —aside from a pregnant wife. He believed in the play when he agreed to produce it. How could he have lost faith overnight? It wasn't even his money involved—it was his wife's. Which was probably why he wasn't about to risk losing any more of it.

Willa was magnificent. She turned on the producer with a fury I hadn't seen since she attempted *Medea*. How dare he allow a second-rate critic, who was known to be an unproduced playwright himself, to still an original voice in the theater? And how much money could he possibly save by closing the play in one night—before the second-night critics even had a chance to see it?

The producer explained the economics involved, then Willa asked him to delay his decision for a few more hours while she tried to raise enough money to keep the play open till the end of the week. The producer asked where David was; he'd been trying to reach him all morning. Willa started to cover for him, but David suddenly grabbed the phone and said this was probably the best play he would ever write, and he was going to do all he could to give it a New York run. We had ten thousand dollars in our savings account, which he was committing to the production right now. He wanted an ad in the Sunday *Times*, which he intended to lay out himself with the ad agency. By the end of the day he hoped to raise enough to keep the play open—on the condition that he have control over how the money was spent. The producer finally agreed, even began to seem excited at the prospect of making a fight for the play—especially with someone else's money.

When David put down the phone, Willa turned to Paul and said he took the easy way when he turned down the play to do a movie. Now he was going to pay for it. She was putting him down for five thousand dollars.

"But I want you to know, David," Paul said with a smile, "I'm not doing this for you, I'm doing it for Willa. The play will be done all over the country, whatever happens in New York. You'll be attending productions in colleges and community theaters for the rest of your life—going backstage to meet actors who've never met a playwright before. But Willa may not have another chance to play this part—and she deserves to be seen in it." With that, he wrote out his check for five thousand dollars. Willa smiled a smile that acknowledged Paul had given her her due, nothing more.

I then called my father in Texas and told him I wanted to make an investment in my husband's future. It has been a tradition in our family beginning with my grandmother that a woman owed the man she loved any resources she had at her command. Only by sharing the risk did she earn the right to share any later success. My grandmother had used the inheritance from her mother to back her husband in business. My mother had married my father when he was a struggling young lawyer still in debt to his father for his law school tuition. Now it was my turn.

I have no money of my own. The few savings bonds I brought to our marriage were spent long ago. I haven't earned any money since we left New York, and any cash gifts have been immediately transformed into tangible goods. But when my grandmother dies, I know I'll inherit something. I have no idea how much, but my father, having drawn up her will and amended it countless times, knew exactly what was coming to me. I told him I wanted it now—to invest in the play. I was sure Grandmother would not only understand but approve. He asked how much we needed. I assured him I only wanted an advance on my inheritance.

"I'm writing you a check for ten thousand dollars," he said. "I want to invest it in the play—in my name. You may need your inheritance later."

What a lovely man. What a perfect father-in-law. What an ass I've always been.

Finally David called his mother. She greeted the news that the producer had threatened to close the play with a sigh of relief that we would be coming home soon. The dishwasher had broken and she didn't know who to call to fix it so she was washing all the dishes by hand. David explained that we were not coming home—not if we could raise enough money to keep the play running. He said all we needed was another five thousand dollars.

He waited for Eula Lee to offer us the money. Since moving in with us, she has had no expenses aside from her weekly trips to the beauty parlor and the checks she presents each of us on birthdays and at Christmas. But she was silent on the other end of the phone. Finally David told her that my father was sending us a check for ten thousand dollars. "He's always been nice and he's always been rich," she replied. "Where will you get the rest?"

David said he was afraid she'd be hurt if he didn't give her a chance to invest in the play too. Another long silence. Finally she said, "You'll never know how much you hurt me by writing

167

that play, David. I never told the neighbors a thing, though they would've loved to know. Now you've told New York and you want to keep on telling it! I hate that play. I always have and always will."

"Mother, how can you say something like that?" David asked in disbelief.

"I'd never say it to anyone but you," she replied.

David hung up the phone. "Who am I kidding trying to keep this play open? If it were any good, it would've gotten good reviews. And it would be running without any help from me. Come on," he said, taking me by the hand. "Get Julia. We've got to pack. We're going home."

Willa suddenly drew back her fist and punched David in the mouth. "Don't ever send me another play," she said. "I can't take the pain of being part of your life." And she locked herself in the bathroom with the shower running. Molly and Paul rode down on the elevator with us and helped us into a taxi.

The phone was ringing when we got back to the loft. It was Wyatt calling from our house in Los Angeles. "How much more money do you need?" he asked. David said we would have to invest every penny of our savings to keep the play open, and it just wasn't worth it.

"How much more?" Wyatt repeated. David told him another five thousand, and Wyatt said he was good for it. "How many people in their lifetime create something that will live after them?" Wyatt asked. "If there weren't plays, there wouldn't be jobs for actors or directors or set designers. I'm investing in my own future when I invest in your play." I couldn't help shedding a tear at the smile on David's face when he realized the play had been saved.

Then Wyatt added that once we had the play on its feet, maybe he could help us replenish our savings by getting David work writing for his soap opera. They were looking for new writers—and seemed impressed with anyone who came from the theater.

Wyatt thought I might be offended at the prospect of writing daytime drama, as the network executives pre-ferred to call it. At this point in our finances, I was grateful

for any job. I thanked him and said to see that Mother got
the dishwasher fixed, so she'd be in a pleasant mood when
we arrived.

☐

WE RETURNED TO CALIFORNIA in triumph tonight with
Anybody Home? still running on Broadway—and a rave review
in *Time*. It was Julia's first flight and she was so excited until she
saw the plane on the ground waiting to be boarded. Then she
suddenly grew very quiet. As the plane took off, she began to
cry. I assumed she was afraid—until she asked what had happened to the bird.
"What bird?" I replied.
She explained that giant birds were supposed to carry people
up to the sky to get on the plane. I said that with modern planes
that was no longer necessary. She suddenly burst into uncontrol-
lable sobs—apparently at the thought of being born too late—
and was still sniffling when we landed in L.A. No miracle of
modern science can compare with the wondrous inventions of a
child's imagination.
We arrived home without a penny in our pockets. Though the
play is still running, it's not paying royalties. However, our savings were well spent. If we hadn't kept the play open, the *Time*
review would not exist. I just hope the soap opera job works out
—but unfortunately the producer is out of town for the holidays,
so we won't know anything till after New Year's.

☐

I'LL NEVER FORGET this Christmas—but I've got to if I'm
going to stay married to David. I used my parents' Christmas
checks (now that they're separated, each one sent what they
used to send together) to buy him a new digital watch—with a
card saying I would love him till the end of time—

Liar.

and a big picture book on the history of Broadway, which I
inscribed "to my favorite playwright." He opened the book first,
but when he saw that it was written by a New York theater

169

critic, he threw it at the tree. The tree swayed, and a dozen ornaments fell to the floor, shattering into silver splinters. Julia began to cry and David began to shout. How could I be so insensitive? Didn't I know better, after a decade of marriage, than to give him anything written by a *critic*—especially in hard cover? I grabbed the book apologetically and promised to return it to the store for credit. "You can't," he said, turning to the page I'd inscribed. "It's ours forever." And he ripped the page out of the binding.

Why do I sound like a madman when she tells it? It happened just the way she says—at least I suppose it did—I don't really remember that Christmas—but the pain is missing. She never understood what I was going through.

The irony is, you're no less vulnerable when you have a hit. I was told about a playwright who wrote one of the most successful comedies in recent Broadway history and was given a theater book by his wife last Christmas. He was reading along when he came to a paragraph knocking his play. So what if he didn't throw the book at the Christmas tree or at his wife? It still hurt.

Eula Lee told Julia not to pay any attention to her parents, just to keep opening her presents, but she was so frightened she picked up her remaining packages and ran into her room, slamming the door. Eula Lee retreated to the kitchen in tears while I got a broom and dustpan and began sweeping up the shattered ornaments. Suddenly I heard David shouting at Julia to get back into the living room with her presents—Christmas was a family occasion and if she'd been selfish enough to open any of her presents in private, he was returning them to the store personally. When he discovered she'd pushed her bed against the door to keep him out, he threatened to spank her. I followed him into the room and found Julia hiding under the bed clutching her new toys, open boxes scattered everywhere. She screamed that if her toys had to go back to the store, she was going with them. I reassured her that no one was taking her presents away from her and no one was going to spank her as long as I was alive. "She's my child, and I'll spank her any time she deserves it," David said, pulling her out from under the bed.

"Not as long as you're married to me." I don't think I've ever defied him so openly before, but I found myself standing up for Julia in a way I've never been able to stand up for myself.

"I'm not going to live in a house where I don't have any authority." Then he stormed out of the room. In a few minutes I heard the front door slam.

As the car pulled out of the driveway, I called Braniff and reserved two places on their next flight to Dallas. Then I called a taxi. I told Eula Lee I would be in the bedroom packing and to let me know when the taxi arrived. I also asked if she'd put some things in a suitcase for Julia. She started to cry, but I said I couldn't talk about it.

The next time I looked at the clock, over an hour had passed—and no taxi. I found Eula Lee stretched out on her bed pretending to be ill so that Julia could try out the stethoscope from her new doctor kit. She said there had been no sign of a taxi.

I was on the phone with the cab company, crying that I was going to miss my plane, when David walked through the front door loaded with presents. He told Julia he'd met Santa Claus on Ventura Boulevard, and his sleigh was full of presents he'd forgotten to leave at our house.

On the other end of the phone the dispatcher was explaining that a taxi had arrived at our house only to be told I'd changed my mind. Eula Lee! I should've known. "Who's calling?" David asked as he put his arms around me.

"Wrong number," I replied, hanging up the phone.

I can't believe how close I came to losing the two people who mattered most to me in the world. Thank God Mother was guarding the pass. Dear Julia, will you ever forgive me?

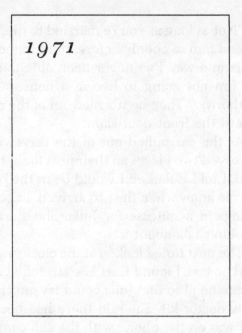

1971

I KNEW WE WERE IN TROUBLE when David came through the front door, took one look at the mushrooms I was slicing, and said we couldn't afford luxuries like that anymore. Any other time I would've argued with his definition of a luxury, which is anything I like that he doesn't, but I could see he was too upset for a fair fight. He then explained that he not only didn't have the soap opera job, but was going to have to audition for it—a sample script for $200. And then, even if his writing proves acceptable and he gets the job, the fee is only $250 per script. It is so much less than we had imagined.

☐

IT'S AFTER MIDNIGHT and David is still typing. He's been through five drafts of his sample script since his meeting yesterday but is still not satisfied. As far as I can see, the fifth script is no better than the first, but how much can a writer do when the characters and situations are handed to you? Writing a soap opera script is about as creative as filling in the blanks of a coloring book. But David has absolutely lost perspective. From the time and care he's put into it, you would think this half-hour episode of *World Without End* was about to open on Broadway.

☐

THE PRODUCER LIKED the sample script—at least enough for another meeting. Over drinks at the Polo Lounge this afternoon, David learned that husband-and-wife writing teams are preferred, so he quickly said that I was a writer too.

Talk about opening Pandora's box.

Now I have to go to the next meeting and convince everyone—starting with myself. Help!

I haven't thought of myself as anything but a wife and mother for so long I don't know how I'll get through a meeting posing as a writer. What happened to all the confidence I had at eighteen when I marched into the newspaper and demanded a job? I had no doubt at all about my ability then. I could type finished copy directly from my notes and turn it in ahead of deadline. Now I can't even write a letter home without making a first draft.

☐

THE MEETING WENT WELL. I pretended I was an actress playing the part of a professional writer and even dressed for the role, digging out of the closet a black coat dress I wore constantly in New York.

Remember the pink coat she dyed in the washing machine? She was still wearing it!

It somewhat disguises the fact I'm seven months pregnant. I added a paisley scarf and circle pin at the neck and wore dark stockings and low-heeled black leather pumps. David, wearing his usual khakis and V-necked sweater, prevailed upon me to leave my gloves and pillbox hat at home.

The producer of *World Without End* turned out to be a woman about ten years older than I am. She appeared somewhat harassed but very friendly. Within ten minutes I discovered an amazing fact which put me completely at ease—I'm brighter than she is. She's probably earning $25,000 a year. Who knows what's ahead for me if I put my mind to it.

Even the fact that I'm pregnant turns out to be an advantage. The producer is unmarried, and I suddenly found myself speaking like an expert about what life is like for women who stay at home with their children—the show's typical viewer. I think I even surprised David by speaking so forcefully about what women like me want to see on television—but no more than I surprised myself. By the time the meeting ended, I'd become one with the part I was playing. Though I had not put pen to paper, I was now a professional writer. I didn't even care whether we got the job.

Well, I sure as hell cared. In fact, I was counting on it. I remember when the producer asked why I was willing to write for a soap opera, I wanted to shout "Money, you bitch, we need the money." But I lied—something about what a powerful force soap opera can be—and she hired us.

The phone was ringing when we got home, David's agent calling with an offer from *World Without End* for our services as a husband-and-wife writing team. I guess from now on I'll have to say "our" agent.

Until he became "your" agent exclusively.

☐

EVEN THOUGH I WORK AT HOME, the fact that I'm earning money for the first time since we moved to L.A. has changed the way I live. After breakfast I no longer feel any guilt about leaving Julia in Eula Lee's care and secluding myself in our bedroom to work. My mother-in-law is less than thrilled about my professional emergence—especially after I had the audacity to suggest she begin doing the laundry for the household along with her one load a week. I don't think she believes David and I are actually working when we're in the bedroom with the door closed.

I reappear to prepare lunch for the family, then work again while Julia naps. No time for naps of my own now, but I no longer need much sleep. I often lie awake for an hour or two after David turns out the light just looking forward to tomorrow.

Until now I've always been afraid to try writing fiction, but dreaming up dialogue for *World Without End* is hardly making a bid for literary immortality. I'm beginning to think of the characters as part of our family—even though I have never personally known anyone with amnesia.

Much less two amnesiacs living on the same street. They would meet for coffee and reminisce about their lack of memory.

□

WHERE DID DAVID ever get the idea I could write dialogue? Where did I? This morning after rewriting a scene three times to try and please him, I announced I was quitting. Left to my own devices, I would never have attempted to write soap opera, so what was I doing pretending I could hold up my half of a writing team? I was about to have a baby and that was career enough for any woman.

What happened to all my talk of equal rights for women, David demanded? For the first time in our marriage, the soap opera is providing us an equal employment opportunity but instead of being grateful, I'm trying to get out after only two weeks. He reminded me that we'd invested our life savings in a play that wasn't even paying royalties. If it weren't for *World Without End*, we'd probably be in the unemployment line. We couldn't make it without this job—and he couldn't make it without my help.

Choking back tears, I said I wanted to do my share to earn the living—but on my own terms. As soon as the baby was born, I'd go out and get a job doing something I knew how to do. Taking me in his arms, David told me to stop behaving like a spoiled child. Anybody who could write sentences could write soap opera. I was lucky to have a husband who loved me and wanted me to work with him and a job that allowed me to stay home with my family. Then he sent me back to the typewriter for another try.

Looking back, I do marvel at my ability to put things into the proper perspective.

☐

TODAY I WROTE A SCENE David hardly had to rewrite at all. He was on his way to lunch with Ben Weisman and said I'd done such a good job with my scene, he was letting me write his.

What an operator—not only getting her to do my work but to consider it a reward.

When he came home, he read over what I'd written, shrugged, and said it was as good as the show deserved. Not exactly a compliment—still I'm grateful for every scene I get past him without an argument.

Ben had taken him to Perino's for an expensive lunch to celebrate a huge writing contract he's just signed at Universal. He said David was the only friend he had in Hollywood who wouldn't be jealous of his good fortune. Ben thinks we're getting rich off royalties from the play. David didn't disillusion him by confessing that *World Without End* is our only source of income.

☐

I WAKE UP EACH MORNING with my stomach in knots, which only begin to untangle when I've written my scene for the day. Whatever made me think work would be liberating? I live like a prisoner in my own house, not daring to leave the bedroom until David has read and approved what I've written. When I come downstairs, Julia is clamoring for my attention, and I divide the afternoon between child care and housework. David does all the errands so I'll be free to work. He thinks he's doing me a favor—but I'm losing my mind living under house arrest.

House arrest? Did she really think I got a thrill out of waiting in line at the bank and the post office and the filling station? I often used to wonder how much money I'd have to make to justify hiring someone who would do for us all the things Joanna took for granted.

□

SUSAN SAVAGE CALLED this morning to say she's in Pasadena; her mother has been hospitalized with a stroke. Sad news —but I was thrilled to think she was close enough for a visit. I drove over as soon as I finished my writing, taking Julia to play with the two Savage children, Toby and Lucy. Lucy is six but seems more like three; four-year-old Toby treats her like one of his toys. Julia seemed to accept her easily, and the three children were soon playing wood tag in the citrus orchard behind the old frame house where Susan spent her childhood.

When I asked Susan how long she was staying, she said she had no reason for returning home. Brad is having an affair with Elaine West—and Susan blames David. Right after David turned down the playwright-in-residence post to risk everything on having his play produced in California, Brad got tenure. Susan invited their friends to a party to celebrate but Brad came home drunk and insulted them, saying they were all failures because they'd failed to try.

I pointed out that David has had his share of failure. It's part of the game.

"But Brad has always been afraid to play the game," Susan said quietly. "Remember *On the Waterfront?* What was that word Marlon Brando used? A 'contender.' You're married to a contender, Joanna. I'm not."

However, she's not prepared to walk out on him. Despite Elaine, despite everything, she still feels he needs her. She began to cry. I put my arms around her and said there were people here who needed her too. Susan admitted that her children are happier in California. And she has more time for them. She's begun teaching them at home—and loves the challenge.

Watching Julia play hide and seek among the orange trees with Toby and Lucy, I asked Susan if I could pay her to take on another pupil. I said I enjoyed my work when I wasn't terrified of it but worry that I'm neglecting Julia. Eula Lee doesn't mind baby-sitting—as long as that's all it is. If I put out clay or paints, she says distastefully that Julia makes such a mess when she gets creative. I invariably come downstairs at noon to find Julia sitting in her grandmother's lap watching television game shows, her hands and face neatly washed, waiting for me to fix lunch.

Susan said she would love having Julia to keep her children company any day I could bring her. Then she added how much she envied me for having another child. Was I going to have a third? She'd always wanted a big family, but after discovering that Lucy was handicapped, Brad was afraid to have more. When Susan became pregnant a second time—and refused to have an abortion—he stopped sleeping with her.

Laughing softly at the irony, Susan confessed that she'd refused to marry Wyatt because she wasn't sure what kind of sex life they'd have. She asked if he was involved with anyone in Los Angeles. I said as far as we knew, he lived alone—and had ever since he left New York. She obviously wishes they could be friends again. Her mistake was wanting more in a husband. Instead she got less.

Driving home, I couldn't help thinking how lucky I was to have a husband who loved me, a healthy child and the prospect of another one, and a job I was beginning to master. Hearing Susan's troubles made my life seem manageable again—until I walked in the bedroom and found David typing furiously. He berated me for leaving the house before he'd approved my scene. Reminding him he was at Universal having lunch with Ben, I asked what I was supposed to do—bring my scene to their table at the commissary and stand there while he read it? I promised to rewrite the scene as soon as I cooked dinner, but he said never mind, he'd done it for me. I knew the real problem wasn't my scene—and how bad it was—but Ben's nonstop boasting about his three-picture deal with options to direct while David hacks out scripts for a soap opera.

☐

JULIA ASKED ME TODAY why she wasn't enough for us. Wrapping her in my arms, I assured her she was everything we ever imagined in a child. Then why were we having another one? she demanded. How would I feel if another wife came to live in our house? I said children were different—having a brother or sister was like having a friend to sleep over every night—but I could tell my answer didn't really satisfy her.

When I asked David what he would've said, he suddenly blurted out that he wasn't sure he could love another child any more than he could love another wife. He was giving everything he had to Julia and me; he didn't know how large families had enough love to go around.

Holding me close, he said he couldn't stand seeing me go through childbirth again. I promised it would be easier this time —for both of us. Maybe for me, he said. At least I had the illusion I was in control. For him it was worse than taking a plane.

David hates to surrender control. As long as he's at the wheel, he feels all of us are safe—even though he knows the chances of an accident are much greater in a car than in a plane. Not I. My spirits lift with the plane, knowing that I'm just a passenger, not responsible for anything. How does a marriage survive when both partners want to be pilots?

☐

GRANDMOTHER DIED QUIETLY in her sleep last night— in her own bed in her own apartment, just the way she planned it. She was determined to go out under her own power—no doctors, no machinery to keep her alive once her own will had failed her.

At the time of her death her only daughter—my mother—was living within walking distance. Since she and Daddy separated last year, she has made three trips to Europe, but never staying for more than a month at a time. I realize now that when she and Daddy disagreed about where they would live once he retired, what she really wanted was not to live anywhere.

She wanted an apartment which she could abandon without compunction and to which she could return without ceremony. What she has to have—which I doubt my father will ever understand or accept any more than David could—is the freedom to come and go at will. But Daddy has always lived by the rules, and there was simply no precedent in his experience for the kind of relationship Mother had to have. Though he was the one who insisted on beginning divorce proceedings, he cannot bring himself to move out of the house. He says he's only waiting for a buyer, but his asking price is absurd and he refuses to lower it.

Grandmother never knew that my parents had separated. She thought Mother was a young debutante again, always on her way to some glamorous party or off to Europe with friends. When Mother was in Italy, Daddy would visit Grandmother on his way home from the office. Thinking he was courting her daughter, she would beg him to propose as soon as she came home—before she fell in love with one of her European suitors and left Texas forever.

Mother always resented giving Grandmother the time and attention she regarded as her due—until Grandmother suffered a final stroke, from which she never really recovered. From then on, Mother spent hours at her bedside. She would walk over early each morning in time for breakfast and again at dusk to say good-night. Her authority diminished, Grandmother ceased to demand love, allowing Mother once again to offer it freely, as she had as a child.

It was Mother who called to tell me Grandmother had died. She was not crying—she had made her peace with the woman who had tried to live so much of her life for her. She said I must not consider coming home for the funeral—it would be foolhardy to travel in the last trimester of pregnancy. I had given Grandmother the gift she cherished most—her first great-grandchild—and in her lucid moments she had understood that another baby was on the way. There was nothing more I could do for her.

Fortunately Mother has no travel plans till summer. By then she hopes to have closed out Grandmother's apartment and distributed her possessions. She has no room in her new apartment, and Daddy hardly needs any more furniture with his house on the market, so it is up to the grandchildren to speak for anything they want. My sister will be flying in from San Francisco tonight, and my brother and his wife are driving up from Houston. The funeral is tomorrow.

"I'm glad you don't have to go through it," Mother said matter-of-factly. "I wish I could get out of it. Promise me—when my time comes—you'll have my body cremated and the ashes scattered. And no ceremony. Of course, unless your father dies first,

I won't have a prayer of getting away without a fuss. Now let me know if there's anything of Mother's you want. I dread going through her things. She could never stand to throw anything away."

Suddenly she began to laugh, remembering when she helped Grandmother move from her house into her apartment. Mother knew there wouldn't be room for everything and finally talked Grandmother into giving a truckload of furniture to Goodwill. The truck was loaded, pulling out of the driveway, when Grandmother suddenly changed her mind. Shouting at the driver to stop, she ran into the street after the truck, insisting she needed to go through everything one more time. Fortunately, the driver didn't hear her. Mother promised to go to Goodwill later and get anything she really missed, but once the truck was out of sight, Grandmother was fine. She just couldn't bear the moment of actually parting with anything.

Mother's laughter changed suddenly to tears. "The doctor said she died peacefully but I don't believe it. I'm sure at the last moment she demanded one more day."

All I could think about was how much I wished she could have lived to see another great-grandchild. Suddenly I heard myself promising that if we had a girl, we were naming her for Grandmother.

I'd always liked the name Jessica. Good thing, because there would've been no way of talking Joanna out of it. Always before when she had an idea, she made it seem as if it had originated with me and she was just jogging my memory. This time there was no attempt to manipulate me. "If the baby's a girl, I'm naming her after my grandmother," she announced with an authority Jessica the first would've applauded. She didn't even bother with the editorial we. We were into the second decade of our marriage and the terms, they were achangin'.

☐

JULIA NOW SPENDS three mornings a week with the Savage children. Some of the other young mothers in the neighborhood have asked Susan to teach their children too, so she has a full-scale kindergarten in her home, for which she has finally agreed to accept payment.

At first I drove Julia to Pasadena, and David went back for her in the afternoon. But last week Eula Lee said she would enjoy getting out of the house and asked if she could do the driving. I was amazed. She never goes anywhere on her own except the beauty parlor.

I thought Eula Lee might be jealous of Susan, but the first time she drove Julia to school, Susan invited her in for coffee, and she stayed all day, reading stories to the children and even visiting with Susan's father, Marvin Armstrong.

Today, to my surprise, she suggested that Julia spend five mornings a week in Pasadena instead of three, saying it was good for her to be with people outside her family who liked her as a friend. I realized she was talking about herself as well as Julia. She told me how sorry she felt for Mr. Armstrong because his wife was ill and how sorry she felt for Susan because her husband was unfaithful.

For my mother-in-law pity has always been the most elemental bridge to other people. I don't think I've ever heard her come right out and say she likes someone, but she's quite comfortable expressing pity—perhaps because it places her at an advantage in the relationship. I'm convinced the two of us would be much closer if I came crying to her every time David and I have a fight, but something in me stubbornly refuses to give her that satisfaction.

However, Susan seems to enjoy confiding in her. She tells her she's afraid her mother will never get well and her father won't be able to manage without her and her husband has written that unless she comes home by the end of the month the marriage is over. Susan has not said a word to me about an ultimatum from Brad, but we haven't talked in over a week. I think I'll invite her to dinner.

☐

JESSICA CERTAINLY timed her entrance to attract the largest possible audience. How her great-grandmother would have applauded!

182

I was cooking for a dinner party I'd planned for Susan last night when I felt a familiar twinge—but decided not to say anything to David, hoping to spare him the agonizing wait he had when Julia was born. Besides, I was looking forward to the party.

I'd invited Wyatt—after telling him Susan and Brad were separated (which is at least geographically true). Then, just to keep things off balance, I asked Paul Gaines to come too.

I suggested Susan bring Toby and Lucy, then at the last minute I remembered to include her father. When I told Eula Lee she'd have to entertain Marvin Armstrong, she said she wasn't feeling well—and would probably go to bed early. I suggested she take a nap until time for the guests to arrive.

I was packing my suitcase for the hospital when the doorbell started ringing. David had gone to get club soda, and Eula Lee was nowhere in sight. Julia came running from her grandmother's room saying Nanny had tried on every dress in her closet but didn't like the way she looked in any of them, so she was going back to bed.

I opened the door for Susan, her father, and the two children. While Julia took Toby and Lucy into her room to play, I left Susan and Mr. Armstrong in the living room and hurried in to Eula Lee. I said I thought I was in labor but was not telling David till I was sure.

To my surprise she gave me an excited hug and said how happy she was to be with us this time. Then she warned me that second babies come much faster than first and suggested that I rest in her bed while she finished dinner. It was such an amazing and unexpected offer I almost took her up on it, but said I'd be fine as long as I had her to help me.

I seldom stop to acknowledge—even to myself, let alone to Eula Lee—how much I've come to depend on her. But how comforting to know that while I'm here at the hospital, there's someone I trust at home looking after David and Julia. I cannot imagine my own mother giving up her life for even twenty-four hours to help me live mine.

While I finished preparing dinner, Eula Lee served drinks, even though she has never touched liquor herself and suggested early in our marriage that we fill the crystal decanters we got as wedding presents with colored water. Knowing she was needed seemed to put her at ease, and she took a seat at the table beside Marvin Armstrong without any prompting.

Susan was helping me load the dishwasher when the pains became more pronounced. I said I hated to spoil the party but it was time to leave for the hospital. While I began to practice deep breathing, David got my suitcase out of the closet and started the car. To my surprise Wyatt, Susan, and Paul climbed in the back seat, saying the party was coming with us.

But I was in too much pain to appreciate the gesture. Clenching the steering wheel, David drove like a madman. "Why didn't you tell me your pains started before dinner?" he demanded, swerving to avoid an oncoming car.

I whispered that I was trying to save him another long wait at the hospital. But I couldn't help grimacing with pain. "So you decided to let *me* deliver the baby en route?" he raged.

Suddenly numb with anger, I began to shout. "Enough, David. No matter what I'm going through, you always find a way to be the injured party. Well, this is *my* show tonight. *Your* turn to sit in the audience."

The tires screeched as we pulled into the emergency entrance. While David hurried to find a wheelchair, the admitting nurse handed me a long form. Returning with the chair, David grabbed the form and said if she didn't get me on the table, I'd deliver the baby on her desk. Finally a nurse wheeled me to an elevator. The last I saw of David, he had collapsed into a chair. Susan was holding his hand, Wyatt had his arm around his shoulder, and Paul was offering to find him a drink. It looked as though it was going to be his show after all—he had the audience.

But less than an hour later, Jessica, her dark hair combed into a little curl, was rolled from the delivery room in her glass-enclosed bed to greet the fans gathered for her opening-night party, her proud mother close behind. A night to remember!

I was awakened this morning at 6 A.M. by a phone call from Willa (it was 9 A.M. in New York—she forgot about the time change), congratulating me on Jessica's arrival. I asked how she'd heard so quickly. She said David told her last night when she called after the final performance of the play.

The play closed? What a bleak event to be forever connected by the calendar with Jessica's birthday. Poor David. Why didn't he tell me?

According to Willa, the producer called our house late yesterday afternoon and said he was closing the play unless David was prepared to put in more money to keep it running. David told him that we had not only invested our life savings but used up any future credit we might have with family and friends. Enough was enough. The play was being published, and there were enough good reviews in print to assure it a life outside New York. Universal owned the film rights and maybe some day they would get around to making the movie. He would've loved a long run—not to mention royalties—but he was not prepared to subsidize it.

Listening to Willa, I realized David must have gotten the call just before he went out for club soda. No wonder he was in such a rotten mood on the way to the hospital.

We had cartons of club soda. I was trying to figure out how I could tell my two best friends they were each five thousand dollars poorer for knowing me. I'd headed west on Ventura Boulevard—trying to get as far from Broadway as I could drive. But when I reached the San Diego Freeway, I looked at my watch and saw that the party had already started. So I turned back, cursing Joanna all the way home for planning a party on a night when I'd just gotten another kick in the balls.

I'd calmed down by the time I pulled into the garage and resolved not to share my bad news until after dinner. But Joanna—and Jessica—upstaged me. Not until we were driving home from the hospital (Paul at the wheel, thank God —he was the only sober one among us), when nothing except the fact that Joanna had survived childbirth one more time seemed very important, did I raise my glass to the final performance of my play. Then turned into a blubbering fool. Both Paul and Wyatt were quick to assure me they never expected any immediate return on their money; they considered it an investment in the future. What fu-

185

ture? You, your mother, and Jessica were all I had going for me.

I was so stunned to learn David's play had closed, I had a hard time concentrating on the rest of what Willa was saying—something about wanting desperately to have another baby before it was too late but refusing to get married again. Did I think it was wrong to become pregnant by a man without telling him what you were doing?

I seem to remember saying I thought it was selfish, but at that moment David was coming through the door, and I couldn't wait to walk with him to the nursery to see Jessica. I suddenly felt very generous for having elected to share the experience of parenthood with him when from a biological point of view, his role had ended with conception. I wonder who labeled women the weaker sex when nature leaves it entirely up to them whether or not to allow a man to become a father?

I didn't realize how entirely until I read these journals. No wonder men pass laws outlawing abortion—seeking a legislative antidote for their basic impotence. Such a theory seems obvious now but it would never have occurred to me then, which proves, I guess, that Joanna finally succeeded in raising my consciousness along with my income.

☐

THE NEWS THAT GREETED ME on my return from the hospital today made me want to turn around and check in again. David has gotten an assignment at Universal to write an hour episode for a new series and expects me to start drafting all the scenes for the soap opera as soon as I'm able to work.

And I thought of myself as a pioneer woman when we brought Julia back to our one room at the Montecito and I had nothing to do all day but take care of her! I'm in over my head— but so is David. Ben set up the meeting with the producer, and David said he couldn't turn down the chance to write for a series. If they like his first episode, there might be more.

☐

186

BRAD ARRIVED IN LOS ANGELES last night—and says he's not going back to Chicago without Susan. He told her Elaine has resigned her teaching post and returned to New York. He swore their affair was over and assured Susan it was always more intellectual than physical anyway. Is that supposed to make her feel better?

Susan can't decide what to do. Her father needs her, and the children cry at the thought of leaving California.

☐

DAVID HAS FINALLY ADMITTED that there is another woman in his life—Jessica. Having a baby in the house makes everything seem worthwhile, he says, even *World Without End*. He hopes now we will never be without one. I wouldn't mind. I'd forgotten how sensual life becomes with a new baby. Where do women get the idea motherhood makes them less desirable to men?

From men—where else? Presumably the types who aren't turned on by Rubens's nudes.

☐

SUSAN'S MOTHER has made her decision for her—by dying. Now Susan has to stay with her father—at least for a while. And Brad is returning to Chicago alone.

☐

THIS MORNING the producer of *World Without End* called to say one of the actors was ill and a scene was needed to explain his absence. She wanted it within the hour, sooner if possible. David was at Universal so I was on my own.

My heart pounding, I inserted a blank page into the type-writer, knowing I had to get the scene right on the first draft without any help from David. Once I began to type, however, the characters, as if sensing my desperation, came to my rescue and started carrying on a conversation inside my head. I could hardly type fast enough to get their words down. It was an experience totally alien to me—and thrilling beyond measure.

The scene had the reality of a newspaper story; I had been nothing more than a reporter taking down a confrontation as it occurred. When I called the producer and read her the scene, she said I'd saved her life—plus a lot of money.

A huge bouquet of flowers was being delivered to our front door as David returned home. He read the thank-you note from the producer and asked for an explanation. Hesitantly I showed him the scene I'd written without him. He read it without changing expression while I waited nervously for his reaction. "What a load off my back," he said finally, sinking into a chair with a long sigh.

Then he confessed he'd taken another assignment at Universal—for a half-hour comedy pilot—and will no longer have time to read, let alone edit, my scripts for *World Without End*. However, if he told the producer I was doing all the work and deserved solo credit, he was afraid it would cost us the job. I said not to worry, remembering how Colette learned to write by churning out pulp fiction under her husband's name. She said it was a good apprenticeship—despite the fact he kept her chained to the bedpost. At least I have the run of the house.

I wonder if Colette's husband ever regretted teaching her his tricks. As I recall, he had no sooner unchained her than she left him.

□

LAST WEEK ELAINE SENT DAVID a rough draft of her first novel—a thinly veiled fictional account of her affair with Brad. It is a devastating portrait of a man who can only be described as an intellectual and emotional parasite. David wrote her that he found the relationship implausible—despite the fact that it really happened.

When I read the manuscript, I agreed with him—and felt I should show it to Susan in case she was considering going back to Brad.

Joanna's definition of the "right to know" is somewhat broader than mine. She has always felt she had the right to

read anything that helped her understand people better—
including their mail.

I questioned the ethics of showing Susan a manuscript
Elaine had sent to me, but Joanna thought Susan had the
right to see Brad as Elaine saw him—and insisted she was
only doing for Susan what she hoped Susan would do for
her if the situation were reversed. I swore it never would be.
I learned from reading Elaine's novel what a mistake it is
to have an affair with a writer. You'll pay for it later in
print. It took me longer to learn how much more vulnera-
ble marriage makes you. I lived with Joanna for years with-
out realizing how many things she was storing in her mem-
ory long before either of us had any idea how she'd use
them.

□

SUSAN RETURNED THE MANUSCRIPT yesterday, saying
it had stripped any remaining scales from her eyes. She has
decided to fly to Chicago next week with the children to ask
Brad for a divorce—and to pack their things for shipment to
Pasadena.

However, she worries about leaving her father alone for two
weeks, so I've promised to look in on him frequently. Actually,
he's in very good health for a man his age. His eyesight is excel-
lent and he's quite capable of driving anywhere he wants to go,
but since his wife's death he has only left the house at Susan's
suggestion—and with her at the wheel. I have never seen a man
abandon the role of head of household with such alacrity.

□

THIS AFTERNOON I DECIDED to take Julia and the baby
to Pasadena to visit Mr. Armstrong. I invited Eula Lee to come
with us, but she said she was exhausted from taking care of the
children all morning while I was writing. I think she has missed
Susan's school this summer more than Julia.

Marvin Armstrong was dozing in a lawn chair when we arrived. He seemed more pleased to see the children than to see
me. I could sense how worried he was about losing his grand-

children if Brad talked Susan into staying in Chicago. I assured him they would all be returning as planned and invited him to come home with us for dinner. When he declined, I told him how worried I was about my mother-in-law; I said she was exhausted from baby-sitting all day and needed a diversion. Perhaps a movie tonight after dinner. Then I excused myself and went in the house to feed Jessica.

When I returned, he was bouncing Julia on his knee. A newspaper open to the movie ads lay on the table beside him. He asked if he should call and extend a formal invitation, adding that he hadn't escorted a woman who wasn't his wife anywhere in almost fifty years and hardly knew where to begin. Or where to end. I couldn't stop myself from kissing him on the cheek, then suggested the best strategy would be to let the idea occur to him spontaneously during dinner, when David and I would be on hand to second it.

On returning home, I found Eula Lee in her bedroom with the door closed. I knocked and told her we had company coming for dinner, but she said she wasn't hungry. I countered by saying I wasn't hungry either but I had to fix dinner and needed help with the children. Then I told her Marvin Armstrong was very depressed over his wife's death and I'd invited him to join us. Trying to enlist her pity, I said how sorry I felt for him. She said she was sorry for him too, but that didn't mean she had anything to say to him. She didn't mind being friendly as long as his wife was alive, but things were different now. And with that she closed her eyes and pulled the cover over her head.

Mr. Armstrong arrived at our front door promptly at six, carrying two bouquets of flowers. He presented one to me and said the other was for Eula Lee. Pretending she was still getting dressed, I sent Julia into her with the flowers. Then leaving Mr. Armstrong alone in the living room holding Jessica, I found David and asked him to get Eula Lee out of the bedroom. He said forget it; much as she loved going to the movies, she wasn't about to let another man into her life. She had enough unhappy memories from her first marriage to keep her in bed with the covers over her head for the rest of her life.

Somehow we got through dinner. I don't know how I can face

Marvin Armstrong again—or how Eula Lee can face me in the morning.

> *It never entered my mind that your mother would try to get your grandmother married and out of the house again. So I sat like a spectator at a tennis match, my head pivoting from side to side as one made a move and the other countered. It wasn't that your grandmother was a better player, it was just that she'd been at the game longer.*

☐

SUSAN HAS RETURNED FROM CHICAGO, ready to make Pasadena her permanent home. I drove the children over for a visit this afternoon and found Wyatt hard at work helping her convert the downstairs living and dining rooms into play space for the children when her school resumes in the fall. Last we heard he was going to Hawaii for his vacation, but it seems he decided to spend it with Susan instead.

Mr. Armstrong inquired solicitously after Eula Lee's health. I said I was sure she would feel better once Julia was back in school. After the way Eula Lee behaved the night he came to dinner, I didn't dare offer him any more encouragement than that.

☐

TODAY DAVID SAID YES to Universal. When they discovered how many projects he was working on simultaneously, they decided the only way to keep him exclusive was to put him under contract. The studio will own everything he writes for the next three years, even plays, but David says he doesn't have any more plays in him. He's tired of putting so much of his life into the theater and getting so little in return.

David told the producer of *World Without End* that he would be leaving the show at the first of the year but I was free to continue writing scripts. In fact, he confessed to her that I'd been doing most of the work for the past six months. She obviously didn't believe him—and said the show was only interested in working with us as a team.

David reminded her that in the beginning they had only been

interested in his services. He was the one who suggested that we work as a team, and now I'd proved that I was perfectly capable of writing the scripts alone. Had she forgotten the flowers? Patiently she explained that she could hire David without me because he was an established playwright, but she couldn't hire me without David because I'd done nothing on my own.

Nothing except the work. I can't help wondering if a male producer would have dismissed Joanna so quickly. Or with such ill-disguised glee.

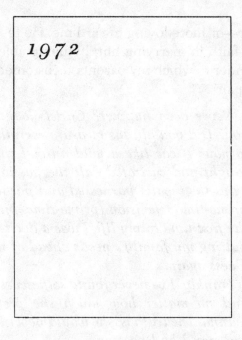

1972

I AM NOW UNEMPLOYED. I never felt unemployed before I had a job, but now I do. I told myself I was only writing for *World Without End* to help David earn the living—until the work came to an abrupt end, forcing me to acknowledge, at least to myself, how much I've come to depend on it.

For the first time in our married life, David now goes to work every day in an office. He meets friends in the commissary for lunch and usually stays late in the afternoon for screenings. He comes home ready for dinner, full of news and ideas. At first he would ask what I'd done with my day, but as I never had anything of interest to answer, he finally stopped asking.

Julia now insists on wearing pants every day—and screams if I suggest how nice she would look in a dress. At the age of five she's decided she wants her father's life when she grows up, not her mother's. Who wouldn't?

For the first time we're able to project our income more than six months ahead. We're putting a new roof on the house this summer, and by next year we may even have enough in our savings account to build another bedroom so Julia and Jessica can each have rooms of their own. David has never been happier—or more loving toward me. He feels he's finally justifying my faith in marrying him by being able to care for me in the manner to which my parents accustomed me. Why am I in such despair?

Never been happier? Christ, Joanna, how blind were you? Did you always measure everything by my response to you? I was like a wild animal that had finally been caught and castrated—all the passion that drove me toward the theater harnessed and put to work grinding out prime-time television (prime-time, but hardly prime). For the first time in my life I was a docile, solicitous husband putting my family's needs ahead of my own. But happy? Guess again.

Frankly, I've never found selflessness much of a turn-on, and no matter how much she pretended, neither did Joanna. The truth is, she would never have agreed to marry the man I had become.

□

I'M GOING CRAZY never getting out of the house. This morning I told Eula Lee I'd drive Julia to Pasadena and she could stay home with Jessica, but she seemed so disappointed, I changed my mind. She really looks forward to helping Susan with the children and visiting with Mr. Armstrong. She says she enjoys talking to him when there are other people around, but gets nervous at the thought of being alone with him. Susan makes her feel special and important—something I've never been able to do, probably for lack of trying—and she's not about to return to the role of full-time baby-sitter.

So then when I kissed David good-bye, I asked if he was free for lunch. I thought maybe Jessica and I might join him in the commissary on our way home from the park. He looked embarrassed and said he had plans. Then what about tomorrow? I persisted. He shook his head again. I should've stopped while I was ahead, but I just can't get used to the idea that we're leading such separate lives. Until this year we always kept a single datebook, with all our appointments written in it. Now he has his own.

194

Trying not to sound like a nagging wife, I said that since he obviously wanted to play hard to get, why didn't we make a date for next week. That's when he pulled out his datebook to show me he was booked for lunch for the next month. I knew some of the names—they were actors, writers, producers—but most of the ones I didn't recognize were women.

I ran into the bedroom and slammed the door. For a minute I was afraid he wasn't coming after me but then he did. I couldn't help crying as I asked how he'd feel if I met a man for lunch. He told me to grow up, these were business lunches, nothing more.

I suggested we invite all those people to dinner now that I'm not working and have plenty of time to cook. But to my surprise he said we were through with all that. People in the business would much rather have lunch at a studio where they can be seen. Besides, this way he can get rid of people in two hours instead of wasting a whole evening on them. But the best thing about not giving any more dinner parties, he said, is that I'll finally have time to concentrate on work of my own, so that if we're hired as a team in the future, I'll be taken seriously as a writer.

Did I really use the phrase "taken seriously as a writer"? In Hollywood? And she bought it? What I hated was the fact that she would stop writing a week before a dinner party and start poring over cookbooks, planning menus, polishing silver. I remember screaming at her, "Who are you trying to impress? These people don't matter. They're bums!" They weren't bums, of course—they were our best friends. I was just trying to put it in perspective. Was it Steinbeck who said if you want to be a serious writer, you have to give up being gracious? To this day I haven't been able to break your mother of the habit. Except with me, of course.

Work of my own? Where do I start? I've never been more frightened. Until now I've always been told what to do with my life. I was an honor student in school, but I'm at a loss without a teacher to please and other students with whom to compete. I was a dutiful daughter until I left home to get married and then I concentrated on becoming a good wife, trying to put my husband's wishes ahead of my own. Now I've been given my freedom—at least intellectually—and I have no idea what to do with it. I feel like one of those slaves freed by the Civil War who begged to be allowed to stay on the plantation.

I have no idea what she's talking about here. I never gave her her freedom, intellectual or otherwise. And I never will!

☐

DADDY HAD A HEART ATTACK last night. His condition is stable but he'll be in intensive care for another week. He was alone when the attack occurred, around midnight, but fortunately keeps a phone by his bed and so was able to call for help. It frightens me to think that if he'd been even a few feet from the phone, he might have died there by himself. Mother had just left for Venice, where she has rented a villa for the summer. I talked to her this morning, urging her to stay in Italy. It would only make Daddy worse to think she'd changed her plans on his account now that they're no longer married and legally obligated to each other.

My brother and his wife are driving to Dallas today and will stay until Daddy is out of intensive care. My sister is trying to rearrange her vacation schedule so she can take him home from the hospital and stay in the house until a private nurse can be hired.

My brother and sister made all these plans without even consulting me, for which I feel grateful and guilty at the same time. They said they realized it would be hard for me to get away, since I have two small children and a demanding husband—actually they didn't say a "demanding" husband but I knew that was what they were thinking.

Why shouldn't they say it? It's true. But I've found the only chance of getting what you want out of life is to ask for it—to demand it, if necessary. Joanna never understood that. She thought if I loved her, I'd know what she wanted without being told. How could I when she seldom knew herself?

The truth is, I enjoy being married to a man who demands me at his side every night. If my father had felt that way about my mother—and had told her so occasionally—he wouldn't be alone now.

I haven't been home for a visit since we moved to California, and no one from my side of the family has even seen Jessica, who is already walking everywhere.

Once she left Daddy, Mother stopped going through the motions of asking me to come for a visit; there is no room in her small apartment or her crowded life for visiting grandchildren. I think she may also have suspected—based on her experience with her own mother—that one mother-in-law to a marriage was more than enough, and she had no intention of competing with Eula Lee for the role. After she established her own residence, we politely asked her at six-month intervals to include us in her future travel plans. She always thanked us and promised the first time she traveled west, she would stop in Los Angeles for a long visit—she really would like to see our house some day, she said—but so far every time she's left Texas, her destination has been Italy. What draws her there? I wonder if she has a lover.

The thought crossed my mind when she walked out on her husband. I was convinced she either had one or, more likely, was looking for one. But for once in our marriage, I refrained from sharing my suspicions with Joanna. Not out of any sensitivity on my part, I just didn't want to put ideas in her head. I once read that if you want to know what your wife will be like when she grows old, take a look at her mother. I did—and the prospect paralyzed me.

☐

TODAY IS MY TWELFTH WEDDING ANNIVERSARY— and I'm sleeping alone in the bed where I came of age. Daddy is asking such a ridiculously high price for the house I doubt that it will ever sell. Mother suspects that was his plan from the beginning, but as usual he was more farsighted than the rest of the family. "Why do you want to keep living in that big house with all those empty rooms?" we would ask. But now all the rooms are full again.

I've only been here a week, but the past exerts such a powerful hold on my imagination, I know this is where I belong—at least for now. I wake up feeling so safe and necessary to the well-being of everyone around me. Sometimes I find it hard to believe I have a husband, a home, and a twelve-year marriage waiting in California. It is only at night, after David's phone call, that I fall asleep aching with longing. But during the day with Rosie, the cook who did as much as Mother to raise me, bringing me breakfast in bed and assuring me she can keep an eye on my children while she cleans house, just as she used to do when I was little, I feel pampered and indulged.

Tonight after dinner (when I didn't have to do anything but eat—what luxury not to have to cook or clean up), I wrote a long letter to David trying to describe just how he makes me feel and putting into words all the thoughts we've never had the time— or the inclination—to express out loud.

I haven't had this much time alone since college, and I find myself examining all my relationships and putting them into perspective. Why do I feel so much fonder of people at a distance? Maybe because at a distance I'm allowed to shape my image of them, heightening the qualities I like and ignoring the irritating habits that set my teeth on edge. To my surprise, after I wrote David I even wrote a warm, friendly letter to my mother-in-law describing how the children spend their days and how much they miss her. She has so few interests in her life —I wonder how she passes the hours without the children to occupy her?

☐

TODAY, WHILE DADDY AND THE CHILDREN were napping, I had lunch with my best friend from high school. We used to spend every Saturday night together, taking turns sleeping at each other's houses. As we got ready for bed, putting our hair in soft rollers, we would discuss endlessly the largest challenge the future held for us: how we would manage to curl our hair at night once we were married. We finally decided the only solution was to wait till our husbands were asleep to put in the curlers, then remove them before they were awake, thus keeping their illusions about our natural beauty intact.

Over crab soufflé at the club, I tried to explain to my friend how abandoned I felt when David began going to an office every day after working at home all the years of our marriage. "You mean you've been fixing lunch for him for the past twelve years?" she asked in amazement. "But what happened when you wanted to go out with your friends?"

Her question made me realize that marriage had cost me not only my family but friends of my own. However, only now—away from David—can I see clearly how lonely I've been in the last few months. Through twelve years of marriage my husband has been not only my family but my best friend. We've always shared everything—work, friends, children—but now suddenly he has a life of his own that does not include me, at least during the day. In Los Angeles I am David's wife, period. I no longer know who I am without him. But in Dallas I have an identity of my own, securely rooted in family and friends who loved me long before I loved David.

An identity as what? The older daughter? The high school valedictorian? The rich girl who played at the newspaper on her summer vacation? How could she have felt more secure in those outgrown roles than she did with me? I saw her as a complicated, exciting woman whose innocent sexuality as a bride had been enhanced by motherhood—a woman who was on the verge of discovering a new career as a writer. I was prepared to guide her into the unknown territory that lay ahead of us. Why was she so afraid of following me?

She wasn't afraid of anything when she agreed to marry me and share my struggles. But then it was my ass on the line. How many years did she take refuge in the role of David's wife? And if my career had worked out the way we hoped, she'd still be living happily in my shadow. But when the sun stopped shining on me, I could no longer cast a shadow big enough to hide her. She had to come out from behind me.

When Joanna fled to Dallas that summer, she wasn't running from the role of David's wife. Far from it. She was terrified of admitting that my life was no longer big enough for both of us—it wasn't even big enough for me. She had to become her own person. It's only now that I'm beginning to understand what a frightening prospect that was for her.

□

TONIGHT, WHEN DAVID CALLED to ask if I was ever coming home, I was evasive. How could I tell him I was already home—and couldn't face the terror of returning to Los Angeles, where I'm supposed to *do* something to justify my existence? In Dallas no one expects me to *do* anything. I am a daughter to my convalescent father, a mother to my two daughters, and a wife to my absent husband—more than enough, by the reckoning of everyone I know, to account for what I do with my days. And so, for the moment, it is enough for me.

It's been a long time since I've lived so immersed in the present. Life seems rich and textured when you savor each moment without thinking about what will happen next. Why do we allow anxiety about the future to color so much of our daily experience of life?

I've never enjoyed my father more than on this visit. For the first time the two of us have really begun to talk one on one. When I was growing up, I was almost never with him without Mother, and the conversation was usually a feminine dialogue, with Daddy interjecting occasional comments. But now we've begun to confide in each other, and I'm seeing for the first time how alike we are—and how different he is from David.

David was so angry when he hung up tonight—and my father was so understanding. He thinks I should stay here until I've made up my own mind about what I want to do.

And to think I was feeling sorry for him because his wife had walked out on him! Now I find out he was encouraging my wife *to leave me.*

How many times in the past have I condemned my father silently for what I perceived as a lack of passion, a tendency to reserve judgment? I realize now I was always comparing him to David, and the qualities I disliked in my father were the very ones David abhors in me. What once appeared to me as flaws—in my father and in myself—seem to me now to have great sustaining value over the course of a lifetime. If my father had been the kind of man who passed judgment, he would've judged David and forced me to make an irrevocable choice between them. I would've chosen David and cut all ties with my family. Though my relationship with my father has been more form than substance since I put another man at the center of my life, we've never lost touch, and now once again, for the first time since childhood, we're close enough to embrace. And do. Often.

I'd always wanted daughters because I'd heard they fell in love with their fathers at an early age. That was something I had yet to experience, and Joanna assured me her father had never been anything to her but an amiable, somewhat distant figure in her upbringing. However, I realize now she began falling in love with him that summer while I was alone at home without a wife or daughters. Even Mother had abandoned me. Once Joanna's absence forced her into having to fix dinner every night, she began accepting Marvin Armstrong's invitations. She would always offer to make something for me, but I was depressed enough about my life without having to face her cooking.

☐

DAVID IS HERE! I found him talking with Daddy this afternoon when I came home from a fashion show at the Zodiac Room. "David has asked me to move to Los Angeles and live in your house," Daddy said, obviously pleased by the invitation. And that is how I learned that my mother-in-law was marrying Marvin Armstrong.

What a swell fellow I thought I was that day. I could tell from her letters that Joanna was falling in love with her

*father, so I thought I'd make a grandstand play by inviting
him to move in with us. Of course it never occurred to me he
might accept.*

Eula Lee has been so much a part of our family since the children arrived, I have a hard time imagining how we'll get along without her. I'm guilty of taking her presence very much for granted. How many other young mothers can leave home on a moment's notice without worrying about a baby-sitter? I really can't imagine my father—or anyone—taking her place.

Daddy must have seen my hesitation. He was quick to assure me he had no intention of moving in with us permanently, though he would love to come for a visit. But not yet. He showed us a letter that had just arrived from Mother. She's returning to Dallas this weekend—and will stay as long as he needs her. "I hope she's not coming home on my account," he said shyly. "I wouldn't want her to change her plans."

"I'm sure she misses you," I said, giving him a hug. I can't seem to stop hugging people since David arrived.

"I'd like to believe that," he replied. "I haven't stopped missing her."

□

MOTHER ARRIVED FROM VENICE this afternoon laden like Marco Polo with presents for everyone. She usually hates to spend time shopping in Europe—or anywhere, for that matter —but today she seemed to want to present us with tangible evidence that she was at least thinking about us during her absence.

Daddy could not hide his happiness at having his family around him. "I thought it would take my funeral to have all of you gathered around this table," he said as Rosie brought in the roast turkey with oyster stuffing he'd ordered for Mother's homecoming dinner. He then offered a prayer of thanksgiving for his family, in case the significance of the turkey had been lost on anyone.

After dinner, Mother, who had already made a six-hour exception to her rule of going straight to bed after a transatlantic crossing, said she was exhausted and would like to go to her apartment. David offered to drive her and mentioned casually that we were returning to Los Angeles tomorrow and taking Daddy with us. "For how long?" Mother asked in amazement. My father, a shrewd lawyer who understands the uses of an effective bluff in and out of court, smiled and shrugged as if his fate were now in other hands.

"As long as he'll stay," I hurried to answer.

"But where will you put him?" Mother asked, as if he were some outsized relic from the past. David told her Eula Lee was getting married, so we'd have a spare room. I don't know which Mother found harder to believe—that we wanted Daddy to live with us or that there was a man who wanted Eula Lee to marry him.

I do.

"But you can't leave just like that—without any warning?" she protested frantically, suddenly forgetting how exhausted she was by her trip.

"Why not?" he replied. "You did."

"But that was different," she countered weakly.

"Oh? How?" he asked calmly. For the first time I was able to imagine my father cross-examining a witness. It made me sad to think I'd never once in all the years I was growing up gone to court to see him argue a case. But I was seeing him in action now, fighting for the verdict of a lifetime from a judge who held his future happiness in her hands—my mother.

"Well"—she hesitated—"you were here to take care of everything."

"And now you're here," he answered, refusing to let her off the hook.

Suddenly Mother said she was too exhausted to think about anything but getting to her apartment and going to bed. Tomorrow would be time enough to discuss what the future held for all of us.

☐

2 A.M. I've been wandering through the house for the past hour trying to decide just where I belong. I left David sleeping

in the bed where I spent so many years dreaming alone. Nothing I imagined as a naive and impressionable young girl about what goes on between men and women prepared me for what a difficult, complicated, day-to-day arrangement marriage is for everyone. Growing up, I assumed my parents and all their friends were happy, and they were careful not to let me see or hear anything to make me doubt that every wedding ceremony was the beginning of "happily ever after." Only now, coming home as an adult, have I begun to realize that all was not as it appeared. A suicide here, an alcoholic there, infidelity here and there.

Watching my parents at the dinner table tonight, I could see how much they still care for each other. Why can't they live together? And why does it matter so much to me where they live? Would I feel better about my own marriage if my parents got back together? As happy as I am to be sharing a bed with David again, I'm not sure I can live the rest of my life with him.

I had no idea she was having doubts. Now I learn that while I was sleeping soundly for the first time in weeks, thinking my marriage was finally back on course, Joanna was lying awake beside me contemplating her options. I imagined our hearts were beating as one that night. But then I imagined the same thing last night.

I wish Daddy were coming with us. At least then I'd have another adult at home to keep me company during the day.

Another adult? Someone who would question her motives, confront her prejudices, challenge her ideas? That was the last thing she wanted. No, she wanted her daddy, who would assure her everything she did was wonderful. That's not love, Julia, and don't ever be deceived into thinking it is.

☐

I AWOKE THIS MORNING to find Mother fixing Daddy a breakfast tray. She said it was nonsense for him even to consider traveling to Los Angeles. He wasn't well enough. Furthermore, as long as she was alive, she had no intention of allowing him to move in with us. It was hard enough to keep a marriage afloat without in-laws clinging to you for support. It looked as though we were finally getting David's mother off our back; the last thing we needed was to have my father take her place. Didn't David and I ever want to be alone? I refrained from pointing out that she and Daddy never thought about living apart *until* they were alone. Sometimes I think being alone creates more pressure in a marriage than supporting a family.

I said we couldn't leave Daddy here by himself—not after what had happened. Mother said not to worry. She'd gotten out of her lease in Venice and canceled her reservation for a Mediterranean cruise in the fall. She was here for "the duration." I didn't dare ask for her definition of that dour word.

☐

HOMECOMING! How could I have ever doubted that this is where I belong!

I spent the morning cleaning the kitchen (I get the feeling it was hardly used in my absence) and thinking about what happened yesterday.

Eula Lee and Mr. Armstrong met us at the airport holding hands. David whispered to her as we waited for our luggage to appear on the carousel that the children knew nothing of her plans. "I'm so glad you waited for me to tell them," she said, squeezing his hand.

I could see that she was a changed woman. In the old days no matter what anybody said or did, she found a way to come out of it the injured party. Mother had spent a lifetime collecting grievances. Now at last she'd met a man who, by praising every move she made, had broken her of the habit—something neither her father nor her husband nor her son had ever been able to do. My hat was off to Marvin Armstrong. Sometimes heroes come in very unprepossessing packages.

"I'm finally able to give you something I've never been able to give you before," Eula Lee said to the girls on the ride home from the airport. Julia was cuddled close to her. Jessica was climbing on Mr. Armstrong's lap, looking inside his coat pocket for the candy he always keeps hidden for her.

"I know what it is," Julia began to scream with excitement. "You don't have to tell me. It's the only thing I want that nobody ever gives me." Breathless with anticipation, she plunged ahead. "A pony! A pony of my very own! Is it waiting for me at home or do we have to go to the stable to get it?"

Jessica's attention was fully engaged for the first time. "Pony! Pony!" she squealed with delight, bouncing up and down on Mr. Armstrong's knee.

"No, no!" Eula Lee hurried to correct the mistake. But it was too late. "Not a pony. A grandfather."

"We already have a grandfather," Julia said, tears of disappointment spilling out of her eyes. "We have everything except a pony." All the emotion of the reunion with her grandmother, reinforced by anticipation and disappointment, suddenly overcame her and she began to sob. Jessica had no idea what was happening, but it always frightens her to see her older sister cry, and she began to whimper in sympathy.

"Darling," I interrupted, pulling Julia into the front seat and cuddling her in my arms. "Your grandmother is going to marry Mr. Armstrong. He'll belong to our family just the way he does to Toby and Lucy."

Until then, it had not occurred to Julia that the man in the back seat, whom she had grown to love going to school in what was once his living room, was in any way involved in the news her grandmother was announcing. She stood up and leaned over into his arms. I held on to her knees to keep her from tumbling into his lap alongside Jessica, who was contentedly stroking his white beard.

"You're going to be our grandfather?" Julia asked in wide-eyed delight.

"Yes indeed," he said, smiling happily. "And please start calling me Marvin—all of you." Then he asked Julia if she would like to be a flower girl at the wedding.

"Will I get to wear a long dress?" Julia asked.

"And matching shoes and hat," Eula Lee promised. "Susan is going to make dresses for you and Jessica and Lucy. We've already picked out the pattern and the fabric."

"Then you've already made all your plans?" I couldn't help being a little surprised at how much had been decided in my absence.

"I told Susan at the beginning of the summer I wanted to marry Eula Lee if she'd have me," Marvin confessed shyly. "I had to make sure she and the children would be all right without me."

"It's different for you and David," Eula Lee hastened to add. "You have each other. You won't even notice when I'm gone."

"Where are you going, Nanny?" Julia asked fearfully, realizing for the first time that gaining a grandfather might mean losing a grandmother.

"We've found an apartment we like in Santa Monica—right by the ocean. We signed the lease the day Marvin proposed." Eula Lee began to blush as if she were confessing an illicit arrangement.

"So you'll be setting up housekeeping?" I couldn't imagine Eula Lee doing any of the things I'd been doing for her ever since she moved in with us.

"Actually it's more of an apartment hotel," Eula Lee continued. "Maid service every day. And a dining room for meals."

"Unless we decide to go out," Marvin interjected. "There are a lot of wonderful restaurants within walking distance. I don't want Eula Lee to lift a finger."

No wonder she looked so happy.

You really are a bitch about my mother, Joanna—you really are.

"It's a two-bedroom apartment, so you and Jessica can stay overnight whenever you like," Eula Lee explained to Julia, who was about to cry at the thought of her grandmother leaving home.

"And any time your mother and father have to go out or away on a trip, we'll stay with you at your house," Marvin assured her.

"And wherever we are, we'll go out to eat," Eula Lee added with a smile approaching rapture. Marvin Armstrong had clearly discovered early in their courtship that the way to her heart was through the doors of a restaurant.

Plans for the wedding occupied us all the way home. Susan

wants to have it in the orchard behind their house in Pasadena on a Sunday afternoon in August. She and Eula Lee have worked out everything including the minister, the music, and the menu for the reception. I was already feeling excluded when, just as we pulled in the driveway, Marvin said to David, "And I want you to be my best man. You're everything I ever wanted in a son." David put his arm affectionately around his prospective stepfather's shoulder as they unloaded the car. I was happier about David finally getting the father he deserved than I was about Eula Lee finding an affectionate and attentive husband so late in life. I waited for my mother-in-law to ask me to be her matron of honor and say that I was everything she ever wanted in a daughter. Instead, she offered to help the children unpack while I fixed dinner.

My heart sank at the thought of returning to a life that revolved around the refrigerator, buying groceries to fill it up, then emptying it again for yet another meal.

"Marvin is a wonderful man," I said to Eula Lee, thinking enviously of all the restaurant meals ahead of her. "I know you're going to be very happy."

Once the children were asleep, David came into the bathroom while I was taking a bubble bath and climbed in behind me—something he hasn't done since we left our Greenwich Village apartment with the bathtub in the kitchen. In those days when we used to stay awake till dawn, we would sometimes spend hours in the tub together. Once the children were born, the nights were never that long again—nor the bathtub quite so central to our existence.

But last night he seemed to think there was nothing more important than making me happy. Gently he began to soap my back and massage my shoulders. I've never known him to take so much time to make me feel good without wanting anything in return. When I tried to turn and face him, he insisted I stay where I was, encircled by his legs and arms. Finally, just as I was feeling relaxed and thoroughly loved, the back of my head resting against his chest, my eyes half closed, his hands caressing my breasts, he whispered into my ear, "Are you upset by any of this?"

"Any of what?" I couldn't imagine ever being happier.

"The wedding plans."

Eula Lee might as well have climbed in the tub with us. Furious at David for breaking the mood, I got out and wrapped myself in a towel. "Mother was afraid you might be hurt," he continued. "She asked me to explain how it happened."

"Hurt? What are you talking about? Are you telling me the only reason you got in the tub with me was to talk about your mother?" I'd never felt more betrayed.

Suddenly David looked ridiculous still sitting in the tub, as embarrassed as Adam when he bit into the apple and realized for the first time he was naked. I began to laugh and crossed to the door, where his terry cloth robe was hanging on a hook. "Here," I said, holding it open for him. "Now get out and tell me what's on your mind. And don't touch me again until you've said everything you have to say about your mother."

"I know," he began hesitantly, "that when Marvin asked me to be his best man, you must've expected her to ask you to be her matron of honor."

"Why would I?" I lied. "It's her wedding. It has nothing to do with me."

David was visibly relieved. "I'm so glad you feel that way. I've been dreading telling you."

"Telling me what?"

"Why she asked Susan to be her only attendant." A long explanation followed, but I couldn't listen. I kept drying myself briskly with a towel so David wouldn't notice the tears. He was saying something about knowing nothing until everything had already been decided. Apparently Marvin and Eula Lee had been having dinner with Susan, making plans for the wedding, when Marvin announced he was going to ask David to be his best man. Eula Lee immediately reciprocated by asking Susan to be her matron of honor. Not until she got home later that night, she told David, did she realize I might be hurt by her choice. But she hoped I would understand she felt sorry for Susan because she didn't have a husband.

"Of course." I had to laugh—and admit to myself, if not to David, that I'd gotten what was coming to me. Being married to her only son did not automatically make me my mother-in-law's best friend. I had no interest in that role and had never made any effort to earn her affection. Susan, on the other hand, genuinely liked her—long before there was any prospect of a family tie between them. Sometimes I wonder how Eula Lee and I would've felt about each other had we not met through David. Would we ever have been friends?

People like Joanna do not meet people like Eula Lee except through people like me.

☐

A BUYER HAS TURNED UP for my parents' house—a businessman from the East. His company is moving to Dallas—part of a trend to relocate in what is beginning to be known as the Sunbelt—so he's willing to pay the absurd price Daddy has been asking in the hope of never finding a buyer. Since his illness Daddy has given up his dream of retiring to a small town and accepted Mother's invitation to share her apartment. She has no room for any more furniture and wants to know if there is anything from the house we would like. I asked for the two antique chests my grandmother used to keep in her front hall filled with Liberty silk scarves and kid gloves ready for her to seize on her way out the door. She was always in a hurry, creating the impression of being continually off on some grand adventure. I wanted Julia and Jessica to have the chests—and with them the promise of adventure just beyond the front door.

Though Daddy seems to be recovering nicely from his heart attack, he has to avoid overtiring himself—which leaves the dismantling of the house entirely in Mother's hands. As hard as she has struggled to be free of family obligations, they always seem to catch up with her. She had no sooner left her husband than her mother claimed her total attention. Now she is single-handedly trying to sift through the artifacts of over thirty-five years of marriage, knowing she will have to find space in her already overcrowded apartment for whatever she deems worth saving. Hearing her plaintive tone over the telephone, I took pity on her and said to send me anything involving any family history and I would find a place for it in our house.

We were about to say good-bye when I impulsively asked her to ship the furniture from my girlhood bedroom, including my double bed. Now that Eula Lee is establishing a separate residence, I plan to see that her mahogany bedroom suite follows her to Santa Monica. Finally we will have a guest room we can furnish to our taste.

☐

THE WEDDING WAS AN OCCASION of real joy. For at least one afternoon everyone present was overflowing with affection for everyone else. Seeing Susan look so lovely, I could almost forgive Eula Lee for asking her to be matron of honor. Marvin had invited a few friends from the past, none of whom he had seen since his wife's funeral. Eula Lee was represented by David and me and her two grandchildren, who are in fact the only friends she has ever wanted.

She wore a soft pink chiffon dress that enhanced her already glowing complexion. "You know, this is my first wedding," she confessed as I fastened her pearls for her. "I ran away with David's father. I knew my parents would never give their permission for me to marry that man. I should've listened to them, but if I had, we wouldn't have David, either of us—so it was worth it, wasn't it?"

"Absolutely," I replied, impulsively kissing her cheek.

Everything in the garden appeared to be in bloom as the string quartet Susan hired for the occasion played the wedding march. Jessica was the first flower girl to toddle down the aisle, but instead of casually strewing rose petals from her basket, she insisted on placing each one in a straight, unbroken line to the lilac-laden arch Wyatt had built, where the groom and his best man were waiting. David caught my eye as I stood in the front row and gestured for me to get the show moving—at the rate Jessica was progressing, it would take her ten minutes to get down the aisle—but I just shrugged pleasantly. I was not an official member of the wedding party. What could I do?

Your mother has always had the ability to make her point without making a scene. I might have gotten further down the road if I'd had that gift. But no, when my feelings are injured, I yell bloody murder. I remember so well —and so often—how your mother would just step back

211

from the fray and smile sweetly. I'm afraid you girls are like your father. Too bad. But not too late to change. Maybe not too late for all three of us to change.

Unable to restrain his impatience, David met Jessica halfway down the aisle and swooped her into his arms. She began to howl at the indignity of having her first public appearance cut short. Embarrassed, David quickly deposited her on the seat beside me. I consoled her by promising she could throw her remaining rose petals on Julia and Lucy as they walked down the aisle side by side (Susan worried that Lucy would forget why she was there without Julia to guide her).

Jessica hurled the petals with glee, but still had a few left when Eula Lee marched proudly past. David had offered to give her away but she said she was not his to give and if she couldn't make it down the aisle under her own steam, then she was too old to be getting married. I blew her a kiss and Jessica threw a last handful of rose petals, which clung to her hair as she recited her vows.

The sun was setting when the bride and groom kissed all of us good-bye. They're planning to spend their wedding night in their new apartment, then fly to Honolulu tomorrow for a week at the Royal Hawaiian. I've never seen Eula Lee so happy. Why can't David be happier for her?

I was happy for her. If I seemed sad, it was because I was grieving for all the years lost in her first marriage. I wished her youth to go along with Marvin's love.

☐

JUST WHEN I BEGIN TO FEAR marriage is an impossible arrangement, everyone seems to want to try it. Last night after the wedding we brought Toby and Lucy home with us and this morning when Susan came to claim them, she told me Wyatt had asked her to marry him. But she swore after her divorce from Brad that she would never commit to a permanent relationship with anyone again—so she has refused Wyatt for the second time in twelve years. However, she is willing to share his bed this time. Progress of sorts.

Did Joanna envy Susan and Wyatt their less than perma-
nent relationship? Was she suddenly putting ours on the
same basis without bothering to inform me that the terms
had changed?

I wonder how many times she might have walked out on
me if we hadn't been married. Often the only thing that
keeps you together is knowing how hard it would be to
separate.

Once we had a child and Mother came to live with us, I
knew I was making it next to impossible for Joanna ever to
consider divorce. No matter how angry she got at me, I
counted on the fact that she would never be able to talk you
and Jessica into leaving your grandmother. I deliberately
set out to weave a web of family so complicated she
wouldn't be able to extricate herself. However, when
Mother married Marvin, my web began to unravel.

☐

MARVIN AND EULA LEE returned from their honeymoon
in Hawaii with presents for everyone. They came to dinner
tonight with Wyatt and Susan and her two children.

As soon as the presents were distributed, Julia took her grandmother by the hand and led her to her former bedroom, now
furnished with my girlhood furniture. To my surprise Eula Lee
said it was just the room she would have liked when she was
growing up. Then she asked what I'd done with her furniture. I
was quick to assure her that it was safely stored, waiting to be
moved to her new apartment.

To my amazement she announced that she had no desire to
see it again, admitting she never liked it but it was the best she
could afford at the time. "I was afraid I was going to have to live
with it the rest of my life," she laughed. "But Marvin has promised we're going to buy everything new for the apartment.
There won't be one piece of furniture to remind us of the past."

☐

SUSAN STARTED HER SCHOOL again today. There are
now a dozen children in daily attendance. At eight Lucy is the

oldest in years, although mentally she will probably never get beyond kindergarten. But the other children take their cue from Toby and Julia, instinctively making allowances for her limited ability while always finding a way to include her in their games. Jessica, at eighteen months, became the youngest student this morning. She couldn't bear to see Julia go off to school without her, and Susan encouraged me to let her stay. She finds the age mix healthy, operating the school on the principle of the one-room schoolhouse.

I came straight home and sat by the telephone in case Jessica changed her mind about staying—or Susan changed her mind about having her—but so far it has not rung.

It feels so strange to have the house to myself. With Eula Lee in her own apartment, David in his office at Universal, and both children at school, I am at a loss trying to figure out what I'm supposed to be doing with *my* life.

So far all I've done with my first free morning is read the help-wanted ads to see if there are any jobs for which I'm qualified.

☐

LAST NIGHT I TOLD DAVID I wanted to work and showed him the jobs I'd circled in the ads. He exploded—said he didn't sign his life away to Universal so that his wife could start punching a time clock. Women have a choice between working or not working—a luxury a man can never afford. Why didn't I enjoy my options instead of panicking the minute I was home alone? I had every right to work, but I should have the courage to set my own terms—and not rush into the first paying job I could find just to avoid thinking about what I might accomplish if I weren't so terrified of my freedom.

I believe this more than ever. It infuriates me to see women, for all their talk about the quality of life, fall into the same trap as men, measuring their worth by the size of their paychecks. The actress wife of one of the most successful television producers I know claws to get commercials when she could be producing plays in Equity-waiver theaters, playing leads and providing work for other people, maybe even giving a new playwright a chance at produc-

214

tion. But she sits around in her elegant Beverly Hills home waiting to be hired—then deposits her paycheck in a separate account which barely covers her Christmas shopping.

I'd indentured myself to Universal so that we could finally have a little financial security. I'd be damned if I was going to let Joanna tie herself down to some dumb job. No matter how much it scared her, I was determined that she would use her freedom to take chances—for both of us.

□

WHY AM I SO RESTLESS? I have a loving, attentive husband—

And faithful—don't forget faithful. You always took that for granted.

two daughters who are everything I ever wanted or wanted to be—and yet I sit in my kitchen feeling as if I'm surrounded by a moat and David is the only one with drawbridge privileges.

What privileges? I always hated leaving home—risking attack every time the drawbridge was lowered. Surely she'd noticed.

I hate women who whine about their lot in life—even in the privacy of their journals—and I'm not going to turn into one of them. Still, I have all these questions.

Does marriage make everyone so insular? I long for closer ties with people outside this house, starting with my own parents, but I seem to spend all my emotional energy on my immediate family.

□

I'VE DECIDED TO SEND CHRISTMAS CARDS to everyone we know. Not one of those self-congratulatory annual reports—just little notes to friends past and present saying they're in our thoughts.

Today I got out all my old address books and started going through them. How many people have passed through our lives! It's a sobering experience to go through the names and see how many have been lost through death, divorce, or simple neglect. I'm making David an up-to-date Rolodex for Christmas. With each new card I type and file, I feel a little richer, knowing that's one more friend we can count on. Now I understand why he gets such pleasure from making lists of our assets. From now on, whenever I'm feeling lonely and depressed, I'll just bring the Rolodex up to date.

It got to be a rather select list. Joanna had a way of editing our friends that I found very disconcerting. People we hadn't seen in a while or with whom we'd had a falling-out or who had failed to repay our invitations would just disappear from the files without a trace. People always made the mistake, when they first met Joanna, of thinking she was easy to please. The truth is, she expects too much of everyone, including me. She's probably going through her Rolodex even now, while I'm writing this, purging names.

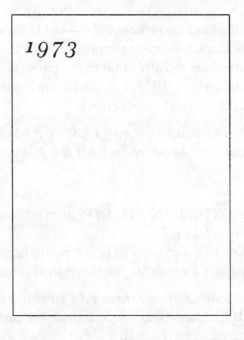

1973

MY NEW YEAR'S RESOLUTION is to forget about finding a job and try to be better at the jobs I already have—wife, mother, and daughter.

I know David expects more from me. He thinks I'm wasting my mind at home, and yet he ridicules every reason I come up with for stepping outside the front door. According to him, exercise classes are a waste of money, volunteer work is for women with time on their hands, and extension courses are designed for dilettantes. He keeps saying I should have the courage to do something creative—something unique that no one else would be able to do. But what am I equipped to do? I know he would like a better wife, but I don't know how to become what he wants.

I've been a full-time mother all year, since *World Without End* did—and I can't see that the children are any better off. In fact, I sometimes think they prefer playing without me hovering over them, making suggestions. When I'm out of sight, Julia has complete authority over Jessica, and that's the way she likes it.

So, until I get a grip on myself, I'm as good a wife and as good a mother as I know how to be—but to be a better daughter seems like a much simpler proposition. All I have to do is give a little more time and attention to my parents. So when I called to wish them a happy 1973, I invited them to come out for a visit. To my amazement, they accepted.

To her amazement! I had to go to bed with a wet towel over my head when I got the good news.

☐

MOTHER AND DADDY arrived last night. One day down, six more to go!

David is not used to being polite to people around the clock. How am I going to get through this visit?

Joanna always insisted I treat her family like company. Which seems to me to defeat the purpose.

I'm not sure it's possible to be a good wife *and* a good daughter at the same time. Whatever made me ask my parents to come?

And whatever made them accept? I never saw two people so uncomfortable in the presence of their own flesh and blood.

☐

STRIKE ONE FOR MY PARENTS. Two more and they'll be out and on their way home to Texas. David was being his most charming last night. Once he puts his mind to it, nobody does it better. We took them to Chasen's for our favorite meal—chili and hobo steak. David was regaling us with stories of his father (how he can take such horror stories and make them into high comedy never ceases to amaze me) when my mother suddenly pulls out her compact and begins powdering her nose and putting on lipstick.

Just as I was getting to the punch line. The woman is a killer!

In protest—though nobody got the message but me—David excused himself from the table. This left Daddy with the check, which made him very happy. Until tonight, much to Daddy's distress, David has insisted on paying for everything. Daddy doesn't feel in control of a situation unless he's picking up the tab.

David didn't say a word all the way home. I was so tense I could hardly breathe—but tried to cover it by talking nonstop about nothing.

David—thank God—waited until my parents were in bed before putting me on trial for my mother's bad manners. I made the mistake I always do when he puts me on the defensive—and tried to downplay the importance of what had happened. Oh, God, when will I ever learn? The only defense with David is a strong offense. He would've been thrilled if I'd attacked my mother at the table and asked how dare she take out her compact in the middle of his story? But like a fool, I tried to explain that for some women, repairing their makeup after they eat is a reflex action and in no way indicates lack of attention.

"You're never going to be able to write until you start looking beneath the surface," David said. Didn't I see the significance of the fact that my mother chose to look at herself rather than listen to him? The incident captured their whole relationship.

I said if being a writer meant getting your feelings hurt every time you turn around, then it wasn't the profession for me.

"It means being sensitive," David roared. "A quality no one in your family appreciates."

So now it's us against him. Battle stations, everybody! I turned off my light and wondered how I was ever going to get to sleep —not to mention getting through the rest of their visit.

But David wasn't through with me yet. As we lay side by side in the bed—trapped in a marital version of trench warfare—he said in a low voice, "If you saw one of the children do something rude, wouldn't you feel it was your responsibility to reprimand them?"

"Of course," I muttered between clenched teeth, "but that's different. They're the children and we're the parents."

"You don't think adults have the same responsibility toward each other?"

"No, I don't. I think beyond a certain age people ought to

respect each other for what they are—and not try to change them."

"That's ridiculous," he scoffed. "The more you love a person, the more you should expect of them. You're not the girl I married and I take most of the credit."

What an ego! I would laugh if it weren't true.

Damn right. Nice of her to notice.

I never said half of what I was thinking or feeling before I married David. I still don't talk back to my parents—but that's a choice made out of respect.

Come off it, Joanna. You'd sell your soul for their approval—even now after all these years. It's true. Admit it. Otherwise, I'd be saying these things to your face, instead of writing my rebuttal. Why am I bothering? Why do I still get so upset over events long past? This is all history now— or is it?

However, I'm finally learning to fight with David. When he started telling me how he'd had to get his mother in shape when he moved her in with us so we'd all be able to live together, I hit the ceiling. I said I had a very different relationship with my parents than he had with his, and I was proud of it. They would never put themselves in a position where they were dependent on me for anything—and so they didn't have to put up with my opinions about how they should behave. Frankly, our marriage wouldn't survive if he insisted on treating my parents the way he treats his mother.

He seemed stunned by this accusation. He honestly thinks he's a wonderful son—and I suppose he is, considering his rotten childhood. He's often told me that his first memory was lying in his crib with his mother on one side and his father on the other, screaming insults at each other. No wonder he grew up feeling he didn't owe either of them a damn thing. And I suppose he's earned the right to reprimand his mother whenever he feels it's necessary. But my parents did everything they were supposed to do for me. My childhood was safe, sheltered, secure . . .

So what if they never told her they loved her? From a material point of view they provided generously—but I was the first person who ever made her feel beautiful and talented and capable of things she'd never dared. The irony, of course, is that everything they left unsaid created a need to be loved so desperate it kept her with me through everything—all the anger, all the abuse. I exploited her need, I admit it. If they had loved her as I've loved my daughters, she would never have stuck it out with me. Dearest Julia, sometimes I think I've loved you so much you'll never be able to live with a man—or at least one who's worthy of you—but I can't say I'm sorry.

Sometimes I think David feels he's in competition with my parents for possession of my mind. But that's ridiculous. He's the only one who ever wanted to possess me—they've always prided themselves on their ability to let go.

□

STRIKE TWO! After a long day of sightseeing, we stopped for dinner at a show business watering hole we thought my parents might enjoy. We were all getting along fine till the waiter, who spent the whole time he was taking our order auditioning with his jokes, showed up without David's hamburger. David quickly said he and I would share, then when the waiter left the table, muttered that he was taking the missing hamburger out of his tip. Daddy immediately announced dinner was on him. While David went to get the car, Daddy paid—and couldn't resist telling Julia what a generous tip he was leaving, but warning her not to tell her father. Which, of course, Julia couldn't wait to do as soon as her grandparents had gone to bed. And of course David took it as a personal affront. "Don't you find it significant that your father overtips a waiter who fails to bring me my food?"

By this time I knew better than to try to make a case for the defense. I told David I was taking my parents out for breakfast alone tomorrow—and confronting them with the error of their ways. He loved the idea—and promised to keep his distance until they were ready to apologize.

If this were fiction, I would say she was making a fool out of me. Unfortunately, embarrassing as it is to admit, it all happened just as she has recorded it. It would be civilized if I could look back now, eleven years later, and wonder how I could've been so petty about an addle-brained waiter forgetting a hamburger, but I still get just as angry today thinking of my father-in-law rewarding him while I went home hungry.

☐

MY PARENTS SEEMED DELIGHTED at the chance to have breakfast alone with me—and immediately began telling me what a wonderful trip they were having—and how much they appreciated our efforts to show them a good time. They were so full of praise for David, I couldn't bear to tell the truth about his feelings for them. It would ruin everything—just as they were finally growing to like him.

Then Daddy told me regretfully that they were going to have to cut their trip short—and return to Dallas tomorrow. A case was coming to trial sooner than he'd expected. I did my best to sound disappointed but inside I was flooded with relief—and determined to make our last day together count.

That bitch! She came home and told me her parents were leaving because they felt so badly about the things they'd done to upset me—and they could see they were putting our marriage at risk. Then I felt terrible and wanted to apologize and beg them to stay but Joanna said they couldn't discuss it and had made her promise to stick to their cover story of the court case going to trial early. To think how guilty I've felt all these years! I never knew Joanna had such a gift for getting even.

Suddenly over breakfast Daddy apologized for overtipping the waiter yesterday and said he hoped David didn't take it personally. It seems Mother really gave it to him when they were alone for being such a show-off big-time spender.

Did she really? I like her better than I thought.

But then Daddy began to talk about how he used to wait tables when he was working his way through college—

and though that was close to fifty years ago, his sympathy is still with the waiter, even when he gets flustered and forgets an order.

As we lingered at the breakfast table, he began to laugh about how he had turned down a job for two hundred dollars a month when he graduated from high school and asked his father to lend him the money to go to college. His father was a farmer who didn't have much use for education, but he finally agreed. When Daddy got out of college, he still didn't feel he had the tools to embark on a profession and asked his father for another loan so he could go to law school. His father was even more dubious about this move, reminding his son of the two-hundred-dollar-a-month job he had been offered with only a high school diploma. But Daddy was determined, and graduated from Yale Law School in the middle of the Depression—only to discover there were no jobs to be had at any price. He was still in debt to his father at his death—but continued to repay the loan to his brothers and sisters as their inheritance.

"I just wish my father could've lived to see me in *Who's Who in America*," he laughed. I was stunned. This was the first I'd heard of the honor. I asked when it had happened. Daddy confessed shyly that he'd received a form one day in the mail not long ago and had just gotten around to sending it in.

> *I have to give her credit for not telling me any of this. I always thought being in* Who's Who in America *required a certain amount of risk taking in one's chosen profession—doing something no one had ever done before. I assumed it was an honor much more likely to be awarded a playwright, for example, than a lawyer.*

☐

DAVID WAS ON HIS BEST BEHAVIOR when we put my parents on the plane yesterday. I let him think he was the reason they ended their visit, so he was full of remorse—mixed with relief—as we told them good-bye.

"They'd rather run for cover than try to have an honest relationship—is that it?" he demanded when I told him of their change in plans.

As I watched their plane taxiing down the runway, I began to wonder if he was right. Could the court case have just been an excuse to avoid the confrontation Daddy must have sensed was inevitable if they stayed another day?

I couldn't sleep last night thinking about them. I could feel in my bones the truth of what had happened. My father had just stepped out of my life in favor of my husband.

When David heard me crying into my pillow, he took me in his arms and began to comfort me. But I couldn't bring myself to tell him that I wanted my father *and* my husband in my life. Instead I heard myself apologizing for what I'd put him through by asking my parents to visit and promising I would never do it again. I said I was crying because I loved him so much and yet I knew I continued to hurt him. As he kissed me, he said how proud he was of me for finally standing up to my parents. He was sorry they got their feelings hurt and fled home—but if they were that afraid of an honest relationship, it was their loss. We had tried our best to be open with them—or at least I had.

I continued to sob—I doubt if I'll cry any harder on the day my father dies—but also, traitor that I am, I continued to let David kiss me, and by the time he had pulled my nightgown over my head, my parents were no longer in my thoughts—or on my conscience.

What can I possibly say in my own defense? You were there, Julia, you saw everything. Even at the age of six, you saw what was happening between the polite exchanges. Tell me you'd be happier with the relationship Joanna has with her parents, then I'll apologize for what I put your mother through. Otherwise, I'll let the evidence, as distorted as it is in this account, speak for me.

☐

TODAY WE GOT A FORMAL ANNOUNCEMENT from Willa celebrating the birth of her son—Timothy Mark. There was no mention of the father. Is it Paul? He spent last year making a movie on location in New York and seeing a lot of

Willa, according to the columnists. We haven't heard from him since the night Jessica was born. If the new movie is a hit, it may be years before we see him again. But if it's a flop, we can count on a call inviting us to dinner.

Thinking about Willa raising a child alone made me appreciate what a difference having a father has made in my life. I sometimes forget how much I owe him when David is around. Last summer in Dallas, when the children and I were alone with him after his heart attack, I felt I really got to know him for the first time. I doubt if I'll ever have a chance to talk to him like that again. But at least we can write. I want to get down as much of his life as I can remember on paper while he's still alive to answer my questions.

□

I SAT DOWN at my kitchen table to write this morning as I have every morning this week as soon as the girls are at school and David at the studio. I've been telling myself I was just writing the story of my father's life—a family history to give the girls when they're older—but today I suddenly began inventing incidents that never happened (at least to my knowledge) to make the story more interesting.

I was still writing when David came home. Seeing no evidence of dinner, he asked what time we were eating. I said I'd gotten so involved with what I was writing, I'd forgotten about dinner.

"What exactly *are* you writing?" he asked.

To my amazement I heard myself reply, "I think I'm writing a novel." I could see that, in spite of all his challenges to do something unique with my life, he was stunned.

"How can you write a novel when you've never even sold a short story?" he demanded.

I said he was the one who was always quoting J. D. Salinger's advice to aspiring writers, to "write what you want to read." I like to read novels, so that was what I was trying to write.

Then David asked if he could read what I'd written. I said no, I was just beginning. I wasn't strong enough for criticism. When

225

I'd finished the book to my satisfaction, I'd be ready for an outside opinion.

"An *outside* opinion?" I could see he was hurt. "I'm your husband, for God's sake. When I'm working on a play, I can't fall asleep till I read you what I've written that day."

I said I couldn't work like that. Besides, a play has to deliver for its audience line by line. A novel can start more slowly—its effect is much more cumulative.

"Sounds like you're in trouble already," David said. Then he demanded to see the opening pages so he would at least know if I was on the right track. He said he couldn't stand back for a year while I wrote a first draft, *then* tell me where I'd gone wrong.

I quickly gathered up my pages and said we'd talk about the book some more after dinner.

David put his arms around me and said now that I was finally taking myself seriously as a writer, I shouldn't have to think about dinner. We'd order in pizza. Julia and Jessica were thrilled. It's the first time they've been the least bit impressed by what I'm doing. But if writing a novel means dining on pizza, they're all for it.

☐

I DON'T KNOW how much longer I can keep what I'm doing from David. Once he finds out I'm writing about my father, I'm finished. I'm careful now to put my work away before he gets home. I wrap my pages in tinfoil and hide them in the freezer behind the frozen vegetables—the only place in the house I know he'll never look. It's also the closest thing we have to a fireproof vault. I write in longhand, so there's only one copy. If anything were to happen to these pages, the book would be over before it began.

Last night after we made love, David began to coax me to tell him about the book. I said it was very personal—too personal to discuss. He said in that case I was probably on the right track. But I suspect he searched for my pages after I fell asleep. When I woke up this morning, the papers in my desk were all out of order.

□

THE JIG'S UP. Last night I was in the tub shampooing my hair when David suddenly burst into the bathroom holding my pages. Without saying a word, he walked over to the tub and dropped them into my bath water. So I wouldn't be tempted to look at them again, he explained, assuring me there was not one usable thought or phrase to be salvaged. What I had written about my father was sentimental and obvious. "You make the same mistake writing about your father that you do talking to him. You're terrified of conflict. But that's what drama is—conflict, tension."

"I'll show you conflict," I shouted, picking up my soggy pages and hurling them at him. Then I exploded—and said I'd start being more honest about my father when he took a hard look at his feelings for Eula Lee. His autobiographical play put all the blame for his parents' unhappy marriage on his father's infidelities. But how dare a woman marry a man she didn't love just to get away from a domineering mother—and then subject her son to all the abuse engendered by a loveless marriage? Why had he never been able to admit how much he resented what he'd been put through?

David just stared at me without a word, then disappeared into our bedroom. As soon as he'd gone, Jessica came in fearfully to ask if we were getting a divorce. Close behind came Julia. "I told her Daddy was just helping you with your book," she explained, displaying all her seven-year-old wisdom, "but she wouldn't believe me."

"Your book is all wet, Mommy," Jessica said in a shaky voice, picking up a dripping page.

"I know," I replied, climbing out of the tub. "Have you ever heard the expression 'soggy prose'? Well, apparently, that's what I write."

As I dried my hair, I wondered what it would be like to be one of those wives who never know what their husbands are thinking. I cannot imagine. David can't stop himself from telling the truth, no matter how much it hurts.

I can remember my grandmother sitting on her porch in East Texas one hot summer afternoon with three ladies from the neighborhood. One had her right hand wrapped in a bandage. She'd caught her thumb in the wringer of her washing machine and crushed it so badly it had to be amputated. The other ladies were comforting her, assuring her that she'd never know it was gone. But not my grandmother. She smiled and said, "Mrs. Bass, you're gonna miss that thumb every day of your life. Every day of your life."

When I finally got the children to sleep and screwed up my courage to confront David, I found him in the bedroom writing furiously in the steno pad he keeps by his bed in case a good idea comes to him in his dreams. I tried to apologize for what I'd said about his mother but he said he couldn't talk yet. I'd just given him a great idea for a new play.

When he finally turned out the light, he wrapped his arms around me and apologized for being so rough on my writing. He said he was just doing for me what he wanted me to do for him. Look how he was responding to my challenge about his mother. It hit home and he'd already started a new play. Now what was I going to do about my book?

"Abandon it," I would've said if I'd been honest, but the last thing I wanted to hear was what a compliment he was paying me by taking me seriously enough to criticize me. So I remained silent while he assured me that if he didn't believe in my talent, he wouldn't be wasting his time on me—as a writer, that is. Of course, he assured me with a kiss, my position as a wife was secure.

Is it? I wonder. Sometimes I think being married to "just a wife" is no longer enough for David any more than being one is for me. But I'm terrified that I don't have the skill to be anything else—and I'm too old to learn.

I keep thinking of a friend of ours who just walked out on her husband. She had a featured part in a Broadway musical when they met. He was dazzled by her talent and the whole backstage ambience of their courtship. But his writing career took him to the West Coast shortly after they were married. There were no musical comedies in Hollywood where her talent could shine, and her features were too off-center for the camera. Her only job offers were touring companies of musicals, and she didn't want to leave her husband alone for months at a time. He tried to make it up to her by getting her small parts in his television shows, but the other actors resented the favoritism, and when she wasn't singing and dancing, there was nothing to distinguish her from any other actress. He began to berate her because she was no longer the girl he married. How could she be? Marriage had denied her the chance to do what she did best. When she left her husband, she said she was afraid it was already too late to become the person she started out to be, but at least she would die trying.

Why am I identifying with her? I hardly had a full-fledged career as a journalist going when I met David, and yet I knew I was good at it—and getting better. I don't have any sense of my skill as a novelist, and I can't shake the suspicion that David only pushes me to write fiction because it keeps me conveniently at home. And yet, if he were just indulging me, wouldn't he have praised my pages instead of drowning them?

Damn right! I only did for Joanna what I waited all our marriage for her to do for me. At least half my plays should've been drowned at birth, but she just nodded politely when I read them to her and said they were wonderful. What would I have done if she'd dropped even a page of my dialogue in the bathtub? Maybe she knew better than to put me to the test. But at least she knew how I felt about her writing—that she was capable of the very best. But what did she honestly think of mine—after all these years and so many failures? Did I really want to know? Do I even now? But nothing to fear, she'll never tell, not even herself.

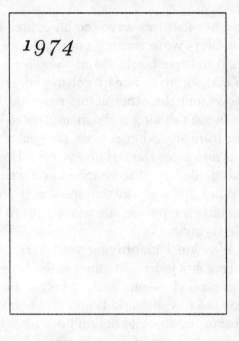

1974

OUR FOURTEENTH wedding anniversary. David is taking me to the Bel-Air Hotel for dinner. I wanted to have a big party to celebrate but when I showed him the guest list, he said why bother with all those people—there was nothing special about the fourteenth anniversary.

Isn't the fact that we're happy and together worth celebrating? I have nothing else to show for the past year—not even journal entries. I feel too guilty writing here when I'm not writing anywhere else.

Why don't I feel I've accomplished enough at the end of the day knowing I've gotten through it without hurting anyone? I've done everything I'm expected to do for my family. We're safe and together. I spend hours each day with Julia and Jessica, playing games, reading books, making clay figures and collages —and trying to feel fulfilled as an artist sitting on the floor cutting shapes out of colored paper.

The more I think about my father, the more determined I am to write about him—without being sentimental. For him just living his life is an accomplishment. He's important in his own city but unknown elsewhere. He's not rich or famous or powerful—but he's lived his own best life. That's all I want to do.

I remember a sermon I heard when I was an impressionable adolescent (are we ever more devoutly religious than we are at thirteen?). The minister told the story of the two bricklayers. When the first one was asked what he was doing, he replied, "I'm laying bricks." But when the same question was put to the second bricklayer, his answer was "I'm building a cathedral."

I'm right there with the first bricklayer—washing dishes, paying bills, listening to grievances from school and studio. I just can't see any cathedral taking shape.

My father does. He looks back on his life with the pride of an artisan who has built something that will last. He took crude, unpromising material and gave it a shape. If I can just find a way to write about his life, maybe I'll feel better about my own.

But where is the conflict David says is essential? My father has made a career out of settling conflicts, resolving differences, negotiating compromises. David, on the other hand, spends his time bringing hidden conflicts into the open, creating tension, heightening differences to make drama. I have my father's temperament, so what am I doing trying to get into my husband's line of work?

Wait a minute! Maybe the conflict I've been searching for is inside me. What if I wrote the book from my point of view? I'm split apart by the two men in my life—my father and my husband. God knows I won't have to make up anything. The conflict exists—I just haven't had the courage to confront it. I wonder if David will keep pushing me to be honest once I start being honest about him?

I'd planted the seeds of my own undoing. Can I honestly say I regret what happened? No. At least not yet.

☐

COLUMBUS DAY—a holiday I've never noted before, but this year I feel I'm on the verge of discovering a new world as a writer.

How long has it been since I opened this journal? I seem to spend all my time and energy trying to breathe life into my novel. The details of my own life hardly seem worth recording.

I have a hard time trusting this new career because it's so

convenient for everyone. I can satisfy all my ambitions and still take care of the children, do the laundry, and have dinner waiting when David comes home at night. Most married women have to make such sacrifices to have a career. What's the catch here?

David hasn't asked to see what I'm writing, and I haven't offered to show him anything. I think he knows better. It took me months to get started again after the bathtub incident. It's hard enough to be honest with myself as I write. I just can't take David's being honest with me on top of that. At least not yet. I think back to the early days of our marriage when David kept seeking out Elaine for her opinion. He's always been so unsparing with his own work, he finds it impossible to hold back with someone else's. Whereas I find it almost impossible to criticize his writing, not because I'm afraid of hurting his feelings, at least not anymore, but because I don't feel I have the right to impose my opinions on someone else's work.

> *By this point in my career I was grateful for Joanna's reluctance to give me an honest reaction to my work. I was having a hard enough time living with my own reaction to it. Was that why I was being so hard on her writing? I'd put away my play until my contract expired—and was spending my time grinding out episodes for a television show I preferred not to discuss. But it paid the bills.*

☐

THERE WAS A BIG CHRISTMAS PARTY at Universal tonight. I was introduced to everyone as David's wife, including his producer, whom I've met on at least three previous occasions. But I didn't remind him. He shook hands cordially, asked me to repeat my first name as if he actually had some intention of learning it, then asked me what I did. Always before, I've let this question put me on the defensive. In the beginning I used to go into my adoring wife routine and say being married to David was a career in itself. Once I had children, I would add motherhood to my accomplishments—at the risk of losing the attention of the audience. But tonight, for the first time, I just said simply that I was a novelist. What a difference one word can make! He looked at me as if he were seeing me for the first time. In fact, he was. Before he could ask what I'd published, another producer joined us, and to my amazement I heard myself being introduced as "Joanna Scott, the novelist." No mention of David.

I can't wait to get back to the book. Why do I feel for the first time that I know what I'm doing when I pick up my pencil? Is it simply that "you are who you say you are"?

In a city of pretenders like Hollywood? You bet. I didn't know what had happened to Joanna that night. She came home sparkling like a Christmas tree. I assumed someone had made a pass at her.

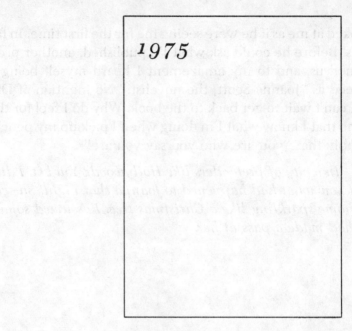

1975

DAVID is a free man again. Now he can finish his play. His contract with Universal expired at the end of December. They wanted to renew it but he said no. We have a little money in the bank, so he's going to concentrate his energies on the theater.

In my career I've been like a man pursuing a mistress who keeps rejecting him. The theater is the only mistress I've ever wanted—it has teased and tormented me more than any woman ever could. Or so I thought until I began reading these journals. Joanna and the theater—how much can one man be expected to take?

□

DAVID has almost finished the first act of his play about his mother. He is fearless about facing his complicated feelings for her. Why can't I capture—at least on paper—my struggle to free myself from the influence of the two men in my life? Perhaps because I lack the courage to invent the confrontations I have spent my life avoiding. Whenever I try to imagine the angry words that would come out of an argument, I see Daddy or

David reading the book over my shoulder, asking what gives me the right to malign them like that. I don't have an answer, so the bold confrontation I know I have to write shrivels to a polite quarrel.

Thank goodness being a wife and mother provides me with another acceptable career, so I don't feel guilty on the days when I don't get any writing done. When I started this novel, David suggested hiring a housekeeper so I'd be free to write full-time. The idea terrified me. If he were actually paying someone to take my place around the house, then the pressure would be on me to produce something that would earn more money than he was spending. I said no thank you, and I've never been sorry. I suspect David was relieved. He'd made a gesture to appease the guilt he feels when he sees me wielding a mop or broom. Now his conscience is clear, but our overhead remains low.

Pow! Right in the kisser!

Usually, I find housework a welcome change of pace from the mental agony of trying to furnish a fictional world, and I can do it at my convenience. What I do resent, however, is the daily obligation to feed a family—not the actual work of preparing meals but the time I spend *thinking* about food, planning menus, making grocery lists, deciding each morning what to defrost for dinner. Sustaining life would be such a simple matter if I lived alone—a bowl of cereal when I woke up, a bowl of soup before I went to bed. I'd be thinner and healthier.

> *My real competition with Joanna was never another man —at least as far as I know—but this romantic image she carried of the monastic life. I actually heard her tell someone once that she was perfectly capable of living alone in a single room, preparing her meals on a hot plate. I found this fantasy more threatening than some Candlelight Romance dream of a dark, handsome stranger who would sweep her onto the back of his horse and gallop away.*

Would I find it easier to write if I could live more like a real writer? While I was emptying wastebaskets and making beds this morning, I remembered an interview I read recently with a successful male novelist describing his day. He takes a long walk every morning to "sift his thoughts," writes till lunchtime, naps, devotes the afternoon to correspondence, and spends the evening reading or being with friends. He never has to clutter his mind with thoughts of what to have for dinner or when the children are due for a dental checkup. And yet without these chores to root me in reality, what would I have to write about?

However, I worry that the relative domestic content in which I take such comfort isolates me emotionally from the world around me. It has been years since I walked through a city alone, open and vulnerable to the feelings of people I passed on the street, imagining what I could not know. Now I experience the world from my kitchen table, with electric appliances humming in accompaniment. Is it necessary for a writer to be always emotionally at risk?

☐

LAST NIGHT I dreamed David died—I was so relieved to wake up and find him still sleeping peacefully.

I've never slept peacefully and she knows it.

I'm so worried about what I'm doing to him and to our marriage by bringing him into this book. Every day I find myself saying things as I write that I would never say to his face. He seems to be taking over the book just the way he took over my life.

Nature abhors a vacuum.

☐

WRITING A NOVEL is like blind men trying to describe an elephant—it appears entirely different from every angle. Will I ever finish? Why did I have to begin with something so long and unwieldy? I could have a collection of short stories by now—or several unproduced screenplays in circulation, like everyone else in Hollywood.

☐

TODAY I FINISHED THE FIRST DRAFT. I don't want to show it to David—or anyone—yet. Just knowing I have eight hundred and fifty-four handwritten pages (enough for a novel even if they're not good enough) gives me a gigantic feeling of satisfaction. I feel like Clark Kent—still the same innocuous wife on the outside but now with a secret that may just possibly transform me.

Clark Kent? I just saw a woman who was no longer shy about wanting sex. At the time I took it as a compliment.

☐

I'VE SPENT THE LAST TWO WEEKS immersed in holiday cooking, decorating, and gift buying. In the past I've sometimes resented all the work Christmas requires, but with my novel completed, I've thrown my whole heart into the holidays.

I bought rolls of white paper for the children to color, so this year all the packages under our tree are wrapped in hand-painted paper. Every night after dinner Julia and Jessica join me in the kitchen and we make popcorn balls or iced sugar cookies or divinity from a recipe contributed by Eula Lee. Jessica calls it "Nanny's infinity."

Tonight we decorated the tree. David always insists on supervising, which used to annoy me when we were first married (except for setting up the tree in its stand and stringing the electric lights, my father left Christmas to my mother). But now I've come to depend on him. He's decided we should clear all the bookshelves and table tops in the living room and decorate them in the spirit of the season too. And tomorrow he's outlining the roof in colored lights. Christmas has become a cottage industry at our house.

The explanation was simple: except for a couple of movie rewrites, I had been unemployed since I left Universal. I was out of work—and stuck on the second act of my new play. Joanna wasn't the only one making a career out of Christmas that year.

☐

CHRISTMAS DAY. For once we got to sleep late. Last night we had a Christmas Eve party for our extended family. Eula Lee and Marvin are just back from a three-month cruise to the Orient. Eula Lee used to refuse to travel because she hated packing and unpacking—but once she discovered cruises, she and Marvin spend more time on the open seas than they do at home.

Wyatt and Susan came with her two children and armloads of presents for everyone. Julia immediately led Toby off to play. Now that she attends our neighborhood school, she misses seeing him every day and welcomes any chance to be with him. They can amuse themselves for hours just talking. Jessica becomes frustrated trying to force them to include her in their friendship, but consoles herself by ordering Lucy around. She finds it very satisfying to give orders to someone older than her older sister.

At Jessica's suggestion the children improvised a Christmas pageant (parroting the lines from her nursery school play in which she portrayed an angel—only this time she cast herself as the Virgin Mary). When the pageant concluded with the children singing "Away in a Manger," Wyatt brought out a bottle of champagne and announced that he and Susan are expecting a child in June—and she has finally agreed to marry him. They haven't set a date, but it will be sometime this spring. I'm so happy for both of them.

We had invited Marvin and Eula Lee to spend the night so they could watch Julia and Jessica at the tree in the morning. They were about to retire to her old bedroom when the children began begging to open their presents. That suddenly seemed like a terrific idea. Too much champagne had been consumed for anyone to drive, and the thought of being able to sleep late this morning was irresistible to David and me.

We started by letting the four children open the gifts they were exchanging, but soon the adults got in on the action, and we didn't stop until the tree had been stripped of presents.

Susan and Wyatt cooked breakfast for everybody, then Julia and Jessica begged to have Toby and Lucy spend what was left of the night. Jessica said we could pull out her trundle bed for

Lucy, and Julia insisted Toby take her top bunk bed so they could fall asleep talking. I wonder if they'll have as much to say to each other when they're grown as they do now at the age of nine.

1976

DAWN. David is finally asleep, but I'm afraid of what I'll dream if I close my eyes.

I was awakened in the middle of the night by ungodly noises coming from the bathroom. When I opened the door to see what was wrong, I found David kneeling on the floor, vomiting into the toilet. I held a wet washcloth against his forehead, then helped him back into bed. If I didn't know better, I would've sworn he was pregnant.

As he lay weakly back on his pillow, he gasped, "What was that dish you fixed for dinner?"

I mumbled evasively that it was an Indian recipe—from the international cookbook he gave me for Christmas, I added hurriedly, hoping to placate him.

"Indian as in India? God, I must have been suicidal to give you an *international* cookbook," he moaned, motioning weakly for me to plug in the hot pad. "You know I can't stand curry in anything!"

I apologized—and promised to stay away from the Asian chapters in the future.

But this wasn't what David wanted to hear. "Why do you have to get so creative in the kitchen?" he stormed. "You should be spending that time and energy on your novel. For the sake of my stomach, if nothing else."

So then I had to confess that I'd finished the novel—at least the first draft. "Why haven't you shown it to me?" he demanded, as if I was betraying a wedding vow by not sharing immediately every thought I committed to paper. I muttered something about a cooling-off period so I could be more objective when I went back to it.

"You'll never be objective about your own work," he was quick to assure me. "You need me for that. Now go get me your pages. I'm too sick to go back to sleep."

My knees were trembling as I returned to the bedroom with my pile of handwritten pages. Handing them to David, I felt a wave of nausea sweep over me. I hurried into the bathroom and bolted the door. Then I lay flat on the floor wishing I could disappear—or at least blame the way I was feeling on what I'd eaten for dinner.

I fell asleep on the rug—only to be awakened by David banging on the door. I opened it in a daze and barely got out of his way before he was sick again. While he was in the bathroom, I looked at the pile of pages stacked at his side of the bed to see how far he'd gotten. All the pages had been overturned. He knew everything. Where could I hide? I was in bed with the covers around my ears when he came out of the bathroom. "If I should die before I wake," he muttered, ignoring my attempt to appear asleep, "I want you to know that somewhere in those pages you've got yourself a novel."

I jumped out of bed and threw my arms around him. "I was so afraid it was what I'd written that made you sick the second time." I was crying with happiness—and relief.

"It was," he groaned, turning the hot pad to "high" and pressing it against his stomach. "Your creative efforts are killing me."

"You said I didn't have any conflict in the novel I was writing about my father," I reminded him. "So I decided to bring you into it."

"But did you have to change the title from *Keeping the Faith* to *Disturbing the Peace?*"

"I'm just trying to be honest about the effect you've had on me."

He laughed and admitted the title was accurate—then he said I hadn't gone nearly far enough. I was still holding back. Why didn't I have the courage to face what the book was really about? A woman who has accepted the world on her father's terms until she meets a man who seduces her, not with sex but with a dream. When the dream eludes them, what keeps them together? She has to start over—alone.

"That's not the book I want to write," I protested.

"So what? This isn't the life I wanted to live. You have to use what you've been given. As a writer, that's all you've got." Then to my surprise he reached over and pulled me to him. He said he was proud of me for not abandoning the book after he dumped my first set of pages in the bathtub. "I knew you had talent," he said, "from that first letter you wrote me at Yale. But if you're going to make it as a writer, talent comes second—after staying power. I never believed you'd stick with it. Now keep proving me wrong."

He kissed me for a long time and I thought we were going to make love, but then he said he had a lot of ideas and I should get them on paper before he forgot them. So I pulled down my nightgown and took out a pencil and pad.

Now he's asleep and I'm in despair. If I do what he says and make this into the story of a woman who marries a failure, how can our marriage survive? On the other hand, if I resist a tough ending, he'll be furious. How did I get myself into such a no-win situation?

Reading those pages was like coming face to face with myself naked. First there was a horrifying shock of recognition, then gratitude that Joanna could see me so clearly and still be willing to share my bed, not to mention my life. In a funny way I felt more secure about my marriage that night than I had before—or have since.

I remember being stunned, reading what she'd written, to realize how deeply Joanna felt about how many things. I had always assumed my tortured childhood entitled me to a special vision. But here was my wife, the product of a comfortable, middle-class childhood, revealing on paper passions and perceptions of which she had shown no evi-

dence in fifteen years of marriage. Those pages were a double whammy—to realize that she could see right through me while I had no idea who she was.

☐

I WAS FIXING BREAKFAST for the girls this morning, trying not to think about last night, when David suddenly appeared in his bathrobe and asked to speak to me privately.

Following him into the bedroom, I braced myself for what I knew was coming. He was going to tell me he couldn't live through the novel he was forcing me to write and wanted a divorce. I was wondering how we were going to tell the children when he suddenly pulled out his steno pad. "I woke up with a dozen ideas for your book," he said. "Now, sit down and let's go over them while they're still fresh in my mind."

I stared at him in amazement—and asked how he could separate himself so completely from his character in the book. He reminded me that I'm writing a novel, not a biography. Starting today, I have to forget that the characters are based on real people. What really happened is unimportant. Fiction has its own logic. "You have to face the truth first," he said, "but finally, you must free yourself from the facts and create a lie that tells a larger truth."

When he finished going over his notes, I thanked him for his help and said I felt guilty taking time away from his own work. "Don't be a fool," he said. "I don't know where I'm going with my play. I don't know how to end it. As much time as I've spent with my mother, she remains a mystery. I can't get anywhere near the truth of that marriage and until I know the truth, I can't do what I've been telling you to do—move beyond it."

I realize now David has done for me something Eula Lee will never do for him—and that is, open her life to him. Why is she so ungenerous? It seems to me people who really love each other should be willing to share their experiences as freely as they share their worldly goods. Parents always pretend they want a better life for their children, yet they would rather die than admit their mistakes openly. How can you learn anything from people who want to go to their graves maintaining the illusion

243

they always knew—and did—the right thing? My parents are as guilty of this as Eula Lee. Whatever mistakes David and I make with our children, at least we allow them to see we're human. But I hope they also see how much we love each other. Never more than today.

From that moment on she thought she was writing a love story. She even had me convinced—until yesterday.

□

I'M STILL NOT SURE what happened last night. David was in a rotten mood trying to end his play, which he's calling *The Mother Lode.* Marvin and Eula Lee were spending the night with the children while we went to a party Paul Gaines was giving at Chasen's to celebrate the success of his current film and to welcome Willa Crane back to Hollywood. She's making her first film in ten years and staying at the Chateau Marmont with Molly and her three-year-old son Tim.

Paul suspects he is Tim's father but Willa refuses to confirm or deny it. Not that Paul wants to get married or assume any of the responsibilities that go with being a parent, but his ego rebels at the thought of having a son who will never know who his father is. Paul has gone through life breaking hearts with abandon— Willa is the first woman who has ever had the upper hand with him.

I was looking forward to the party, but David said we weren't leaving the house until he finished his play. It got later and later. Finally I announced I was going without him—he could join me later. He threw his papers in the air in a fury, saying if I had no respect for his work, why should he? However, I knew it was the play that was making him crazy.

Marvin was asleep when we got home from Chasen's, but Eula Lee was watching the *Tonight* show on the little television set in the kitchen. I told her good-night and went to check on the children. Suddenly I heard David shouting, "You made me live through it, damn it. I've got a right to hear your reasons."

The next thing I knew he had stormed into the bedroom, and Eula Lee had awakened Marvin. Ordering him to get dressed, she announced they were driving back to Santa Monica tonight.

She begged me tearfully to tell the children good-bye and said if they wanted to talk to her, they would have to telephone. She wouldn't be coming to our house again. Marvin just shrugged helplessly and followed her out the door.

Mercifully the children slept through her exit, so there was nothing for me to do but go to bed. David was writing furiously when I entered the bedroom. He held up his hand for silence, then said with great excitement, "I've finally found a framework for the whole play—and it gives me just the ending I need."

What price art? Kindness, courtesy, consideration. But at that price it better turn out to be art. Too frequently in my case, I fear, temperament exceeded talent.

☐

EULA LEE CALLED to tell the girls good-bye. She and Marvin are leaving on a cruise through the Panama Canal. Fortunately, she did not ask to speak to David, so I was spared having to lie and say he was out. He doesn't want to risk talking to her again until he has a first draft.

I remember reading his first play at Yale and being shocked at how much his characters fought. When I read Eugene O'Neill, I found his family portraits even more depressing. Why is it so hard for me to acknowledge how many honest differences separate even people who love each other?

☐

DAVID HAS DECIDED he wants to hear *The Mother Lode* read aloud in front of a few friends. It has always been his contention that a play is meant for the ear, not the eye. He can't decide who to cast in the role of the mother. "The problem is, I've written another role for Willa Crane, God help me," he said.

Much as I hate to admit it, I can't see anyone else in the part either, so I suggested he send her the script. She finishes filming next week—and is never more dedicated to the theater than when she's just made a lot of money in a movie.

☐

DAVID is the man I married again. With a new play under his belt, all systems are go. He is so full of energy and ideas. I get a charge just being around him, listening to him make plans. At times like this, being David's wife is my one and only raison d'être—especially since I'm getting nowhere with my novel. I just pray that *The Mother Lode*, which he and I both feel is his best play, will take him everywhere he wants to go. And all I ask is that he take me with him.

Why did she have to keep doing that to me? Copping out on her own ambitions, placing the whole burden of our happiness on my career? Watch out, Julia—women deserve to be treated like second-class citizens as long as they keep settling for second best. And anything is second best when it's someone else's best instead of your own.

☐

THE READING WENT WONDERFULLY. I'm too excited to sleep. Paul and Willa came together, along with Molly and three-year-old Tim, who is adorable—he looks nothing like Willa and suspiciously like Paul. Susan and Wyatt brought Toby and Lucy to spend the night with Julia and Jessica.

Willa said she'd been waiting for this part all her life and would go anywhere to play it. In that case, Wyatt suggested, we should look for a small theater in Los Angeles and raise the money to put on a production ourselves. I think he was trying to tell David as kindly as possible that it is a mistake to sit around waiting for lightning to strike on Broadway. The only realistic way to work in the theater is to protect yourself as much as possible by setting your own terms. That thought appealed to all of us, so Wyatt and Susan invited us to their house tomorrow to continue the discussion. They're planning their wedding for Mother's Day—that way they can celebrate their prospective parenthood at the same time. Susan has asked me to be her matron of honor, and Wyatt wants David for his best man.

Willa wanted to talk, so Molly put Tim to bed in our guest room (formerly Eula Lee's bedroom—I wonder if she'll ever occupy it again? Or ever forgive David for writing this play?). Willa seems to love talking about Tim—especially around Paul.

She says she finds motherhood the most creative experience in her life. When she decided to have another child, she was determined to avoid the mistakes she made the first time and to approach motherhood with the same concentration she brings to an acting role, avoiding any entangling alliances.

Poor Molly! How must she feel about all this? From what I observe, she's the one experiencing motherhood. Willa talks about Tim, but Molly is the one who takes care of him. She graduated from high school last year and, at Willa's suggestion, is taking some time off before deciding what to do with her life —besides baby-sitting.

"People who see the three of us together always assume Tim belongs to Molly," Willa laughed. "I love watching their faces when I tell them he's mine. For some reason I just don't strike people as the motherly type."

Starting with her own daughter.

☐

SUSAN IS DEAD—and so is the child she was carrying. I am numb with shock. A drunk driver ran into their car last night as they were headed back to Pasadena from our house. Wyatt was driving, with Susan beside him. He received only a few bruises but she was thrown from the car and suffered fatal brain damage. The baby was removed by Caesarean section but did not survive.

I let the children play all morning—until Toby and Lucy asked when they had to go home. Then I took them in my arms and told them about Susan. Toby cried, but all Lucy understood was that they were staying with us another night. She thinks her mother is waiting for her at home.

Toby went into the backyard and climbed the avocado tree. When I called him to come in the house for lunch, he said he wasn't hungry. So I packed the sandwiches in a basket and told the girls they could have a picnic. They decided to make their camp under the branches of the avocado tree. When I looked out the window just now, Toby had climbed down and joined them. Sometimes I think children are better at comforting each other than adults are.

I wish there were something I could do for Wyatt. I tried to get him to come stay with us when he was discharged from the hospital but he said he just wanted to be alone in the house where he and Susan were so happy.

David told Wyatt he would contact Eula Lee and Marvin. He finally reached them when their ship docked in Puerto Rico. Eula Lee was very cold and distant until she heard what had happened. Then she broke into tears, beginning to apologize as if she were somehow to blame for the accident.

David asked if he should talk to Marvin, but Eula Lee said she would tell him. Suddenly all her thoughts were for him, and David said later she showed a strength and composure he had never seen before. From the time he came of age and convinced her to leave his father, he has thought of her as another dependent. Her marriage to Marvin has provided him with a temporary reprieve from responsibility, but today I think he felt for the first time since childhood that his mother could take care of herself and anyone she loved.

☐

I HATE WAKING UP to the shock of remembering that Susan is dead. My grandmother disappeared from my life by degrees, but until now I've never lost anyone close to me to such a sudden, violent death. I move through the day in slow motion, weighted down by grief.

Toby and Lucy are staying with us until tomorrow, when Brad arrives for the funeral. Wyatt wants Toby and Lucy to continue living with him in Pasadena. He says they are the only children he will ever have and he cannot imagine life without them. Unfortunately, however, he is not their legal father.

☐

FAMILY AND FRIENDS gathered today in the orchard, where Susan had planned to have her wedding, to celebrate her life—and try not to mourn the fact that it had come to such a tragic end at the age of thirty-nine.

Brad and his new wife, who's expecting her first child in the fall, asked Toby and Lucy to move to Chicago and live with them but seemed relieved when the children begged to stay in California. Wyatt immediately accepted Marvin and Eula Lee's offer to give up their apartment and move back to the Pasadena house so they can help with the children.

How unpredictable life is. Eula Lee saw her second marriage as an escape from responsibility—and for a time it was—but now she is in it again up to her neck. When you fall in love with someone—for whatever reasons—you make yourself doubly vulnerable to the accidents of fate. And yet what other choice is there except to live alone and refuse to care what happens to anyone else?

☐

OUR SIXTEENTH WEDDING ANNIVERSARY. We decided to celebrate quietly at home and include Wyatt, Toby, Lucy, Marvin, and Eula Lee. The idea of a man and woman celebrating their anniversary alone seems incongruous anyway. Look at all the unrelated people whose lives are now intertwined just because Wyatt and Susan fell in love.

I miss Susan so much. She was the first and only best friend marriage has allowed me. I always had a best friend in school, but they have receded now into that prehistoric past before I pledged my life to David. Marriage—or at least my marriage—cannot accommodate lesser allegiances.

Joanna missed Susan. I missed Wyatt and Susan to-gether. After her death I found it almost impossible to be around him. He didn't talk about her—it wasn't that—but to be with him without her made me think of what my life would be like if I lost Joanna, and that is something I cannot bear to contemplate, even now when I have no choice.

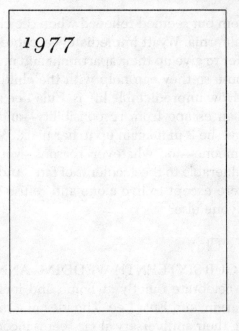

1977

WYATT IS LEASING a small theater in the Valley, which he's naming the Susan, as a showcase for new plays. He wants *The Mother Lode* to be the first production. He and Susan were talking about producing the play themselves as they were driving home the night of the accident. By going ahead with their plan, Wyatt feels he will be keeping part of her alive. He has become very successful designing sets for television in the past few years but misses the theater. Fortunately, television has provided him with the means to indulge his passion for the stage.

Wyatt took David to lunch today, then over to inspect the theater. David left Julia and Jessica in Pasadena with Toby and Lucy. We'll probably bring all four children home with us tomorrow so Marvin and Eula Lee can have a weekend to themselves. Marvin insisted on hiring a full-time housekeeper to cook and clean and help care for the children, but even so Eula Lee finds the responsibility of raising two children exhausting. And of course Lucy requires special attention at all times. Eula Lee keeps saying she doesn't understand how Susan managed to do so much—and to be so happy doing it.

Susan never seemed to experience the conflict between work and family that tears so many women apart. She wove all the elements of her life together as skillfully as if they were threads on her loom—Wyatt, her children, her school, painting, cooking, sewing all had their place. Always the artist, she designed her life to accommodate all her passions.

"It's possible to have it all," she said in one of our last conversations when she showed me the sketch for the wedding dress she was designing, "but not all at once. If one of the children is sick, I forget about doing any work of my own that day. Sometimes weeks go by with no time to paint, but that doesn't keep me from thinking about what I'm going to paint next. I feel rich just knowing I have a talent that encourages me to look at the world more closely than most people. Even on the days I don't put it to work, I take comfort in knowing it's there."

Why can't I feel that way about my writing? Maybe because David is beginning to treat me like a professional, and I'm not comfortable with it.

"Did you get any writing done today?" he asks every night at dinner. Usually I lie, my stomach in knots, and say, "A little." The truth is, my heart has not been in my writing since Susan died. I am too full of questions about my own life. But like Susan with her painting, I must learn to take comfort in the knowledge that my characters are there waiting for me when I'm ready to be with them again.

David can't understand why I'm not more excited about rewriting my book and submitting it to a publisher. But no success in the outside world can compare to the sense of accomplishment I felt when I finally finished my first draft and had a full-length manuscript I could hold in my hands.

I once asked Susan if I could take some of her paintings to a friend who owns an art gallery in the hope of arranging a show. "Why would I want a showing?" she asked in amazement. "My paintings aren't for sale, and I don't need a critic to tell me I've done good work—or bad. I'm the best judge of that."

When I told David what Susan had said, he shrugged. "What do you expect from an amateur?"

I was stung by his reply. An amateur. It seems like such a putdown. Yet the word is rooted in the Latin verb *amare*, "to love." Since when is money a nobler motive? At the turn of the century, when the Olympics were revived by English gentlemen, they insisted on amateur status for the contestants to keep the money-grubbing lower classes from competing and destroying the high moral purpose of the games. Yet today *professional* has come to mean "someone who takes his work seriously," while an amateur is considered a dilettante.

Why are men so quick to call women amateurs, intending it as a slap? Women are much more comfortable with the label— perhaps because we've never been paid for the work men pretend to honor, the work of making a home and raising children.

Sometimes I suspect men harbor a deep-seated resentment at having the role of family wage earner forced on them by society. With wives and children dependent on their support, earning money has to take precedence over enjoying the work. What irony that women are leading the revolution in the workplace, demanding equal pay and equal opportunity, when to my mind men are the more oppressed. Even the most militant women today are asking only for the right to choose whether to work or stay home with the children. How often does a man have that choice?

David may not realize it, but sometimes I think he must resent the fact that I write only when and what I want to write. Though he was always determined to be a writer—even when our finances were at low ebb and he was forced to take other work—he can only afford to speculate on a play between paying assignments. Whereas everything I write is on spec. It doesn't seem fair, and yet it was the unspoken bargain we struck when we married. I gave up any professional ambitions of my own to follow my husband wherever he traveled to seek our mutual fortune. It was marriage that made me into an amateur, and yet, like Susan, I consider it a privileged position.

Maybe, thinking of her, I'll be able to write tomorrow.

> *My favorite definition of the difference between an amateur and a professional is that a professional doesn't have to be in the mood.*
>
> *Reading this journal, I'm beginning to understand why it took Joanna so long to finish her book. The guiltier she*

felt about not writing, the longer and more complicated these entries become. She's damn near written a book explaining why she wasn't writing a book.

☐

I CAME AS CLOSE to leaving David yesterday as I did the Christmas before Jessica was born. He was spending the afternoon with Wyatt, helping him remodel the theater. Julia and Jessica were staying overnight in Pasadena, and I was supposed to be working on my novel.

Before I started writing, I looked in the refrigerator to decide what to cook for dinner. I knew my mind would not be clear to write until I'd planned the menu.

Excuses, excuses.

We were out of several essential items, so I made a list—then began to worry that David wouldn't be home in time to go to the store before dinner.

He treats grocery shopping as recreation once his writing for the day is finished. He says he can't afford for me to shop alone. He has a much better eye for bargains than I do and actually enjoys clipping coupons and comparing prices. It began when we had no money, but now seeing how much we can save has become a game to him. Sometimes we even go to more than one store to take advantage of all the bargains. I try to share his enthusiasm, but the truth is, I'm no more interested in saving money than I am in making it.

Why would she be? From the day she was born, everything was provided for her. But I grew up working for my father in his grocery store—every afternoon after school, every Saturday, every summer vacation, until I was eighteen. It gave me great pleasure, once I married, to stand on the other side of the counter as a customer, watching someone else sack my groceries.

I couldn't write, knowing how much I needed before I could fix dinner. So I drove to the store and soon began to enjoy being out on my own. I almost never get a chance to go shopping alone —even for clothes. During the day when the girls are in school and most of the wives I know are hitting the stores, I'm at home trying to write, waiting to fix lunch for David. We usually go shopping as a family at night or on the weekends. By the time we've finished buying things for the children or the house, I'm too exhausted to shop for myself—unless something happens to catch my eye as I'm riding an escalator.

The prospect of an afternoon to shop alone was so seductive I set out for Fashion Center, ignoring the groceries in the trunk of my car. Two hours and several hundred dollars later, I pulled into the driveway, eager to show David my new wardrobe. He's always taken great interest in how I dress—more than I have lately—and I thought he'd be pleased with my purchases. When he heard the car, he came outside to meet me, his face ashen.

"What's happened?" I cried. "Has there been an accident? Are the children all right?" He just stared at me in silence. "Why don't you answer me?" My heart was pounding.

"Those same questions flooded my mind when I came home and found you gone. But no one was here to answer me. I've been in hell for the past hour. I was ready to start calling hospitals."

"Why would you assume I'd been in an accident just because I wasn't here? Didn't it ever occur to you I might want to get out of the house for a while?"

"And do what?"

I decided not to mention the new clothes. "Well, I had to get some groceries before I could cook dinner."

"And you couldn't wait for me?"

"I thought you might be late."

"Then we could've gone out to eat. Why do you make yourself into such a galley slave? When you cook dinner, I feel obliged to eat it. Christ, it wouldn't hurt either one of us to miss a meal. How much weight have you put on since we married anyway? I bet you outweigh me by now. God, you've let yourself go. Do you know how unbecoming that dress is? Why don't you ever buy any new clothes? We can afford it. It reflects on me when you go around dressed like a bag lady."

I unloaded the groceries in silence. "Don't fix dinner for me tonight," David said as I was stocking the refrigerator. "I'm too upset to eat. I'm going to unplug my phone and work for a while."

I waited until he made his exit, slamming the door behind him, before going out to the car and bringing in my new clothes. I went into Julia's room and closed the door then stripped to the skin and stared at myself naked in her full-length mirror.

I am almost forty years old—halfway home—and what do I have to show for my life? Compared to Susan, I feel I've accomplished so little. She really lived every moment. Too often I feel I'm just marking time.

When I look at myself naked, however, I don't feel old—or fat. To me my body still looks innocent and inviting. I remember the first time I undressed in front of David. He kept saying he'd never seen anyone as beautiful as I was. At the time I thought he'd probably been with a lot of women, so I was wildly flattered. Later I realized I was the first woman he'd ever seen naked.

No one had ever told me I was beautiful before. My parents always praised me for being well-behaved and making the honors list in school, my friends liked the fact that I was a good sport and an attentive listener, but David made me feel like an exciting, seductive woman, and so I gladly surrendered my life to him. I was as much in love with his image of me as I was with him. Looking at myself through his eyes, I began to believe I was as beautiful as he said I was. I realize now his praise has always worked on me like a drug, artificially inducing an unreal state of euphoria. Deprived of it, I plunge into despair, losing all inner sense of who and what I am. Because I believed David long ago when he said I was beautiful, I have to believe him now when he says I'm fat. Or do I?

I try never to read reviews of my plays, though it's hard not to want to bask in them when they're good. But if you believe the good ones, then you have to believe the bad ones. Of course, like any critic, I had complete confidence in my own opinion, certainly when it came to Joanna. She was still beautiful but she was fat—especially dressed.

I tried on my new clothes and really like the way I look in them. I realize that subconsciously I've come to resent my total dependence on David—shopping at his convenience and only buying the clothes he approves. However, on the surface I remain compliant and eager to please, partly because I was raised to be a dutiful daughter and a submissive wife, partly out of my guilt at having had such a comfortable childhood, both emotionally and materially, while David's was an exercise in survival. I was determined to give him a happy marriage to make up for his unhappy childhood. And still am—though no longer at the expense of my own happiness.

I was raised to believe that privilege implies responsibility. "Unto whomsoever much is given, of him shall be much required" was the text for many a college sermon. If I'd been a child of the sixties instead of the complacent fifties, I would probably have committed myself to a political cause or joined the peace corps. I got married instead. A selfish choice perhaps, and yet I'm convinced that all the instincts that set countries at war and threaten the peace of the world are present in the relationship between two people struggling to share their lives. Until two individuals can learn to live under the same roof, neither attempting to dominate nor possess, what hope is there for the world?

How did we get from her weight problem to world peace?
No wonder I always left the room to avoid an argument.
Who could follow her reasoning?

How can I keep loving David without letting him overwhelm me? How can I be my own woman but continue to share his life? He sets all the terms for our relationship, and if I protest, I pay the price.

I crawled into Julia's bunk bed and fell asleep. Whenever life gets to be too much for me, I have a hard time keeping my eyes open. Sleeping is cheaper and safer than drinking. It keeps you from saying or doing things you'll regret later, and though you may have nightmares, you won't wake up with a hangover. I recommend it wholeheartedly.

In the middle of the night I felt David's arms around me. "Don't you know I can't sleep if you're not in bed with me?" he whispered.

256

"You're lucky I'm still in the same house with you," I muttered, turning away from him.

"This was supposed to be our weekend alone—without the children," he continued, stroking my back. "Remember?"

I can take anything but tenderness. The tears I had suppressed all night out of anger suddenly overflowed.

"I know I'm not rational about your taking the car and going places by yourself," he admitted. "But after what happened to Susan, I live in terror of losing you. Please try to understand."

"If you love me so much you can't imagine living without me, how can you say things you know will hurt me?" I had to know.

There was a long silence. David sat on the edge of the bed with his head in his hands. "To try to love you less—so if anything were to happen to you, I could go on." Then he began to sob. "But it's not working."

What a cheap line. But she bought it.

Enclosing him in my arms, I pulled him back into Julia's narrow bed. I had to bite my tongue to keep from pointing out that Wyatt was driving when Susan was killed. Why does David feel safer when he's at the wheel than when I'm driving alone? But I'm acting on the assumption that his fears are logical and whose fears ever are? "Please don't torment me again," he begged. "Promise you won't ever leave the house without telling me where you're going."

I promised. What else could I do? I love David and would do anything to spare him unnecessary suffering. We spent the rest of the night in Julia's bed sealing the pact.

All this from the woman whose favorite song is "Someone to Watch Over Me." Or was. Little did I realize how rapidly "I'll Walk Alone" was moving up the charts.

I returned to my book this morning with an excitement I've never felt before. I realize now that writing is my way of leaving the house and traveling on my own, without causing anyone concern. And it is much more rewarding than shopping.

I'm very grateful to David. By keeping me at home, he has made me into a novelist in spite of myself. Left to my own devices, I would probably have been a journalist, following

257

other people around the world and writing down what they were doing. But marriage has forced me to recreate the world in my imagination, and I suspect I'm the richer for it.

□

TO PROTECT THE PLAYWRIGHT, Wyatt has decided to run the Susan as a club—selling subscriptions to a series of plays to prospective members and thus circumventing the critics. Who needs reviews when the theater is filled every night with subscribers? We give the critics their power by asking for their help selling tickets, but a bad review can kill a new play at birth. Wyatt's plan will give a play a chance to get on its feet in a protected environment before taking its chances in the outside world.

The Mother Lode goes into rehearsal next week, Willa in the lead. With no reviews hanging over our heads, we may enjoy an opening night for once in our lives.

That production made me remember why I got into the theater. I'd almost forgotten what fun it could be when nothing matters but the work. Knowing we were invulnerable to the critics even put Willa on her best behavior.

□

DAVID IS HAPPIER than I've ever seen him. No matter what we're doing, he manages to get to the theater every night in time for the final curtain. Hearing the applause and seeing all the responsive faces in the audience, I can understand why he can't stay away. Will I ever hear applause for something of mine?

About time she came out of the closet and admitted to having a little ambition of her own. I can't believe how much of this journal is devoted to my career. Why does she keep hiding in these pages behind what was happening to me? Did she play the self-effacing wife at night in her journal out of guilt at what she was doing to me by day in her novel?

258

☐

I'M FINALLY READY to show David my rewritten version of the novel. But sometimes it comes so cruelly close to the truth of our marriage, I'm terrified of what he'll say. So I've decided to make a second copy and send it to our agent at the same time.

I don't believe it! At that point in our marriage she was still leaving her letters to her parents unsealed for me to approve before they were mailed. Now I learn she was planning to weigh my opinion against an agent's!

☐

DAVID SPENT YESTERDAY at the theater rehearsing a new scene he wrote to open Act Two. During this six-week subscription run he's been able to do a lot of work on the play. Next week his high-powered New York agent, Abe Peters, is coming out to see it. David hopes he'll like it as much as the audiences do. Oh, God, so do I.

While he was out of the house, I called Eliot, our Hollywood agent, and said I had something to show him. When he learned I was finally going to let him read the novel I'd been working on for four years, he said he'd send a messenger.

The smartest move he ever made. It bought him Joanna's loyalty long after mine was exhausted.

Last night David took me to the theater with him to see the new opening for Act Two. It worked like a dream. When we came home, he was too excited to sleep, so I screwed up my courage and handed him my revised manuscript. I fell asleep to the sound of pages turning.

She fol' ͻwed most of my suggestions—and left me with no place to hide. That night I forgave Mother for refusing to come to The Mother Lode *and wondered how I would survive if by some miracle* Disturbing the Peace *were ever published. However, I was pretty certain the odds were on my side.*

259

I crept out of bed this morning while David was still asleep and was helping the girls make Father's Day cards when Eliot called, enthusiastic about my book.

So the first reaction was from him! I feel like a man who assumed he married a virgin only to find out years after the fact that he was not her first lover.

He said he knows nothing about publishing but has a high school friend working at one of the top houses in New York. Without making an official submission, he can send it to her for a reaction. That will give us a better idea of what we've got—and how to market it.

I was so excited I began dancing with Julia and Jessica—but I warned them not to say anything to their father—I didn't want anything to get in the way of his reaction.

When he finally made an appearance, Jessica slammed the bedroom door in his face, saying they were making him a surprise for Father's Day. "Can't they ever *buy* me anything?" he muttered as I followed him into the kitchen. Moaning that he had a terrible headache, he asked me to try and keep the children quiet for the rest of the day. When I leaned over to kiss him and rub his temples, I would've sworn, if I didn't know better, that there was liquor on his breath. But David doesn't drink— except for the occasional glass of wine at parties. He can't get close to a bottle of whiskey without remembering how his father behaved when he was drunk.

But reading her book the night before, halfway through the bottle of bourbon her parents left behind from their visit, I began to sympathize with my father and her father and all husbands everywhere who married one woman and watched her change before their eyes into another woman they barely knew.

Finally he took my hand and said I should consider the novel finished. He couldn't promise it would ever get published—the marketplace was too unpredictable—but I had done what I set out to do, and I should take great pride from that.

I waited expectantly for him to say he would give the manuscript to Abe Peters when he came out to see the play. He handles lots of authors and, unlike Eliot, is well connected in publishing circles. But David just continued patting my hand and saying how proud he was of me.

Finally I said I thought I'd show the novel to Eliot—not revealing I'd already done so. Then, if I ever wanted a job in television, at least he would know I was capable of writing on my own.

David said frankly he thought it was a waste of time but if I was that eager for outside approval, go ahead. However, he warned me not to expect a Hollywood agent to get very excited about a client who's written a book. "And don't pay any attention to his critical opinion," he added. "That's my territory, not his."

And I thought her novel *was hard on me! We could all pretend that was fiction, but these are the facts—and they're hanging me. Dear Julia, what can I say? Was I really that reluctant to see her novel leave the house? Or, as I prefer to think, had I been through enough rejection in the outside world to want to protect her as long as possible?*

☐

ELIOT'S NEW YORK CONTACT, making it clear all the while what a great favor she was doing us by reading the manuscript so quickly, called him personally to say the novel was unpublishable in its present form. She strongly suggested I change it to third person before submitting it elsewhere. Hesitantly Eliot asked me what I wanted to do. I said I wouldn't know where to begin making such a radical change, and even if I did, I wasn't sure it was right for the book.

David found me crying over my cookbooks when he came home from the theater. After confessing everything that had happened, I said from now on I was confining my creative efforts to the kitchen. When I described the new recipes I was planning to try, he offered to show my manuscript to Abe Peters if I'd promise to fix pork chops for dinner.

"What if he thinks the book should be in the third person?" I asked timidly.

"Then you'll have two votes in favor," David replied matter-of-factly. "But only two. And as the author, you always have the deciding vote."

☐

IT'S BEEN THREE MONTHS since David sent my manuscript to Mr. Peters. I know he's busy and important, but how dare he treat me like a . . . like a *wife!* Is there anything worse in the eyes of an agent? Why couldn't I have just kept my manuscript on ice, along with any ambition for a career outside my kitchen. But it's too late now. I can't stop after one rejection. I have to know whether the book stands a chance of being published.

☐

I WAS HAUNTING THE MAILBOX hoping for a letter from New York when the phone rang—Mr. Peters for me. David answered and I could tell he was as stunned as I was. I had long since abandoned hope of getting anything more from his agent than a polite letter of rejection—a phone call had to mean good news, didn't it? Motioning to David to stay on the line, I hurried to another extension. I felt that, having put his relationship with Mr. Peters at risk for me, he was entitled to hear every word of our conversation.

Apologizing in passing for his delay in getting back to me, a very intimidating voice informed me with ill-concealed surprise that I had written an intriguing book. At times perhaps I told more about my characters than the reader cared to know, but that was something an editor would ultimately decide. Thanking him profusely for his response and already feeling guilty for taking so much of his time, I started to hang up when he asked wryly if I was interested in where he planned to send the book.

"Then you're willing to show it?" I blurted out.

"My dear lady, why else would I be calling you?"

David is right. Women are amateurs. But I was too happy to care how foolish and naive I sounded. Promising to send the book off to the first publisher on his list, my new agent said he would keep me informed. "My best to David," he added just before he hung up. "Tell him I continue to have high hopes for his play."

High hopes—but no prospects of a production. The workshop had gone so well I'd begun to feel like a playwright again—but I still had a family of four to feed, a fact Abe preferred to ignore.

Whenever we talked, he would urge me to move to Connecticut and concentrate on a career in the "theatuh." It seemed pointless trying to explain to him how much easier I found it to concentrate on a play when I knew there was enough money in the bank to pay the bills.

At least Eliot understood my dilemma, so when he called with an offer to rewrite a movie, I told him to take it and, in the words of a struggling actor I know who refuses to let his agent negotiate price for fear of losing the job, "to hold out for minimum."

☐

ANOTHER CHRISTMAS with barely enough money in the bank to fill stockings for the children. David was counting our assets after dinner, trying to combat depression, when we got a phone call from his father and stepmother in West Texas. Their hot water heater had just exploded, causing their trailer to burn to the ground. They escaped without injury and are staying the night with a neighbor. But they have no prospects, no insurance, no money. All they have is David.

He offered to bring them to Los Angeles to live with us but was visibly relieved when they said they didn't want to leave Texas. However, no one seemed to know what to suggest next. Finally the neighbor took the phone and said she knew of a trailer comparable to the one they lost that could be purchased for three thousand dollars. David agreed to pay.

It amazes me that he ever found the courage to marry and start his own family with parents who are more helpless than children. It doesn't seem fair that he should have the financial burden of supporting a father who never had a kind word for him when he was growing up.

Eula Lee started this whole mess by marrying Bartlett—but

freed herself of any future responsibility by divorcing him, leaving David to see his father through old age. Something is wrong with our whole idea of family when men and women can fall in and out of love at random, leaving their offspring with no choice but to pick up the pieces. You can only choose to divorce someone you first chose to marry. Children are forever bound by blood to parents they never chose.

□

BARTLETT AND MABEL called today from their new trailer. When David asked how they liked it, Mabel said, "It's nice, David—for a *used* trailer." Had they actually expected him to buy them a new one? David said he hoped they would be happy there, because that used trailer was what all of us were getting for Christmas this year.

I hate the tone of this entry. She makes it sound as if Mabel and Bartlett shouldn't have wished for a new trailer. Just because people are poor shouldn't keep them from wishing big. The thing I regret most is that I never took them to Disneyland. They never actually asked to go any more than they asked for a new trailer, but they were clearly disappointed when I took them to Knott's Berry Farm instead. I chose Knott's because I thought it would be less familiar—and, of course, cheaper. Poor people hate the less familiar. Mabel and Bartlett wanted to go back to West Texas and brag. I still grieve that my dad died without ever being able to say he'd seen Disneyland.

264

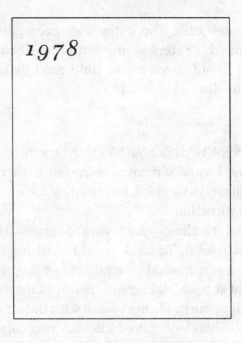

1978

DAVID IS BACK at Universal. On Christmas morning there was an envelope under the tree with my name on it. When I opened it and found his copy of a new three-year contract, I burst into tears. I can't stand the thought of his going back into bondage. He's no happier about it than I am, but he's pretending to be—and was furious at me for ruining Christmas.

"But what about *The Mother Lode?*" I sobbed.

"What about it?" he challenged. "I wrote it on my own time. I own it. And whenever someone decides to produce it, I'll be in the front row. But meanwhile, I've got to earn a living."

If only someone would publish my book! Then maybe I could bring in a little money for a change. God knows it's my turn.

☐

I FINALLY HEARD from New York today—a polite rejection letter from an editor who liked the book personally but was overruled by the sales manager, who questioned its commercial value. His exact words were "You can buy it, but don't expect me to sell it."

Why does a rejection on paper seem so much more final than

a phone call? The letter was accompanied by a cheerful note from Abe Peters saying not to be discouraged, the next move had already been made. But I can't shake my despair. If I'm not a novelist, what am I?

☐

WE SHARE EVERYTHING with our children, but sometimes I wonder if we're being fair to them. I always felt I was too sheltered as a child, but we may have gone too far in the opposite direction.

Before filing—and trying to forget—the rejection letter, I let Julia read it. Today I found her sitting on the floor in her bedroom surrounded by a pile of her favorite books. When I asked what she was doing, she answered matter-of-factly that she was finding me publishers—and with the air of someone who has just single-handedly saved a floundering career, proudly handed me a list of a dozen now obsolete publishers of children's books. I gave her a hug and decided to keep the list, just in case.

☐

NO FURTHER NEWS from New York but today an East Coast editor on a West Coast scouting mission had lunch with Eliot, who sent him back to his hotel with a copy of my manuscript. Explaining that someone else was showing it in New York, Eliot said he could only give him twenty-four hours to make a decision. How can I sleep knowing someone who can shape my future has taken my book to bed with him?

☐

ELIOT just called to say that the editor, Clement Turner, wants to publish my book. I don't care how little money I make or how few copies I sell, by this time next year I'll have a card with my name in libraries across the country. I could die happy tonight.

She had turned our marriage inside out and exposed all the seams—but she'd made it pay off so I forgave her.

Hurrah for me! How happy we were that night. Why couldn't we make it last?

☐

CLEMENT has now read my book three more times and is writing me a detailed letter with his editorial comments. I was terrified when he began to talk about changes, but his voice sounded so warm and reassuring, I relaxed immediately. Soon he was talking about my characters as if they were mutual friends of long standing. Clement says that having spent every waking hour with my book for the past two weeks, he probably knows the inside of my head better than my husband. I wouldn't be at all surprised.

I didn't know how to react to the relationship between Joanna and her editor. At first I refused to learn his name. How could I be so jealous of a man who was only interested in my wife's mind? Perhaps because I was as possessive of her mind as I was of her body. I hated the thought of another man putting his ideas into it. I'd gone over every word of that manuscript before it was submitted to anybody, and I wasn't about to let Joanna make any changes in it without my approval. Yet I knew she had to pretend to agree with him—the way I always pretended to agree with a director until he committed to a play. Time enough, once he was involved, to argue.

Actually the changes he suggested were very minor—but to hear Joanna thanking him over the phone, anyone would've thought his suggestions were saving the book. When she came into the bedroom, where I was trying to write, to tell me about their conversation, her cheeks were flushed and her eyes shining. I tried to recall the last time I'd caused such a change in her appearance. I couldn't.

☐

MOLLY CRANE, who has turned into a lovely twenty-year-old woman, appeared at our door without any advance warning last night and asked if she could stay with us for a while. She said she couldn't stand living in New York with Willa another day. If she were going to spend her life looking after a child, it was going to be her child.

A few weeks ago she fell in love with a young actor who was working with Willa on a scene for the Actors Studio. A Hollywood director was in the audience and promptly cast the actor in his next film. Willa was furious when he accepted the offer, but Molly encouraged him and he asked her to come to California with him. However, by the time they'd driven across the country, Molly realized she was not in love with anything except the idea of leaving Willa to cope with motherhood alone. So she asked the actor to drop her off at our house.

The girls consider Molly a big sister and begged her to live with us. David and I offered her the guest room for as long as she wants to stay. Since Eula Lee moved away, I've really missed having an extra adult in residence to keep an eye on the children, but I must be careful not to take advantage of Molly. I can understand how Willa became so dependent on her.

David insisted Molly call Willa to tell her how and where she was, but Molly wouldn't agree until he promised to get on another extension and come to her defense if Willa got mean. Which she did as soon as she realized Molly was safe—and unmarried. What hurt her most was not the fact that Molly had chosen our household over hers but Los Angeles over New York. Willa considers her daughter's defection a betrayal of everything she holds dear.

As her parting shot, Willa announced that she had to turn down the lead in a Broadway play last week because she couldn't find anyone to stay with Tim. David reassured Molly later that either the play was no good or the part was not big enough. He'd never known Willa to turn down anything she wanted—except for something she wanted more.

"It was so much easier doing a play in Los Angeles," Willa lamented to David, "knowing I could count on Joanna for help. I wish we lived in the same city." To my amazement I heard David inform Willa that she could no longer count on my services as a baby-sitter no matter where we were living. I had my own career now. My novel was being published, and I was working with my editor on changes. I couldn't believe how proud he sounded.

"Little Joanna has written a novel?" I heard Willa ask in amazement as I listened on the other extension. "Why, she never said a word about it to me."

"She probably didn't think you'd take it seriously until she found a publisher," said David.

"Did you?" asked Willa.

"Yes," he replied without hesitation. "I wasn't sure she'd get it published, but I knew it was a good book from the day she started writing it."

I hung up the kitchen phone with great care so neither David nor Willa would know I'd listened to their conversation. David could not understand why I insisted on scrubbing his back in the bathtub and performing other acts of gratitude that kept us awake until late last night.

My friends kept waiting for me to turn on Joanna—or, more likely, for her to turn on me. But in my experience, failure is the home wrecker, not success. I had no idea what was in store for us once her novel was published, but just the fact that she was now out there playing the game, too, doubled our chances of winning.

□

TODAY IS MY FORTIETH BIRTHDAY. My mother and her friends formed a club called the Old Crows to get them past this dreaded milestone. They would dress in black and write lugubrious verses mourning the passing of their youth whenever they gathered to welcome a new member. Within a year the new member had usually become pregnant once again. Perhaps a book is my way of defying old age and beginning a new life as a writer.

Clement is in town on business and invited me to lunch at the Beverly Wilshire Hotel. I didn't tell him it was my birthday, but that didn't stop me from celebrating privately. I had no clear image in my mind of what he would look like. I guess because he represents such an authority figure for me, I expected someone older and a little gray around the edges. I was amazed to discover that he is younger than I am. However, there was instant rapport between us. We even ordered the same thing for lunch, something David and I have never done in a restaurant.

As we ate, we found ourselves finishing each other's sentences. Is it possible that I have finally found someone for whom I will never be too old or too fat? Someone who will not exact promises or demands? Someone who likes me just the way I am?

Lots of luck. Okay, I was jealous, I admit it. And I had no right to be, considering how many women I've taken to lunch. But to me food is food and sex is sex. Whereas Joanna was always making subliminal connections between the two—so for her having lunch with another man was not as innocent as it appeared.

There are few moments in a relationship as intense as the first meeting between two people who are excited about learning everything there is to know about each other. Clement and I covered every possible point of contact, seeking out common interests and associations. He grew up in Georgia and feels his background gives him a broader base than most New York publishers. He's looking for books that will appeal to readers across the country and not just to the eastern critical establishment.

Listening to him talk, I couldn't help thinking of David and wishing a play could get a shot at a national audience before being stopped at the pass by a handful of Broadway critics.

She couldn't help thinking of poor David while sharing confidences with a man who was already finishing her sentences? Heartwarming.

David had briefed me with questions to ask Clement about the publication of the book—the size of the first printing, the possibility of a paperback sale, book clubs, serial rights, translations. But our conversation began on such a personal note, I was reluctant to turn it into a business discussion. However, I knew I couldn't face David without hard facts to show for my two hours at table, so I cross-examined Clement as casually as possible while he walked me to the front door of the hotel. When I told David what I'd learned—a first printing of 25,000 copies—I could tell he didn't believe me.

I didn't—until a letter from her editor the next week confirmed it. I didn't read what Joanna wrote back. She no longer asked me to edit her letters. And her return address no longer read "Mrs. David Scott." She was now "Joanna Henley Scott" to everyone—even when she was just paying bills.

☐

MOLLY CALLED WILLA to wish her merry Christmas, but Paul answered the phone, explaining Willa had invited him to spend the holidays with his son. This was the first official acknowledgment of his fatherhood we'd had from either him or Willa. Neither David nor I was surprised, but Molly was stunned. She burst into tears and ran from the room. David quickly took the phone to assure Willa that Molly was very happy in California and already planning to attend UCLA next semester.

I ran after Molly to try to console her, but she said she could never forgive Willa for giving Tim a father when she had never had the chance to know hers. Then she confided that she and Tim often talked about their fathers and tried to imagine what they were like. One day last spring—just before Molly left New York—Willa overheard them. She told Tim that his father never knew he had a son because she didn't want to share Tim with anyone. Then she informed Molly that her father had died; Willa only found out when she read his obituary in the newspaper. He left four ex-wives, ten children, and apparently no money for any of them. When Molly began to cry at the news that she had lost her father without ever knowing him, Willa said to Tim, "You see how lucky you are not to have a father. Fathers only cause their children pain." But now she'd given Tim a father and Paul a son, and Molly couldn't understand why.

Hugging her, I said I was sure Willa was so lonely without her, she changed her mind about letting Paul become part of the family. People who live alone, or even in twos or threes, have a hard time getting through the holidays. That's why we were having such a big crowd for Christmas dinner.

271

Molly set the table while Marvin carved the turkey, Wyatt made the gravy, and David carried platters of food into the dining room. After dinner Eula Lee put the children to work clearing the table as she loaded the dishwasher. Molly said it was the first family Christmas she'd ever had, and it really didn't matter that she wasn't related to anyone in the room.

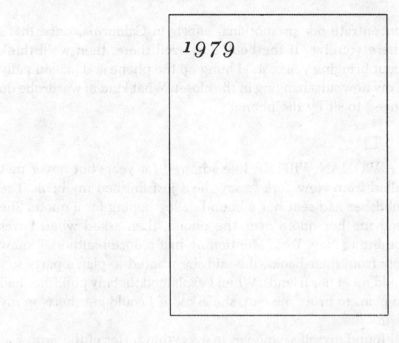

1979

A BOUND COPY of my book—the first one off the press—arrived in the mail today. I guess I expected a trumpet fanfare, but the package didn't even come special delivery.

The official publication date is not for another month, but I can tell already that it's nothing like opening night in the theater—merely a date the promotion and sales departments use in their work. Apparently reviews dribble in for months, and sales build slowly, especially with a first novel. So when will I know the verdict?

I don't think I'm even going to be sent on a promotion tour. I asked Clement when I would be coming to New York, and he said he wasn't sure it was necessary. I can't believe I'm just expected to sit home and do nothing while my book makes its own way in the world.

"But what about interviews?" I persisted. "I know some authors would rather be at home writing than out meeting people, but I really don't mind. I've never been on television, but when the *Today* show asks for me, don't say no."

Was Clement laughing on the other end of the line? "You're being very cooperative," he said finally, "but we're going to concentrate our promotional efforts in California, since that's where you live. If the book does well there, then we'll think about bringing you east." I hung up the phone and looked sadly at my new suits hanging in the closet. What kind of wardrobe do I need to sit by the phone?

☐

A WOMAN WRITER I've admired for years but never met called from New York to say she'd just finished my book. The publisher had sent her a bound galley hoping for a quote. She read me her quote over the phone, then asked when I was coming to New York. Mentioning half a dozen authors I know only from their books, she said she wanted to plan a party so I could meet her friends. When I explained that my publisher had no plans to bring me east, she asked if I could get there on my own.

I found myself saying yes to everything. Her enthusiasm was contagious. I couldn't believe someone I'd never met, who knew me only through my book, was suddenly shaping my life. "I'm calling your publisher today," she announced. "They don't know it yet, but they're giving this party with me. They owe it to you. And I'll suggest that as long as you're coming into town at your own expense, they might as well take advantage of your presence and arrange some interviews. Let me tell you something about publishing," she continued. "No one cares about a book as much as the person who wrote it. Your publisher has a new list coming along every six months, but how long will it be before you have another book?"

Probably never, I thought to myself. One book was more than I ever expected to write.

When I told David about the phone call, he reacted like a general planning a battle campaign. "She's right," he said. "It's up to us to make your book a success. It's not like a play, where your fate is in the hands of a producer. No one can close a book —no matter what kind of reviews it gets." We began to map out an itinerary to send Clement, telling him that our summer vacation would be taking us to all these cities and I would be happy to do anything I could to promote the book while I was in town.

*Our friends were always pulling Joanna aside at parties
to ask how I was taking her emergence. When she told Paul
about my strategy for promoting the book, he just laughed
and said, "David has been poised at the starting gate for
twenty years waiting for someone to fire the damn gun."*

☐

JUST ONE MORE WEEK TO GO on this book-flogging tour.
Will my marriage survive? I feel as if I'm using up all the credit
I've accumulated in nineteen years of following David around
the country with productions of his plays.

Every morning I leave him and the girls asleep in their hotel
rooms and go off with sales representatives to bookstores and
radio interviews and an occasional local television show. (Not
being a big-name author, I rank last on the list of visiting celebri-
ties—after television stars, country singers, diet experts, and
dog acts. I was heavily booked in Cleveland, but Chicago
couldn't have cared less.)

☐

IF I COULD'VE LOOKED into the future when I first married and witnessed the scene that took place today in a Minneapolis bookstore, I would've been convinced Central Casting
got the two leading roles confused. I'm still not sure how I ended
up with my part.

I was serving my time at a two-hour autographing session,
trying to ignore the stack of unsold books on my table, while an
embarrassed clerk blamed the lack of business on bad weather.
Suddenly a woman wearing a drab raincoat with a kerchief tied
unbecomingly around her hair entered the store carrying a
large shopping bag. At last a paying customer! Then she pulled a
copy of my book with a clearly visible discount sticker from her
bag, and the clerk started to turn her away. Though her back
was to me, I could hear her admit she bought the book somewhere else, before she knew I was going to be in town. But she'd
already read and loved it. Didn't that count for anything?

"It does with the author," I shouted, crossing to her quickly
and asking how she wanted the book inscribed.

275

"For Elaine," she replied.

"Elaine what?" I asked.

"Just Elaine," she said quietly. I looked at her curiously. Elaine West? Living in Minneapolis? Was it possible?

"I thought you'd never recognize me," she said with a laugh. I gave her a hug and pulled up a chair next to mine, urging her to stay and keep me company. As she could see, business was not exactly booming.

She took a seat and began to talk rapidly, covering the missing years as if seeking my approval for her choices. After her affair with Brad ended, she fled back to New York only to discover that she preferred living in the Midwest, where life was less pressured.

She's now head of adult education in a small suburban college —and finds it very rewarding working with people old enough to admit they've made mistakes. She says she's in the business of putting lives back on the track, including her own. She feels her mistake was starting out with such publicly declared ambitions. From the time her first book of poetry was published, everyone was watching to see what she'd do next. "You don't know how lucky you are, Joanna. No one expected anything from you." I didn't like admitting it, but I knew it was true.

Then to my surprise she confessed that she continued to write and had three unpublished novels in her trunk. Embarrassed, I began telling her about my rejections and saying how much depended on luck. I offered to send anything she'd written to my publisher, along with a letter of recommendation. In a matter-of-fact voice, daring me to be surprised, she said she'd already sent her last book to my publisher with a note saying we were old friends and I was enthusiastic about her work. But the book had been rejected anyway. So there was nothing more I could do for her—unless I was free to have dinner.

I said great. Our plane didn't leave till eight, and I was sure David would be as happy to see her as I was.

"David?" She seemed disoriented. "Is he here? I assumed, after reading the book, you had to be divorced." In fact, she said, my book had made her feel better about not being married herself. That was the reason she sought me out, thinking we could finally be real friends. How could I write so convincingly about the price women had to pay to sustain a relationship and still be married?

I explained I was married, for better or worse, to a man who was as interested in exploring the bonds of matrimony as I was—and never let me leave home without him. In fact, he and the children were probably camped in the hotel lobby now with our luggage, waiting to go to the airport. I urged Elaine to come back to the hotel with me, but she suddenly said she'd forgotten about an appointment, gave me a quick hug, and sent David her best. "Tell him he was right about my first novel," she added as an afterthought. "It *was* implausible—just like my life."

Joanna never told me about her meeting with Elaine. Why? Perhaps because she knew I was finding my life equally implausible, waiting with the children while she went from interview to interview trying to become a famous novelist.

□

SEVERAL NASHVILLE BOOKSTORE OWNERS planned a party in my honor tonight, and I made sure David and the children were included. But when I told him about the invitation, he begged me to make some excuse and let them eat in peace at the hotel. He said he couldn't stand being identified by one more well-meaning stranger as Joanna's husband then asked what *he* did for a living.

I pointed out that at least he could reply with an accredited profession. He had no idea how it felt to be "just a husband."

Oh, no? In Washington Joanna and I were asked to appear as a working couple on a local TV talk show that I'd done twice before when I had plays premiering there. Our billing in The Washington Post *listed us as "novelist Joanna Henley Scott and her husband." Remember, Julia? You and Jessica thought it was so funny you called me H.H. (short for "her husband") for the rest of the trip. I laughed too—ha, ha.*

Little wonder women are so angry—and so determined to change the world for their daughters. In that one month

of following Joanna around the country, I began thinking
of myself as a second-class citizen. There's an old Indian
saying, "Before you can understand a man, you have to
walk a mile in his moccasins." I walked my mile that
month—and felt I'd finally made it up to Joanna for taking
her away from her typewriter in the newsroom.

☐

WE'RE HOME AGAIN, but it feels like a foreign country.
Now when the phone rings, it's for me as often as it's for David.
And twice this month photographers have come to the house to
take my picture. But the most exciting thing occurred today
while Julia and I were shopping for back-to-school clothes. Suddenly, at the age of thirteen, she's decided to start wearing
dresses. She said she'd given the subject a lot of thought and
finally realized women were better off than men. Women could
be writers plus have babies. Men could only be writers.

My bright little darling, it took your mother forty years
to figure that out—and Betty Friedan to help her.

☐

TONIGHT I made the mistake of asking David if he'd heard
from Ben lately. He said he never expected to hear from him
again. I asked if they'd had a fight.
"Of course not," he smiled. "It was your book."
"How could it possibly have been my book? He wrote me a
lovely letter after it was published."
"Yes—*right* after it was published, but *before* he knew how
well it would sell."
I refuse to believe I ended their friendship—though it appears to be as finished as Ben's first (and only) marriage. Looking
back, I realize Ben and David have always had very little in
common—except their careers and their mutual respect for
each other's talent. I can remember Ben shouting at David
once, "You've never even read *Ulysses* yet you *re*read Salinger."

He also said I should listen to more Mozart and how dare
I spend money on the complete score of The Most Happy
Fella.

Thinking about Ben and David, I find myself pondering the nature of friendship. Marriage is for better or worse. Friendship is too often only half the vow—for better and better, or worse and worse.

Susan was a friend for better and better. In fact, I hesitated to share my disappointments with her because she so delighted in good news. Ben, on the other hand, would come running in the middle of the night still wearing his pajamas if there was a problem, the worse the better. But once we were on our feet financially, we saw less and less of him. Whoever included "for better *or* worse" in the wedding vow really knew what he was doing.

Like Salinger, as I read these journals, I'm beginning to miss everybody—even Ben.

☐

WE'VE NEVER gotten as many Christmas cards as we have this year—and most of them mention my book. I've heard from people out of the past I thought were lost to me forever: my third-grade teacher, my first boyfriend—who moved away in the sixth grade just as he finally found the courage to hold my hand in the movies—and Adam Greenfield, who is now teaching history at the college where his sister Kate and I roomed together almost twenty years ago. He retired from the foreign service last year after his wife's death.

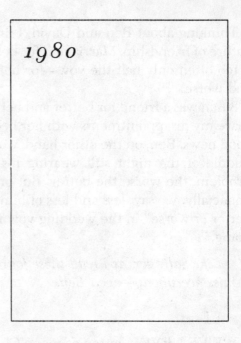

1980

MY MAIL IS BEING CENSORED—by David! I've never felt more violated.

Lately he's been coming home for lunch instead of meeting someone in the commissary. He says my life is more interesting than his and he can't wait till dinner to hear about my phone calls and read my mail. He usually brings the mail in with him and slits all the envelopes while I'm fixing lunch. He goes over the bills before giving them to me to pay, then we exchange letters as we eat.

But today he had a luncheon meeting so I brought in the mail and read it alone. Enclosed in a fan letter from Detroit was a newspaper clipping—a letter to the editor challenging a bad review of *Disturbing the Peace*. The letter was signed David Scott.

I was dumbstruck. I never saw a bad review for the book, so I assumed I hadn't gotten any. What a fool I am. But so is David for thinking he can—or should—shield me from criticism. And how dare he write a critic in my defense!

What can I say? I worshiped Harry Truman—I made that clear to Joanna the first night I came to dinner. And

one of the best letters Truman ever wrote was to a music
critic who attacked his daughter's singing.

When I saw his car pull in the garage tonight, I went out to meet him and slid into the front seat.

"Where are we going?" he asked in surprise.

"Nowhere," I said. "I just don't want the children to hear us fighting."

"Fighting?" he asked in amazement. "I'm not upset about anything." I don't think it's ever occurred to him we could have an argument he didn't start.

"I know," I replied. "But I am." I showed him his letter to the editor from the Detroit paper, then told him in no uncertain terms if I was strong enough to write a book, I was strong enough to hear what people thought of it. Just how much had he kept from me?

He shrugged—a few bad reviews, a little hate mail.

Hate mail? For me? I was stunned. All I'd done was try to write truthfully out of my own experience. Why would anybody hate me for that?

David smiled ruefully and said I should see some of the letters he'd gotten about his plays.

"You've gotten hate mail? Why didn't you tell me?"

He said it's hard enough reading bad reviews yourself, but what really hurts is watching the person you love read them, then struggle to come up with words of comfort.

"Well, since you've already read mine, I don't have to watch you," I said. "Now we're going in the house and you're going to hand over every bad review and every piece of hate mail I've gotten."

"Too late," he said. Did I detect a note of pride in his answer? "I destroyed them as soon as I answered them."

"You answered them? All of them?" I couldn't get my breath. David has always hated writing letters.

"I've always wanted to review a critic. It was very satisfying. As for those deranged letters"—he grinned—"let's just say *I* gave as good as *you* got."

I burst out laughing. I knew there was a principle getting lost here somewhere, but imagine having a husband who would go to such lengths to protect his wife from the slings and arrows of public exposure! However, I wouldn't leave the car until he had given me his solemn word that, from this day forward, I would see all my mail and read all my reviews.

"On one condition," he said. "That you won't let it stop you."

"Stop me? What do you mean?"

"From writing a second novel," he said. "Do you have any ideas yet?"

I mumbled something about being busy making notes, then fled into the kitchen before he could question me further. One book is enough for me—it's more than I ever dreamed of doing even in the most ambitious days of my adolescence. Why isn't it enough for David?

He found me hiding among my pots and pans, and told me to save the pot roast for another night, he was taking everybody out for pizza. I said I wasn't feeling well. It was true. I was sick at my stomach at the thought of starting a second novel. I used everything that ever happened to me in the first one. What do I have left to write about?

As soon as David had left with the girls, I slipped into the Japanese kimono he gave me when we first came to Hollywood, poured myself a glass of white wine, and took out my file of unanswered correspondence. I wondered briefly what had been said in the hate letters David had destroyed but soon lost myself in the warm words of people who knew me only from my book. Funny—even though I still spend most of my days at home, since *Disturbing the Peace* was published I no longer feel lonely or isolated. Invisible threads connect me to readers I'll probably never meet. How could a second book add anything to my life?

> *Her absolute disregard for money never ceases to amaze me. Not that I was pushing her to write another book to help pay the bills—though I don't mind admitting I was already enjoying the "comfortable margin" her projected royalties would provide. In fact, I remember Wyatt wisecracking that every husband we knew bought his wife a typewriter for Christmas after Joanna sold her paperback rights. I was even counting the months till my Universal contract expired. Thanks to Joanna's new career, I could*

afford to return to my old one—and write yet another play.
But, more than the money, I was determined before I died
to teach her to enjoy the talent that so terrified her.

I poured myself another glass of wine before rereading Adam Greenfield's long Christmas card, which I've been waiting to answer till the mood was right. He sounds so lonely. He was attached to an embassy in the Middle East when his wife became ill. She died in his arms on a plane to Paris. They had been unable to have children, he confessed, so he's alone now. Kate's family is the only one he has. Her oldest daughter is a freshman at our old alma mater, where he's now teaching. He says she reminds him of me—as eager and excited about life as I was when he knew me. He wrote to me in care of my publisher but said he hoped the card would be forwarded and we could reestablish contact. Can we? I don't know. So much has happened to both of us since the Thanksgiving weekend we spent together when I was still trying to decide whether or not to marry David.

Oh, no, darling, you've got that all wrong. I was still
trying to decide whether or not to marry you.

□

FOR YEARS after I married David, I used to dream I had to leave him and the children and go back to college. The parting was unbearably painful, and once back on campus, I would wander around like a refugee, knowing none of the students or teachers.

Today I am back at college—alone—and it is no dream. I just spent an hour walking around the quadrangle, going in and out of the buildings I remembered, then exploring somewhat more tentatively the ones that did not exist when I was a student. No one spoke to me on my walk. I'm beginning to feel like a ghost.

Now I'm getting ready for dinner. This time I'm not sharing a communal bathroom in a dormitory, I have a private bath in the apartment reserved for guest speakers. After dinner I have to give a speech to the student body. As far as I could see on my solitary walk this afternoon, the only announcement of my presence on campus was a small handwritten sign on the bulletin board. I wonder if anyone will come.

My visit was arranged by Adam Greenfield. When he first proposed it, I said I couldn't possibly leave my husband and children to fly across the country for one night. Then a second letter arrived offering a handsome fee plus plane fare, and David said why turn it down. I think he could tell how much I wanted to go—but of course he had no idea why.

After that Christmas card from that asshole? How dumb did she think I was?

Adam and I have exchanged letters every few weeks since he made contact again. He writes funny stories about the infighting that goes on among the faculty—things he says he can only tell someone at a safe distance. Writing Adam, I'm able to confess the fears and doubts that only depress David when I try to confide in him. He doesn't like hearing me say I feel like an imposter when I'm introduced as an author.

But I bet Adam Greenfield lapped it up. That kind of talk is music to the ears of someone who has grazed in the fields of academia.

Still I was nervous about seeing Adam again, and almost didn't recognize the gray-bearded man who was waiting for me at the airport. He is at most five years older than I; this man seemed to belong to another generation. But a stranger wouldn't have been smiling at me the way he was. "I recognized you from the picture on the back of your book," he said, taking my hand.

"You mean I don't look the way you remembered?"

"Who does?" he said with a shrug, taking my luggage and putting his free hand against the back of my waist as he guided me toward his car. After a few polite, impersonal questions about the plane trip, he became strangely quiet. I kept waiting for him to tell me more of the funny stories that fill his letters, but when I tried to prod him with questions, he became wary and guarded.

"Do you still like to dance?" I asked finally, trying to find some connection between this ill-at-ease stranger and my roommate's

284

handsome brother, who might have given David a run for his money if he'd had the slightest interest in pursuing me.

"What makes you think I ever liked to dance?" he asked curiously, as if I had him confused with someone else.

"You don't remember how much we danced that Thanksgiving weekend when I came home with Kate?"

He stared straight ahead, never taking his eyes off the road, as he confessed, "I probably shouldn't be saying this, but I honestly don't remember ever having met you before."

The smug bastard. If I ever run into him, he'll remember meeting me.

I was prepared for anything but that. I didn't know what to say. "But that Christmas card you sent after you read my book—you said you couldn't cross the campus without seeing someone who made you think of me."

"Kate reminded me when she sent me your book that she'd brought you home for Thanksgiving one year. After reading it, I felt I knew you better than I'd known my own wife, and I began to imagine what you must've been like at twenty. But I couldn't actually place you. Kate was always bringing friends home from school and expecting me to show them a good time."

"Which you certainly did," I had to admit.

"I was all set to lie to you today," Adam confessed, "to pretend I remembered everything you wanted me to remember. I knew you'd give me enough clues so I could bluff convincingly. But I couldn't go through with it. I had to let you see me for the fool I am. I must've been myopic not to see in you at twenty the woman you would become."

I just smiled and accepted in silence what I was sure he intended as a compliment. How could I make him understand that the woman I was to become depended on the man I was to marry? I've never missed David more than I do tonight.

When her alumnae magazine arrived later that spring, Joanna looked in vain for a story about her triumphal return to campus. But there was no picture and nothing in print to indicate she had ever been back to her alma mater.

Adam Greenfield wrote to thank her, but she never an-swered his letter.

□

WHY AM I STILL TREMBLING from what should have been a routine phone call? I'm forty-two years old, married, with two children and a published novel—why do I crumble when confronted with authority in any form?

A new theater in Pittsburgh suddenly slotted *The Mother Lode* as their next production; apparently something fell out at the last minute. Willa arranged everything and is already there rehearsing.

David immediately made plane and hotel reservations for the four of us, but left it to me to inform the children's principal that they will be a month late starting school this year. Explaining our plans, I began to feel like a truant schoolgirl. In a stern voice the principal said he couldn't possibly condone what we were doing—it was unfair to the children.

Furious that he would presume to tell me what was best for *my* children, I informed him coolly that I wasn't asking for his permission to take Julia and Jessica with us. They were going in any case. I just wanted to get their assignments so they could keep up with their classwork.

But he accused me of putting unnecessary pressure on the children by taking them out of school for such a lengthy period. And then asked if there was no one who could stay home with them. I knew who he had in mind—me.

Trying to explain my rather unique marriage, I said I happen to have a husband who values my presence and my opinion and never travels without me. I had feared once our children were born, I'd have to start staying home, but David, happily, continues to want all of us with him.

I then explained that I grew up with a father who went to an office every day. Neither his wife nor his children had any idea what he did there. Our children have been raised differently. They know what we do—and how much failure goes before any success. We spent last summer traveling around the country to promote my book. Now it's David's turn with a play.

The principal interrupted to ask when Julia and Jessica got their turn.

Just as soon as they're ready for it, I heard myself promising, and David and I will be there to applaud. Then I paused, waiting for him to give his blessing to what I was sure I had painted as a rather remarkable family. But he remained stubbornly silent.

Growing desperate, I suddenly asked how many of his students came from broken homes. He didn't seem to know, so I said, judging from my children's friends, I would guess at least fifty percent. And not a week goes by without another child coming to school in tears because his or her parents are getting a divorce. "But who cares as long as the children never miss a class—right?" I was close to tears now but before he could interrupt to ask what my point was, I continued, revealing more of my inner struggle than I realized, "It's very hard staying married these days—keeping a family together. Why won't you help me?"

I was ready to hang up the phone in defeat when I heard him ask the exact dates we would be away. Then he said he would speak to the children's teachers personally and get their assignments.

"Thank you. I'm so grateful," I said in a whisper.

"You're welcome. Have a safe trip. And wish your husband good luck with the play."

☐

DAVID TOOK AN UNPAID LEAVE from Universal so we could be in Pittsburgh for the entire rehearsal period. We're staying in the same hotel as Willa so Tim can play with the girls while she rehearses.

David tells everyone I'm working on my second novel—but the truth is, I still don't have an idea for one. And frankly, after being on the firing line all year—answering questions, going into bookstores and introducing myself, smiling endlessly—I'm relieved it's David's turn at the front. It's so easy slipping into the well-worn role of backstage wife. It's even kind of relaxing to be around Willa, who ignores me as relentlessly as she always did. I wonder if she ever got around to reading my book. Considering how many hours I've spent watching her onstage, I think she owes me that.

I thought so too—and mentioned one day during a break in rehearsal that Joanna's book could be adapted into a play. Willa bought the book the next day but never mentioned it again.

Molly is going to UCLA full-time and living on campus. Once Willa admitted that Paul was the father of her son, he began to treat Molly like an adopted daughter. He takes her out to dinner at least once a week and often invites her to be his date for screenings. The gossip columnists don't know what to make of the relationship, and I suspect Paul likes to keep them guessing.

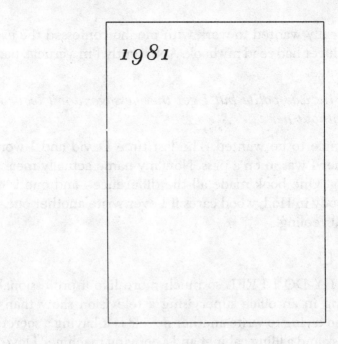

1981

A NEW YEAR—and David is back on the open market. Whatever happens in the years ahead, I pray he'll never have to sign another long-term contract. He must stay free to write plays.

> *At this point I was beginning to wonder how truck farmers felt about their careers when they hit forty-five. But then I remembered Shaw didn't write* Saint Joan *until he was sixty-seven—and I was once again a playwright, off and crawling.*

□

"HOW'S THE NEW BOOK COMING?" David asked casually tonight at dinner. I said I was still making notes—I just couldn't seem to get started writing.

Maybe I needed a change of pace, he suggested. Would I mind putting aside the book for six months to produce thirteen episodes of a half-hour television show with him?

Mind? I was flooded with relief at a legitimate excuse to escape outside my own thoughts for a while, and I could tell David was thrilled to get such a good offer. When I asked if he was sure he really wanted to work with me, he confessed the executive producer had read my book. Apparently I'm a crucial part of the package.

He was polite but I got the message: don't leave home without her.

It's nice to be wanted. The last time David and I worked together I was in on a pass. Now my name actually means something. One book made all the difference—and one is enough. Nobody in Hollywood cares if I ever write another one. What a great feeling!

☐

WHY DO I FEEL so much more like a professional writer sitting in an office supervising a television show than I do at home trying to write another novel? Is it having a secretary and a desk and a filing cabinet and a copying machine? I love getting dressed and driving to work with David every morning. It's fun having adjoining offices and going out to lunch together. When we're both at home, immersed in separate projects, we tend to take each other for granted. But at work, watching how good David is at what he does, I find myself as attracted to him as I was when we first met on the newspaper.

Jessica and Julia often come to the studio with us. There's an unused office across the hall which we've claimed for them until someone more qualified comes along. They have their own typewriter and a desk full of office supplies. And despite being only ten and fifteen, they're collaborating on a script for the show which is funnier than any we've commissioned. Jessica dictates while Julia types. When they're not working on their script, they write long letters to their grandparents in Texas, to Eula Lee and Marvin, who are cruising in the Aegean, to their friends at camp, but mostly to Toby and Lucy, who are spending the summer in Chicago with Brad and his new family, which now includes a four-year-old son and a baby daughter.

Julia and Jessica would be very lonely this summer without Toby and Lucy if they didn't have the novelty of going to an office every day. But they love sharing our lives—and frankly are more familiar with current television shows than David and I. In fact, when writers come into the office to pitch story ideas, we usually arrange to have our daughters positioned discreetly in the background; they're our best defense against secondhand plots. "We saw that on *The Brady Bunch*," they'll say—and another writer bites the dust.

☐

WE HAD A WRAP PARTY today after taping our last show. The girls performed a skit parodying the series. The cast adored it, and afterward an agent who represents child actors gave me her card. However, I don't expect I'll be using it. Julia and Jessica both want to be writers—despite the fact that, with the series in the can, their parents are out of work, and the next job is nowhere in sight.

Monkey see, monkey do. Poor, brave monkeys.

☐

I STILL CANNOT BELIEVE how David handled the death of his father. When Mabel called last night to say Bartlett had died in his sleep, David sympathized with her heartbreak and then offered to pay for the funeral expenses. However, he reminded her that since his father had lived poor, he should also expect to be buried poor.

Mabel assured David that she was arranging as inexpensive a funeral as possible—the coffin would cost less than three thousand dollars. His voice suddenly exploded. Three thousand dollars? Ridiculous! There must be cheaper caskets. Yes, but the one she'd chosen was "real pretty." And Bartlett was already in it. "Well, get him out of it," demanded David.

Mabel said she didn't think that was possible. Apparently the mortician was standing beside her, shaking his head. David asked to speak to the mortician, who insisted Bartlett was in a nice, middle-priced casket—their prices ranged from $891 to $6500.

David said he'd take the $891 one. The mortician said it was little more than plywood. David said that would be fine. The mortician then confessed that he'd measured Bartlett and he wouldn't fit in the $891 model. "Push," was David's response.

The mortician said his father might fit into the $1100 model. However, he did feel compelled to tell David that it was not lined. David said he still preferred the $891 model. The mortician said he'd never wedged a customer into a casket in his career—and he refused to start doing it now.

Finally David compromised—the $1100 casket. He then talked to Mabel again, urging her to buy an inexpensive plot and a small marker. He added that he loved her—especially for loving his dad so much—hung up, and took us all out for a Mexican supper. The only thing he ever said to me about the conversation was how much his dad would have loved hearing him haggle over the price of his casket. I suppose it *was* Bartlett's kind of humor. And it's also David's. But I couldn't even finish my enchilada.

I finished it for her.

☐

DAVID HAS AN IDEA for a new play but says he cannot make a career out of being an unproduced playwright. So for now—at least until something more happens with *The Mother Lode*—he's going to concentrate on *my* career instead. Help!

It was a simple matter of logistics. My plane was stuck in the hangar. She had an open runway.

He's even taking out an insurance policy on my life—since my royalties are now helping to support the family. I have to admit I'm flattered. It would certainly never occur to my father, conscientious head of household though he is, to take out an insurance policy on my mother's life.

Then he asked how I was coming on the new book. When I said I didn't have anything good enough to show him, he lectured me for betraying my talent by not working harder at my writing. I went to bed early as I always do when I'm depressed—but I can't sleep. Just by writing one book, I've done more with my life than I ever expected to do. Why do I allow him to make me feel so inadequate? And why is it impossible for me to be happy with him unless I'm convinced he's happy with me? From the beginning our relationship has revolved around how he feels about me, never how I feel about him. I suspect it's because as long as he's happy with me, I'm happy with him. The reverse, unfortunately, is not true. I can be very happy with him only to discover abruptly, like a thunderstorm intruding on a sunny afternoon, that he is unhappy with me. When this happens, my universe turns inside out and I wander disoriented in the dark like a solitary voyager, deprived of map or guide, no longer certain of who I am or where I'm going.

You see why she needs an editor.

I remember being very sure of myself and my ultimate destination the day I left for college at eighteen, standing in the door of the train as it pulled away from the station platform, waving my family good-bye without a tear as I set out for the unknown country that lay east of Texas.

Whatever happened to that confident young girl? She fell in love with an even more ambitious young man, and in place of the dowry parents once were expected to provide to entice an eligible young man into an arranged marriage, she freely entrusted him with her life.

And now she has come to depend on her husband to tell her who she is and what she wants. She thought he would make her happy—and he has—but she had not realized she was also giving him the power to make her unhappy at times when she could've been quite content alone.

It was true—and yet I couldn't stop myself from wanting more for Joanna than she wanted for herself.

I know David well enough to know he would never leave me —he is too loyal for that. But I also know he is quite capable of living with me, continuing to feel responsible for me, long after he has ceased to love me. I cannot bear for this to happen. I am not afraid of living alone. I never have been. But I am terrified of spending the rest of my life with a man who no longer loves me.

There I was, out of work, terrified of starting a new play, and she was worried that I had stopped loving her. Why did I never consider the possibility that she might be disappointed in me? I refuse to believe it was because she loved me more than I loved her. In fact, I'm now convinced just the opposite is true.

☐

HOW MUCH LONGER can David live with me? I keep waiting for him to explode as he did in the old days when he felt my parents were being unfair to him. But there are no villains in the scenarios we've been acting out since my book was published—just subtle shifts in focus that leave everyone uncertain of their lines.

The exchange that took place yesterday would probably have left no impression on the casual observer—in fact, all the way home I kept hoping it hadn't hurt David as much as it had hurt me for him. His silence even deluded me into thinking perhaps the remark hadn't registered on him. But when we were in bed, with the lights out, he said in a voice so low I had to lift my head from the pillow to hear him, "The irony, of course, is that all you've ever wanted is for someone to say to you what Michael said to me today. I wish it were enough for me—but it's not." Then he turned away. I was afraid to touch him. By trying to console him, I would become an accomplice in the slight no one intended.

It all began so innocently. We went to a play starring an actor we've known since New York and I talked David into going backstage afterwards to congratulate him on his performance—something David prefers doing by phone later. Why did I have to say I wanted to speak to Michael too? It's just that for so many years no one cared what I thought about anything. But ever since my book was published, people actually listen when I express an opinion—and I'm afraid it's gone to my head. Now that I know my praise carries some weight, I'd rather pay a compliment than receive one.

Michael greeted us warmly, accepted our praise with becoming modesty, then, quickly changing the subject, congratulated me on my book. If only the conversation had ended there! But then he looked at David in the way people do at a husband after just complimenting his wife on some public success, as if there were a marital communications law demanding equal time. "And congratulations on your . . . on your life," he said, clearly at a loss for words.

All actors are at a loss for words without playwrights.

I hardly slept all night. Fortunately David was having lunch with a television producer today, so I invited Wyatt to come here. I told him I desperately needed to talk about what was happening between David and me, and he is the only person we know who loves both of us equally—the only friend I can count on not to take sides. My married women friends take me off in a corner at parties and tell me I'm their fantasy—that I'm out there for all of them. My unmarried women friends, like Elaine, assume now that I'm financially independent I'll want to be emotionally independent as well, and sooner or later, they expect me to leave David. I'm sure David's men friends feel he has grounds for adultery any time he's in the mood, and I also doubt if they'd be surprised to see him start hitting the bottle, as if the two of us were some bus and truck company of *A Star Is Born*. But what obvious choices—all of them. David has always taken pains to avoid clichés in his work—so how could he consider them in his life?

Thank you, my sweet.

I told all this to Wyatt over salmon mousse.

Salmon mousse. Ugh!

But then I began to cry, confessing how helpless I feel to comfort David when someone makes a remark like Michael's. "Why does everyone feel David deserves some kind of consolation prize?" I blurted out.

"What do you think he deserves?" Wyatt asked.

The question was so unexpected it stopped my tears. "A success equal to his talent," I replied.

"He's hardly the first to have to settle for less," Wyatt said.

"But how many of those who had to settle for less were married to wives who got more?"

"More success than they deserved? Is that what you feel you've gotten?"

I nodded. Suddenly Wyatt reached across the kitchen table and took my hand. "Would you feel that way if you weren't married to David?"

I'd never thought about it before. Then I had to admit, "I'd still feel lucky. But no, I wouldn't feel guilty."

"Then you're not being fair to David—or to yourself—worrying so much about him. Marriage is supposed to enhance your good fortune, not diminish it."

Well put, Wyatt.

I could see that, beyond listening to my confession, Wyatt wasn't going to be much help. He's still such a romantic about marriage. I have no doubt that David is happy for me—he knows as well as I do that I would never have written a novel if he hadn't pushed me into it—but he can't go on accepting compliments on his life when he should be writing plays and winning prizes for them. He's the writer in the family, not I. How do I know? Because he cannot *not* write. Whereas that appears to be what I do best.

Hemingway once blamed an unsuccessful love affair on "unsynchronized passion." How much more threatening to a marriage is unsynchronized success? It's easy enough for a woman to live in her husband's shadow all her life. We're trained to play the role of "the woman behind the man"—or at least have been until quite recently. But even if a man is suited by temperament or talent to be a supporting player—which David never was and never will be—society refuses to allow him to relax in the role.

I know all this is costing David more than he will admit. How much longer can he continue taking it? I grow more frightened with each new hurt he swallows. If only he would allow some outward release, but everything is turned inward.

When Wyatt kissed me good-bye, he said he would nudge David to write a new play with the promise of a production at his theater. "All it takes for David to feel successful is to be writing something he believes in. It's the work that counts—not how much money it makes or what people say about it afterwards. Just get him started on a new play and you won't have to worry about what people say or don't say to him. He'll be invulnerable."

I said I couldn't imagine pushing David to write the way he does me. "He's pushing you because he's not writing himself," Wyatt said. "Or at least not writing anything that matters to him."

"I know that, but I can't do to him what I don't want him to do to me. I just want him to leave me alone to work at my own pace, find my own rhythm. With the next book—if there is a next book—the pressure has got to build from inside, like a volcano, until I have no choice but to erupt in writing."

"Maybe what you see building in David now—what you're so afraid of—is just a play."

"I pray you're right," I answered. "If not, it may end by destroying us."

She was right. When I look back now, I realize I was slowly going mad—and there was no one I could blame. In the past when the pressure built, I could always count on losing my temper—and regaining my composure. But this time the instrument of my undoing was the woman I loved —and let's be fair, the woman who at that time, before I read these journals, had never given me any reason to doubt she loved me. And I had made her into my reluctant rival by forcing her to take chances she would never have taken on her own. I wasn't kidding when I said she would have been thrilled to be congratulated on her life. But of course no one ever feels the need to offer parallel congratulations to a wife. It is assumed she shares in her husband's success. The one thought that comforted me was that at least Joanna hadn't written a hit play. Nor had I spent my life struggling to become a successful novelist. I had my turf and she had hers. Still, the more threatened I felt by her success, the more I kept pushing her to try to repeat it. Why?

☐

IF THIS HAS NOT BEEN the worst day of my life, it has certainly been the most puzzling. David is somewhere in Indiana tonight—and while I know the facts, I'm not sure I understand them.

He left an hour ago. We were just sitting down to dinner when there was a phone call from a woman in West Texas who said she was Linda's mother. David took the call in the bedroom but as I hung up the extension in the kitchen, I could hear her crying hysterically, telling David her daughter needed his help.

Jessica and Julia kept asking what was wrong, but I didn't know how to answer them. I only knew Linda was an old girlfriend, but David hadn't mentioned her in years.

We'd finished dinner by the time he returned to the table. I took his plate out of the oven, but he said he didn't think he could eat anything. He reassured Julia and Jessica that nothing had happened to anyone in our family. However, an old friend had just lost her husband in a hunting accident. Her mother wanted him to know.

"But why would she call you after all these years?" I asked.

"Linda's all alone in Indiana. And her mother's too ill to travel."

"I still don't understand why she called you. You haven't heard from Linda since we married, have you? She didn't even send us a wedding present."

I couldn't tell Joanna that ever since that trip to West Texas by bus—when she thought I was in Rome—I'd kept in touch with Linda's mother by phone, usually calling every year or so to check on her and confess my current frustrations. She continued, of course, to believe I'd be happier married to her daughter—and I have no doubt she saw the tragedy she called to report as a second chance for both of us.

Without further explanation, David left the table to call Linda. He'd promised her mother. The next thing I knew, he was packing a suitcase. He said I had to understand there were prior loyalties that even marriage couldn't obliterate. Linda had no children, no brothers and sisters, her father was dead and her mother bedridden. There was no one else she could turn to. With that he called a taxi to take him to the airport.

He then took Julia and Jessica in his arms and explained that he had to help his friend. But when he'd gone, they turned to me and asked if Daddy and I were getting a divorce. Trying to hide my own fear and confusion, I assured them everything was fine. I didn't understand why their father felt he had to make this trip, but I was sure he'd be home soon.

☐

DAVID FINALLY CALLED THIS MORNING. "The situation is worse than I thought," he began. "It wasn't a hunting accident, it was suicide—but Linda doesn't want her mother to know. The crazy thing is, she somehow blames us."

"Us?"

"Yes—us."

"For her husband's suicide? What are you talking about? How could she possibly blame us?"

"She's obsessed with you, Joanna."

"How could she be obsessed with me? I've never even met her."

"She read your book—and apparently believed every word of it. She thinks I ruined her life by not marrying her—then ruined my life by marrying you. And she didn't bother hiding her feelings from her husband."

"And that's why he killed himself?"

"Apparently."

"You can't seriously believe that?"

"What matters is what she believes."

"Are you staying in her house?" I was ashamed for asking, but I had to know.

"Of course not," he assured me. "I'm at a motel." He gave me the number, then gave me Linda's number, too. He asked to speak to the girls, but I said they were still asleep. Then I told him to try to get some sleep himself. I didn't know what else to say.

He asked if we needed anything. I said we were okay for now

—just do what he felt he had to do for Linda and come home. He seemed relieved and said he'd call again tomorrow.

But what *can* a man do for a woman who wanted him to love her all his life? Will anything less make any difference? I have sympathy for her and what she's living through, of course. And I can also understand her need for David. But why his need for her? Is a helpless female really that appealing to him? There have to be more than selfless motives behind this trip. What is he looking for that I haven't given him?

Always you, *Joanna. Always looking for the* you *in everything!*

☐

DAVID IS LEAVING INDIANA TOMORROW—but not coming home. He's taking Linda to her mother in West Texas.

"She's a grown woman," I protested. "Why do you have to take her home to her mother? Can't she go by herself?"

I have to admit my patience is wearing thin. Or am I just afraid that if David goes back to his roots, he'll become so entangled in them, he may never find his way home?

"She won't go without me," he replied. "She can't face her mother alone. She feels she's failed at everything. She's never had a job, she couldn't have children, and now her husband's killed himself."

"So she's bringing you home as some kind of consolation prize." I was so angry I almost hung up the phone, but I couldn't bear to break the connection.

Ignoring the crack, David explained patiently that he was just encouraging Linda to be practical. She couldn't support herself alone in Indiana. If she went back to Texas, her mother could take care of her financially—and Linda could take care of her mother physically.

"But why are you so involved?" I protested. "You're taking charge as if you were part of the family."

"They have no one else. And besides . . . I almost was."

"How long are you planning to stay in Texas?"

"I honestly don't know." I wanted to shout at him to spare me any more of his damn honesty—I'd had all of it I could take. But I just said to call when he arrived and give me a number where he could be reached.

When I hung up, I thought of my trip back to college after my book was published—ostensibly to make a speech but really to see Adam Greenfield and discover if any of my past was still alive in the present. Is this what David is doing? The instinct that leads to *la recherche du temps perdu* is in all of us—Proust just gave it a name. The difference, however, is that I was only away one night, whereas David refuses to say when he'll be home. What would he have done if I'd said I didn't know how long I was going to be away?

How is it possible to be married to someone for twenty-one years and still know so little about him? I feel as betrayed as I did when he told me he'd been married before, but this time he's living a play instead of writing one.

And I'm still not sure which is more difficult.

☐

TONIGHT WHEN HE CALLED from West Texas, David suddenly put Linda on the phone. She began by saying how much she loved my book, and how brave I was to be honest about my marriage.

"That's *not* my marriage in the book," I protested. "I mean the facts were just a starting point—the rest is fiction."

"I understand how you feel," she said in a sweet, shy voice. "At first I couldn't tell anybody that my husband committed suicide. But now even my mother knows, and it makes it so much easier."

"I'm very sorry about your husband," I said, ignoring her other implications. "I think losing a husband must be the hardest thing a woman has to bear."

"I just wish I could have loved him more," she said finally, then thanked me for letting David come.

"It was his decision," I replied. David came on the line again. This time I didn't make the mistake of asking how long he would be away. Instead I said that as soon as the children got out of school on Friday, we were flying to West Texas to be with him.

They knew almost nothing of his life before he married—and neither did I. It was time to fill in a few blanks.

"Don't do that. Don't bring the children here. I want your word."

"Well, you're not getting it," I replied—and hung up.

☐

I HAVEN'T HEARD FROM DAVID since our last phone call —three days ago. Tomorrow is Friday. I have our plane tickets, but I don't look forward to using them if he doesn't call before we leave.

☐

DAVID IS HOME! I'd taken the children to school and just finished packing for our trip to Texas this afternoon when I heard his key in the lock. But I was still too confused and hurt by his silence all week to greet him warmly. I had the eerie feeling a stranger had just entered the house. He began stalking the living room, stopping to look at the paintings, the books, even pieces of furniture, as if he'd never seen them before.

"You're back, then," I said, moving quickly to a chair so I'd be seated if he were planning to tell me he wanted a divorce. And when he began to talk, I was sure that was where he was headed.

Listening to him describe Linda—how frail she was, how eager to please—I realized for the first time he'd really been in love with her at eighteen. Was he still? Refusing to marry her couldn't have been as easy as he made it sound when he first told me about her—mocking her passion for early American furniture. Whenever we'd be browsing in an antique store and come across something quaint like a butter churn or a chamber pot, he'd threaten to send it to Linda—something to remember him by, he'd say, and we'd laugh together. But now I know David only makes jokes to avoid his real emotions.

Suddenly he was confessing he knew even at eighteen that to marry her would mean mortgaging all his ambitions. He couldn't face repeating in his marriage the life he saw everyone living in that little town. So he began to run and he was still running last week, when his round trip ended, back in that barren place where it began.

Staying in the spare bedroom of the house where he used to come calling for Linda, he said he tried to imagine what his life would have been like if he'd married her. Each morning he'd take long walks around his old neighborhood.

"I kept seeing it through your eyes—then through Julia's eyes and Jessica's. That's why I wouldn't let you come, why I couldn't let you bring them. I began wondering what your grandmother would've thought if she could've seen that run-down shack where I grew up. She was always so gracious to me, so generous to accept me on my own terms, but only because I'd done everything I could to erase my past. It's always been a point of pride with me that I never kept up with anyone I knew before college. But when I talked to Linda the night her mother called, it all came flooding back, all the guilt. That's why I had to take her home to Texas, to try to make amends for believing that the only way I could better myself was to leave her behind."

I was still afraid to ask where all this left me, so I just continued to sit quietly, clutching the arms of my chair while David prowled the room, picking up objects from shelves and tabletops, as if rediscovering the room through the sense of touch.

"But when I got back to that town I never planned to see again, I realized I'd reached the end of the road. I could finally stop running."

"What were you running from, David? Me?"

"No, darling—from us. From all the good things I've been too guilt-ridden to enjoy. I'm guilty of only one thing, Joanna, of having made all the *right* choices. Maybe now—finally—I can start enjoying them."

He said it didn't all fall into place until yesterday—when he went to visit his stepmother, who still lives in a neighboring town in the secondhand trailer he bought for her and Bartlett. "She took me t ny father's grave and said she'd been grieving because she couldn't afford to buy him a tombstone. 'A man needs to leave his mark on the world,' she said. So I drove her to the stone cutter and we decided on one. It cost me more than it should've, but I figured Dad had it coming, considering how much I'd saved on his funeral. We agreed to put his name on the

303

stone, and the years of his birth and death, then Mabel said she wished there could be a few words. She'd been racking her brain since he died, but she hadn't had any more luck coming up with the right words for his tombstone than she had coming up with the money to pay for it. So it looked as though she was to be beholden to me for both of them. I said it had taken me a whole play to find the right words for my father. 'Well, what do you want on your tombstone when you die?' she asked. I'd never stopped to think about it before. But then I began to look back on my life, on all the things that have happened to me—you, the children, the plays, Broadway, Hollywood—and suddenly I realized that all this time I've been living the dreams I had when I was a boy. I just haven't stopped to enjoy them. I told Mabel I supposed I'd just want to say thanks.

" 'Thanks? Is that it?'

" 'Thanks—as in thanks for the use of the hall.'

"At that Mabel clapped her hands with delight. 'Thanks for the use of the hall. That's just the way your daddy would've put it. But then he always said you were a chip off the old block!'

"I couldn't have been more surprised. 'He said that about *me?*'

" 'Yes. Coming home on the train after we saw your play. He was so proud of you, David, of all the things you've done with your life. Didn't you know that?'

" 'How could I? He never told me.'

" 'Well he told me, and now I'm telling you. I hope that's good enough for you.' I smiled and said of course it was. On the way home from the stonecutter, Mabel said that when Dad knew he was dying, she asked him what he wanted on his tombstone. He said he didn't need one as long as he had me to write about him. Then she squeezed my hand and thanked me for giving him my own epitaph."

By the end of David's story I was so moist-eyed I didn't see him coming toward me. It wasn't until he took me in his arms that I dared believe he was home to stay. He began touching me the way he'd been touching the things in the room, as if to make sure I was real and not just part of a dream. Then he took me into the bedroom and we had the use of it. I've never known love like we made it—until time for the children to come home from school. We've been married twenty-one years and I feel our marriage has finally come of age."

What do I add? We both thought we'd solved everything that afternoon. But obviously, we hadn't. Just as no one ever really learns to write a play—or Tennessee Williams would have died with hits on Broadway—I fear the same is true with marriage. We never really learn how. We may survive it but we never conquer it. Which, of course, makes it as exciting as playwriting.

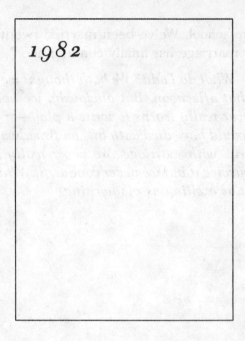

1982

DAVID HAS DECIDED that whoever said "Living well is the best revenge" was right. So next week, as soon as the girls get out of school, we're leaving for London, where we plan to spend the summer. A screenwriter friend is renting us his flat on Kensington Square. It has four bedrooms—plenty of space for visitors. Toby and Lucy will be going to Chicago, so we're trying to talk Wyatt into joining us. He finds the house in Pasadena unbearably lonely without the children, even though he knows he has no legal right to their presence. Marvin and Eula Lee are taking a Baltic cruise but will stop in England on their way home.

☐

OUR TWENTY-SECOND WEDDING ANNIVERSARY. This has probably been the happiest year of our marriage. We had dinner at the Savoy Grill to celebrate—and could almost believe Noel Coward and Gertrude Lawrence were sitting at the next table. I love being in London, especially at this time of year when everything is in bloom. I wish I could look forward to spending our anniversary in a different city every year.

We gave the children the option of choosing which plays they want to see. However, they've elected to take their chances with us. Last week they sat uncomplaining through a four-hour production of *Hamlet,* but yesterday Jessica said of a contemporary playwright, "He reminds me of Shakespeare. He takes a great idea and makes it boring."

☐

IT'S FUNNY to be celebrating American Independence Day in England. Walking along King's Road this morning, we passed a sign that said, "We're celebrating *our* liberation from those damn Yankees."

Wyatt arrived in time for lunch and brought a welcome surprise with him—Toby. Brad decided to send Lucy to a camp for handicapped children this summer, so Wyatt persuaded him to let Toby travel to London—at Wyatt's expense. Julia and Jessica were overjoyed to see him and immediately began planning excursions for the rest of our stay.

We spent the afternoon at the newly restored Covent Garden. As a designer Wyatt was fascinated by the way the old food market has been transformed into a chic collection of boutiques and restaurants. When Jessica and Julia took Toby off to explore the stalls, Wyatt told us that Brad and his wife want Toby and Lucy to live with them permanently. That was the only reason they agreed to let Wyatt have Toby for the summer. Toby knows nothing of his fate, and Wyatt thinks it's better not to tell him till fall. He's had a hard enough time adjusting to the separation from his sister.

"Why can't they just leave the children where they are?" I blurted out before I realized how unfair I was being to Wyatt, expecting him to maintain a house for another man's children. Apologizing, I said I wasn't thinking about how difficult all this has been for him. Toby and Lucy are Brad's responsibility, not his.

Wyatt looked at me as if I'd lost my mind. "I can't imagine life without them," he said in a voice so drained of emotion I hardly recognized it. "But I have no legal recourse. Brad had every right to reclaim them when Susan died. I have to be grateful that he was willing—for whatever reason—to leave them with me for as long as he did. But, God, I'm going to miss them." And he put his head in his hands.

David asked if his mother and Marvin knew what Brad was planning.

Wyatt shook his head. They'd already left on their cruise when Brad called to say he was sending Lucy to camp for the summer and if that worked out as well as he hoped, he was enrolling her in a special school in the fall. Brad thanked Wyatt for keeping the children after Susan died and said starting a new family had left him financially strapped. But he's just been made head of the theater arts department, with a nice raise in salary, so he can finally afford to have all his children under one roof.

Wyatt had flown to Chicago with Toby and Lucy and seen that Lucy was safely installed in camp before leaving for London. Only the excitement of his first trip abroad assuaged Toby's anxiety at being separated from his sister. "He's always looked after her, from the time he understood that she was different from other children," Wyatt said, "but since Susan died, he seems to feel personally responsible for her safety. He's always having nightmares that the house is on fire and he has to go back for her, or she's fallen in the swimming pool and he has to save her."

No wonder he seems so much older than his age.

"I wonder if the nightmares will stop once someone else begins taking care of her," David said reflectively. I could tell he was remembering the relief he felt when his mother married again.

I've never experienced that kind of crushing dependence. It's different with children. They're helpless in the beginning but you know they're growing day by day into your equals. You don't look ahead to a lifetime of feeling responsible for them—as David did with Eula Lee and as Toby does with Lucy.

"We're going to make this summer into the best time Toby has ever had in his life," David vowed.

"That's what I had in mind when I asked him to come," Wyatt said with a smile.

It was the best time any of us had ever had. But if I'd known then where it was going to lead . . . Of course that's why we don't.

☐

EULA LEE AND MARVIN are in London with us now, so all four bedrooms are full. Sometimes I feel I'm living the dream I had in New Haven when David and I were first married. Sleeping under the eaves of that old house, listening to all the sounds below us, I kept wishing the other rooms were filled with people we loved. Here on Kensington Square I've finally gotten my wish. If only the summer didn't have to end and we could stay forever.

But tomorrow Wyatt takes Toby back to Chicago. He's decided Brad should be the one to tell him where he'll be living— and why. Time enough to break the news to Marvin and Eula Lee when they're safely back in Los Angeles.

☐

HOME AGAIN. David has started a new play. I asked him today what it was about, but he just smiled and said he wasn't sure himself. This is the first time since Yale he hasn't read me his new play scene by scene as he was writing it. Why? What's happening to us?

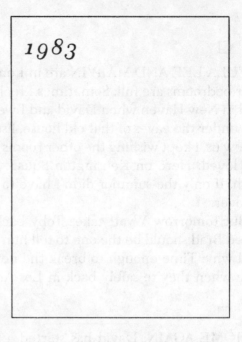

1983

NEW YEAR'S DAY. Christmas was very sad this year without Toby and Lucy. Wyatt decided to fly to Boston to be with his married brother and nieces and nephews, most of whom he hasn't seen in years. He said he always wanted a large family, but now it looked as if the only one he'd ever have was the one he was born into.

He stopped in Chicago for a visit with Toby. They drove to Lucy's school and spent the afternoon with her. Wyatt reports that Toby is not unhappy living with his father's family but misses everyone he left in Los Angeles. Lucy is going back to camp next summer, and Brad has been looking into camps for Toby, but Wyatt convinced him to let Toby spend the summer in Los Angeles with us. That news was the best Christmas present any of us could've received.

Julia misses Toby so much it is painful to watch. She writes him every night before going to bed and gets frequent letters in return. I have no idea what they say to each other but I'm pretty sure there are no secrets between them. Sometimes I wonder what my relationship with David would be like if we'd grown up together and had a chance to become friends before becoming entangled in the complicated role playing of male and female.

When Toby and Lucy moved to Chicago last fall, Marvin was so devastated he wanted to sell the house in Pasadena and move back to Santa Monica. He assumed Wyatt would move into a place of his own closer to the theater now that they no longer made any pretense of being a family, but to his surprise Wyatt said he loved the house and if Marvin wanted to sell it, he'd like to buy it. However, if Marvin and Eula Lee wanted to stay, he would happily continue sharing expenses as they had in the past.

So the three of them have stayed on together in the old house. Wyatt says as long as the rooms are there waiting, he has to believe the children will be back to occupy them for at least a few weeks a year.

Marvin could not face the holidays at home this year without Toby and Lucy, so he took Eula Lee on a South Seas cruise. We had a New Year's Eve party last night to welcome them home, and Wyatt greeted them with the news that Toby would be spending the summer in Pasadena.

☐

EULA LEE CALLED before sunrise to say she thought Marvin was having a heart attack. An ambulance was already on the way. David met her at the hospital. The girls were still asleep and I was waiting by the phone when David called to say Marvin was in serious condition but the doctor thought he would recover.

I began to cry, then I called my parents in Texas to tell them and to make sure my father was feeling better. He's been complaining of pains in his legs since Christmas, but the doctor can't find anything wrong.

Sometimes I worry that I've forgotten my own family in my concern with the extended family I've acquired through marriage. I suspect the biblical injunction to a wife to leave her family and cleave to her husband was designed to spare her the guilt that floods me when I think what a small fraction of my life since marriage has been spent with the man and woman who gave birth to me.

No wonder David answers adamantly in the negative when

anyone asks if Julia has started dating, insisting that his daughters will never marry and leave home. He says they can bring anyone they like to the house and he will be happy to add on as many rooms as they need. He's also made it clear to both girls that any babies resulting from any relationship they form, permanent or otherwise, are to be welcomed and turned over to their grandparents at the earliest opportunity. Sometimes I suspect David would be quite happy, as our daughters come of age, to convert our house into a home for unwed mothers. Our friends just laugh at him and call him the Reverend Brontë (though Charlotte and Emily's possessive father looks reasonable next to David), but I'm afraid he's serious.

Still, I cannot imagine sending either of my daughters into the world to marry quite as easily as my parents did me. The irony is, if I'd had a father like David, he would never have allowed me to marry a man like David. And David has changed the shape of my life.

True. But that's asking a lot of a husband. Too much. Wouldn't it be better to find the shape of your life before you marry?

Why was it so much easier for me to leave home—to take the plunge into marriage and into life—than it is to imagine my daughters living on their own? Perhaps because I had no idea what was ahead of me, but I know no matter how much happiness is in store for them, there will be at least equal parts pain.

Equal parts? They should be so lucky.

So why do I resist when David insists he's going to keep them at home as long as he can? Because I still believe in life. Like Piaf, *je ne regrette rien*. My friends all color their hair to hide the gray. Not I. I've earned every gray hair.

Every parent wants more for his child. And so do I. Not more wealth or more fame or more power. More life.

Such a brave toast—why can't I drink to it? Because I honestly don't think I could survive the breakup of my family.

☐

MARVIN IS HOME FROM THE HOSPITAL and convalescing comfortably. Eula Lee is convinced the heart attack was caused by the excitement of Toby's impending visit. She said Marvin had steeled himself against the pain of relinquishing the children to their natural father, but he was unprepared for his joy at the prospect of having his grandson for the summer.

It is one of the large ironies of human existence that the more you love someone, the more vulnerable you make yourself to the pain of losing them. And the more people you love, the more you increase your chances of being hurt. Love makes you strong—and at the same time leaves you defenseless. How is Marvin going to live through Toby's arrival and departure this summer?

For the past month our life has been centered around the hospital. We persuaded Eula Lee to move back in with us, then David and I took turns driving her to visit Marvin. Julia and Jessica devoted themselves to making her comfortable. Julia brought her breakfast in bed every morning before going to school, and Jessica climbed in bed with her every night to snuggle and sing her lullabies.

In the past I think Eula Lee took the proximity of her grandchildren for granted, but this year, seeing the pain Marvin has experienced being deprived of his, she has come to appreciate her good fortune. "Nobody stops to consider what divorce does to grandparents," she said to me one night as we were clearing the dinner dishes. "You're always reading about children being the innocent victims of divorce. What about grandparents? If you decided to leave David and go back to Texas, I might never see Julia and Jessica again. And I wouldn't even have a case to take to court. Grandparents have no legal rights."

"That's true," I agreed, "but Marvin hardly knew his grandchildren *until* Susan got divorced. Marriage causes its own estrangements." I wasn't thinking of Susan.

☐

THANK GOD David was not at home when the mail came today. Even though he's stopped screening my letters (I hope), he still scans the envelopes. If he'd seen one addressed to me from *Who's Who in America*, he would've known what I am determined he will never know. I tore up the form and dropped it down the disposal. Why me and not David? How dare they! And who are they? He's devoted his life to writing; I'm the reluctant author of one book—terrified of trying to write a second. It's so unfair.

I'll be damned. How could she deny herself such an honor? Did she really think I wouldn't be happy for her? What kind of person does she think I am? What kind of person am I? Is it true that I stand between her and everything that happens to her? Can't she enjoy anything without worrying first about how I'm taking it?

All I wanted when I started writing was to establish a separate identity for myself—to be someone besides David's wife. But it's gotten out of hand. I don't like seeing David take a back seat to me any more than I liked taking a back seat to him. He jokes with his friends that I'm supporting him now, which is simply not true. In fact, it is only because he makes such a good living as a writer that I have the freedom of writing exactly what I choose, without being concerned about whether it will make money. Sometimes I think it's a miracle our marriage has survived one book. I'm convinced now that I mustn't push my luck by trying to write a second.

What a lousy cop-out! How dare you do that to me, Joanna! I never blamed you for any of my failures. I admit I may have laid it on a bit thick with my friends about your success, but that's because I knew how much they envied me.

Adjusting to a successful wife is a lot easier for a man than those women's magazines would have you believe. Especially if the man is middle-aged and exhausted from his own efforts to make his mark on the world. Why shouldn't marriage work on the principle of the relay team? Frankly, I was winded—and eager to pass the baton to Joanna. So why was she so reluctant to run with it? If only I'd seen that letter from Who's Who. *What a lovely celebration we could've had! And I would've made sure she*

314

filled out her form and had it back in the mail the next morning. I wonder if they'd still accept her? I'll write a letter tonight, say her form got lost. Of course they'll accept her. I'm breathing easier already.

☐

I WANT ANOTHER BABY. David has no idea.

Another baby? When was this? Last year? My God, she was forty-five. Was she that terrified of writing a second book? Or, for all her brave talk, of being left alone in our empty nest?

Today I had my I.U.D. removed. I've been reading how dangerous they are. But pills are even worse—especially at my age —and using a diaphragm would be like going back to gaslight after living with electricity. I can't believe how little modern science has done for women. I'm just going to put myself in the hands of mother nature and see what happens.

Without even asking me?

☐

ALL LAST WEEK I thought I was pregnant—but it turns out I'm not after all.

So, on top of everything else, I'm now sterile! Is it any wonder?

Why do I feel like a failure when a new baby would throw what is beginning to be a well-ordered life into complete chaos? Could it be that there's something a bit boring about a well-ordered life? I've felt young and sexy this past week thinking I might be pregnant. And also relieved thinking what a great excuse I had for not writing a second book.

Just as I suspected.

☐

JULIA GRADUATED from high school today, a year ahead of her class. Once we began taking her out of school to travel with

315

us, she found classrooms impossibly confining and doubled up on her course load so she could graduate early. When people ask what she plans to do next year, she replies happily, "Live my own life—for the first time in sixteen years." I envy her assurance—and her answer. She's doing something I've never had the courage to do. But that's why we have children.

I watch David falling more in love with her every day but feel helpless to do anything about it. For the first time in our marriage I know I have a legitimate rival. When David tells Julia how beautiful she is, I hear words he once used to praise me and me alone—and I react with a mixture of jealousy and pride. How can I feel such a sense of competition with my own daughter when she is my creation as much as his? Perhaps because she contains within her own unique persona all the unused possibilities of my younger self. It is not just David's praise of her youth and beauty that I covet, it is the long, still formless life ahead of her.

David never wanted a son. He said he knew they would be natural enemies, just as he was with his father, but I never imagined that I would regard a daughter, even on the most subconscious level, as anything but an ally. Has David always been wiser than I?

Always.

If we had a son, would I find myself falling in love with him the way David is falling in love with Julia? I wonder how he'd react to that?

Even during times of mental chaos, David has never considered going into analysis. He thinks it is death for a writer to try to understand rationally all the terrors that propel him to the typewriter. However, he would probably be the first to agree he is in the throes of a typical oedipal involvement with his older daughter. And the jealousy that is turning me inside out is so common, it would be considered a cliché if I were to attempt to put it to any literary use.

□

316

DAVID FINALLY LET ME read his new play, *Rehearsal*—about a young girl falling in love with her father's best friend. It's the finest thing he's ever written—but the most threatening to me personally. He's found a terrific theatrical framework for exploring all his conflicting emotions about Julia and her future, but I can't help identifying with the best friend's wife, who conveniently dies at the end of the first act.

No wonder most writers are so maladjusted. Who could get along with flesh-and-blood people after playing God with your characters all day? Any time a fictional wife gets on your nerves, off with her head! I'm beginning to be more sympathetic with what Eula Lee has gone through watching her life transformed into drama. Even if your only ties to a writer are legal, you eventually find yourself related by blood.

> *Why does she still insist on making it sound as if there were only one writer in the family—me? And talk about blood ties—I have to live the rest of my life with the portrait of a husband she painted in her novel.*

☐

WYATT wants to produce *Rehearsal* at his theater. David is so happy to be going into production again, and the Susan provides such a warm, nurturing climate—just like its namesake. Will I ever stop missing her?

David has asked Wyatt to direct the play as well as design the sets—and I think it's a terrific idea. Wyatt has worked with so many directors as a designer, he's probably learned everything he needs to know from seeing their mistakes.

Listening to Wyatt and David talk about the play today over lunch (I made a sensational seafood quiche), I understood for the first time what Wyatt tried to explain to me years ago—all that matters is the work, not how much money it makes or how many prizes it wins. David is so alive bringing a new play to life. I envy him the experience and want it for myself.

☐

THIS MORNING I started my second novel, but this time I'm not telling anyone until it's finished—at least to my satisfaction. I have to prove I can write a book by myself.

Why?

☐

REHEARSAL OPENED TONIGHT. David has never written a better play or received a better production. The actress playing the daughter is a brilliant new discovery making her stage debut. Like Willa, she understands David's rhythms instinctively. She has none of Willa's temperament but all of her talent. Why wouldn't she? She's Willa's daughter.

Willa was in the opening night audience to applaud Molly. Paul was seated on one side of her and Tim on the other. The opening night party was a giant celebration of friends and family who've traveled with us since the early years of our marriage, so it was appropriate that it took place on the night of our twenty-third anniversary. David wrote the play; Wyatt produced, directed, and designed the sets; Molly starred; Toby (who's here for the summer) worked as an apprentice, alongside Julia and Jessica; and I played my usual role as a member of the audience (though since the theater is nonprofit, I also doubled as ticket taker).

David and I were married in 1960, when I was twenty-two. I have now spent more of my life married than unmarried, and every year the scales will tip further in favor of my identity as a wife.

Sometimes I think marriage is like a play in many acts, with a new conflict occurring in each act. In the early years we argued about money, sex, in-laws. I thought once those questions were resolved, we would live happily ever after. What a lie those fairy tales feed us. Marriage is the beginning of the drama, not the end. You no sooner resolve one conflict than another one appears in its place.

Both David and I have had a hard time adjusting to the fact that after being totally dependent on him for the first half of our marriage, I now have an identity and an income of my own. But I think we're finally comfortable with the idea of being equal partners in this undertaking called marriage. What happens next to upset the balance? Where do we go from here? I feel to some degree as I did at twenty-one—as if I were standing on a new threshold.

God, I wish I were standing on a new threshold. How does she keep coming up with these attitudes and phrases? Joanna has this uncanny ability to continually run totals on her life. I threw away my abacus years ago.

☐

WE PUT TOBY ON THE PLANE to Chicago yesterday, and last night Marvin died in his sleep. Eula Lee is being very brave. She said she never expected life to provide her with a second chance at marriage.

"Did I ever tell you how much Marvin reminded me of the first man who asked me to marry him?" she said when we kissed her good-night. Our guest room has become her bedroom again and will be, I expect, for the rest of her life.

"You did tell me once that Dad wasn't the first man who asked you to marry him," David replied, "but you never said who was."

"Yes—and you said I owed you some answers," Eula Lee admitted. "But I couldn't tell you the truth without facing it myself, and I'm just beginning to find the courage to do that." Then she described the man. He was a schoolteacher. They were both teaching in the same little town, boarding with a big farm family. They'd sit at the kitchen table at night after dinner and play checkers. "It felt as though we were already married," she remembered. "On the weekends he'd drive me home in his Model T to visit Mama and Papa. They took it for granted we would be getting married. So did he. But I was young and I guess I thought falling in love should be more exciting. So when my best friend moved to West Texas and wrote me to come for a visit, I was on th‿ next train. When I came home again, I was married—to your father."

David asked what happened to the other man.

"I never asked. I didn't want to know. But I used to dream about him. In my dreams we were always sitting at that table

playing checkers. Nobody was talking—we never did talk much
—but I felt so safe. Once I married Marvin, I never had the
dream again."

☐

WYATT INVITED ALL OF US to Pasadena today for Thanksgiving dinner. He was very surprised and touched to learn that
Marvin had left him the house in his will, but assured Eula Lee
their bedroom would remain unchanged, and she was welcome
to stay in it whenever she liked. However, she said her home
was with us now and urged him to remodel the house and make
it his own.

I cannot imagine Julia and Jessica allowing their grandmother
to leave home again. Especially Jessica, who will not go to bed
each night until she has written Eula Lee a note saying how
much she loves her. It's become a game. She hides the note
inside the sugar bowl or the clothes hamper or the refrigerator
so Eula Lee will find it during the day while Jessica is in school—
and know someone is thinking of her.

Jessica got the idea from watching Eula Lee wait for the
postman every day. She never writes anyone, so it's not as if
she's hoping for an answer, but she's always the first one to the
mailbox—and acts cheated if someone else goes through the
mail before she does. David once asked what she was expecting
from the mail, offering to send it to her, whatever it was. She just
smiled and said all she had to look forward to in life was something she was *not* expecting.

Molly spent the afternoon in the kitchen with Wyatt, cooking
the turkey and trimmings. They've become very good friends
since the play. When I told David I thought they were falling in
love, he just scoffed and said I was being ridiculous. Wyatt is at
least twenty years older than Molly. "The same age difference as
the characters in your play," I pointed out.

"The theater allows for suspension of disbelief," was his answer. "Life doesn't."

Sometimes I think David is the last to see the dramas taking
place in front of his eyes every day. I know Toby and Julia began
making plans this past summer to share their lives. Toby is going

to Northwestern when he graduates from high school next spring, and Julia is filling out an application so she can join him. David knows nothing about it. He was delighted when Julia announced last summer she was ready to start living her own life—but assumes she plans to keep doing it under our roof. Julia is waiting to confront him until she is sure she has been accepted.

1984

I READ A SURVEY TODAY that compared the mental health of four different categories of people: married men, married women, single men, single women. I asked David to rank them, starting with what he considered the happiest group. "Probably in the order you said—married men, married women, single men, single women—though single men might come after married men."

"Wrong," I replied, then read him the results of the survey. "Your first choice was right—married men are the happiest, best-adjusted group."

"I knew that without a survey," he said, giving me an affectionate kiss.

"But single women come close behind. Then single men and finally married women. According to the survey, married women are the least happy because they have the least control over their lives."

"I've never put any faith in statistics," David said finally. "Now I know why."

☐

I TOOK JULIA WITH ME to the doctor today and suggested she talk to him about being fitted for a diaphragm—just as a precaution. I promised that whatever decision she made would be private—I just wanted her to be informed and responsible for her actions.

Julia, we have to talk. Don't let your mother push you into adulthood before you're ready.

When I went in to see the doctor, he told me what I already knew. I'm pregnant.

Pregnant? You mean I'm not sterile?

I want this baby desperately. I don't have any proof yet, but I know it's going to be a boy. I can't tell David—he'll say I'm too old to be having another baby.

Of course you are. I can't let you risk it.

I must keep the news to myself until it's too late for an abortion.

When's that? When was this damn entry written? Why doesn't she ever date anything?

□

WYATT AND MOLLY did not realize when they chose today for their wedding that it was our twenty-fourth anniversary. But they took it as a good omen, saying they couldn't ask for more than to be as happy as David and I have been.

We offered to have the ceremony, but Wyatt said his house owed him a wedding. Looking around at the guests, I felt that in twenty-four years of marriage, David and I had created a family infinitely more far-reaching and complicated than the two daughters who stood beside us. As Wyatt and Molly recited their vows in the orchard, all kinds of cross-connections, personal and professional, were in evidence, weaving our lives into a fabric so strong and startling in its colors, it would have delighted Susan. She was very much present for me on this occasion, as I'm sure she was for Wyatt and for Brad, who came out with Toby and Lucy for the wedding.

Toby was Wyatt's best man, and Molly asked Julia to be her

maid of honor. Molly came down the aisle on Tim's arm. Though he's only eleven, he rose admirably to the occasion. When Molly told him she was getting married, he said maybe now she'd stop grieving that she never knew her father. "Oh, God, you don't suppose everyone will think that's why I'm marrying Wyatt, do you?" she asked.

"Who cares what people think?" Tim replied. Certainly not Willa's children. Willa and Paul always look happy when they're together, but they have no intention of ever sharing their lives. Willa stays with him when she comes to California, and he knows her door is open to him any time he's in New York. But neither can imagine living together—or on the opposite coast.

After the ceremony Toby and Julia came down the aisle arm in arm behind Wyatt and Molly. They held hands all through the reception—until Julia broke free to catch Molly's bridal bouquet. When it grew dark, David and I left with Eula Lee and Jessica. Toby promised to have Julia home by midnight.

□

2 A.M. I can't sleep—and I can't face tomorrow until I finish writing about today. What do I want for Julia? I'm not sure I'll know until I decide what I want for myself.

It was almost midnight before Julia returned with Toby. Still wearing her dress from the wedding, she came into the bedroom where David and I were reading, and climbed into bed between us, her eyes sparkling with excitement. I told her how beautiful she looked. For once David appeared not to notice. He asked if Toby had left. Julia shook her head and said he was waiting for her downstairs.

"Waiting for what?" David demanded.

"He wants me to go back to Pasadena with him," Julia said, "and stay at least till Wyatt and Molly get home from their honeymoon."

David sprang out of bed as if he'd just received an electrical shock. "You're not staying alone in that house with Toby. You're still a child, for God's sake."

"I'm almost eighteen," Julia replied with surprising dignity. "I'm old enough to live my own life, and I want to live it with

Toby. I might as well tell you now I'm going to Northwestern next year, so we'll be together sooner or later. I just hoped you would understand why we didn't want to wait."

"Northwestern?" David was reeling with shock. "Why go all the way to Chicago when there are perfectly good schools in Los Angeles? Why doesn't Toby come here? We'll add on a room."

"He can't be away from Lucy," Julia explained patiently. "He visits her every weekend. He feels responsible for her. You of all people should be able to understand that."

Climbing back into bed, David turned off his light. "I think I'm having a heart attack," he said. "I can't talk about it any more tonight."

Julia got out of bed and kissed him affectionately. Sometimes I'm in awe of her maturity. "I don't want to hurt you—or do anything behind your back," she said, "but I've been sleeping with Toby one way or another since I was nine years old. I've always known we'd be married one day."

"I knew it was a mistake getting you those damn bunk beds," David muttered. Then he said he was feeling nauseous and asked me to bring him a wet washcloth to put over his eyes.

"I'll tell Toby to go home tonight, and we'll talk about all this tomorrow," Julia said, patting David's arm reassuringly, then tiptoeing out the door.

David groaned and asked me to turn off my light so he could go to sleep. I said we had to talk first. It was time to face the possibility that sooner or later our daughters were going to want to lead their own lives and I had to know whether we would still have a marriage once that happened. In the beginning there were just the two of us and that was enough, but I wasn't sure it was anymore. I was just about to tell him I was pregnant when he turned over on his stomach, put his pillow over his head, and said he was in too much pain to talk about the future. The way he was feeling, he wasn't even sure he'd be with us tomorrow.

Defeated, I turned off my light, but my head was churning with all the things we had left unsaid between us—tonight and for the past twenty-four years. When I heard David breathing regularly, I crept out of bed, picked up my journals, and closed the door behind me. It was just the bedroom door and I didn't slam it as Nora did when she left the doll house, but for me the action was equally definitive. I can no longer be married to a man who expects me to lie awake in the dark for fear of disturbing his sleep.

I went into Julia's bedroom to see if she wanted to talk, but she was asleep—or pretending to be. Perhaps she could sense that what we were feeling was too complicated to be translated into conversation. I know she loves Toby and I want her to be happy, but I also sympathize with David. She still seems so young to me —though at eighteen she's much wiser than I was when I married at twenty-two. However, she has seen enough of our marriage to make up her own mind.

My parents conducted every aspect of their marriage behind closed doors. I had no idea what was going on between them most of the time. David and I have been much more open with Julia and Jessica, and yet how much have we continued to hold back, not only from them but from each other? Tomorrow, when Julia confronts David about her future, I cannot remain silent as I did tonight. I have to get into the argument and in so doing, determine the shape of my own future.

□

JULIA DARLING, I'm directing this final entry to you. By the time you read it, I will be in Dallas. I cannot say how long I will be away. Knowing how close I am to losing my firstborn makes me realize that I still have unfulfilled obligations to my own parents. This is the first time since my marriage that I've gone home alone, without the excuse of illness or business, simply to spend time with them. Too often in the past I've been so busy being a wife and mother I've forgotten—or perhaps chosen to forget—that I am still a daughter, and will be as long as my parents are alive. Marvin's death has made me acutely aware of how little time we may have left together.

David finally made his peace with his father and mother. Now I must do the same with mine. I hope he will understand—and forgive me for leaving at dawn to avoid an argument. It was realizing the loss we will feel when you leave home—and knowing how unbearable life would become if I thought I was going to see as little of you as my parents have seen of me since I married—that made me aware of the debt I still owe them.

I'm sure David will be hurt and angry that I've left without a word to him, but my feelings at this moment are too complicated to risk putting anything on paper. For David, his family is his fortress. He only feels safe when everyone is at home behind locked doors. Perhaps I'm trying to make it possible for you to leave by leaving first.

I thought about waking Jessica and asking her to come with me, but David needs her now more than I do. Please try to help her understand where I've gone and why.

You'll know by now, having read to the end of these journals, that I'm expecting another baby—a boy this time—around Christmas. I've had the tests and everything is fine. But I am determined to finish my new book before he's born. Once it's drafted and I know how it ends, perhaps I'll have a better idea of what I'm going to do with the rest of my life.

I'm still not sure what to tell you about your life—and when and if you should begin sharing it with Toby. I love him almost as much as you do and would welcome him into the family, but my affection for him must not influence your decision. The sexual revolution may have created new options for some, but I know the kind of people you both are. For you and Toby, living together will be as momentous a decision as marriage was for your father and me.

How can I tell you what marriage is like when it is different for everyone, even the two people involved? A husband and wife often come to very different conclusions about the same marriage. On balance, I think David and I would agree that we have been happy—though perhaps not as happy as other people would like to believe. However, there are times, even after twenty-four years of marriage, when I feel we are still strangers to each other. The only advice I can give you is to trust your own feelings, taking into account the feelings of all of us who love you, but not allowing any of us to make your decision for you. All I can leave you as a guide is the elusive truth of my own experience. But no matter how closely you read, nothing in these journals will tell you what to do tomorrow. That you will have to decide for yourself.

I am only a phone call away whenever you feel like talking. Or, if you're not sure what you want to say, I find writing a letter helps clear my thoughts. Whatever you decide, I continue to love you more each day.

Dearest Julia—thank you for telling Toby you couldn't see him until I'd read these journals, even though you never imagined it would take me so long and I would have so much to say in response. Neither did I.

Jessica and I are leaving for Texas immediately. I don't trust your mother to write an ending without me. If you're not here when we get back, we'll know where to find you.

I wish you were coming with us—now and for the rest of our lives.